PIRATE ALLEY

Also by Stephen Coonts

The Disciple
The Assassin
The Traitor
Saucer: The Conquest
Liars & Thieves
Liberty
America
Saucer
Hong Kong
Cuba
Fortunes of War
The Intruders
The Red Horsemen
Under Siege
The Minotaur
Final Flight
Flight of the Intruder

With William H. Keith:

Deep Black: Death Wave
Deep Black: Sea of Terror
Deep Black: Arctic Gold

With Jim DeFelice:

Deep Black: Conspiracy
Deep Black: Jihad
Deep Black: Payback
Deep Black: Dark Zone
Deep Black: Biowar
Deep Black

Nonfiction:

The Cannibal Queen

Anthologies:

The Sea Witch
On Glorious Wings
Victory
Combat
War in the Air

To Alyson Hagy
All the best to a fellow scribbler

PIRATE ALLEY

STEPHEN COONTS

Nov 7 2013

St. Martin's Press New York

This is a work of fiction. All of the characters, organizations, and events portrayed in this novel are either products of the author's imagination or are used fictitiously.

www.stmartins.com

Library of Congress Cataloging- in-Publication Data

Coonts, Stephen, 1946–
Pirate Alley : a novel / Stephen Coonts.—First edition.
p. cm
ISBN 978-0-312-37284-2 (hardcover)
ISBN 978-1-250-02331-5 (e-book)
1. Maritime terrorism—Fiction. 2. Political fiction. I. Title.
PS3553.O5796P57 2013
813'.54—dc23
2012041268

St. Martin's Press books may be purchased for educational, business, or promotional use. For information on bulk purchases, please contact Macmillan Corporate and Premium Sales Department at 1-800-221-7945 extension 5442 or write specialmar kets@macmillan.com.

First Edition: May 2013

10 9 8 7 6 5 4 3 2 1

To Deborah Jean

PIRATE ALLEY

PROLOGUE

Mogadishu, Somalia

The little drone made a low buzzing sound, a bit more than a dragonfly. It was about twice the size of that insect and weighed three and a half ounces.

We were on the roof of a three-story building. The locals would have been unhappy if they knew, but so far, our presence was our little secret.

I'm Tommy Carmellini, and sneaking around is what the CIA pays me for. It's in my job description somewhere. I was here today with Travis Clay and Joe Bob Sweet, who were what the agency likes to refer to as "covert operatives."

I watched the drone soar above our heads, watched Clay maneuver it around with the joystick on the control unit until he was sure it was functioning properly and the telemetry was good. I checked the small television screen, adjusted the contrast and brightness, then nodded at Trav.

He flew the drone off the edge of the roof and dropped it gently, stopping at each window as it came up on the monitor.

We thought our guy was in this three-story apartment building—or what had once been an apartment building back when the people of Somalia paid rent and obeyed laws. They didn't do either anymore.

Before we went in to get him, we wanted to know where in the building he was and who else was there, and in what rooms.

I watched the monitor over Travis' shoulder, and when he flew the thing to the next window, I glanced around. We were squatting near a water tank. People on the street couldn't see us, and people some distance away, or across the street in that dump building, who could couldn't tell who we were or what we were up to.

Mogadishu reminded me of some sections of Newark and Detroit, only worse. Dirt streets, trash, abandoned vehicles and ruined buildings, the stench of raw sewage, dirty people in rags carrying weapons . . . all in all, I thought it looked like hell might look when I got there. Seventeen years of civil war had brought them to this.

Believe it or not, when I joined the CIA I thought I would be spending my time in Europe or Russia or exotic places like China or Istanbul. I did a little of that, sure, but these days it seemed that the third—no, make that the fourth—world had my name upon it. Tommy Carmellini.

Using a device that picked up electromagnetic energy, I checked the satellite transceiver mounted on the roof one more time. It was hot. As amazing as it sounds, someone in the building was on the Internet.

After the drone had looked in every window, Travis flew it back to the roof and we conferred. The third-floor rooms were empty except for one man, who we thought was the guy we were after. Travis stowed the drone in his backpack.

I checked across the roof. Joe Bob Sweet was hunkered behind the remains of a chimney, keeping watch on the street below, the main drag.

Like me, Travis and Joe Bob were wearing dashikis and sported unruly beards. They also wore sweatbands that kept long, unkempt hair out of their eyes. Compared to them, I looked like a boot recruit. We smelled as bad as we looked.

I nodded at my two colleagues, who had their backpacks on and their weapons in their hands, then opened the door that led down into the building. I was following the wire from the satellite antenna. The installation expert hadn't bothered to drill holes in the walls or floors to get the wire out of the way; he had merely unrolled the thing, so it ran down the steep stairs, then along the poorly lit, trash-infested hallway to a closed door. The insulated wire ran under the door.

My little EMI receiver indicated the wire was hot.

Travis and Joe Bob already had silenced MP-5s in their hands. I put the electronic gizmo away and got out my Ruger with the silencer on the barrel. Travis looked at me and I looked at him as I slowly turned the knob on the door. Didn't see any locks. After all, locks only kept honest people out, and in Somalia, there weren't many of those folks left alive.

The door moved a millimeter.

I took a deep breath and opened it slowly, oh so slowly.

There was a guy sitting at a table by the window with his back to me. He was staring at a computer monitor. Didn't see anyone else.

I walked across the space between us as slowly and silently as I could. The man must have seen my reflection in the computer screen, because he turned suddenly, startled. I jammed the silencer barrel against his teeth, and he froze.

Travis was right behind me. Joe Bob charged for the open doorway that led into another room, a room we couldn't see.

Fear. I could see it in the eyes of my guy. He was one scared fella, which was fine with me. He had a right to be. If he even twitched, I was going to kill him as dead as a man can get. Maybe he saw that in my face, because he remained frozen, immobile, as I turned him slightly and began checking him for weapons.

Behind me I heard a single shot, then a stutter from the MP-5. Then another. I didn't even turn around.

Travis went charging for the other room. He was in there too long.

"Guys?"

"Joe Bob caught one."

Shit! I thought this floor was empty!

The shot must have been heard all over this building. We had mere seconds.

"Help me," I said urgently.

Travis whipped out a plastic tie and secured my computer guy's hands behind his back. Then he pulled out a preloaded syringe from a bag on his belt. "Sweet's gut shot," he said. "A fucking kid."

"Where'd he come from?"

"Oh, fuck!"

The computer guy was trying to watch Travis and me; his eyes got big as saucers when he saw the syringe. Whatever he had been expecting, that wasn't it.

Clay didn't bother pulling up the guy's sleeve or any of that nurse stuff; he merely jabbed the syringe needle through the dirty shirt straight into the muscle and pushed the plunger.

The guy collapsed before Clay could get the syringe put away. Clay stepped quickly back into the other room.

I stowed the Ruger and checked out the computer, which was an old IBM clone. I was prepared to operate—take out the hard drive—but saw that the computer box wasn't very big. I jerked the plugs off it, stuffed it into my backpack and carefully put both arms through the armholes.

I ran the three steps into the other room. Joe Bob had taken a slug right in the gut, then put three into the kid's heart. I merely glanced at the kid, sprawled across a filthy mattress. I saw he was small and dead; his pistol lay near his hand.

Joe Bob was on one knee, bleeding.

"Help me get him up," I grunted at Travis. The two of us lifted Joe Bob onto my shoulder. He weighed about a hundred and eighty, so I wasn't going to move fast with him there. "Goddamn fat slob," I told Sweet as I walked into the other room. Travis picked up the computer guy like he weighed about fifty pounds and tossed him over his shoulder. Clay weighed maybe a hundred and fifty, but it was all muscle and bone.

"We got him," I said into my headset and received two mike clicks in reply.

Away we went, back the way we had come onto the roof. Kept going to another roof, then another. I wasn't going fast, not with Joe Bob draped over my shoulder and his MP-5 in my hands. If anyone was curious about the gunshot, they were waiting for the news to find them.

I could hear the chopper coming. Glanced around, saw it and stepped out where the pilot could see me. It was an Italian chopper and carried the markings of an Italian petroleum company.

There was just enough room on that roof. The pilot eased that thing in there slick as a whistle, and Travis tossed our prisoner through the open door onto the floor, then scrambled aboard. The crewman on the chopper helped me with Joe Bob, then grabbed my hand and I vaulted in.

The floor came up and threatened to hit me in the face.

I turned and glanced at Travis, who was bent over Joe Bob working on him. He didn't have to say anything to me. I could see Joe Bob's pasty face and see his eyelids flutter as he tried to remain conscious. We were going to have to get him to a doctor quick or he was going to die.

The bad news was that the nearest doctor and surgical facility were at a French base in Tadjourah, Djibouti, which was at least eight hours away by chopper.

I looked at the unconscious computer guy and wondered if he was worth the life of Joe Bob Sweet, a twenty-nine-year-old Texan, a Special Forces sergeant on temporary duty with the CIA, an all-around good guy and father of two little towheaded kids.

The chopper flew us northwest toward our base. Joe Bob bled out during the flight. After a while the brown eyes in his chalk face focused on infinity, and Travis and I could get no reaction from him. No pulse. No respiration.

I took a seat by the door and watched Africa go by.

A V-22 Osprey delivered us to the desert two weeks ago, to a site the experts had picked for us. Actually it was in Ethiopia, not Somalia, but I am probably not supposed to say that. I don't think anyone in the American government asked the Ethiopians if we could use their desert, but I am something of a cynic. It was about as lonely a place as one could find on the planet, and conditions were a bit Spartan. We hammered a tube into the ground to piss in and dug a hole to poop in. We erected four tents, built up dirt berms around them to stop shrapnel and bullets, and between them built a food and ammo dump below ground level. Two of the tents were for the other guys to sleep in, one housed the com gear, and one was mine. All mine. With my own cot and vermin and flashlight. I felt like an Eagle Scout.

We did some serious camping. The sand and dirt got into everything, including our food. We bitched a lot, but that didn't help. Gave up shaving. And bathing. Worked out every day, cleaned our weapons and played cards. At one point I was $152,000 ahead, but I lost twenty grand and the deed to my ranch the next day when one of the guys filled an inside straight. I tried to keep my gambling wealth in proper perspective; the bastards would never pay off.

This afternoon when we arrived in a cloud of dirt, the other guys got busy refueling the chopper while I sent an encrypted message via satellite telephone to my current—and I hoped temporary—boss, Jake Grafton, head of Middle Eastern covert ops for the CIA, telling him we had Omar Ali and one KIA.

Walk into a room and collect a bullet in the gut from a kid.

Truth was, I suspected, that Joe Bob hesitated half a second when he saw it was just a kid . . . and the kid drilled him while he hesitated.

You can train and train and train until you are eligible for your pension, but in the real world, you are going to hesitate for just an instant.

So the boy shot Joe Bob, and he still had to kill him.

We put Joe Bob in a body bag and settled in with beer to wait for Ali to wake up. He slept the rest of the afternoon.

Our two interrogation experts checked him from time to time to ensure he wasn't oversedated, and we got on with the evening meal, which consisted of MREs and Tabasco sauce. Man, you eat that stuff for weeks, you become a hot sauce junkie.

The interrogation guys, Joe and Skeeter, talked to me over a beer, ensuring they knew precisely the information we wanted from Ali. This certainly wasn't the first guy this team had snatched and, if the world kept turning, wouldn't be the last. In fact, snatching bad guys was our mission, why the Company sent us here in the first place. What with all the Islamic fundamentalist rebels, terror groups and jihadists, we were in no danger of running out of bad guys any time soon. Looked like a career to us.

What happened to them after we squeezed them dry kinda depended on how bad each dude was. Real bad actors went into a hole in the ground. Guys from mud-hut villages who were doing the bad-guy thing because they were bored, or it was the only game in town, could be sent to Gitmo, there to rot while American politicians wrung their hands and wept. Gofers and kids and hangers-on could be relocated in the middle of the night and turned loose with an admonition to go forth and sin no more. No one knew if they did or didn't—sin anymore—but there is a place in this world for hope.

Omar Ali was a case in point. He was the computer geek for a pirate named Ragnar up the coast from Mogadishu. This past summer Ragnar's boys captured a yacht with four adults on it, two men, two women, and Ali got busy on the Internet trying to find out what these four captives might be worth in the ransom market. Then the gig went sour, somehow, and the pirate captain on the yacht killed all four of them.

So our boy Omar Ali was up to his nuts in conspiracy, piracy and murder. He also knew all about the pirates, who, what, where, when and why, how they operated, and so on. Hence the snatch.

That night we sat in the African dirt, stuffed with food containing enough preservatives to mummify King Tut, which we had washed down with Tabasco sauce and beer, looking at the stars on a black African night while we waited for Omar Ali to wake completely up. We talked about everything on the planet except Joe Bob Sweet. Finally the encrypted satellite phone started buzzing.

It was Jake Grafton, my boss.

Now don't get me wrong; I personally like Grafton and have worked for him several times through the years. It's just that the stuff he handled these days was usually red hot, and in dump places, like the Middle East and the horn of Africa. I am on the Company payroll as a tech-support guy, which means I crack safes, plant and monitor bugs, tap telephone lines, diddle with other people's computers, stuff like that, usually in fairly decent places, like Europe or China or Japan or Australia or Canada or California or Washington or . . . Oops, I'm probably not supposed to mention the stateside stuff. Anyway, Grafton borrowed me from time to time to handle chores for him. Like I said, I liked him well enough but wanted our professional association to be temporary, and the more temporary, the better.

Tonight, after exchanging pleasantries with me, he said, "The Osprey is coming for Ali. Put him and Sweet on it."

"You want us to find out what he knows before we send him?"

"No. That wouldn't play well in an American court."

I couldn't believe it. Just when you think there are no more surprises left in life. "They're actually going to try this guy? Let him lawyer up and cry for the cameras?"

"Justice thinks they got enough on this dude to lock him up for life. They want to give it a whirl."

"Yessir. But after the press release, don't plan on us going back to Mogadishu to snatch anyone else. It'll be impossible."

"I'm sorry about Joe Bob, Tommy. I'll write a letter to his wife, and we'll send someone to see her, get the process started. Ain't much, I know, but Joe Bob signed on for the king's shilling and knew the risks."

Sympathy was not one of Grafton's major virtues. Maybe he had seen too many corpses.

"Yeah," I said.

"Tell the guys to hang tough, Tommy."

"We need more beer and gasoline for the generator."

"You got it."

Omar Ali went flying out of our lives an hour later. After we had offloaded the fuel drums and some boxes of rations, we put Ali on the V-22 Osprey with his computer. We strapped him to a stretcher and gave him another shot, so he was sleeping like a baby. Joe Bob's corpse went on, too. The tilt-rotor Osprey lifted off, raising the usual cloud of dirt, and flew away low with its lights off, across the desert toward the sea.

Good-bye, shipmate.

We put on flea powder and cleaned our weapons again and used the hole in the ground.

"Next time it could be you or me," Travis Clay muttered. "Any one of us. Or all."

"Yeah," I said and tossed him another beer.

CHAPTER ONE

GULF OF ADEN, NOVEMBER 9

At dawn the sea was moderate, with a four-foot swell with a nice distance between the crests. The rising wind occasionally ripped spindrift from the tops. The boat rode well, topping the crests and shipping just a little water over the gunwales that collected at the bottom.

Mustafa had two men with cans bailing as water accumulated in the boat. There wasn't much of it, so all it really did was soak clothes and weapons. There were a dozen men, so they took turns bailing. The activity helped keep them warm and alert.

They had left the island of Abd Al Kuri off the coast of Somalia in the middle of the night. Above them was a high overcast layer that hid the stars. Mustafa used a compass to hold a northerly course. It was in the hour or so before dawn that Mustafa first saw stars. The wind freshened.

The handheld radio in his pocket came to life. Mustafa held it to his ear. "She is doing thirteen knots, at coordinates—" and the voice read them off. Mustafa wrote the numbers down, then repeated them.

Yes, he had them right. He typed the numbers into his GPS, a little rectangular thing not much bigger than his hand, and watched the numbers light up. Now he had a course and distance. Only forty miles. Three-three-zero degrees.

Of course, she was heading northeast, along the coast of Yemen, so he would point a little more to the east to intercept.

Another voice, distinctive. "Mine is at—" and he read off the coordinates. "They will pass each other in two hours and ten minutes."

There were three other boats in sight in the early light, before the sun rose. They had followed the little light on the masthead. Mustafa turned it off.

The dawn revealed a clear sky and a restless, empty sea. There was a freighter to the east, but Mustafa ignored it and held his course. They were in the sea lanes that ran into and out of the Bab al Mandeb, the asshole of the Red Sea. Only twenty miles wide, that strait handled all the traffic headed to and from the Suez Canal, twenty-three thousand ships a year, almost two thousand a month, an average of sixty-three ships a day. The narrow Gulf of Suez, the Red Sea, and the Gulf of Aden were a maritime superhighway, perhaps the busiest on the planet—and it was infested with pirates. Pirate Alley, some people called it, and for good reason. Still, ships had to go through these waters to get to the Suez Canal, or else they had to transit all the way around the continent of Africa, down around the Cape of Good Hope, a place that Mustafa had never been but had heard about. Mustafa had never actually seen a world globe, but he had been told all this and had looked at rough sketches in the dirt, and like many illiterates, he had a good memory.

Mustafa al-Said was good at his job and made a fine living working at it. No other job in Somalia paid as well as being a pirate captain, except of course being the pirate sheikh, a warlord, and having a dozen or so captains with their own boats working for you. Pirating was dangerous work, but so was fishing on the open ocean, and pirating paid so much better.

Better to die at sea than starve to death, Mustafa thought.

So here they were, under a cloudless sky, on a wide, empty, restless ocean. The men were looking around in every direction, searching the horizon for a mast, a wisp of smoke, anything. The weather was far from ideal for a pirate ship: Every minute they were here increased the chances that a patrol plane would fly over to check them out. Or that the mast peeking over the horizon would turn out to be a warship.

Mustafa didn't know how radar worked, but he knew the warships could see through night and fog and his chances of spending the day here at sea undiscovered were slim. Further, he knew the warships could easily outrun his skiff, which normally had a top speed of perhaps twenty knots in a calm sea. In this swell, with ten men and weapons aboard, something less. However, for this mission the boat sported a new engine, one that pushed it at thirty knots when run flat out. The other two boats following him to the left and right were similarly equipped.

Mustafa listened to the steady throb of the engine and smiled. German. For this victim they would need the extra speed.

The men sensed their precarious position, and they were restless, even though they said nothing to Mustafa, in whom they had confidence. He had earned it. He had been to sea fifteen times in the past year and had taken six vessels, which had put plenty of money in the pockets of the men who sailed with him. The men knew his reputation and vied to crew for him. Sixty men had volunteered for this voyage, and he had picked his crew from among them. Some of them had sailed with him before, and he trusted them to obey orders. The others were recommended by powerful men in the village and on the coast, warlords, so he had taken them to preserve his relationships.

He was thinking of relationships now, of the political riptides that ruled the villages along the coast, of the money to be earned, of the protection he needed when ashore to ensure no one stole his money or killed him to take it. He needed a warlord and the warlord needed him.

He also needed the warlord's organization to ransom the ships and crews he captured. He, Mustafa al-Said, couldn't demand ransom from shipping and insurance companies spread around the globe, but a warlord could. His was Sheikh Ragnar, and he had the contacts Mustafa lacked. Without a warlord, Mustafa was merely a poor bandit with a boat. With Ragnar, he was a successful pirate, with money and women and a future.

He kept the skiff heading northwest for another hour. He got another call on the radio, from a different fishing boat. His victim had been sighted again. Mustafa updated his GPS.

"They will pass each other in an hour and twenty-two minutes."

Mustafa looked at his watch, then at his GPS. He throttled back a few hundred RPM.

The boat rode better taking the swells at an angle. Mustafa wished he could increase his speed. The faster he went, the less chance he would be intercepted by warships. Still, today he didn't want to arrive early. Timing would be the key to this capture.

He had sufficient fuel to run all day at this speed, then turn back for the Somali coast this evening and make the village on the island with a comfortable margin.

One of the men pointed out a plane running high, merely a speck against the blue sky. The dawn was here, and in minutes the sun would be rising.

Mustafa checked the engine RPMs, oil pressure, temperature and the boat's heading. He glanced at the GPS. Soon, he thought. Soon.

"Allah akbar," he shouted, *God is great,* and the men responded. One fired his weapon into the air. The reports were flat, lost in the vastness of this wilderness of sea and water. Still, all the men cheered. They were confident and ready. They drank water and ate and stared into the distance, looking for a smudge of smoke, a mast, some telltale mark upon the horizon.

If only they could find that ship . . .

Soon, Mustafa thought.

The captain of *Sultan of the Seas* was a Brit—all the officers were British, Australian or South African. His name was Arch Penney. In addition to his professional qualifications, which were absolutely top-notch, he had another trait that fueled his rise to the top in the cruise ship business: He had an uncanny ability to remember faces and names. He knew—and used—the names of every officer and man and woman in the crew, and he was quickly memorizing the passengers on this voyage. This morning as the sun peeped over the eastern horizon he was walking the deck, saying hello to early risers. He called most of them by name.

Captain Penney was a few years over forty, looked eight or so years younger and was about five feet eight inches tall. He was tanned from years of standing on open bridge wings and wore his hair short so the sea winds wouldn't mess it up or put it in his eyes. His looks were only average, but his personality made him unforgettable. His smile lit up his face, and he used it often because he was a genuinely nice guy who liked people. His officers liked to speculate about when he was going to retire from the cruise line and go into politics, where his charisma, personality and phenomenal ability to put faces and names together would undoubtedly be richly rewarded.

What his officers didn't know was that he had been offered the rank of senior officer of the cruise line, in charge of the operations of all five of its ships, and he had turned down the post. He liked what he did, and he liked having his own ship.

Whenever possible, his wife and children accompanied him on his various cruises. Arch Penney was that rarity, a truly happy man.

Last night, leaving his officers to complete the transit of the Bab al Mandeb, he walked about the passenger lounges murmuring names. "Mr. Bass, Mrs. Bass." He shook hands, smiled, asked the routine questions about how were they enjoying the cruise, were their accommodations adequate, and how was the service?

A German who still used the old "von" was aboard, Von Platen. He was accompanied by three men who apparently were his lieutenants in a car manufacturing company, Juergen Hoff, a man named Schaffler, and a young man with an unruly mop of hair, Boltz. There were some Italians, an Irish construction mogul named Enda Clancy who was apparently out of the house-building business after the housing market collapse, a retinue of British dowagers and the usual mob of Americans, which comprised about half the passenger list.

Last night he greeted the sisters, Irene and Suzanne, by name, and the Denver radio talk-show host, Mike Rosen, a genial, intelligent man with the demeanor of a college professor in mufti. The Americans liked to be called by their first names, so Arch Penney obliged. "Keith, Dilma, Ari, Buck, Chad, Chuck, Betty, Toby, Obed . . ."

Then there was Meyer Brown, a sixty-something retiree on the make, if Arch's instincts were right. What he didn't know was that Irene and

Suzanne called Brown "Putty," since he had made a remark at the bar last night that set them giggling. "I'm just putty in a woman's hands, although everything I have isn't all putty."

Brown apparently had an American woman, Nora, in his sights. Nora's daughter was nowhere to be seen. Brown was hovering over Nora, trying to keep his eyes off the striking cleavage, and entertaining her with stories of his many adventures.

The North African, Mohammed Atom, was reading something and studiously avoiding his fellow passengers, so Arch passed him with only a head nod, which Atom didn't return. Penney knew Atom's reputation, that he was an arms dealer to rebels all over the Middle East, including al Qaeda, although no one had yet caught him with enough evidence to prosecute.

This was, Arch Penney thought, a typical passenger list for this time of year. Almost no children and many gray heads.

This morning there were only three exercise nuts on the upper deck, jogging to burn off alcohol and last night's gourmet feast. Penney completed his circuit, greeting the crewmen he met by name, running his eye over everything, and headed for the bridge, where he found his first officer had things well in hand, just as Penney knew he would. The chief officer was Harry Zopp, from South Africa. It was, Penney thought, just a matter of time before Zopp got his own ship.

"Captain," Zopp said respectfully.

"Harry. How goes it?"

"We're smack in the middle of the northern eastbound traffic lane. We're five miles behind an empty tanker, matching his speed, which is thirteen knots. Six other ships on the radar, closest point of approach will be four thousand yards."

"Fishing boats?"

"Fifteen."

"How are the engineers coming on repairing that evaporator?"

"Expect to be finished by noon, sir."

"Where and when do you expect to pass this tanker that's ahead of us?" The *Sultan* couldn't remain on schedule if she loafed along at thirteen knots for more than a few hours.

Zopp told him, referring to the chart and the radar screen.

Arch Penney nodded his approval.

Zopp handed the captain three sheets of paper stapled together. Today's Somali Pirate Update from the NATO shipping center. The captain took the time to read every word.

"November 15, Somali Basin. Latitude 07 01 S, Longitude 041 22 E. Alert Number 165/2011. Warning—Warning—Warning—At 0403 UTC November 15 a merchant vessel is currently under attack by pirates in the above position.

"Alert Number 164/2011." The position followed. "A Pirate Action Group consisting of 2 x skiff with 5 POB, weapons and ladders reported in the above position."

There was more, two pages of it. Arch Penney read every entry, taking the time to refer to the chart to check the various positions.

"The murdering bastards are busier than they were last month," Zopp remarked. "The international task force has a chopper patrolling this sea lane this morning. He went over about twenty minutes ago, heading northeast, probably to check out the *Stella Maris.*" The *Stella Maris* was another cruise ship, one that had sailed from Doha and was on its way to the Suez Canal, backtracking the route just traveled by the *Sultan.* They were scheduled to pass each other this morning.

Penney nodded and handed the report back without comment. He went out onto the open wing of the bridge to catch a few moments of peace before the passengers all woke up and the day really got under way. There was a high overcast and a nice breeze from the west. This time of year the wind wasn't warm, but it was very dry.

Novembers had wonderful reputations for perfect weather in the Red Sea and Gulf of Aden. The summer monsoon was over, and the heat of the deserts to both sides was beginning to dissipate. Truly, the Red Sea was something special. Without a river running into it carrying silt and debris, it was the cleanest ocean on earth, with clear water and hundreds of coral reefs.

The Gulf of Aden, however, was another matter. This was merely an arm of the Indian Ocean. Windy and choppy this morning.

Captain Penney drew in a deep breath of the wind off the Arabian

Peninsula. Clean and dry. "Pure," the Arabs liked to say, "like Islam." Penney thought the desert wind smelled empty, like nothing at all. As he stood there, he watched a freighter with rusty sides pass his ship to port on its way into the Red Sea.

Arch finally walked inside the bridge and took a careful look at the radar picture. He spent a few minutes discussing traffic with his first officer.

The radar was always full of contacts; avoiding collisions required the most careful diligence. Harry Zopp was up to the task, Penney knew. He trusted him. Still, he was the captain, legally, morally and ethically responsible for this ship and the lives of everyone aboard her, so he monitored the bridge team in narrow waters, mentally weighing every decision, every order.

Fortunately they were out of the Bab al Mandeb, so the *Sultan* had more room to maneuver. Not only did the bridge team need to avoid other ships and fishing boats, they needed to be able to outrun and outmaneuver pirate skiffs.

When Harry Zopp had passed the tanker ahead of them and the *Sultan* was steaming northeastward at nineteen knots, paralleling the coast of Yemen, Arch Penney went below to have breakfast with his wife.

"She's up to nineteen knots now," the voice on Mustafa's radio said. "Should meet the other ship in forty-one minutes."

Mustafa typed the new coordinates into his GPS. The speed increase meant he was going to be a few minutes late. Just a little. He jammed the throttles forward and adjusted his course.

The men heard the change in the engine's song and felt the prop bite deeper into the sea. They hung on tightly and ignored the spray coming over the bow when the boat nosed into a swell. Their eyes were on the horizon. Soon.

Suzanne's husband was dead and Irene wished hers were, so they escaped Denver four times a year by going on ocean cruises. This late-autumn cruise from Istanbul to Doha was their thirteenth. Everyone they met on the *Sultan* tried to think up something witty to say when that number came up in conversation. Actually, comparing numbers of cruises was a popular topic of conversation among the passengers, most of whom, if they were to be believed, spent a significant portion of their lives leisurely sailing from port to port, seeing the planet on a floating luxury hotel.

"I've gained four pounds already," Irene remarked to her sister as they surveyed the choices on the breakfast buffet.

"The ship's paper says Denver is getting an early winter storm," Suzanne remarked, because she didn't want to discuss her weight, which was ten pounds more than Irene's. After all, the price of the cruise was all-inclusive, so the gourmet food was already paid for; why not eat it? Indeed, so were the drinks. After loading her plate with eggs Benedict, extra ham, a few potatoes, a slice of tomato and just a taste of smoked salmon, Suzanne helped herself to a Mimosa—after all, a little champagne with the orange juice wouldn't hurt much, would it?—and followed Irene across the dining room to a door that led to the porch overlooking the wake. The table they normally sat at for breakfast was empty, so they seated themselves. The waiter came over immediately, and Irene ordered coffee.

"Oooh," whispered Irene, staring back through the window at the buffet line, "there's Warren Bass and his new trophy wife."

Suzanne eyed the skinny fifty-something babe with obviously fake tits who came in with Bass. He was, Suzanne knew, a Texas oil mogul. Rumor had it the woman with him was his fourth or fifth wife. Her name was Theodolinda, and she said everyone called her "Dol." Bass was in his mid-seventies, with a full mane of gray hair, which he brushed straight back. He sported a matching mustache in a tanned, lined face. His hair stood up in the back, giving him a comb that reminded Suzanne of a woodpecker.

"She's had some plastic surgery," Irene said, scrutinizing Dol Bass, who was helping herself to one little spoonful of scrambled eggs.

"Liposuction, too, probably."

"I watched her at dinner last night. She didn't eat four bites."

"One of those, eh?"

"A gal's gotta do what a gal's gotta do."

"You need a set of tits like that," Suzanne remarked.

"Right."

"I'm thinking of getting a set when I get home," Suzanne continued. "My Christmas present to myself. D's, I think."

"Look, there's Atomic Man." Sure enough, Mohammed Atom, accent on the first vowel, came strolling into the lounge. He was wearing a blue blazer, a shirt and tie, gray trousers with a knife-edge crease and polished loafers. "He's from somewhere in Africa, I think. Stole a pile of money from the starving masses and now rides around enjoying it."

After Atom had seated himself several chairs away on the porch and ordered coffee, the sisters saw Mike Rosen working his way through the breakfast line. He was about five feet nine inches tall, reasonably thin and relatively good-looking. An economist by trade, he held forth on a Denver talk radio station for three hours every morning. He sat down at the table between Irene and Suzanne and the Basses. Irene heard him order coffee from the waiter.

Suzanne looked at her watch. "Thirty seconds . . . a minute . . . ninety seconds . . ."

Just before the second hand showed two minutes, Nora Neidlinger and her daughter, Juliet, came out of the dining room, looked around and zeroed in on the talk-show host. They brought their plates over, and he stood and graciously invited them to join him.

The daughter was addicted to hats with wide brims, which she liked to shape so that the brim hid half her face. Her long brown hair swept down her back. Nora, on the other hand, wore her hair relatively short, the better to showcase her striking features, which people noticed when they tore their eyes from her surgically enhanced figure.

"Double D's," Suzanne whispered to Irene. "Mine will be a bit more modest."

"That's wise, dear. After all, you have to carry them around."

The swirling sea breeze played with the brim of Juliet's hat. She adjusted it.

When Rosen nodded at Nora, she smiled and held his eyes.

"Ten bucks she lands him before Doha," Suzanne murmured to Irene.

"No bet," Irene shot back and glanced around for a waiter.

Rosen was making conversation with Nora and Juliet; Suzanne and Irene couldn't help but overhear. "Did you take the tour to Luxor?"

"Oh, yes," Nora said and began discussing the bus ride from Al Qusayr and the ancient monuments by the Nile.

It was all very pleasant, with the blue sea and the light wind off Arabia and the sun shining down.

Irene winked at Suzanne and asked the waiter for more coffee. Suzanne ordered another Mimosa.

Harry Zopp glanced at the surface radar—and was surprised to see four small targets approaching from the south. They were on a collision course and closing. He picked up the closed circuit telephone, which rang in the captain's stateroom.

"Pirates, I think," Harry Zopp said. "Maybe fifteen minutes out."

"Radio the navy and activate the boarding prevention plan," Captain Arch Penney ordered, then added, "I'll be right up."

Zopp dialed the preset radio frequency into the box in front of him and picked up the handset. "Red Ryder, Red Ryder, this is *Sultan of the Seas.*"

"This is Red Ryder. Go ahead, *Sultan.*"

"Looks as if we have four high-speed boats approaching from the south on a course to intercept us. About fourteen minutes out. Over."

"We'll get the chopper headed your way. Nearest surface warship is seventy miles northeast of you."

Two hours, Harry Zopp thought. He used the intercom to call the bosun. "Activate the boarding prevention plan. Pirates less than fifteen minutes away."

Zopp walked out on the starboard wing of the bridge with his binoculars. He was standing there trying to spot the boats on the horizon when Captain Penney joined him.

"Just got a glimpse of one of them," Zopp said. "Radar says they are making thirty knots."

The captain told the helmsman, "All engines ahead full." Full speed for the *Sultan* was thirty-one knots, but with the pirate boats on the starboard quarter, there was no way he was going to outrun them on this heading. He went inside the bridge and looked at the moving map display on the GPS. He was twenty miles offshore. If he turned tail to the pirates, he would be heading toward Yemen. He could buy some time, but he couldn't sail through sand and stone.

Penney glanced again at the radar. He could see the symbol for the *Stella Maris,* fifteen miles ahead. She would pass down his left side if he kept on this course. "Come left ten degrees," Penney told the helmsman. This course would take him very near to the *Stella Maris.* He picked up the radio handset and dialed in the proper frequency, then called *Stella Maris.* Better tell her captain what was going on.

That was when he got a bad shock. The voice of the *Stella Maris*'s captain rang in his ears. "*Stella Maris* is under attack by pirate boats, apparently from Yemen. Three of them. They are shooting up the ship. Mayday, Mayday, Mayday!"

Lieutenant de vaisseau Gilbert Louceck surveyed the instruments in the cockpit of his Panther helicopter and checked the radar distance readout to the ship currently under attack, eighteen miles from the Yemen coast. In his headset he could hear the captain of the ship calling Mayday in English, and the controller aboard the French destroyer talking to him in French. Long ago he had learned to sort all these voices out. His copilot was answering the controller just now, giving him a range and how many minutes they were from the ship under attack, the *Stella Maris.* Ten miles to go. A little less than five minutes.

Now he was listening to the panicky voice of the ship's radio operator. Apparently the captain was busy conning the ship.

"They are shooting at the bridge." The words were in English, although heavily accented. Idly, Louceck wondered about the speaker's nationality.

"Now they are approaching again." While he held the microphone open, Louceck could hear a beating sound that he took to be automatic gunfire. "Three boats. Maybe ten men in each boat."

Louceck could see the ship materialize out of the haze, which seemed thicker the higher one got. By now he had the helicopter in a descent, accelerating.

"About three minutes, *capitaine,*" the copilot said, quite unnecessarily.

Automatically Louceck checked his fuel. He had enough to stay over the cruise ship for perhaps twenty minutes, then he would have to fly back to the *Toulon,* his ship.

"Call the ship," he told the copilot. "Get them heading this way." If the ship could close the distance, that would save a few gallons, give him another minute or two over the cruise ship.

As the copilot made the call, Louceck turned the safety sleeve on the master armament switch and lifted it, arming the Giat 20 mm cannon carried in the external pod. Just in case. He could see the boats now. He lowered the nose still more, intending to make a low pass.

The pirates knew the game. His orders did not permit him to open fire on the pirates unless they fired at him, which of course they would not do. They knew his orders as well as he did. Still, if he could intimidate them, make them turn away . . .

"I'm taking photos." That was the crewman in back.

"They are alongside." The voice was high-pitched, the words nearly impossible to understand. "I leave microphone open and move away from radio."

The copilot, Pigot, fidgeted in his seat.

Sure enough, now continuous cacophony sounded in the helicopter crewmen's ears.

A burst of gunfire came over the radio, then the transmission ceased abruptly.

Lieutenant Louceck was at fifty feet, making 180 knots, coming down the port side of the cruise ship. One pirate boat was against the side.

People, all over the ship, running, some leaning over the rail, trying to see. Like ants on a corpse!

Louceck roared right over the pirate boat, then threw the chopper into a hard turn while he pulled up on the cyclic. The chopper quickly lost speed, slowing dramatically as it came around in the turn.

The captain of *Stella Maris* was holding his ship steady on course. Why didn't he turn into the pirate boat, force them away from the ship?

While Louceck was wondering, a hole appeared in the Plexiglas to his left. Then another.

"They're shooting," Pigot roared into the ICS. His voice drowned out the cacophony coming over the radio.

Automatically Leucock dumped his nose and began accelerating. Fortunately he was pointed right at the pirate boat. His finger found the trigger on the stick and he squeezed off a burst. A handful of 20 mm shells struck the water right beside the pirate boat, then Louceck was overhead and saw a man shooting at him with a rifle, then he was going away, his tail rotor pointing at the danger as the massive slab sides of the ship slid by the cockpit on his left.

She looked like a floating hotel, with rows of balconies and white faces and people waving their arms at him. At him!

Louceck checked the engine instruments and hydraulic gauges. All seemed okay . . . for now. Here he was, over hostile pirates, a hundred miles from the *Toulon.* If this machine stopped flying, he was going into the sea.

"Any damage back there?" Louceck asked the crewman.

"Don't see any." The kid's voice was none too steady. Well, neither was Louceck's or Pigot's.

Louceck climbed and turned again and looked for the other pirate boats, which were on the starboard side of the ship, toward Yemen. They were still fifty yards or so away from *Stella Maris,* angling in.

Why didn't the captain turn his ship?

Louceck came smoothly around and lowered his nose for another pass at the pirate boat on the port side, which was still almost against the ship, with grappling hooks being thrown up toward the ship's railings.

Louceck flew the gun's pipper into the pirate boat and squeezed the trigger. He held it down, walking it the length of the boat, then released it.

"Don't hit the ship!" Pigot roared, and automatically Louceck slammed the cyclic left, lifting the right side of his rotor disk. The ship was right there, close enough to touch. He was so engrossed in shooting at the pirates . . . how he had failed to hit the liner he didn't know. A miracle.

The pirate boat fell rapidly behind the cruise ship, foundering in the wake.

Louceck crossed the cruise ship's bow and began a circle of the two other pirate boats. They seemed to be holding their distance from the cruise ship *Stella Maris.*

He could hear Pigot talking to *Stella Maris*'s captain, telling him to speed up and turn into the pirates. He didn't catch the captain's reply, but he heard Pigot call him a fool.

Down Louceck went to ten feet off the water, slowing, flying between the pirate boats and the cruise ship.

He had done this a dozen times in the last four months. Prevented the pirates from closing on their victim. Pirates had never before shot at him.

To his horror, the pirates in the nearest skiff were also shooting. He saw at least four men with automatic assault rifles pointing at him, saw the muzzle flashes, felt the bullets striking the helicopter.

He heard the crewman groan on the ICS.

Louceck already had picked up the tail and was accelerating away. He would come around and sink this boat, too.

Halfway through his turn Pigot pointed to the left engine instruments. The engine was overheating, losing power. Now he looked back as he turned. Black smoke behind him.

Falling oil pressure.

The crewman was on the ICS. "I'm hit," he said. "In the leg."

Pigot began unstrapping as Louceck shut the left engine down and turned toward the *Toulon,* one hundred miles away. Pigot maneuvered himself out of his seat and went aft to look after the crewman.

Damn, damn and double damn.

CHAPTER TWO

Mustafa and his pirates had *Sultan of the Seas* in sight. He was on her beam. She was making at least twenty-five knots. He had to hold in eighty degrees of lead as he closed to keep her from moving to his front.

The men in the boat grasped their weapons. A few fired short bursts into the air in celebratory anticipation. The reports sounded flat.

Mustafa's radio was alive in his hand. He could hear the other boats attacking *Stella Maris* talking to each other. He breathed a sigh of relief when he heard the helicopter had left trailing smoke. One skiff sunk. If anyone who had been aboard was still alive, he was on his own; Mustafa needed all his boats if he hoped to capture a cruise ship. The men knew that, knew the risks, and had come anyway. At least there were two more skiffs to harass *Stella Maris,* which was only ten miles to the northeast.

"Mustafa, this is Ahmed."

"Yes."

"We are closing from the north on *Sultan*. Do you have us in sight?"

"No."

They had the cruise ship in a classic trap. Pirates were closing from two sides, so whichever way *Sultan of the Seas* turned, she would be intercepted.

Yes! The plan was working!

Captain Arch Penney was facing his worst nightmare: a pirate attack on his ship. He had two boatloads of pirates to port and four to starboard. Ten miles ahead, two or three pirate boats were attacking another cruise ship.

Penney was on the radiotelephone to the Task Force 151 tactical action officer on duty this morning. The navy guy had a calm, baritone American voice.

"Nearest surface warship is an hour and a half away," the American navy dude said, "but we will have a helo overhead in twenty minutes."

"Send it."

Penney handed the phone to Harry Zopp and consulted the computer screen that showed all the surface targets in the area, their course and speed, and the prediction of where they would be in a minute, or five or ten, if they didn't change course or speed. The computer's information was derived from the radar. The computer operator had to designate which targets were which.

Arch was not without a plan. He and the other captains of the cruise line, together with the senior captain, had worked out a contingency plan for just such an attack and presented it to management, which had insisted upon some changes designed to protect the company from lawsuits, then approved it.

The plan was The Plan. Unfortunately cruise ships did not carry weapons of any kind, not even a pistol to take down a raving, homicidal berserker. So The Plan relied upon speed and mild maneuvering to keep boatloads of armed, homicidal pirates at bay. However, the cruise line was not willing to have the pirates slaughter a great many of its customers, so if the pirates persisted in shooting into the cruise ship, the captain was supposed to surrender, on the theory that the pirates would then ransom ship, passengers and crew. It all sounded very logical in the boardroom of the cruise company in London.

"We have insured against the risk," the chairman told Captain Penney.

Ah, yes. Insurance. Even if the company had to refund fares and ransom ship, passengers and crew and pay a few families damages because they lost a family member, the cruise line wasn't going to lose money. Comforting, that.

Sultan of the Seas carried 490 passengers and 370 officers and crew. Eight hundred sixty defenseless people. Still, the international task force, Task Force 151, was out there on patrol, just over the horizon, ready to intimidate those naughty pirates and protect honest people from violent, unwashed, starving Africans.

"Don't worry, Captain," the chairman had said. "You can outrun them. The allied navies can deal with them."

Arch Penney looked again at the computer display. If he maintained this course and speed, the helo would arrive eight minutes after the pirates.

Eight minutes. How many people would the pirates maim and kill in eight minutes?

He picked up the mike for the ship's public address system and flipped it on.

"This is the captain. As you may know if you are on the weather decks, we are being intercepted by at least six small boats, which may contain pirates. We will do all we can to protect you and this ship. I request everyone to clear the weather decks and move to the interior of the ship, away from the windows, balconies and portholes. If your stateroom has a balcony, please step out into the passageway and remain there. I will keep you updated."

He switched off.

Harry looked at him with a raised eyebrow. "Going to panic the old pussies, aren't you?"

Arch Penney shrugged and used his handheld radio to call the bosun. "Are you ready?"

"Two minutes."

"Use the LRAD whenever they get in range." The Long Range Acoustic Device aimed a powerful sound blast in a narrow cone. At one hundred yards, the high-pitched wail was painful. At fifty yards, it was capable of rupturing eardrums. The ship had four LRADs installed, two on each side.

Now Penney asked the computer operator, "Where's that chopper?"

"One-two-two degrees true at forty-eight miles."

"Our speed?"

"Twenty-eight knots and increasing," Harry Zopp said. "We are full ahead, sir."

"Very well. Helmsman, use slow rate on the turn and come starboard to course one-two-zero degrees. Steady on it." These new cruise liners had no rudder, but instead had engines in pods mounted below the hull. The helmsman was actually turning the pods. Maneuvering up to a pier, the pods allowed the ship to be turned in its own length and dispensed with the necessity of using tugboats.

"Slow rate on the turn," echoed the helmsman. "Come starboard and steady up on one-two-zero degrees, sir."

The slow rate of turn wouldn't tilt the deck very much, although the ship would take a while to get through the turn. With luck, Arch Penney thought he could get the pirates into his rear quarter. At the very least, the last two boats, out of Yemen, would be behind him in a tail chase.

U.S. Navy Lieutenant Buck Peterson was the pilot in command of the Sikorsky MH-60R on its way toward the two cruise ships under attack by pirates.

This had started out as just another day at sea, with coffee and eggs and reams of paperwork awaiting his attention. USS *Richard Ward* only carried one helo, three pilots, two enlisted crewmen and two aviation mechanics. As the senior aviator, he owned the flying machine and the officers and men—and was responsible for everything.

When the call came from the task force commander, he had mounted up with the senior copilot and senior crewman, a first class named Wilsey. The captain already had his ship on a rendezvous heading, and he turned into the wind just long enough to let the chopper lift off.

Now Buck Peterson was on the radio to the flagship. Pirates had fired on a French Panther over *Stella Maris,* and the Frenchie had sunk one boat, then retired. Still iffy whether he was going to make his base ship or go into the drink. Two boats were still shooting at *Stella Maris*; the captain was in a panic, but he said he thought he could outrun them. He was slowly pulling away, leaving them behind.

The flagship gave Peterson a heading to *Sultan of the Seas.* It was being intercepted by six boats, which had it boxed.

"Wilsey, you got that gun loaded?" Buck asked on the intercom.

"Yes, sir." As crewman, Petty Officer Wilsey was in charge of the helicopter's only defensive armament, an M-60 machine gun mounted in the door. It wasn't a cannon, but it threw a nice stream of 7.62 mm NATO slugs that could slaughter a boatload of pirates in seconds. Peterson had never had to order the gunner to fire; the sight of the gun pointed their way was always enough to dissuade even the most ardent buccaneers. There was just nowhere to hide, nothing to get behind, in an open boat. Every single pirate thought that gun barrel was pointed precisely at him.

Peterson checked the mileage to the *Sultan* while he listened to her captain talking on the radio to the Task Force 151 duty officer aboard the flagship.

Peterson's copilot was Crash Pizzino, a big rangy man with a wicked sense of humor. He wasn't smiling now. He was tightening his straps, running through the checklist, securing loose objects in the cockpit. Crash was also listening to the *Sultan*'s captain describe the tactical scene, the pirate skiffs closing in . . .

"My God, Suzanne! Pirates!"

"We could be in Hawaii this very minute, sister of mine. I wanted to go to Hawaii. Remember?"

"We've been to Hawaii five times," Irene said distractedly. They were crammed into a passageway just forward of the ninth deck aft dining room and the outside portico where they had eaten breakfast. Someone had spotted the open boats on the horizon, and people had idly turned to watch as the skiffs closed on a collision course. Then the captain had galvanized everyone into action.

Chairs were scooted back; people hurried to get inside the ship, away from the windows and open decks. Now Suzanne, Irene, Mike Rosen,

Nora and Juliet were packed together in the passageway along with almost two dozen other people. A cook was also there—he looked like a Filipino—and he was obviously frightened. One of the crewmen spoke to him sharply in a language Suzanne and Irene didn't understand, and the man calmed down somewhat.

Suzanne got tired of standing. She sat down on the deck and put her back against the passageway wall, or bulkhead, or whatever they called it. Irene joined her on the deck but kept her legs tucked under her. Suzanne was not limber enough and let hers stick out straight. *Actually,* she thought, *for a woman of my age, they aren't bad legs.*

"Hawaii," Suzanne grumped. "Egypt is filthy, the Egyptians are filthy, Aqaba is a dump. No human in his right mind would pay money to ride that damn bus across the desert to Luxor. I still can't believe we did it. See Aqaba was number nine thousand and twelve on my Before-I-Die Bucket List."

"Scratch it off."

"You won't admit it, but this is the worst cruise we've ever been on. Pirates, no less!"

Irene sighed. "Next time, Kaanapali Beach."

"You bet your ass," Suzanne shot back.

Sultan's turn seaward, into his little squadron of onrushing boats, gave Mustafa al-Said a bad moment. The ship kept turning, and he tried to turn away, then buttonhook back and come alongside, but the constantly changing course made that impossible. Now the ship was doing at least thirty knots. Mustafa's engine was howling at the red line, and the skiff seemed to leap from swell to swell. Two of the boats couldn't make this speed, but the turn into them had given them a chance.

Finally *Sultan* steadied up on a southeasterly course, directly away from the land. The captain instinctively went for sea room, Mustafa realized, although that would do him no good. The four pirate boats in front of him converged.

Mustafa S-turned once and then bore in for a rendezvous on the liner's starboard side. He well knew if he fell astern he could never catch

Sultan. He swept in, turning hard to parallel, keeping his boat closing. Another boat was ahead of him and went in fearlessly against the side of the ship.

Then he heard the noise. High-pitched, a scream, rising in volume. He put on his sound-supressor headset, a simple set of mufflers, one over each ear, as the other men in the boat hastily pulled theirs on, too.

Mustafa could hear the wail anyway. It was insanely loud.

The men began shooting at the LRAD installations. A sailor stood behind each unit, aiming it at the nearest pirate skiff.

"Kill them, kill them," Mustafa screamed, but no one heard it.

Nuri was manning the machine gun, and he bent down and tried to aim, which was difficult in the bucking, heaving boat. He began firing bursts at the LRAD units.

The sailors manning the LRAD units disappeared. Probably down behind the railings. Two more long bursts, then the sound stopped.

The skiff nearest the ship was not under control. The helm wandered; the boat nosed in against the towering side of the Sultan, was caught in the wash and overturned instantly.

Mustafa ignored the pirates in the water. If they drowned, they drowned. They were in it for the money, just as he and his men were. If Mustafa didn't press the attack, there would be no money for anyone.

"The bridge," he shouted to his men and pointed. Three of them fired AK-47s at the bridge.

Radio talk-show host Mike Rosen was not huddled in a passageway inside the ship. He didn't have it in him. He was on the eighth-deck gallery, and from his vantage point he could see the sailor manning the amidships LRAD transmitter. He heard the wail, of course, but it was focused on the pirate boats, so it was merely unpleasant.

Rosen saw the machine-gun bullets striking around the unit, saw the sparks, felt the impacts, and he saw the sailor, an officer apparently, fall heavily to the deck.

More bullets. The sound stopped.

The man on the deck wasn't moving. Staying below the railing, Rosen hurried to him in the classic combat waddle. Bullet holes everywhere. He turned the officer over. He had been hit at least four times. Some blood, but not much. The officer's eyes were frozen, focused on nothing at all.

At least one of the machine-gun bullets had hit the main transmitter.

Rosen abandoned it and waddled back toward his vantage point, a small gap in the railing that allowed him to watch the pirate boats. He saw the one turn in against the ship and be flipped over by the ship's wash. Men spilled into the water, men without life preservers.

Below, on the fifth-deck gallery, between the lifeboats, Rosen caught glimpses of men connecting fire hoses to fixed, movable nozzles, nozzles aimed over the side. They tried to stay below the railing, out of sight of the pirates.

Oh, man.

Mustafa's skiff was a couple of knots faster than the *Sultan.* It was just enough to allow it to get closer and closer. The men fired long bursts at the bridge; glass cascaded from the windows, a little shower of shimmering reflections.

Now the distance to the ship, less than a hundred yards, began to close quickly. The *Sultan* was turning into him! Faster than thought, Mustafa spun the wheel to bring his bow starboard . . . and the distance began to open.

The machine gun kept burping short bursts. The men with the AKs hosed off whole magazines.

Now the *Sultan* veered left; Mustafa saw her heel. He heard a scream on the radio. Then silence.

One of the other boats gave him the news. *Sultan* had swamped another of the pirate skiffs, then had run over her.

Sultan was steadying again. Mustafa veered in fearlessly to give the machine gunner a better target.

"The masts. The antenna. Shoot them off," he roared over the thunder of the engine and guns at Nuri on the machine gun. That was the plan, but in action men forgot things. The pirates with AKs never aimed them. They held them hip high and squirted. Even shooting from the hip in an open boat bucking the swells, the ship was too big to miss. The AKs merely scared people and broke windows, which was fine because scared people surrender quickly.

His boat was about ten yards from *Sultan* when streams of water under intense pressure shot forth. Hard, narrow rivers of water. One of the streams hit the boat, and Mustafa went down. He hung on to the wheel as the stream of water went forward in the boat, threatening to swamp it and sweeping two men over the side.

Mustafa veered away just in time.

The engine still ran fine. Men were bailing like mad.

One of the men had an RPG-7 launcher. He brought it to his shoulder, then waved at Mustafa, who cranked the wheel over and once again started in toward the ship.

The third grenade did the trick. It burst the last of the movable nozzles and let water merely pour over the ship's side.

How much longer? Mustafa asked himself. The captain must be thinking of the passengers and crew—and, of course, his own life, the infidel dog.

Better scare them some more. Mustafa saw Ahmad looking at him, a silent question. He had the rocket-propelled grenade launcher reloaded. Mustafa gestured toward the bridge.

This RPG hit behind the bridge, went through a big window and made a nice bang. Glass and smoke blew out.

Buck Peterson kept the Sikorsky coming down. The pirates were shooting up the ship. They were not yet aboard. The ship was at flank speed.

Now Buck saw the pirate boat on *Sultan*'s starboard side. It was the closest, so he went for it. Began slowing his chopper, coming around so that he could fly between the boat and the ship. Fortunately that put his door-mounted gun on the side of the pirate boat.

"Get ready, Wilsey. Fire a burst into the water short of their boat."

"Aye aye, sir," Wilsey said, as if he had been asked to make coffee.

That Wilsey was a good man, cool under pressure. Buck wished he had Wilsey's kind of calm.

He brought the Seahawk around and came up the wake, nearly over the ship. Heard the M-60 vomit out a burst, saw it turn the water to foam near a pirate boat.

That ought to sober up the bastards.

Buck Peterson was over the ship's railing, amidships, with the pirate boat on his beam, when an RPG exploded inside the Seahawk. The explosion was unexpected, violent, and the chopper began to buck.

Right engine . . . losing power! Hydraulics going . . . warning lights flashing.

Buck Peterson turned away from *Sultan,* the only thing he could do, right across the pirate boat, and picked up his tail trying to gain speed.

He felt the thumps as bullets smashed into the Seahawk, then realized he couldn't keep the machine in the air. He tried to lower the tail to cushion the impact with the sea.

It wasn't even a controlled crash. The impact of the collision with seawater at speed collapsed the windshield and killed Peterson and Pizzino instantly. Petty Officer Wilsey was already dead, killed by the RPG.

The splash site soon subsided into a roiling mass of bubbles as the *Sultan* and Mustafa's boats swept away at thirty knots.

Arch Penney's hopes sank with the remains of the Sikorsky. The American duty officer said there were no more helicopters available and the destroyer *Richard Ward* was over an hour away. The safety of his passengers and crew weighed heavily upon the captain.

Just as his hopes reached low ebb, the radio squawked again. "*Sultan,* we have jets ten minute away."

Harry Zopp replied, "The pirates are shooting machine guns into this ship and launching grenades. We are defenseless. Do you people understand that?"

"We are unable to contact the helicopter that was in your vicinity. Is it still there?"

"The pirates shot it down. It crashed into the ocean."

"Roger." The voice was tired, cold.

Penney grabbed the radiotelephone from his chief officer. "Are these jets going to just fly around, or will they do something to actually defend this ship and the nine hundred people aboard her?"

"We are assessing the situation."

"Bloody Yanks," Harry Zopp said.

Another burst of machine-gun bullets thudded into the bridge ceiling. Penney and his bridge team were huddled on the deck, out of the line of fire. The helmsman was sitting on the deck, reaching up to turn the steering controls. The RPG had exploded behind the bridge in the navigator's office; now a small fire was emitting acrid smoke. Fortunately no one on the bridge had yet been killed, although one sailor had some shrapnel in a leg from the grenade blast. Penney wondered if any of the passengers had stopped a bullet. No, he thought, the question was, How many?

There would be more grenade blasts, Penney thought bitterly. This wasn't a warship; his crewmen weren't trained warfighters. Hell, they didn't have any weapons to fight with. And the passengers: For Christ's sake, they were mostly middle-aged and old men and women, from all over the world. The only thing they had in common was the fact they could afford the fare for the cruise.

Another hatful of machine-gun bullets arrived and took out more of the forward glass. There wasn't much glass left. Little pieces of insulation rained down from the damaged ceiling. The sea wind swept the bridge.

Penney sneaked a peek over the railing. One of the skiffs, the one with the machine gun, was close on the starboard side, no more than fifty yards away. He scuttled across the bridge and looked on the port side. Two boats there, closing. With his naked eye he could see the men in the boat wrestling with a grenade launcher.

"Eight minutes," Harry Zopp said, glancing at his watch.

Two more grenades slammed into the ship. Penney felt the thuds the explosions created.

Huddled under the rail on the port wing of the bridge, the captain thought he heard a woman screaming. It was high-pitched, and faint.

The Task Force 151 commander was U.S. Navy Rear Admiral Toad Tarkington. He stood in the tactical flag spaces aboard his flagship staring at the flat-screen situation display. The French chopper had been shot up over *Stella Maris* but was still airborne, on its way back to its mother ship. The American Seahawk had ceased transmitting; *Sultan* said the pirates shot it down.

Tarkington took a deep breath. The pirates really wanted these ships and were betting everything they could get them. Fortunately *Stella Maris* looked as if she were outrunning the two skiffs that had attacked her.

Two F-18s patrolling from a carrier three hundred miles to the north, toward the Persian Gulf, were on their way. Fuel would be tight. They could stay over *Sultan* for no more than five minutes. The carrier was launching a tanker, but it was at least a half hour behind the fighters. If the fighters stayed over *Sultan* until the tanker arrived, they would be lost if they couldn't take fuel from the tanker, for any reason. Should he risk two planes and the lives of two pilots by keeping them over *Sultan*? Should he order the pilots to shoot at the pirates?

Tarkington knew the Rules of Engagement cold, and he understood the political climate in which he operated. He would create an international incident if he ordered the jets to use their weapons, an incident that would probably have serious political repercussions in European capitals, perhaps jeopardizing the continued existence of the antipiracy task force. On the other hand, the pirates had shot at his helicopters, perhaps killed the crewmen. He had spent his career in the U.S. Navy; self-defense was instinctive, institutional, ingrained. Overaggressiveness in the face of a threat could be forgiven; excessive caution, never. Then there were all the people on that cruise ship . . .

Toad Tarkington made his decision. "Tell Sea Wolf flight to sink the pirate boats. Weapons free."

"Aye aye, sir."

Lieutenant Commander Dieter Gerhart was leading Sea Wolf flight. Lieutenant (junior grade) Tom Borosco was on his wing. Gerhart listened to the orders, then asked Borosco, "You get that, Tom?"

"Roger."

"You take the boats on the land side, I'll take the boats on the seaward side. Strafe and sink them."

"Got it."

Gerhart consulted the mil-setting table on his kneeboard, found the mil setting he wanted and dialed it into the gunsight. He adjusted the brightness of the reticle, trying to find a setting that would not overpower a hard-to-see target on a gray ocean on a hazy day. Finally he toggled his master armament switch on and selected GUN.

He pushed the nose over, left the power up. He had the cruise ship on radar . . . if indeed it was the right ship. She was twenty-five miles away. He wished visibility were better.

Waiting was difficult as the jets plunged deeper into the atmosphere and the range marched down. Gerhart set his radar altimeter to sound a warning at 1,100 feet above the sea. At 1,100 feet, he would open fire, and hold the trigger down for no more than a second. At 900 feet he should be off the gun and pulling out, right or left, to avoid any ricochets off the water.

He was at six miles when he saw the ship embedded in the haze. There, one, two, three skiffs on the starboard side. He didn't see the fourth, but he could only attack them one at a time, so he picked the closest and went for it.

Power back, down to 420, now 400 . . . speed bleeding off, angle steep because he was diving toward a point well ahead of his target, which was paralleling the ship, moving toward a point perhaps twenty degrees right of his six o'clock.

He raised the nose to establish a ten-degree dive angle, put the pipper short of the boat, slightly left . . . saw 1,500 feet on the radar altimeter, 1,500 on the pressure altimeter, airspeed down to 350. A touch fast for his taste, but okay.

He would be shooting in three seconds.

Captain Arch Penney felt the heavy thud of a nearby grenade blast. Idly, he wondered how many grenades the pirates had brought along. Probably enough to murder hundreds of people.

Three minutes.

"Here come the jets."

Penney risked a look. He saw only one, coming in fast, slanting down. It was coming from about ten degrees left of the bow and crossing over the extended centerline of the ship toward the starboard boats.

Even as he saw the jet, Penney realized it wasn't going for the skiff nearest the ship, but one half a mile away.

He watched, mesmerized. The fighter came plunging down like a hawk.

The F/A-18 Hornet dipped low, perhaps a thousand feet, and began its pullout. The pirate boat disappeared in a cloud of sea spray as the audible buzz from the jet's cannon reached him, seconds late.

"There's a fighter over here, too," someone called. "Hammered a boat."

What would the skiff right by the ship do?

"Stick it to those balmy bastards," another man yelled.

Mustafa al-Said was so intent on getting more RPGs into the *Sultan*'s bridge that he didn't see the jet fighters at first. One of his men pointed . . . then he saw them. Saw one of the boats disappear under a hail of cannon shells. The jet was pulling out, climbing and turning for another pass.

Mustafa spun the wheel. The fighter pilot might not take the chance of shooting so close to the ship. Mustafa expertly brought his skiff to within ten feet of the speeding cruise ship. The sea between ship and boat was a river of foam.

The RPG man fired another grenade right into the bridge wing.

The explosion of the grenade smashed into the officers and sailors huddled on the deck of the bridge. The concussion momentarily stunned Arch Penney. He found himself sprawled on the deck. Blood. Everything was covered with a fine spray of blood. He looked around. Smoke . . . carnage . . . a severed arm lay nearby on the deck. Bodies all over. Harry Zopp was coming around, bleeding from the head. He met his gaze.

"Bloody hell," said Arch Penney. He crawled to the engine controls and moved the handles to ALL STOP.

. . .

"Strike, Sea Wolf One Oh Five. The cruise ship seems to be slowing. There is a pirate skiff alongside."

"Can you attack it?"

"Too close to the ship."

But one boat wasn't. Gerhart steadied up, checked his dive angle and pulled the pipper onto the boat. Closing . . . now! The radar altimeter deedled, he squeezed the trigger, the gun vibrated, then he was pulling.

He glanced back. Spray obscured the skiff. As it exited the cloud of water, he could see that the boat was losing way, that people were jumping into the sea.

The screws of the *Sultan* were no longer churning the ocean into foam. She was obviously decelerating. A pirate boat was alongside.

Dieter Gerhart turned back for a closer look.

"Gear, the bastards are climbing aboard." That was Tom.

Gerhart got a glimpse of men going up the ropes hand over hand, assault rifles on slings on their backs.

Shit!

They had lost. The pirates were aboard! Two more boats were closing from astern. By the time the fighters got into shooting position, those two boats would be too close to the ship.

There wasn't a damn thing two fighter jocks could do about it.

"Join on me, Tom. We'll make a low pass, then go home."

That is what they did. The two jets went over the *Sultan* just above the top of the radar mast at three hundred knots. Dieter Gerhart got a good look at two men climbing a rope up the ship's side. He turned to the northeast, began climbing, and keyed his radio.

As he listened to Sea Wolf lead's report, Admiral Toad Tarkington smote his thigh.

"Send a Flash message to Washington," he ordered curtly. "Pirates just captured a cruise ship."

CHAPTER THREE

Admiral Toad Tarkington stared at the flat-screen display. The destroyer, *Richard Ward,* was about an hour away from *Sultan of the Seas.* His flagship, *Chosin Reservoir,* an amphibious assault ship with the majority of a Marine Expeditionary Unit, an MEU, embarked, was two hours away. The ship was at flight quarters; the helicopters were being readied.

But for what?

The MEU, with 2,200 marines, was a fast reaction force that carried its own logistics. It had choppers, landing craft, artillery and armor, plus the ammo and food to sustain itself anywhere it was inserted. One of the marine units was a Force Recon team, the tip of the marine spear, and was specially trained to board ships under hostile fire.

Toad looked around the ops space. Sure enough, the colonel commanding the MEU was behind him, watching the whole evolution. Toad motioned to him.

The marine's name was Maximus Zakhem, and he didn't have two pounds of extra fat on him. With square shoulders and a square face, hair in a buzz cut that made it almost invisible on his tanned head, he looked every inch a professional warrior. Some of the naval officers referred to him as the marine from central casting, behind his back, of course. Still, Colonel Zakhem did a hundred push-ups every morning just to get the blood flowing and then worked out on the flight deck with his men. There wasn't a private or lance corporal in his command in better physical shape. He could even go step for step with the sergeants of Force Recon, who were fifteen to twenty years younger than he was.

The admiral's chief of staff and his operations officer joined them.

Admiral Tarkington summarized the situation. Since he had been watching for the last hour, Colonel Zakhem had no questions.

"The pirates will probably take the cruise ship south to a Somali port," Toad said with a sigh, then paused to listen to a call from the bridge of *Sultan.*

"Pirates are aboard. At least a dozen. They will undoubtedly be upon the bridge, what's left of it, in seconds." There followed a burst of gunfire; then the radio went dead.

Colonel Zakhem broke the silence with the remark, "That captain had a tough decision to make. He was trying to save the lives of his passengers and crew. Surrendering was the right thing to do."

He and the admiral knew the pirates would kill just enough people to horrify and frighten the cruise ship owners, but no more, so they could demand a big ransom and get it. Like politics and prostitution, piracy was all about the money.

"We could intercept them on the way to Somalia," Toad Tarkington said, musing aloud. "What do you think?"

"Board the ship?"

Toad shrugged. Boarding was only one possibility.

Zakhem took a deep breath. "It could be done, Admiral . . . if you are willing to accept civilian casualties. A packed cruise ship . . . my men will have to go after the pirates aggressively and defend themselves."

Toad stirred uncomfortably in his chair. Over eight hundred civilians. Scenes of slaughter ran through his mind. He listened to the thoughts of his chief of staff, a navy captain, and his operations officer, a commander, but he had already decided.

"We'll intercept the liner," Tarkington said, his mind made up. "Try to intimidate the pirates with a show of force. Ops, get the task force on a course to intercept. Have *Richard Ward* close and stay out of rifle shot off their beam while we get more ships there. In the meantime, I want a helo over the ship continuously. They are to stay out of range of RPGs and machine guns."

"Aye aye, sir."

"We've lost a chopper off the *Ward.* Launch a couple from this ship to search for survivors and take photos. I want shots of that cruise ship from every possible angle."

"Sir, how about picking up pirates from the ocean?"

"Anybody they can find," the admiral said. "I'd like some prisoners to interrogate to see if we can find out just what we're up against."

He addressed his next sentence to the chief of staff. "Send a message to the strike group commander." This was the admiral aboard the carrier three hundred miles northeast. "I would appreciate it if he would bring his force to rendezvous with all possible speed, if his operational commitments will allow it. We could certainly use an E-2 as soon as possible." The E-2 Hawkeye carried a huge radar dish on its back and could act as an eye in the sky, relaying messages and data-linking contacts.

He eyed Zakhem. "We'll use all your marines. Transfer as many as practicable to *Richard Ward.* I want them lining the decks of both ships, armed, in helmets, apparently ready to shoot if even one of those sons takes a pot shot. Actual shooting will be done by snipers, on officers' orders. Force Recon marines will be overhead in choppers and Ospreys, ready to rappel down. I want to put the fear of God in these people, show them overwhelming military force. Saddle up your troops and brief them."

"Yes, sir," Zakhem said. "With your permission, sir, I want to be in an Osprey, ready to go down the rope if we get to board."

Toad paused. Zakhem might be needed later to lead his entire command. Allowing him to go into combat was a calculated risk. Still, Max Zakhem was no headquarters paper-pusher. He had fought in three wars and had the scars to prove it. In an opposed boarding of a cruise liner packed with noncombatants his experience and judgment might prove invaluable.

The admiral smiled grimly. "Of course, Colonel."

The colonel and Toad's two staffers hustled away, leaving him to stare at the tactical situation display. Time was on his side. He had plenty of time to marshal his troops and make an overwhelming show of force. That tactic, he thought, had an excellent chance of success with little downside. Although the pirates could murder a few people to prove they meant business, killing passengers wouldn't make the navy and marines go away. Regardless of what they did, the pirates had to be made to realize they couldn't win.

And if the show of force didn't work, he could try to put a SEAL team aboard. If everything failed, hell, maybe the politicians would elect to pay the money the pirates would demand.

Mustafa al-Said walked confidently through the passageway that led to the bridge. He knew exactly where this passageway led because he had carefully studied the deck plan for this ship. Someone had downloaded it from the Internet several weeks ago.

Two men accompanied him. They held their AKs at hip level, ready to fire. The people sitting on the deck against the bulkhead pulled in their feet and looked at the three Somalis curiously.

The door to the bridge was sprung. No doubt from the RPG.

Mustafa gestured, and his men forced it open. Mustafa walked through into a scene from a slaughterhouse. He had seen shot-up bridges before and expected it.

The captain was the man in uniform with four stripes on his tabs, bloody, trying to stand erect near the steering station. An arm and a disemboweled body lay on the floor, and a bloody mist had turned everything pink. Even the captain's uniform. One sailor, the helmsman, sat on the deck beside the steering station, bleeding from a leg wound. Two other sailors appeared uninjured. They were trying to staunch the flow of blood from another injured officer.

Mustafa could see the captain was unarmed. They all were. His two men spread out to cover them with their weapons anyway.

Mustafa walked out to the port wing of the bridge and looked aft.

Men were climbing from a skiff up ropes attached to grappling hooks. There were only two men left in the skiff. They secured a rope to a machine gun on a tripod, and the men on deck hauled it up. The last rope went around a box of ammo. When gun and ammo were aboard, the last two men on the skiff abandoned it and began climbing hand over hand up the ropes.

Mustafa walked across the bridge to the other side, ignoring the dead and wounded men lying there. He merely walked around them without a glance.

On the starboard side was another skiff, with only three men in it tying up boxes of RPG launchers and ammo. Mustafa's empty skiff was drifting about a hundred yards from the ship. He waited until the men in the skiff alongside were climbing the ropes and the skiff was drifting away before he turned and came back toward the center of the bridge.

"Captain Penney?"

"Yes."

"Get your ship under way. All ahead one third." Mustafa had a thick accent, but Penney was used to heavy accents and had no trouble understanding him. He reached for the engine controls and advanced them.

"Set course one-eight-zero."

Penney glanced at the helmsman. "Medium rate of turn starboard. Steady up one-eight-zero." Without getting up from the floor, the sailor used one hand to turn the indicator knob. The engines responded. It took perhaps ten seconds for the screws to bite and the ship's head to begin swinging.

"You are going to talk to the crew and passengers on the ship's loudspeakers," Mustafa said, eyeing Penney. He held out a piece of paper. It had been folded into quarters and was damp. "You will say what is on the paper. Nothing more, nothing less."

Penney unfolded the paper and began reading. The words were all in caps and legible, although the sentences appeared to be written by someone who wasn't familiar with English syntax.

When Penney didn't immediately respond, Mustafa pointed his rifle at the helmsman and pulled the trigger. One shot. In the head. The man's head literally exploded.

Mustafa nudged Penney with the barrel of the rifle. "You steer. And talk."

The dead helmsman was an Englishman from the Midlands who had been going to sea on merchant ships since he was eighteen. Now he was dead, at the age of thirty-nine. His name was Harry Hamm.

Mustafa nudged Penney again.

Looking at his dead and injured bridge team, the captain was past caring. "Shoot and be damned," he said.

Mustafa spoke into his ear. "I kill you. I kill all them. All. I don't care. Four boats of my men dead. In the sea. We live between life and death. For us, this only way. I kill as many as I want. Even you. You want to see them die? I shoot those two over there if you want. You want? We put you in water with my men, for the fish."

Arch Penney watched the compass heading come slowly around. When it read due south, he zeroed out the rate indicator. He didn't lead it enough. The compass settled on 185. Without conscious thought, he used a very slow turn rate to bring her back to 180.

Two more gunmen came in, and Mustafa gestured at the corpses. Without a word, the men picked them up, carried them to the side of the bridge, and threw them over. When the dead were gone, they picked up the wounded and threw them into the sea.

"No," one of the bridge team screamed. They shot him in the stomach and threw him over, too.

Irene and Suzanne were sitting side by side, shoulder to shoulder, when the first pirate came in. He was dressed in dirty slacks, a pullover shirt, and tennis shoes. He carried his weapon nonchalantly. He was grinning.

"A happy man," Irene whispered.

The grin vanished and the rifle was leveled at her. The man made a gesture, his hand across his throat, and looked around. Silence. Dead silence.

Another pirate came in. He breezed by the first one, ignored the passengers and headed straight for the buffet line. The food was still in serving trays. He reached in and grabbed a handful of something and tried it. Tossed it on the deck and snatched up a pancake, which he rolled up and began eating. He grunted at the first guy, who came over and did likewise.

They surveyed the drink table and sampled the juices, jabbering to themselves, with only an occasional glance at the thirty or so passengers huddled in the passageway. One of the women was audibly sobbing, on the verge of hysteria, Suzanne thought.

As the sisters watched, other pirates came in, six total, helped themselves to food, then left. Two of them actually used dishes, but they ignored the knives and forks.

While they were eating someone whispered to the sobbing woman, trying to comfort her.

The first pirate leveled his AK and fired a short burst down the passageway at the door. The bullets went by the heads of the seated passengers. Suzanne felt the muzzle blast, a mere ten feet from her head. The roar temporarily deafened them all.

The spent shells flew out of the AK into the food trays. One wound up in a dish of fruit.

A woman screamed. It was the woman who had been on the edge of hysteria. The pirates ignored her. They looked at the brass cartridge in the fruit dish and laughed.

The loudspeaker came to life with almost no warning. "This is the captain speaking. Our ship has been captured by pirates." There was a pause as Penney converted the tortured text into real English. "You will obey every order," he continued, his voice tired and flat, "or they will kill you. Obey orders and everyone will live. Disobey them and many of us will die."

He paused again, cleared his throat and resumed speaking. "The on-duty crew members will remain at their work stations. Cooks will continue with food preparation. Engineers will remain in the engineering spaces. Off-duty crew members will stay in their quarters. All passengers will return to their staterooms and remain there until summoned for meals. That is all."

The loudspeaker fell silent. Even the sobbing woman was silent.

Irene and Suzanne looked at each other, then at their fellow passengers, one of whom was shaking and talking soundlessly to himself, then finally at the pirates stuffing food into their mouths and looking at them.

Suzanne levered herself erect, grabbed her sister's elbow. "Come on."

The pirates watched and chewed and swallowed. They eyed the watches and jewelry—some of the women still had their diamond earrings and gold and silver bracelets on—but made no move to touch or grab.

Both women seized their purses, then joined the queue of people shuffling forward toward the elevators and passageways that would take them to their staterooms.

When they reached their stateroom, Benny and Sarah Cohen found tiny bits of glass all over the floor and furniture. The gentle sea breeze through the shot-up sliding door and windows seemed benign; it was a nice day.

Silently Sarah began cleaning up the mess so they would have a place to sit and sleep. Benny used a handkerchief to brush off the seat of the chair at the small desk, then sat on it and used a sleeve to clean off the surface of the desk. From his small leather travel case he extracted their passports. Israeli passports.

Benny Cohen sat staring at the covers. He could throw them overboard, of course. But every computer on this ship, and no doubt a dozen printed lists, listed his and Sarah's passport details and their nationality.

Hell, if these pirates were Muslim fanatics, they wouldn't need passports or computers. One look at his and Sarah's names on a passenger list would be enough to get them killed.

He had been just a boy when his parents had escaped Europe after the war and wound up in Israel, penniless and half-starved. His father had died in the War of Independence.

Benny remembered him, young, skinny as a rail, with a mop of black hair and an Enfield rifle hanging from his shoulder with a sling. His face was indistinct, but the hair and rifle were right there when Benny thought of him.

He and Sarah had lost two sons in the 1973 war. One was in the infantry and the other was a tanker. The day they mobilized was a horrific frenzy; then they were gone. Never to return. One of them, Jesse, left a fiancée.

If only he had gotten her pregnant!

Benny felt Sarah's hands on his shoulders. He looked up at the mirror above the desk and saw the reflection of her wonderful face, framed by gray hair. She glanced at the passports in his hand and knew what he had been thinking without a word being spoken. Her hands tightened on his shoulders and a trace of a smile crept across her face as she gazed at his reflection in the mirror.

Heinrich Beck vomited his breakfast into the toilet in his small cabin the instant he reached it. He turned on the sink tap experimentally and found he still had water, so he rinsed out his mouth and washed his face, then sat on his bed.

His stateroom didn't have a balcony or sliding glass door, merely a porthole, perhaps ten feet above the surface of the ocean. It was intact.

Beck took some deep breaths and sat silently looking at nothing in particular until he was sure his stomach would behave. He was a veteran of the East German Stasi, the most feared secret police organization on the planet until it fell apart in the collapse of Communism. Heinrich Beck's Stasi résumé was a secret, one he didn't share with anyone.

His specialty was interrogations. He had learned from experts and enjoyed the work. Inflicting pain on others was one of life's grandest pleasures.

Hadn't done any of that for over twenty-five years, though. These days Heinrich Beck made a living smuggling cocaine. He had two kilos of the stuff hidden in the air ducts leading into and out of this cabin, perfectly safe from any cursory search by a curious maid or lazy policeman.

Now Heinrich Beck sat assessing his chances of getting to Doha and delivering the coke. What would the pirates do to him if they found the stuff? Confiscate it, obviously, but he doubted they would kill him. He would deny he knew anything about it, claim a crewman must have hidden it in his cabin.

He thought about how the denial would go.

Yes, he could pull it off with these people, he thought. With Herman Stehle, who owned the coke and had entrusted him to deliver it, loss of the drugs would be a different story. Stehle had the money and contacts to make it in the international narcotics trade, perhaps the most lucrative and homicidal on the planet. Beck certainly didn't. Stehle gave him the stuff and told him who to deliver it to. Beck was merely a mule; he didn't even see the money.

He had done a half dozen deliveries for Stehle, most to the Mideast, two to China.

Innocence was slippery stuff. Dozens of people had tried it on Heinrich Beck, and he remembered how it was with those who actually were not guilty of the crimes of which they were accused, how they acted, the looks on their faces, the perspiration on their skin, the smell of them. They weren't truly innocent, of course—no one is innocent—but merely not guilty.

He wondered if Stehle would believe him if he said that pirates stole the stuff.

These pirates. Beck had seen them swagger around with their weapons, shooting here and there, enjoying themselves hugely. He hadn't seen them kill anyone, but doubtlessly they could and would if the spirit moved them. Bang. Watch the blood splatter and the look on the victim's face as he died. Smell the fear.

It would give the shooter such a sense of power. Almost orgasmic.

Beck felt warm as he thought about it.

Power. The power of life and death.

Heinrich Beck lit a cigarette and sat watching the smoke rise toward the return duct where the coke was stashed. It swirled a little and dissipated, but the duct sucked it up nonetheless.

CHAPTER FOUR

The capture of a cruise ship by Somali pirates was headline news worldwide, or would be when Europe and America woke up. The Pentagon received the Flash message from Task Force 151 so knew of it first. The bald facts went from the Pentagon's duty officers to the White House night staff and assorted other government agencies within minutes.

Jake Grafton was sound asleep at home when he received a call from the CIA situation room. Half awake, he grunted three or four times as he tried to absorb the story.

"The director wants to meet with you and the other department heads at seven thirty."

"Fine," Jake said and hung up.

His wife, Callie, had awakened. The incident would certainly not be a secret long, he knew, so he said, "Task Force 151 reports Somali pirates have captured a cruise ship in the Gulf of Aden. About five hundred passengers and three hundred fifty crewmen."

Callie came wide awake. "Isn't Toad Tarkington in command of that task force?"

"Yes."

Toad had served as Jake's aide for years when Jake was on active duty in the navy. After Jake retired, Toad went on to various assignments and had obviously impressed his superiors with his competence. Now he was a two-star admiral.

Jake knew Toad had probably had a damn rough day in the Indian Ocean, and, if anything, tomorrow was going to be worse. Every politician from Washington to Doha, Beijing and Tokyo was going to tell Tarkington what he had done wrong. Being second-guessed went with the job. Jake forgot about Toad and began mulling the probable reaction of those same politicians after they stopped grousing and started thinking.

He climbed from the bed and padded into the kitchen, where he fired off the coffeepot. Two in the morning, according to the clock in the microwave. As the coffee was brewing, he turned on the television.

Within sixty seconds Fox News had it. *News Flash*. He flipped channels. Soon all the cable news networks were giving the story a big play. By the time the coffee was ready, one news channel was airing a photo of the ship, *Sultan of the Seas,* probably one the producer had just downloaded from the Internet.

Callie came in wearing a robe over her pajamas, and together they watched the idiot tube as they sipped hot coffee. The news organizations didn't have any more details, just the facts as announced by the Pentagon, so the talking heads began speculating. They wondered how much money the pirates would demand as ransom.

A lot, Jake thought.

"My God," Callie whispered, "I'm glad we aren't on that ship. And Amy isn't." Amy was their daughter.

Jake finished his coffee. "Well, a lot of people *are* on that tub, and I guarantee you they all wish they weren't."

He headed for the bathroom. Might as well shower, shave, get dressed and go to Langley. Before he went to the seven-thirty meeting he wanted to learn everything he could about the capture, read the follow-up message traffic, and talk to the people at the National Security Agency who monitored telephone and radio traffic in Somalia.

In the shower, thinking about the crew and passengers on *Sultan,* he muttered, "Hang in there, people," but no one heard him.

. . .

Mustafa al-Said had thirty-two men, three boatloads, aboard *Sultan of the Seas*. Their main defense against allied warships, airplanes and marines was the passengers and crew that they held captive. The civilians were hostages, pure and simple. If necessary, Mustafa knew he could shoot a handful every hour for a couple of days and still have plenty of people left alive to ransom. Of course, there was a risk. If he started shooting hostages, the enemy commander might decide to attack in order to rescue as many live hostages as possible. Mustafa certainly didn't want to goad that infidel into pulling a big trigger.

After leaving two men who could actually read a compass to keep a wary eye on the captain and his surviving officers, Mustafa went aft and began assigning topside positions to his men.

Any attack, Mustafa thought, would probably come from the air. Helicopters would hover over the only open area topside, the pool area amidships, which was between the forward and aft superstructures. If attacking helos were allowed to machine-gun the top decks, clearing them of Somali fighters, then they could hover and marines could rappel to the deck. Mustafa was a realist; his men were pirates, not trained soldiers. The people they shot at didn't shoot back. If more than a handful of marines got aboard, his men would be outfought, killed or captured.

To keep attackers at bay he placed two machine guns forward, half-hidden inside the skin of the ship, with large windows to fire through. He had the men break out the glass. The third machine gun he placed aft, giving it the best possible field of fire. Men with RPG launchers were spotted inside the superstructure, out of sight of any helicopters that might approach, in position to step out and launch grenades when the choppers were in range and flying slowly.

Finally, he sent below for twenty passengers, whom he had tied to deck chairs beside the pool, in plain sight of any helicopter or jet pilot passing by.

While Mustafa was busy with all this, the first woman was raped on the second deck. She was a cook's helper, twenty-three years old, from Sri Lanka. Three men dragged her to a bunk and took turns raping her while the others held the other three women in the compartment at bay with rifles.

The pirates had been told to leave the women alone, but. They were young, ignorant, illiterate, and bucked with life. They had guns and no one else did. They were going to be rich. Here was opportunity and no one to tell them no. After all, fucking an infidel couldn't be a sin. Didn't the Prophet, may He rest in peace, say to kill all infidels?

At first the woman fought. One blow broke her jaw, and she ceased her struggles. Just for good measure, the pirate whacked her with the butt of his gun on the side of her head, caving in an eye socket. She lay comatose as the man ripped off her clothes and opened his trousers. The sight of her naked body and the excitement of the morning had done their work. He spread her legs and jabbed his erect penis in as his mates laughed heartily.

When they had all had their turn, they left, slamming the door behind them.

USS *Richard Ward* was the first warship to obtain a visual sighting on *Sultan of the Seas.* An E-2 was a hundred miles away and had the ships on radar, so their symbols appeared on the computer-driven tactical displays of every ship in the task force, including the flagship, *Chosin Reservoir.*

Sultan was proceeding south at nineteen knots, which Rear Admiral Toad Tarkington thought was probably her normal cruising speed. If she held this speed, she would make the harbor at Eyl, Somalia, roughly at dawn tomorrow. If she was going to Eyl. Toad certainly didn't know.

The weather was gorgeous, with just a high, thin cirrus layer diffusing the direct rays of the sun. Visibility was thirty or forty miles; wind out of the northwest off the Arabian Peninsula at five knots, a dry wind. Even the swells of the morning had dissipated until the ocean was a gentle, undulating mirror reflecting the sky.

His staff was sorting though the message traffic from his superiors and dashing off replies. They handed him clipboards full of this stuff, which he quickly scanned and handed back.

Washington wanted the impossible: the *Sultan* recaptured without the loss of a single civilian life.

The marine Force Reconnaissance team had taken down pirates aboard several merchant ships before, a bulk carrier and a container ship. Both had small crews. The Force Recon team knocked out topside opposition, boarded, then fought their way through the ship, killing any pirates who didn't surrender. Most of them did.

Yet today the captured ship contained eight hundred and fifty people, literally people in every compartment, under the control of three boatloads of pirates, somewhere between twenty-five and fifty, all armed, headed for a safe harbor where they would anchor and demand ransom. Don't pay, they kill people. Board, they kill people. Pay the money and you get everyone back alive. They'll even give you back your ship. Then, since that went so wonderfully well and the pirates all got filthy rich, they'll recruit hundreds more pirates, buy more boats and weapons, and motor out into Pirate Alley or the great wide ocean to capture more ships and crews and passengers to hold for ransom, all over again.

The fact that the pirates had a safe harbor to operate from and go back to was the crux of the problem, but one that wouldn't get solved today or tomorrow, so Toad didn't waste any time thinking about it. "Above my pay grade," he once told his chief of staff, Flip Haducek, who was expounding on the wisdom of wiping out pirate nests.

A real-time television picture of *Sultan* appeared on the monitor above the tac display. The camera was on one of the helos.

As Toad studied it, Flip Haducek and Colonel Zakhem joined him.

"Washington wants to approve any plan of action you decide on," Haducek said. He wiggled the message board in his hand.

"Gentlemen," Toad said flatly, "my preferred course is an overwhelming show of force. Steam alongside with armed marines lining the rails of this ship and the *Ward,* helos and Ospreys overhead, fighters zipping past at masthead height. That is what I intend to do. When we've given them a good look, marines will rappel down and take the ship. They'll be letting it all hang out. Still, it could work."

Zakhem nodded his concurrence. The pirates could shoot the marines on the ropes, of course. It would take guts to go down those ropes. His marines had plenty.

"But if it doesn't work, if they start machine-gunning captives or shooting marines, we need another plan," the admiral continued. "I am not willing to watch those bastards sail away on the ocean blue with eight hundred and fifty captives to ransom at their leisure."

"A clandestine boarding by SEALs tonight," Colonel Zakhem said. He pointed to the monitor. "Those lines dangling over the side. Those are on the grappling hooks the pirates used to board. They are still there."

Toad stared. The lines were difficult to see on the monitor. "We need real photos, of both sides of the ship. Blow-ups. Flip?"

"Aye aye, sir." He picked up a telephone. The photos had already been taken and were being processed, he was told.

"SEALs," the admiral whispered, staring at the thin lines on the monitor.

"If it were dark enough, a few determined men in wet suits might be able to climb those lines or their own and get aboard unnoticed," Zakhem mused. "After all, the pirates did it. Who knows, if SEALs get aboard, the pirates can surrender or die."

Toad wasn't so optimistic. The pirates would want a shit-pot full of money for all those people, and he suspected they would fight like hell to get it. On the other hand, four or five SEALs sneaking through the ship slitting throats and tossing pirates overboard might convince the remainder they were in over their heads. Might. Or might not.

"Colonel, you and Flip scare up some SEALs and bring me a plan."

The two officers left without a word.

Toad sat staring at the monitor and tac display until his ops officer approached him.

"We've rescued three pirates, sir. There was a fourth, but he had a twenty millimeter round through his abdomen and died five minutes after we pulled him out."

"What do they say?"

"They are from Eyl, Somalia. Their warlord is a guy named Ragnar."

Ops had prepared a message for Tarkington's signature. He read it through carefully. There was a brief description of the *Sultan,* projected time of arrival off the Horn of Africa, intel from the rescued pirates, projected time of arrival at Eyl, the first suitable pirate port, and so on.

He thought if the pirates intended to cross the bar into Eyl, they would wait for dawn. They were seamen, certainly, but *Sultan* was not a fishing boat or pirate scow. Tod signed the message.

He picked up his binoculars and focused them on *Sultan*. Tarkington made a face. Then he began cursing, silently. Ah me.

Toad wondered what was going on aboard that ship.

Whatever it was, the pirates had the initiative. Toad wanted it back. He wanted to force his will upon the pirates, force them to do what he wanted, which was surrender. His primary goal was to make the pirate captain realize he had no other options.

"Every marine aboard is to be topside and on the sponsons with a rifle. We'll make it plain—they can surrender or die."

He glanced at his staff. "Flip, send another Flash message to Washington, Fifth Fleet, everyone on the list. Let's do this as an Unless Otherwise Directed. Tell them Plan A and Plan B. We will go as soon as we get the marines transferred to the *Ward,* and our ships in position. Make that two hours from now. Draft that and let me see the draft."

Haducek looked at his watch. "It's 1130, sir. May we aim for 1430 instead?"

"Okay. Put that in the message, 1430 local time."

"Aye aye, sir." Captain Haducek strode away.

The other members of the staff discussed what had to be done and began making it happen. After another brief discussion with Colonel Zakhem, Toad personally briefed the captain of *Chosin Reservoir.* While they were talking, a first-class yeoman brought Toad a draft of the message dictated by Haducek. Unless Otherwise Directed, UNODIR, this is what I intend to do and when I intend to do it. Left unsaid but implicit was, If you don't want me to do it, say so. Put yourself on record. Or let me proceed on my initiative and my responsibility.

Toad corrected one word, signed the form and handed it back.

When he and the *Reservoir*'s captain were finished, Toad called the captain of *Richard Ward* on a secure voice channel.

On the *Reservoir*'s flight deck, marines in battle dress were lining up to board Ospreys and helicopters. Colonel Max Zakhem didn't believe in fooling around. Neither did Rear Admiral Toad Tarkington.

Toad climbed out of his chair and went to the head. He had needed to go for an hour.

Most of the women aboard the ship were at least twice the age of the pirates, who wanted something younger. Juicier. Fortunately there were several dozen good candidates in the crew quarters. In twos and threes, they went below and assaulted some women. One of the women screamed so loudly they strangled her, and they left another bleeding badly.

Captain Arch Penney got the news via telephone on the bridge. He turned to Mustafa al-Said, who was strutting back and forth, keeping his eye on the airplanes and helicopters that buzzed about at least a mile away from the ship.

"Your men are raping the women. I thought you said they wouldn't do that."

Mustafa's concern showed in his face. His boss, Ragnar, had told him in no uncertain terms that he and his men must leave the women strictly alone. "We will ask for ransom, and they will demand to speak to the passengers and crew. If they report they have been raped or tortured or abused, we risk our political position." Ragnar well knew that his lair of Eyl was only safe because the allied governments had refused, so far, to attack it. He didn't want to give allied decision-makers a reason to change their minds.

Ragnar had been very explicit. "We want money. Not blood. Not revenge or terror or sex or any of that nonpaying shit. Money. Money we can spend. Don't fuck this up, Mustafa." Those were not his exact words, of course, but close enough. "Your men can wait until they are back in Eyl, then they can have all the women they can stand. If they have money, the women of Somalia will line up to fuck them."

Mustafa left his two pirates who could read a compass in charge on the bridge and went below. He didn't really care what the infidels thought of rape or his men; he cared greatly about pleasing Ragnar, who had a nasty habit of killing people who displeased him. People who thought they had a tough boss had no idea what a really tough boss looked like.

. . .

Radio talk-show host Mike Rosen had been using the Internet computers in the computer room just off the ship's library when the pirates boarded the ship. He heard the shooting and the captain's announcement. Pirates had taken the ship.

Rosen was no hero, but he was a journalist, and he knew that he was sitting in the middle of the biggest story he had ever covered. Maybe as big as 9/11. He logged off the Internet and grabbed his computer bag, which held his laptop, and retreated into the office just off the computer room. It wasn't much, just a desk and chair, a computer and monitor, and a telephone. The computer on the desk was an old Dell, just like the ones in the computer room for the passengers to use. Rosen carefully closed the door and turned on the computer. His hands were shaking as he logged on to the Internet.

Voilà! It still worked. He was on. He was busy typing out a flash to the radio station in Denver when an automatic weapon burst went off outside the door.

Rosen grabbed his computer bag, slid the chair back and crawled under the desk.

More bursts from the computer room outside the door. And laughter.

When the blasts had finally subsided, maybe fifteen bursts, he estimated, he wasn't really counting, the door flew open. He didn't see it; he heard it. Another burst of rifle fire, this time so loud he cringed. Bits and pieces of the computer rained down on the carpet.

Then the door slammed shut.

Rosen waited a good five minutes, then went to the door and, as quietly as he could, opened it a crack. All he could see was remnants of the computers that had been lined up on one credenza facing the wall. The entire dozen were shot to shit.

Rosen carefully closed the door and examined the knob. It had a lock button. He pushed it.

He thoughtfully unpacked his laptop, raked the shards of the old monitor and keyboard off the desk and began setting up. The cord from the Internet connection to the late computer was intact, so he plugged it into his MacBook. Automatically he dug into his bag for the power supply and plugged that in to ensure his battery didn't run down.

Then he tried to log on again to the Internet. Holy damn, it worked.

But what was he going to report? He didn't know beans about what was going on.

He began searching the desk. Pulled out a board that acted as a writing extension, and there he found taped in place a list of the ship's offices and phone numbers.

Might as well, he thought. He examined the telephone. It was intact. He picked a number, the ship's head steward, and dialed.

"Yes."

"How many people are dead? How many injured?"

"Who the hell is this?"

"I'm a spy for SMERSH, you moron. Now answer the question."

"At least four dead on the bridge. Two passengers were shot before the pirates boarded; one of those has died. The other is in the infirmary. One woman was apparently raped to death."

"That's seven dead and one wounded."

"There's more wounded."

"How many more?"

"Listen, you bloody American twit. Tying up the ship's telephone lines to satisfy idle curiosity is wasting my time. Bugger off!" The phone went dead.

Rosen called the ship's infirmary, a small space with three beds and one doctor.

A man answered.

"This is the second officer," Rosen said firmly. "What do you have down there?"

"Four raped women. The men who carried them in weren't shot, thank God."

"Injuries?"

"One had a crushed eye socket. Two had all the usual damage of a gang rape. The fourth woman is dead."

"Passengers or crew?"

"Crew."

"Names."

The male voice gave them to him.

"How many dead?"

"At least eight that I know of. Six crew, two passengers. There may be more. Probably are."

"Thank you," Rosen said and hung up abruptly.

He whistled absentmindedly to himself as he consulted the telephone list.

He called the aft dining room.

"Third officer." He decided to give himself a demotion. "What's your situation?"

"Fuckin' pirates are gobbling everything in sight."

"Any casualties up there?"

"Who the fuck are you, mate? You ain't the bloody third."

"Thanks for all your help. I'll call you back in a while."

He tried the radio room. No answer. Ship's cruise director. A cultured female voice.

"Hello, this is Mike Rosen. I'm one of your passengers. Do you know how many pirates are aboard?"

"We have everything under control, Mr. Rosen. Please hang up and leave this line for crew to use. We'll tell you all we can when the pirates allow us to again use the PA system." He could tell that she was frightened.

"I really appreciate that. But do you or anyone there have any idea how many pirates are aboard?"

The woman took a deep breath and whispered, "One of the pool barmen said he thought about three dozen climbed aboard, but he didn't get an accurate count. They're swarming all over."

"I see."

"I have one in the passageway outside my office, strolling up and down, looking rather fierce. Please stay in your stateroom, obey the public address announcements."

"You bet. Thanks for your help."

He called the engine control room.

"What's our speed and heading?"

"Eighteen knots, heading one-eight-zero." Rosen couldn't place the accent.

"What's our destination?"

"Hell, maybe."

"They haven't told you?"

"No one ever tells me shit. You'll get there when the rest of us do, shipmate, then you'll know. Now bugger off." He hung up on Rosen. Australian, the reporter decided.

Rosen thought for a minute, then called the engine room again. The Aussie answered after two rings.

"Why don't you just shut down the engines?"

"You again! There are two nigger pirates down here, and they are primed to kill somebody. If the engines stop, they'll kill the whole bleedin' lot of us. The bastards don't speak a word of English, yet they made that wonderfully clear. Marvelous communicators they are, regular MPs. Don't call this number again." He hung up.

Mustafa al-Said didn't waste time. He asked direct questions and pressed until he found the three that had raped the crew women. They were on the fourth deck, at the head of the ladder leading to the crew's quarters below, along with two other pirates. Mustafa picked one man, the nearest, shoved the AK into his chest and gave him a burst. Blood spewed out his back. With his heart shot to pieces and a severed backbone, the pirate was dead before he hit the carpeted deck.

Mustafa used the butt of the weapon on the side of the head of one of the guilty men. The other jerked his head back as the rifle butt swung and caught his nose, breaking it, smearing it across his face. Rich red blood poured from his nose.

Mustafa backed off and looked at the four men standing there.

"You were told what to do and what not to do. Touch another woman and I kill you and your family back in Eyl. Everyone."

The injured men and the other two standing there looked properly cowed. Without Mustafa al-Said they would be starving in Eyl, a fact of which they were well aware.

"Throw this piece of dog dung over the side." Mustafa gestured with his rifle barrel at the man on the deck with no chest, then turned and headed back to the bridge.

. . .

Mike Rosen figured he had enough information to write a story. He got into his onboard account, addressed an e-mail to the news director at his radio station in Denver, 850 KOA, and began typing.

Halfway through he wondered how much fuel the ship had aboard. Enough to reach the next port, certainly, but precisely how much? What was the range of the ship with her current fuel load?

He called the engine room one more time.

"What's our range with existing fuel, at this sp—"

"Bugger yourself, you balmy bastard." Bang. The phone went dead.

A dried-up source, Rosen reflected. Sources do that occasionally. He went back to typing. He had met the captain the other night, Arch Penney, so he described him, handsome and competent and all that, and checked the name of the cruise line on the stationery in the desk to ensure he got it right. He even found the length and displacement of *Sultan* and salted that in.

Hell of a good story, he thought as he maneuvered the little arrow over the SEND icon and launched his e-mail into cyberspace, via the satellite.

Of course, the cruise line would put the cost of the e-mail on his bill, but he could and would deduct it from his income taxes. Fuck Warren Buffett.

The night news lady at KOA Denver had seen the news of the *Sultan*'s capture, and knew Mike Rosen was aboard, so when she saw she had an e-mail from him she opened it immediately.

Three dozen pirates, a woman raped to death, three others injured by rapists, eight people believed dead . . . This was hot. Very very hot. The news director passed the e-mail to the on-air host, who read it into the microphone verbatim. She also sent it to the wire service. Then, with two keystrokes, she posted the e-mail on the radio station's Web site.

Fifteen seconds after the e-mail hit the Web site, a lady from Littleton who couldn't sleep started reading the story. A minute later she sent it to seventy-six friends. After five minutes, the e-mail had circled the earth twice and was being read by over five thousand people in thirty-two countries.

Ten minutes after Rosen's e-mail arrived in Denver, the contents were on the cable news networks. MSNBC fretted that it was a hoax. A talking head on CNN read it without comment. Fox had the host read the e-mail on camera and ran the text across the bottom of the screen for deaf viewers or viewers with the audio turned off.

The Pentagon had heard all about Rosen's e-mail, the casualties and the rapes by the time Admiral Toad Tarkington's UNODIR message arrived. The duty officer conferred with the White House staff, who called senior government officials all over town, waking them up. The president had spent the evening in a critical meeting with his political advisers and had a full day scheduled for tomorrow with a foreign head of state, so the decision was made not to wake him. After all, the cruise ship was British and would still be captured in the morning. The Joint Chiefs were advised by the Pentagon staff, but in this age of political wars in shitty little places, American politicians ran military operations; all the military professionals did was obey orders and advise. Advise when asked.

The staff of the national security adviser, conferring by telephone, decided to respond to Admiral Tarkington's UNODIR Flash message. They all had fine educations and were politically committed to this administration and its goals, and none of them had ever spent a day in uniform in their lives. Since SEAL Team Six whacked bin Laden, U.S. Navy SEALs were hot commodities, military rock stars who fought for civilization against evil Islamic devil-worshippers. SEAL warriors could accomplish anything, or so the staffers believed, to the greater glory of the administration with the guts to unleash them. Task Force 151 was ordered to attempt a SEAL team takedown of the pirates aboard *Sultan of the Seas.*

In effect, Admiral Tarkington's operational plan was turned upside down.

CHAPTER FIVE

Irene and Suzanne had a stateroom on the fourth deck, which meant they had a porthole, not a balcony. When cruising they didn't spend many of their waking hours in their stateroom, so regarded the extra money for a balcony as a needless extravagance. They were rethinking that now.

Oh sure, the stateroom was very pleasant. The air-conditioning was running perfectly, the porthole was intact, the commode flushed, and they had pretty well cleaned out the minibar refrigerator. The television in the room normally delivered twenty channels through some kind of satellite connection, channels like Fox News, the BBC, CNN, CNBC, and several European channels that broadcast nothing but soccer games. If you weren't a fan of soccer, you were out of luck in the sports department.

On the other hand, Fox, CNN and the BBC were all news, all the time. The women were a bit peeved that they were off the air. When the pirates were spraying bullets around, one bullet, only one, severed a coaxial cable leading from the satellite antennae. Until it was repaired, the boob tube was silent. Which was just as well, because the news on those channels was about the capture of the *Sultan*.

The primary source, indeed, the only source, for news from the ship itself was Mike Rosen, tapping on his computer in the little office off the shot-up e-communication, or e-com, lounge. So it would have been interesting for the ship's passengers to watch one of those news channels, and perhaps more so for the pirates, who might have been unhappy with Rosen's activities. Since Mustafa al-Said remained blissfully unaware, life aboard ship went on under the pirates' direction.

As they contemplated the uncertain, unpredictable future, Irene and Suzanne decided that whatever happened, they needed more booze to carry into captivity. They pocketed their stateroom keys, which were actually plastic cards the size of a credit card with their photos on them. Security, you understand. Suzanne opened the stateroom door and peeked out. No one in the passageway.

They sneaked along the passageway forward to the elevator well and stairs. At the foot of the stairs they stood and listened. They could hear two pirates talking somewhere above them; of course they were pirates, gabbling along in an incomprehensible language and laughing uproariously. These were two truly happy men.

The sisters went up one deck, looked and listened, then tiptoed along the port passageway toward Mike Rosen's stateroom. Actually five of the Denver contingent were berthed on this deck, so if one wasn't in, another might be. Before they reached Rosen's room, however, they smelled something burning. The smell seemed to be coming from a stateroom.

"Something's on fire," Irene said and pounded on the door.

The door opened and a blast of pot smoke almost knocked them over. The room was hazy with it. There was so much it must have overwhelmed the air-conditioning.

Four men. Von Platen, the car guy, and three of his business friends were all smoking weed.

They offered the ladies a joint, but Irene and Suzanne refused. "This place stinks," Irene declared.

"In light of our impending incarceration, we decided to consume our inventory."

Von Platen looked to be in his early forties, the others a year or two younger. Perhaps it wasn't the years that had caused the distinguished gray hairs at Von Platen's temples but the miles. Or the pot.

The six chatted animatedly, getting acquainted, as the men puffed away on little roll-your-own cigarettes. The sisters from Denver pretended that watching people smoke pot was no big deal, although it was a life first for both of them.

Finally Suzanne said, "What the hell." One of the men rolled her a cigarette and she lit up, to Irene's horror.

Aboard *Chosin Reservoir,* Admiral Tarkington listened to his chief of staff, Captain Flip Haducek, his ops officer, Commander Myron Snyder, and his SEAL team leader as they tossed around the possibility of getting some SEALs aboard *Sultan* that night if the afternoon matinee didn't work.

The first problem was intercepting the ship. Helicopters would need to put at least four rubber boats with six men each into the water ahead of *Sultan*. Assuming the *Sultan* didn't turn, for any reason, the SEALs would have to motor alongside, shoot grappling hooks attached to ropes, and climb them about twenty feet to the fifth deck, the first one that had an entrance piercing the hull. The dangling pirate ropes were interesting, but no one had much faith in pirate technology. Besides, the ropes could be a trap.

"Radar?"

"Our rubber boats will be difficult to see on radar, sir."

Toad raised an eyebrow. Cruise ships had good radars, he knew, because they had to constantly avoid small fishing and pleasure boats when going into and out of busy harbors. The real question was, Would anyone be watching the radar scope as *Sultan* charged along in the hour or two before dawn?

"You'll be lucky to get four men aboard," Flip Haducek said to the SEAL officer. "And once aboard, you will . . . what?"

The SEAL team leader was Lieutenant Angel Cordova. With a plain, unmemorable face, he stood about five feet seven inches tall and had wide shoulders, huge arm and chest muscles, and a ridiculously thin waist. The veins in his arms stood out like cords. He looked like a professional bodybuilder, Toad Tarkington thought.

"Once aboard . . . ?" the admiral murmured.

"Fight our way forward and up, sir, to the bridge. Kill the opposition as we go."

"What if they start shooting hostages? What then?"

"We take them out with silenced weapons as we get to them, regardless."

"Hostages or no hostages?"

"Yes, sir."

"So how many pirates are aboard?"

"We estimate between twenty-five and fifty."

"Estimate."

"Yes, sir."

"What is the minimum number of men you need to get aboard to have any realistic chance of handling twenty-five to fifty armed pirates?"

"At least ten, sir."

"Each of your boats holds six men?"

"Correct, sir."

"So you must rendezvous with *Sultan* with at least two boats." Toad looked from face to face. Small rubber boats on a night sea, trying to get alongside a ship doing ten knots—ten knots just now—getting swamped in the wash if they failed to get their grappling hooks to snag. Hoping no one on deck saw them and started shooting while they were climbing the ropes.

"What's Plan B?" the admiral asked.

"We jump overboard. The saltwater will activate our beacons. Someone comes to pick us up."

"Too iffy," Toad said. "We need a better plan that this."

The brain trust was still noodling when a yeoman brought Toad a Flash message from Washington. "Green light for SEAL mission." There were several more paragraphs, but Toad didn't bother reading them. He handed it to Commander Snyder, who actually read it while Toad listened to Angel Cordova.

Snyder interrupted. "Admiral, they want to know when the mission will launch."

"We're not going to do it," Toad said. "Too risky." Cordova's face fell.

"Aye aye, sir." The ops officer headed for the admin office just off the flag plot spaces to draft a reply.

"I don't want you people dead for nothing," Toad told Cordova.

"Yes, sir. I understand, sir."

Time for the showdown, the afternoon matinee. Sea still calm, high cirrus clouds moving in . . .

The admiral's aide, a Hornet pilot, brought him a message. "Better read this one, Admiral. Some guy on that ship has been e-mailing a radio station in Denver. Everyone on the planet is reading his stuff."

Toad read the message, then passed it back. Oh, boy. Stuff like this would light a fire under the politicians, stimulate them mightily. Murders, rapes, brave resistance from the crew . . .

Toad was eating a salad in the raised chair in Flag Plot when another message from Washington arrived. He read it in amazement. The National Command Authority, which meant the president of the United States, ordered him to launch the SEAL team mission.

Commander Snyder was there, wearing a worried look, along with Flip Haducek.

"No," Toad said. "In my judgment, the mission is too risky. What did you tell those people?"

"Just that, sir."

Toad wadded up the message and gave it back to Snyder.

The chief of staff cleared his throat. He tried to resist the urge to point out the obvious because that tactic rarely sat well with the admiral. He lost the inner battle and said, "Sir, that's an order. From the president."

Toad handed his salad to Snyder, took the message and smoothed it out. He removed a pen from his pocket. He began writing on the back of the sheet the reasons he thought the mission would probably fail. If the SEALs couldn't get enough men aboard *Sultan* to win control of the ship, they would die or be captured. Passengers and crew might be caught in a crossfire. Pirates might begin executing hostages.

Toad summed up, "The chances of a handful of SEALs successfully intercepting and boarding *Sultan* at night while under way are small. The chances of those who do successfully board winning the battle for control of the ship are even smaller. When the pirates get *Sultan* into a port, they will undoubtedly demand ransom, which, if paid, means that no civilian lives will be lost. If the decision is made to refuse to pay ransom, a much larger, more capable military force can be deployed against the pirates, one that will maximize the possibility of victory and minimize the loss of life."

He used another paragraph to explain the benefits of a show of force. It could happen quickly; if the pirates were cowed, they would surrender and marines could board the ship, and if they weren't, the navy had risked little and could try something else. A lot of upside, little downside. Those were the best kind of military operations. And he would be ready soon.

Tarkington handed the sheet of paper to Captain Haducek. "Send that," he said, "and copy everyone in the chain of command. That's the problem in plain English."

An hour later, Washington answered Admiral Tarkington's message. He was ordered to launch the SEAL mission.

Toad managed to keep a deadpan look on his mug as he struggled to hold his temper. Overruling the judgment of the officer on the scene was not the way the navy worked. The system was designed to find the best-qualified officer, put him in charge, let him make the judgment calls and hold him responsible for the results. Micromanaging from long distance certainly wasn't unprecedented, but on those occasions in the past when the politicians had tried it, the results were usually not good.

Tarkington summoned Angel Cordova and handed him the clipboard containing the message. Cordova read it with raised eyebrows.

"Looks like you are going to have to give it a try," Tarkington said dryly. He searched for words while Cordova rubbed his chin. "I want you to know that I think your chances of successfully pulling off a boarding are poor. Too poor to justify risking your life and the lives of your men. I made my case and lost. The 'National Command Authority' says go, so you are going."

"Yes, sir."

"That being said, if you do get aboard, or any of your men do, you don't have to do the Alamo trick. I want you to try to disable the engines, stop her at sea. If the pirates aren't going anywhere, we can negotiate a surrender."

Cordova nodded.

"Flip, get the engineers to talk to Mr. Cordova. Brief him on the engineering plant and find him as many demolition charges as he and his men can carry."

Toad frowned. "It's goddamn thin, Cordova. Use your best judgment. Disable the ship if you can. If you can't, kill as many pirates as possible."

"Oh, you can bet on that, sir. But what if they use the crew or passengers as human shields?"

"Kill anyone you have to kill to save your own lives."

Lieutenant Cordova took a deep breath and exhaled slowly. "I'd like that in writing, sir."

"Flip, write a direct order to Mr. Cordova to attempt to board *Sultan of the Seas* and disable her engineering plant. Authorize him and his men to kill anyone to save their own lives, including passengers and crew used as human shields. I'll sign it."

"Yes, sir."

"Then send a copy to Washington. Hell, send it to everyone on the distribution list as info addees. When it's gone with a date-time group, give Mr. Cordova a copy."

"Yes, sir."

Toad Tarkington fixed his gaze on the SEAL lieutenant. "You are being handed a really tough mission. If you don't think it's doable, say so. No one is ordering you or your men to undertake a suicide mission. We don't do suicide missions in the United States Navy."

"We can do it, sir."

Goddamn gung-ho kid, Toad thought.

"You ever been shot at before?"

"No, sir."

"You are about to get an education. Get cracking. I want a complete briefing from you before you go."

"Aye aye, sir."

. . .

Jake Grafton thought he understood what had happened in the Gulf of Aden when he went to the director's conference room at CIA headquarters in Langley, Virginia, for the 7:30 A.M. meeting. He had read all the message traffic and even Rosen's e-mails, which the night duty staff had arranged in chronological order by date-time group.

CIA director Mario Tomazic was a new guy, a retired army four-star who made his bones in Iraq. He got this job, Jake suspected, because he was quite good at not saying things the staffers at the White House didn't want to hear.

"Who are these pirates?" the director asked.

The silence that followed was pregnant, so Jake Grafton stepped in. "Apparently they work for a pirate warlord named Ragnar, which is not his real name but a *nom de guerre.* Either he's a fan of Ayn Rand or someone told him a lie or two. In any event, NSA says he and the pirate leader aboard ship have been gabbling back and forth. Our files say Ragnar's base is Eyl."

"Any ransom demands yet?"

"Not yet, sir. If they hold to their normal routine, there won't be until they get the ship in the harbor and the people into the old fortress on the bluff."

"What's 151 going to do about all this?"

An aide directed the people at the table to the appropriate messages. Of course Jake had already read his copies. Now he reread them as the others digested Adrmiral Tarkington's messages and the national security staff's responses.

The director got it. "The staffers decided they know more about pirates than Admiral Tarkington."

Grafton met Tomazic's eyes. "Oh, man," the retired general said disgustedly. He swept the pile of paper in front of him aside.

"Okay," he said to the aide. "Where the hell is everybody out there?"

That was an easy request to answer. The computer display was soon on the screen on the wall. On the left side was a legend that explained the symbols. An aide pointed out ship positions and enemy strongholds with a white piece of wood, one little more than a large splinter.

"Let's assume the ship reaches port, somewhere," the director said.

"There'll be a ransom demand. That's where the politicians will go into a dither. Pay or don't pay? Shoot or surrender?"

"What if the ship owners or governments or private people refuse to pay ransom?" one staffer asked.

"Those people on that ship will expect the government to pay or rescue them," said another.

"One or the other."

"What about all those foreigners aboard *Sultan*? Should the U.S. government pay ransom to get them back?"

"Their governments can figure it out."

"So we only buy out Americans?"

"Foreigners don't pay taxes or vote. The American taxpayer is tapped out. And in a pretty damn sour mood."

"It's a British ship. Don't forget that. This is really London's problem, not ours."

"It's registered in Monrovia, Liberia."

"So call the Liberians."

"This is amazingly insightful," Tomazic said dryly. He glanced at Grafton, who had been sitting with his mouth firmly closed. "Don't we have a covert team in Somalia?"

"A snatch team camped out in the desert," Jake said with a curt nod. "Eating MREs, shitting in a hole and working on their tans."

Tomazic grunted and glanced at his watch. "Well, I gotta get over to the White House and get told what we're gonna do." He stood and the meeting was over.

The remainder of the afternoon passed slowly with *Richard Ward* and *Chosin Reservoir* keeping station four miles away on each of *Sultan*'s flanks. Ospreys and choppers ferried marines to the *Ward,* just in case. Fighters from the carrier to the northeast flew lazy patterns high overhead.

When he had done everything he could, Toad Tarkington went to his stateroom and tried to nap. He tossed and turned and fumed at the politicos in Washington.

He wrote a letter to his wife, worked his way through a pile of routine paperwork and was on the flag bridge to watch the sun sink in the west.

As darkness settled over the ocean, *Sultan of the Seas* kept every light ablaze as she steamed south, even the ribbon of decorative lights on a wire that ran from the funnel to the masthead, then down at an angle to the bow.

Toad Tarkington stared through his binoculars at the cruise ship. No one on deck that he could see, but *Chosin Reservoir* was now just a half mile to port, behind *Sultan*'s beam. A destroyer was on *Sultan*'s starboard side. It was possible, although not probable, the pirate might jam the helm over and try to ram the warships, so Toad had cautioned the captains to be careful. He also wanted to stay out of range of rifle and machine-gun fire.

The sea had abated and was almost calm. The only wind seemed to be relative, from straight ahead, manufactured by the ships moving through dead air.

Toad wondered what Captain Penney was thinking.

Actually Arch Penney was thinking of possible ways to kill Mustafa al-Said. The pirate's murder of three ship's officers, the helmsman and the bosun's mates who manned the LRAD had filled him with anger. Rage. He had never before felt such a bitter emotion. He eyed Mustafa again. The man would kill him without remorse or hesitation. If Arch had a weapon handy he would use it on Mustafa and enjoy every single second.

But he didn't have such a weapon. Perhaps the gods were looking out for him.

He wondered about his wife, who was in his cabin. He thought about calling her, and looked at the telephone, but decided against it. No use letting this asshole pirate know she was aboard and giving him another weapon to use against him.

He checked his watch. The chief steward had called him on the phone and they had talked about serving dinner to the passengers . . . and pirates. Mustafa had watched and listened to the conversation but hadn't said a word.

Penney obsessed about the murdered officers and crew, one of whom, a woman, was raped to death. The three raped women who survived the experience were in the ship's tiny hospital; the doctor had telephoned him and reported. He tried to clear his mind and focus on the current situation. The dead were dead—his responsibility was to the living.

Penney picked up his binoculars and aimed them at the warship on the port quarter. Amphibious assault ship—all he could see was her running lights, and red lights on the flight deck. The lights of helos and Ospreys flitting across the sky. Destroyer on the starboard side. Both ships were much closer than they had been during the day, but were maintaining their station now. Penney wondered if Mustafa was paying attention.

Peering out the window of the shot-up passenger computer room, Mike Rosen had seen the warships during the afternoon and evening. They were out there, but closer.

He went back to the office and shoved the desk against the door. He had talked to the ship's steward, the bosun, the doctor, every department head on the list.

He stared at the phone. Should he?

Well, hell, no guts, no glory. He dialed the bridge. Got someone who identified himself as the second officer.

"The captain, please."

"Who is this?"

"One of your passengers."

"Kiss my bloody ass, mate."

"God damn you, shithead! Gimme the captain!"

Silence. The line was still open. Rosen could hear himself breathe. Then a male voice came on. "Captain."

"Mike Rosen, sir, a passenger. I am in the computer room, and we still have a satellite connection. I've been e-mailing my radio station in Denver. Do you have an accurate casualty list?"

"No. I know that there are at least three officers dead, the helmsman, two bosun's mates and a woman passenger who was raped to death. Someone told me another passenger, a man, was killed, but I don't know that for a fact. Four or five more have been injured."

"Is there a message you want to get out to the world?"

"I'm not free to talk." The voice was lower.

"Our destination?"

"Eyl."

"Is that in Somalia?"

"Yes."

"Anything else."

"We are doing our best to ensure our passengers and crew remain safe." The connection was severed.

Rosen got on the computer and started typing. He had his lead. The captured cruise ship, *Sultan of the Seas,* with at least seven dead, perhaps eight, was being taken to Eyl, Somalia, by pirates.

Mustafa al-Said decided to feed the passengers at 8:00 P.M. The crew members who cooked and served were ready, so at the appointed moment the captain used the loudspeaker to send the passengers to dinner, deck by deck. He started low in the ship and worked up.

By then Irene and Suzanne were back in their small stateroom, trying to get the marijuana smoke smell out of their hair.

"I didn't know that stuff stunk so badly," Suzanne declared. Actually, she felt pretty good—knew she had a buzz on, and was past caring how she smelled.

"There are a lot of things we don't know," Irene said philosophically. She too had inhaled a lot of that smoke and was feeling very mellow.

"I wonder why those men didn't bring their wives on this cruise."

"Because they're gay, you twit." Irene laughed hugely.

The captain's announcement ended the conversation. Food would be good. Irene and Suzanne locked their small stateroom and hurried up the ladder to the restaurant on the fifth deck.

Under the watchful eye of a pirate with half his teeth missing and the other half stained a putrid yellow-brown, the bar at the restaurant entrance was doing a land-office business. They were serving the drinks free. Anything you wanted, they mixed and poured, then you grabbed it and made room for the next thirsty person behind you.

With a Cosmo in each hand, the two sisters sat at a table that already had a man and a woman at it.

"Do you mind?"

"Of course not. Twila and Harold. We're from Arkansas."

When the introductions were over, the diners began comparing experiences. The Arkansas couple had had a long, boring afternoon. The Arkansas lady's nose twitched. She had caught a good whiff of the marijuana smell on the sisters. "My heavens, what is that smell?"

"It was coming out of our air-conditioning," Irene explained. "Terrible stuff."

"Well, with pirates and all, what can you do?"

Eventually the conversation turned to what might come next.

"These pirates just want money," Suzanne said. "Someone will bail us out and we'll all go home."

"Who?"

"The cruise company or the government or something. The pirates can't keep us forever. And why would they want to?"

"I am worried about what happens when we get to wherever we are going," the lady from Little Rock said. "Are we going to stay aboard ship, be taken ashore . . . what?"

"How much food and water is on this ship?" the husband wanted to know. "How long before the sewage tanks fill up and the commodes stop working? How long can they keep the generators going?"

Neither of the sisters had thought for a minute about those questions, and now they looked at each other and considered.

"We're in a hell of a pickle," Irene said.

Suzanne nodded soberly.

"Well, who *is* going to bail us out?" Irene demanded. "Pay the ransom? I don't have any money and my kids don't. Any pirate who thinks he is getting money from me or any of my relatives is wasting his time."

Suzanne went off to get refills for herself and Irene. The Arkansas couple were sticking to soft drinks, the poor bastards.

"Oh, it will all work out," the Little Rock lady said when Suzanne got back with the booze. "Harold here worked for Walmart for a lot of years, and he always said everything works out in the end, didn't you, Harold?"

"Yes," Harold agreed. "There were days at Walmart—"

"But who is going to pay ransom for us?" Harold's mate, Twila, asked, interrupting her spouse. She then answered the question herself. "Why, our neighbors at the church. Our congregation always sticks together. Or the government. The people in Washington can always print more money and give the pirates some."

"I guess so," Suzanne said pensively, glancing at the pirate standing in the door with his AK-47 pointed negligently in the diners' direction.

"I don't see why not," Irene declared. "They ship money in heaps to every dictator on the planet. Might as well send some to Somalia and spring us. Boy, am I going to be mad if they don't!"

The waiters brought plates heaping with good things, so they all became too busy to talk.

With her mouth full, the Little Rock lady asked the key question. "Do you think the cruise ship company will give us a refund? After all, pirates?"

"Pirates are going to make their marketing more difficult," Irene said, forking chicken. "Even a partial refund would be good PR."

"Walmart always worried about good PR," Harold remarked. "Even a discount on another cruise would be welcome. We always wanted to go to South America. No pirates there."

"Except in Venezuela. That screwball dictator, what's-his-name."

"Chavez. Like the ravine."

"We'll skip Venezuela," Harold said flatly. "Carnival in Rio would be nice."

"Nice," Suzanne agreed and finished her third Cosmo.

CHAPTER SIX

INDIAN OCEAN, NOVEMBER 10

When Angel Cordova glimpsed the lights of the *Sultan of the Seas,* the SEALs had been in their boats for an hour. It was 3:00 A.M. They were only twenty-five miles off the coast of Africa, sixty miles north of Eyl.

The idling engine on Cordova's boat didn't interfere with his ability to hear the handheld radio on the earpiece he wore under his black, waterproof head covering.

"*Sultan* in sight," he reported.

"She's steering one-nine-three and steady at ten knots."

"Roger. Everyone copy?"

"Two, aye."

"Three, aye."

"Four, aye."

Cordova had his boats spread out about two miles apart, so they covered six miles of ocean. At Cordova's order, the coxswains revved the engines and they began the run-in to intercept the oncoming cruise ship.

Sultan looked as if she would pass between Boats One and Two.

Cordova had less than a mile to go westward; Boat Two a mile eastward. Three and Four were farther inshore, and they would have to hurry or the ship would be past them before they could intercept.

The boat rocked and skipped over the swells, with Cordova and his five men hunkered down to keep the center of gravity as low as possible.

Two miles ahead of the *Sultan,* Cordova's coxswain, who knew his business, turned to parallel the cruise ship. He throttled back to let the big ship overtake him. He placed the boat so it would be on *Sultan*'s port side. As the speed bled off, the boat began to rock more violently in the swells. The men held on to ropes, just in case.

Using his night-vision goggles, Cordova could see Boat Two maneuvering closer.

Angel Cordova was scared, and he tried not to think about it. His stomach felt as if it were doing flip-flops. All that training, years of it, the running, swimming, brutal cross-country, obstacle and confidence-building courses, survival and weapons training, cold, mud, hunger, exhaustion . . . all of it came down to this, a real combat mission. He was worried he would blow it, would screw up the mission and lose his men, who trusted him implicitly.

When he had briefed the mission he had watched their faces. Trust. Confidence. He remembered those looks now, and his stomach revolted and he heaved his dinner over the edge of the boat. The other men pretended they didn't see that. When the mission was over, back aboard ship, then they would rib him. Not now. He was the officer in charge, and their lives were in his hands.

Would they even be able to intercept? Get aboard?

The ship was bigger, overtaking at about five knots. Angel Cordova could see every light.

Jesus, it was a big ship! Hell, every ship was big when viewed from this angle, on the surface of the sea as it came steaming along.

Slowly . . . then the bow was there, passing. Cordova could see lights in the lounges and dining rooms, the staterooms, all lit up like a big city hotel.

He could hear the wash of the bow wave, feel it as the boat approached its edge with the engine roaring and the coxswain taking the waves at an angle to keep from overturning.

Here came the ship's side. Wet and dark and slimy. It was so close he could almost reach it. He scanned the well-lit rails above him, looking for people. Not a head did he see.

"Grappling hooks," he shouted into his radio mike, which was against his lips.

"Hooks . . . now!"

Three hooks shot upward. Two of them seemed to catch. Angel Cordova grabbed one, tugged hard and felt the resistance.

He paused for just a second to check the weapons and backpack full of explosives and ammo, then timed the rise and fall of the boat. As the boat came up, he grabbed a handful of rope—it was wet, but there were knots—and began climbing hand over hand with his feet braced against the side of the ship.

Another man was also on a rope. More ropes went up, and two more men came scrambling.

Cordova reached the deck edge and looked around. No one there. This was a lifeboat sponson; the large boats hung from davits over his head. Lights on the bulkheads.

He hooked a heel over a rail, then crawled over. He unslung his weapon, a silenced submachine gun, and lay there for just a second looking around. He was on his feet against the bulkhead, behind a boat davit, when his men came over the rail. One, two, three and four. Got 'em.

"Alpha Team is aboard port side."

"Bravo is aboard starboard side."

Silence.

"Charlie is maybe five minutes out."

"Delta is ten out, but I don't know if I can intercept."

"Roger."

One U.S. Navy sailor quickly unhooked the grappling hooks and dropped them over the side while his mates went forward and aft, checking the doors. They were open, as they always were in good weather. The black-clad men went through the doors with their weapons in their hands.

. . .

Aboard *Chosin Reservoir,* Rear Admiral Toad Tarkington was watching marines in assault gear man three V-22 Ospreys on the flight deck. Each of the giant twin-rotor transports could carry eight combat-ready marines. Toad was still transferring them to the destroyer. Several were snipers who could shoot pirates if they began executing passengers on deck.

Tarkington was worried. The pirates still held the aces, the hostages. Toad had given Lieutenant Cordova permission to shoot anyone he had to, but good sense had to be exercised. Toad didn't intend to give the pirates the chance to slaughter hostages. Everything depended on keeping the pirates confused and off balance. Speed. It had to happen fast.

If the *Sultan*'s engines were disabled, the pirates might think their position was tactically hopeless. Or they might not.

God damn Washington!

Toad left the flag bridge and hustled down the ladders to the tactical flag spaces.

Angel Cordova made his way upward toward the *Sultan*'s bridge. He heard two pirates in the stairwell above him talking, so he checked his silenced submachine gun and eased upward. He saw their legs before he saw their upper bodies. Took careful aim at the legs. Fired a six-shot burst and both men fell, screaming. As they hit the deck he fired a squirt into each head. Blood and brains flew everywhere.

Cordova continued to climb. He had reached the pool deck when he saw another man with a weapon lounging against a wall. Leaning on it.

A black-clad ghost, Cordova pulled his knife, glided a step forward, then another. Grabbed a handful of hair, pulled the head back and cut the man's throat with one swipe. Blood spurted forward and the body collapsed. The weapon fell on the deck.

Amazingly, the butterflies in Cordova's gut were gone. He reached, snaked the AK back into the shadows, then tossed it over the rail. It spun once and fell into the blackness.

"Bravo is trying to get into the engine room."

He merely clicked his mike twice in reply.

From where he sat he could see the machine gun mounted across the pool on the deck above. Saw at least twenty people huddled in deck chairs. They looked cold. Well, the temp was in the fifties and they weren't wearing coats. Some of them had deck towels wrapped around them.

There should be two machine-gun nests above him. Cordova faded back through the door and started up the staircase.

Mustafa al-Said left the bridge and walked aft. The bridge was on the pool deck. He stepped out of the swinging doors, glanced at the people huddled in the deck chairs and looked aft at the machine guns protruding from the corners of the deck above.

The ship's lights were still on. He wondered about that. Should he turn them off? If the Americans came over, would darkness help or hurt them?

Mustafa decided to leave the lights on. They would help the machine-gun crews see helicopters, and give the Americans a good look at the hostages around the pool.

That decision made, he began a circuit of the pool, checking the men on the corners. Less than a minute later, he found the man with his throat cut, lying in an extraordinary pool of blood.

For a moment he thought perhaps a passenger had attacked the man, but when he saw the head had been almost severed from the body with one vicious swipe of a knife, saw the white of bone amid the red gore, he forgot about passengers. This was the work of a trained killer. Americans were aboard!

Mustafa fired a burst from his weapon over the rail. The sound was flat, but he saw his men on deck looking his way. He gestured and two men came running.

One look was enough.

A few tense words . . . then the command, "Find them. Quickly."

Angel Cordova was behind the two-man machine-gun crew when he heard the burst. The crew moved forward, looked down, trying to see.

Cordova fired two quick silenced three-shot bursts. They weren't exactly silent, just guttural coughs. One man slumped down where he was, and the other fell across the machine gun, which was on a tripod. The barrel of the gun moved upward at a crazy angle.

Almost instantly, a burst of slugs from somewhere smashed into the overhead. Someone on the pool deck below was shooting.

Cordova fell backward and crawled out of the area, headed across the foyer in front of the elevators for the second machine gun on the starboard side.

A man stepped out, saw him and swung his AK.

The SEAL was quicker. His burst hit the man in the stomach, and the man triggered his assault rifle. The long burst hammered at the floor, then the ceiling as he fell. The noise filled the stairwell.

Petty Officer First Class Buster Imboden was belowdecks, going for the hatch that led below for the engine rooms. His team of four men followed him, but not too close. They were spread out so a burst that felled one man wouldn't get them all. The passageway was lined with doors, most of which were standing open. They led to four-man bunkrooms. These were crew quarters, and many of the off-duty crewmen and -women looked at the men wearing black wet suits and carrying weapons with open curiosity. Several stuck their heads through the door, but the SEALs motioned them back into their bunkrooms.

The hatch was open, with lights shining up the trunk. Buster took a look, signaled to the men behind him and took a deep breath. There was only one way down, and pirates would be waiting. He could hear them talking.

"Alpha has run into problems. Alpha Two, get behind that forward machine gun and take them out." While the transmission button was keyed, Imboden could hear bursts of AK-47 fire.

Imboden glanced at his men, then slung his weapon around his neck so it would be easily accessible, stepped on the ladder and started down quickly. At the bottom, a door led onto the engine room catwalk. He opened the door and a hatful of bullets stitched him across the abdomen, missing his backbone but puncturing both kidneys, his liver and his intestines. He fell face forward on the catwalk.

Bravo Two, Petty Officer Second Class Neil Irons, didn't hesitate. He pulled a grenade from his vest and pulled the pin. Went down the ladder to the door, released the lever, counted one potato, two potato and shoved the door open with his left hand while he tossed the grenade aft as far as he could.

Bullets spanged off the door, which had automatically started to close. Then the grenade exploded.

Irons led Bravo Team through the door, guns burping out bullets.

Imboden was sprawled on his stomach. He had his head up and was firing his weapon.

The SEALs coming through the doorway ran by him shooting at everything they saw. That turned out to be two pirates, one of whom was already wounded by the grenade blast. The other went down under a burst of submachine-gun fire.

Leaving a man to watch the hatches, Irons ran on as he keyed his mike. "Bravo One's hit."

The attackers were in a large engine room that was two decks high. Running aft, Irons saw the control panel. Two of the ship's engineers were huddled on the deck in front of the panel while another pirate attempted to hide behind it.

The Somali shouted something. Now he threw out his weapon as the SEALs ran at him. As he stepped out from behind the panel with his hands up, Irons shot him.

The other team members jerked the engineers off the deck and herded them toward the catwalk ladder and the door to the upper decks while Irons surveyed the panel and the engines. Then they ran for the watertight hatch that led to the aft engine room.

The engines were what Irons expected, medium-speed four-stroke diesels. There were two of them in this engine room and two in the aft engine room. The diesels turned generators that supplied the power to the four propeller pods under the ship. Any engine could be shut down for maintenance while the others powered the pods.

The propeller pods under the ship were controlled from the bridge, Irons knew, but all the control wires went through this panel. He removed a preprepared plastique explosive charge from his backpack, armed it and wedged it behind the panel. Another satchel charge went on the front of the panel.

Irons set the timers for ten seconds, hit the arming switches and ran to get behind one of the diesels. Two small explosions, almost simultaneous but not quite.

After a last look around, Irons led his two men back to the place they had left their team leader, Imboden. The man seemed to be still alive. Alive or dead, he was going with Irons and the other men.

They picked him up and opened the door to the ladder leading upward. Someone was trying to get into this space from the aft engine room. A burst of submachine gun fire dissuaded him.

Carrying and shoving Imboden, the men started up the forward ladderwell toward the fourth deck. They heard the explosions of the satchel charges. The lights went out. Seconds later low-wattage emergency lights illuminated.

Imboden was badly hit. The men paused in the fourth-deck passageway to bandage him up as well as they could to stop the bleeding, gave him a shot of morphine, then headed up the stairs toward the fifth deck and the sponson where they had boarded.

One pirate came running down the passageway and was taken out by bursts from two submachine guns, which hammered him to the deck. His weapon skittered along the linoleum to a stop.

"Bravo got the control panel and is egressing with one casualty."

"Roger that," Cordova replied.

As they exited to the sponson, two pirates opened fire from behind a davit. They had guessed how the intruders had boarded and were there waiting.

Two of Irons' men threw grenades, and after they exploded, the SEALS went over the side, jumping toward the black ocean below. Two of them had Imboden firmly grasped between them as they went over.

Mustafa al-Said ran to the people huddled around the pool on deck chairs. The emergency lights were just enough to see with. He gestured to the first five he saw with the barrel of his assault rifle, shouting, "Get up. Get up. Go forward."

When one man didn't go quickly enough, Mustafa shot him. A woman screamed and he shot her. The other three ran ahead of him. He herded them forward toward the bridge.

Alpha One, Lieutenant Angel Cordova, saw the murders by the pool. The pirates would kill everyone if this went on. He aimed his submachine gun at Mustafa, but he didn't shoot. The hostages would probably also be hit. Oh, God! Still, if Mustafa fired again, Cordova intended to pull the trigger. He didn't.

"Alpha *and* Bravo egress. Alpha and Bravo egress."

Bullets were spanging around Cordova from the forward machine gun as he ran for the rail. Two of his men behind him opened fire, giving him cover. He rolled behind a stanchion and fired a burst at the machine gun. It fell silent.

"Over the side," he roared into his mike.

Two men ran past and vaulted the rail.

He saw two men going over the rail on the far side of the deck, so he didn't hesitate. Angel Cordova gathered himself, ran two steps and leaped for the rail. Machine-gun bullets followed him. One of them hit him in the leg as he went over.

"*Sultan* is slowing, sir," one of the radar operators reported to Admiral Tarkington.

He could see that. The computer symbol was showing three knots.

"Her engines have stopped, sir." That would be a sonar report.

"Let's get in there and pick up those SEALs," Toad snapped. Each of the SEALs wore saltwater-activated beacons. They were expert swimmers, but at least one man was wounded.

"Launch the alert Ospreys," Toad ordered. He had three birds ready to go. Two were to pick up SEALs, and the third was to cover them as a gunship. The Osprey could hover like a chopper, and the marine versions carried a 20 mm cannon in the left sponson. Toad had the covering Osprey crew briefed. If the pirates started shooting hostages, they were to take them out with the cannon. Ditto if they shot at the Ospreys.

He watched on the flight deck monitor as the three Ospreys lifted off.

Just in case, Toad had a destroyer going after the SEALs, too. Airplanes could develop mechanical problems or be shot down. There wasn't much pirates could do to hurt a destroyer.

CHAPTER SEVEN

In the false half-light before dawn, *Sultan of the Seas* lay lifeless on the surface of the ocean, resembling nothing so much as a large dead whale. DIW, the sailors said, "dead in the water." Her screws were still, and her dim emergency lighting barely outlined her superstructure amid the gloom.

Ospreys with searchlights ablaze picked up the SEALs in the ocean, strung out along the course the ship had traveled. The nearest was almost a thousand yards from where the ship had drifted to a halt. USS *Richard Ward,* a destroyer with searchlights brilliantly lit, crept among the men being drawn from the sea in horse collars.

"One casualty," one of the Osprey pilots reported. "First Class Imboden. Dead when we pulled him out."

A few minutes later another Osprey reported, "Got a Lieutenant Cordova with a gunshot wound in the left calf. It's bleeding, but the corpsman thinks he'll make it okay. We're inbound to the ship now."

"Roger. Switch to Tower."

Two mike clicks.

On his monitor in Flag Ops, Admiral Tarkington watched the Osprey settle on the bow and four stretcher bearers run for it. In less than half a minute they were trotting toward the island carrying the stretcher with the man on it wrapped in a blanket.

Dawn began to arrive. Fifteen minutes after the Osprey delivered Lieutenant Cordova, the *Sultan* was visible on the monitor as a ship, not just a collection of dim lights. She wasn't moving.

Colonel Max Zakhem delivered the news. "Mr. Cordova never got to the bridge. Bravo Team sabotaged the engine room control panel. One of the pirates started shooting passengers by the pool. Cordova thought any further attempt to gain the bridge would result in a bloodbath of the hostages."

The admiral merely nodded. Cordova was the man on the spot, and he made the best decision he could when he decided to get off the ship after the engineering control panel was sabotaged. All in all, Cordova and his men accomplished a lot. More than Tarkington expected, actually.

"Draft a sitrep to everyone in the chain of command," Toad said to his chief of staff, Flip Haducek. "Let me see it before you send it."

Haducek disappeared to prepare the situation report.

Toad spoke to the flag ops officer, and a few minutes later was handed a radiotelephone. He put it to his ear and keyed the mike. "*Sultan of the Seas*, this is *Chosin Reservoir* on Guard, over." Guard was the international emergency frequency, 121.5 megacycles.

No answer.

Toad tried one more time, got no answer and passed the instrument to Ops. "Call them once a minute."

"Aye aye, sir."

He used the Navy Red voice frequency to talk to *Richard Ward*'s captain.

Five minutes later *Ward* crept up alongside *Sultan,* to about a hundred feet, making three knots, just enough to allow *Ward* to answer her helm. She stopped her engines and drifted to a halt alongside the cruise ship. Her deck was lined with armed marines. High in the superstructure, as high as they could get, snipers lying on their bellies focused their scopes on the pirates they could see. A quarter mile away on both sides Ospreys loaded with marines circled like vultures.

Richard Ward played her searchlights on the deck of *Sultan* and on her rows of balcony windows. Faces appeared, people came out. A few waved. Most just stood looking.

. . .

Mustafa al-Said left the three passengers on the bridge with four of his men. One of them put a rifle to the head of a passenger and led him out onto the wing of the bridge so the crew of *Richard Ward* could see him. He merely stood there with his hostage.

Mustafa marched Captain Arch Penney aft and down. "The engine room," he ordered grimly.

In the forward engine room two pirates were watching two engineers assess the damage. A dead pirate lay on the deck. He had bled a good bit before he died, and the red puddle was turning brown. It was also getting sticky where people had stepped in it. Still, no one touched the body.

Ignoring the dead man as best he could, Penney inspected the electrical distribution bus that sent power to the four propeller pods. It was obliterated beyond repair. The diesels were idling, turning generators, but without electrical buses to distribute the power to the engine pods, *Sultan* was not going anywhere.

"How long will it take to wire around these smashed buses?" Penney asked the chief engineer as he surveyed the damage. "Put power directly to the two aft pods?"

"Five or six hours." The man shrugged.

The engineer straightened and wiped his hands on a waste rag. He never even looked at Mustafa. "We can try, sir. But it's damaged, as you can see."

"Do your best, Derek," Arch Penney said. He faced Mustafa. "Seen enough?"

"So the ship cannot move?"

"That is correct."

"Perhaps I shoot someone. Will it be able to move then?"

"Not unless you can fix it yourself."

Mustafa pointed his rifle at one of the engineers and pulled the trigger. The bullet tore through the man's neck; bloody tissue sprayed out his back. Down he went, probably dead, beside the body of a pirate. The body twitched, moving as muscles contracted involuntarily, and Arch Penney got a glimpse of the man's eyes, full of fear. Then they relaxed and focused on infinity. He was dead.

"You have two hours, Captain. Then I start shooting more people. I shoot someone every five minutes until the ship moves."

The fury welled up in Arch, rose like the tide. The dead man was Jerry Robinson, from New Zealand. He saw Jerry's wife's face in his mind's eye, hysterical.

Arch closed his eyes, tried to control his breathing. When he opened them, he focused on the chief engineer, who was fixated upon Jerry's corpse. Arch reached for the man and turned him by pulling on his shoulder until he was facing the captain.

"Wire the generators to one pod. Just one. We'll move on that while you work on the second one."

The man's eyes flicked to Mustafa, then back. He nodded.

Arch Penney headed for the ladder leading out of the engineering spaces. Mustafa stood for a second, watching his back, then trailed after him.

Benny and Sarah Cohen stood at the door to their balcony looking at *Richard Ward* lying there in the gentle sea. Swells were negligible; there was essentially no wind. The gray warship seemed immobile, as if she were fixed to a pier.

Beyond *Ward* they could see an Osprey circling. Even hear it.

"We could jump," Benny told his wife. "They would pick us up."

Sarah held tightly to his arm. They leaned out and looked at the people on the other balconies. Some were talking and pointing. Several were looking down at the water twenty-five feet below. It was a healthy drop. Hit the water wrong and you could break your back. Especially if you were over fifty, and most of them were.

Sarah whispered, "Go if you want, Benny. I'm too old and can't swim very well."

Benny pulled her to him. "We stay together," he said.

They heard a shout. A woman's voice. A man plummeted toward the sea. He had a full head of gray hair. He went in feet first, then rose and started swimming.

Above them a weapon chattered. As the Cohens watched, bullets began striking around the man. He kept swimming. The bullets impacted all around him, churning the water. He was fifteen feet away from the side of the ship, now twenty . . .

Then a bullet hit him in the head and they saw a little cloud of red spray. The man ceased swimming and floated facedown. The pirate on the deck above them ceased firing.

On *Richard Ward* a marine first lieutenant watching through binoculars made an instant decision. "Shoot him," he snapped at the sniper lying at his feet.

The sniper's bullet went through the pirate's chest and he collapsed on the deck. He was several decks above the Cohens, who didn't see him fall or hear the shot.

The Cohens heard a woman screaming.

"It was that Texas oil dude, Warren Bass," Benny Cohen said bitterly. He stepped back into the room with Sarah and pulled the French door closed.

When Mustafa al-Said returned to the bridge, prodding Captain Penney along with his gun barrel, he could hear a loud-hailer from the destroyer lying a mere thirty or forty yards away.

"Throw your weapons into the sea and come out on deck with your hands up. If you do, you will not be harmed." There were men on the bridge in uniforms, one of them holding a loud-hailer. Two men in khaki, two in some blue mottled coveralls. The warship's bridge was a bit lower than that of the cruise ship, so Mustafa could only see the wing of it.

One of the pirates who obviously understood some English had his gun pointed at the deck and was looking around nervously.

Mustafa cuffed him across the mouth. "Bring one of the civilians. The woman."

The man did as he was told. Grabbed her and shoved her forward. Mustafa gestured with his head. The woman was shoved out onto the wing of the bridge. She grabbed the rail and sank to her knees.

The destroyer accelerated away. The aft gun turret went past, then the stern. The wake was boiling white foam.

"You should have surrendered," Penney said as Mustafa shoved the woman into a corner out of the way, beside the others. "They'll be back."

"For everyone's sake, let us hope not," Mustafa said and looked at his watch. "One hour and fifty minutes. You will decide who we shoot first."

The radio loudspeaker was squawking. "*Sultan,* this is *Chosin Reservoir*—"

Mustafa al-Said fired a three-shot burst into the loudspeaker. In the profound silence that followed the burst Arch Penney could hear the spent cartridge cases tinkling as they bounced off the steel deck, which was stained with blood and human tissue.

Arch could feel himself slipping gently away, letting go of this reality in favor of another, gentler one. He ground his teeth together, shook his head violently and forced himself back to the here and now.

He had only a thread to hang on to, so he seized it. Somehow, someway, he was going to kill Mustafa al-Said, even if it was the very last thing he did upon this earth.

"Ah, Jake, come in. Come in, please."

The director, Mario Tomazic, nodded toward a chair, and Jake Grafton dropped into it. Although it was midmorning in Pirate Alley, it was three thirty in the morning in Washington. Only the night shift was left on duty. And the head dogs, who didn't work shifts.

Tomazic was of medium height, balding, but fit and trim, as befits a modern CEO or senior general. The newspapers said he was one of the leading experts in antiterrorism; Jake had seen nothing from Tomazic to prove or disprove that assertion. He had a nice smile and never raised his voice . . . and was absolutely ruthless.

"What do you hear from Tarkington?" Grafton asked.

"The Task Force 151 commander? You served with him?"

Jake merely nodded.

"It's a fuckup. The SEALs stopped the ship. She's DIW. Then the geniuses at the White House realized that the pirates had over eight hundred hostages, and would probably kill a bunch of them on general principles. They chickened out, got cold feet."

"So?"

"So the cruise ship is DIW, the task force is on the scene, and the White House doesn't have the guts to order a boarding." Tomazic sighed. He hated civilians who meddled. Unfortunately, this was the age of meddlers.

"What does Tarkington propose?"

Tomazic sorted through a pile of messages and passed one to Jake. "You know that he wanted to do a show of force and rappel down marines. They are having a big debate over on Pennsylvania Avenue. I don't think they'll tell the admiral to stay away from the cruise ship or allow him to do anything. Those people have never had any experience with combat situations. They are going to have to look at it from every angle, think about political repercussions, get advice. In other words, they're paralyzed."

"They liked the SEAL idea," Grafton remarked.

"Unconventional warfare, commandos, surprise, surgical violence," Tomazic replied. "They thought it would make great television, sorta like a computer game. Military orgasm: the bad guys all fall down, the good guys win again. Ta-daaa." Tomazic paused to clear his throat. "They're idiots."

Grafton didn't bother to reply.

"They need more adult supervision over there than they're getting," Tomazic added.

A smile tugged at Grafton's lips.

Mario Tomazic didn't notice. He said, "The pirates will take the ship and hostages to Eyl. These are apparently Ragnar's men. I want you to get your people to Eyl and wait for the green light to take out that son of a bitch."

"Okay."

"I want one less pirate in the world."

"We'll give it a try," Jake Grafton said, smiling. He liked Tomazic, who could dance between the cow pies with the best of them. Still, after all those years in the army, he knew when to lower his head and charge, and he had the guts to do it. Tough for the bad guys.

Grafton thought about it for a bit, then said, "The government going to pay the ransom?"

"Don't have a demand yet."

"Oh, we'll get one. Pirates are in it for the money."

"I don't think the White House savants have thought that far ahead."

"Oh," Jake Grafton said. "Well, when they get around to it, the money could be our ticket in. We motor right in with the cash, see the man. That would be Plan B. Plan A would of course be a sniper. Less risk to our guys."

"What would you need for a sniper hit?"

"A drone over the city twenty-four/seven. Without a spotter on the ground, a drone would be the next best thing. A sniper will need a good setup location and some lead time, the more the better. And he'll have to have an escape route. However, a sniper can only shoot when he has a target. A sniper isn't going to get a shipload of people out of there if the money isn't paid, either."

Tomazic eyed Grafton under his shaggy eyebrows. "So we have two problems."

"One relatively easy to solve, the other less so," Grafton replied.

The director sighed. "If we pay the ransom, presumably the pirates will release the ship, crew and passengers," he said. "It's good business. On the other hand, if the ransom is not going to be paid, we have to go forward as if it will be and rescue those people before the pirates realize what is going down."

"That's about the size of it."

"Okay. Get the sniper thing going and give me a plan for rescuing the people if the politicians refuse to pay."

"Is that even a possibility?"

"They'll make the decision that they think will do them the most good politically. Whatever that is. They always do."

"Plans are just paper," Jake said. "We'll have to see how the cards fall." He shrugged.

"Just as long as the cards fall our way," Tomazic retorted dryly. Like Grafton, he didn't believe in fair play. Stacking the deck was not only legal in the intelligence business, it was the only way to play the game.

"Do you really think the White House will give you a green light for a sniper hit?"

"I'll get one eventually," Tomazic said grimly. "After the ship's passengers and crew are ransomed, released or whatever, those people downtown are going to have an epiphany. They are going to want us to do something to solve the pirate problem in that corner of the world, or at least make it go away for a while, and they are going to want it done yesterday. When they come to Jesus, I want you and your men ready."

Half a world away from Washington, Toad Tarkington was as frustrated as a man can get. *Sultan of the Seas* lay a mile away from his flagship, drifting on the glassy sea. There wasn't a breath of wind. Surrounding her were gray warships, sprinkled here and there, moving slowly to conserve fuel and yet remain under control. Helicopters and Ospreys droned back and forth overhead, watching and filming and staying far enough away from *Sultan* to present no threat. Miles above an E-2 circled, watching every ship and plane within a two-hundred-mile radius.

If he wanted them, carrier jets were armed and ready on the flight deck of an American carrier coming south from the Persian Gulf. They could be overhead within an hour. With every minute that passed, the carrier closed the range.

Sometimes in the night when he was trying to sleep, Toad thought about the irony of keeping all these ships at sea, the sailors on watch, the airplanes flying, all to prevent pirates from grabbing an occasional merchant ship and demanding some money, a pittance really, compared to the cost of preventing the piracy in the first place. Maybe most crime is like that: It costs more to deter bank robbery and catch and punish bank robbers than they could ever steal. Yet we try to deter bank robbery and catch and punish the evildoers nonetheless.

Toad wasn't thinking about the irony now. He was sitting in his chair on the flag bridge listening to reports and reading messages from Washington, his fleet commander, and his theater commander. Messages poured in, and staffers read them and passed the ones they thought he should see on to him for perusal. Orders, advice, reminders, more orders, suggestions and general bullshit. Toad was used to it. He had been reading navy messages since he graduated from the Naval Academy, back before the glaciers melted and man discovered toilet paper. Back when there were iron men in wooden ships. Or wooden men in iron ships. Something like that, Toad knew. He was an old fart; all these youngsters standing around busily looking at the *Sultan* and trying to be respectful while thinking of ways to solve this military problem just reminded him of it.

The fact that the problem was insoluble right now didn't compute. Gotta work this thing, get it unscrewed, come up with a solution, make it happen. That's what we're here for. Dammit, people, this is the *U. S. Navy* we're talking about.

He decided to write another message to Washington. Reached for a pad of paper and took his pen from his shirt pocket and started in.

When he finished, he motioned to his chief of staff, Flip. "Washington be damned. This is what we are going to do." He handed the captain the draft message.

Haducek scanned it. "But, Admiral, they already told you not to do this."

"No, they told me to do the SEAL thing instead. So I did. Now I'm going with my plan."

"Sir, you *can't—*"

"Yes, by God, I can! There are eight hundred and fifty unarmed civilians on that ship whose lives are being threatened by homicidal pirates. I'm the officer on the scene. *Yes, by God, I can!*"

Tarkington took a deep breath. When he resumed speaking, his voice was again normal. "Get that typed up. Get the ships in position. We go when everyone is ready. Ten minutes before we go, you send that message. Got it?"

"Aye aye, sir."

Mike Rosen left the e-communications center and headed for the buffet at noon. There had been no announcement, but he was hungry—and why not? He passed two pirates on the way. They were standing near the elevators chewing khat and cradling their weapons, looking worried. Perhaps the earlier SEAL assault had unnerved them. The ship was obviously not moving, not getting closer to Eyl and safety, and they must be worried about that, too.

Rosen could see the surface of the ocean through a window in the lounge area as he walked through it. The sea was flat as a plate, with gray naval vessels moving slowly along. Beyond them was the sea's rim, a perfectly straight line. A high, white overcast threw a soft light that made every detail stand out.

There was indeed food, food straight from the coolers. Nothing hot. Still, the toasters worked, and there was plenty of jam. Coffee was a score. The stewards had trouble keeping the big urns full because the passengers were draining it out so quickly. Rosen had to stand in line to get a cup. At least it was hot and strong.

The passengers were subdued, more withdrawn, plainly worried. Some of them had been roped to the lounge chairs during the SEAL attack, and they were badly frightened. Watching that pirate murder two passengers right before their eyes had shaken them to the core. They might not live through this disaster. Tragedy. Death was right there, waiting . . .

Those who spoke did so in whispers, with glances at the pirates huddled together near the door. There were no smiles, no nervous laughs. The SEAL attack was the main item of conversation. Everyone knew a tidbit, no one knew the whole story. They speculated endlessly over what the attack meant and what it had achieved.

What would this day bring? The dead man and woman by the pool—a woman from Germany and a man from Florida. Slaughtered. Thinking about danger, worrying about something that might or might not happen, well, we all did that every day as we wandered through life. The spouse, the job, the kids, the doctors, the lawyers, the damned stock market . . . But to see people ripped apart by bullets right in front of your eyes, to see real people instantly turned into blood and guts and brains and half-digested food—that was a trauma that nothing in your life up to that moment had prepared you for. It changed you. You would never again be the same. Life would never have the same feel it once did. The world would be scarier. More dangerous.

Rosen could see the stress in his fellow passengers' faces. No doubt they could see it in his. He asked questions in the serving line and got answers, though several of the people tried to pretend they weren't talking to him.

He also saw the stress in the pirates, who were obviously shaken, probably by the SEAL assault. The Americans and their allies were fierce warriors; men lying on deck in pools of their own blood with their throats slashed apart proved that point. Rosen wondered if cultural shock had anything to do with the pirates' mood. This morning they looked like children caught playing hooky. More to the point, Rosen wondered if any of this lot would actually murder a passenger. Their body language said no. The AK-47s were no longer pointed at anyone. None of them laughed or swaggered. It was something to think about.

Carrying his two pieces of toast and his full coffee cup, Rosen joined Sarah and Benny Cohen at a table for six. Benny was toying with his food with his fork, glancing at the pirate in the doorway occasionally.

Sarah said hello. Before long she was telling him about the man who had jumped, Warren Bass. About the bullets churning the water and the spray of blood.

"His wife didn't jump. Just him."

"Maybe she was going to jump and chickened out," Rosen ventured. "The high board always scared me."

"Maybe he told her it was every man for himself and leaped."

"Now, Benny, you don't know that. Don't be unkind."

"Maybe," Benny Cohen repeated, scrutinizing Rosen.

"You know I can't swim very well," Sarah said.

Her husband covered her hand with his.

"We wouldn't have made it, Benny," she said.

Captain Arch Penney stood on the bridge of his drifting vessel trying to get his thoughts together. There was an armed pirate on each wing, and Mustafa al-Said walked back and forth, looking at everything, listening to every report on the intercom, every conversation on the handhelds. All that remained of the carnage on the bridge was the bloodstains, and the three hostages seated against the aft bulkhead, out of the way. Two men and a woman.

The woman was about sixty, Penney thought, Canadian or American.

Her name was Marjorie Andregg. She was one tough female. Hadn't complained or cried or even whimpered, hadn't asked to use the restroom, which was right off the bridge, unlike the man seated beside her. He had been in the restroom twice and had still managed to pee his pants. He was shaking now, kept his hands in front of his face. The captain didn't know his name. Penney wondered if he was going to do something really stupid, like jump up and run.

The other man was obviously nervous. His name was George Something, from New York, if Penney remembered correctly, perhaps a worn fifty-five or a well-preserved sixty-five. Somewhere in there. George's eyes swept the bridge like a flashlight, checking on the pirates, watching Mustafa, even glancing occasionally at Penney with a beseeching look. Penney tried to ignore him—and resented the man for his silent pleadings. Bastard!

An hour after they came up from the engine room, forty-five minutes before Mustafa's announced murder deadline, Mustafa left the bridge, whispered to the men on the wing, then went out.

Penney had little to do except try to figure out what was coming and how to handle it. He figured Mustafa would return with more hostages . . . and at the designated time shoot one. Or two. Or three.

Penney wondered why he believed Mustafa's threats. Had the man achieved that much of a psychological advantage?

Yes. Watching Mustafa murder Jerry Robinson in the engine room had made Penney a believer. The man would kill as casually as breathing.

Thirty-five minutes left.

The woman wanted to go to the restroom. Penney nodded and pointed. She rose and took three steps to the door, opened it and went in. Closed it behind her.

Penney used his binoculars to examine the ships in the vicinity. Then he put the binoculars down and looked at the pirates, who were lounging negligently against the railings. One of them was looking at him, the other was looking at the surface of the sea.

Thirty-four minutes.

Thirty-three.

Thirty-two.

Marjorie Andregg came out of the restroom. She looked around, then walked over to him.

"What are we going to do?" she asked softly, so only Arch Penney could hear her.

"I don't know."

"Why are we stopped? Not moving?"

"Engines sabotaged."

"Those commandos?"

"Yes."

One of the pirates shouted at her, gesturing with his rifle barrel.

"Better sit back down," Penney said.

"We only have to die once, Captain," she said and sat back down beside the men.

Arch Penney stared at her. When he finally looked again at the clock, he saw he had only twenty-nine minutes until Mustafa's deadline. He reached for the handset that gave him a direct line to the aft engine room, then put it back on the cradle. They were working as quickly as they could. *Why waste thirty seconds of their time merely to settle my nerves?*

Twenty-two minutes before the deadline, Mustafa returned. He had a woman with him. Julie Penney.

The captain felt the blood draining from his face. He had to put a hand on a control panel to steady himself.

Mustafa said nothing. He told Julie to sit beside the other three hostages, then strolled toward the far wing of the bridge.

Arch and his wife stared at each other. The man with his face in his hands was sobbing.

The moment was broken when Marjorie Andregg squeezed Julie's arm.

Toad Tarkington watched Ospreys ferry more marines to *Richard Ward*. The marines ran aboard, eight of them to a plane; the loaded Osprey lifted off, flew for about two minutes to the destroyer and hovered over the stern. There the marines ran from the stern of the plane and cleared the area as their transport lifted off to go get another load and another Osprey made its approach.

The warships were about two miles from *Sultan. Chosin Reservoir* was heading into the wind, and the destroyer was backing down so the wind came over the fantail. The ships were gradually getting farther apart, but when the transfer was complete, both ships would head for their rendezvous with *Sultan.*

Toad looked at *Sultan* through his binoculars. The pirates had to be watching this evolution and wondering what it meant. They didn't have many options because their ship was DIW, thanks to Lieutenant Angel Cordova.

Four minutes.

Mustafa al-Said put down his binoculars and walked back into the covered portion of the bridge. He had the butt of his AK braced against his hip, the muzzle pointed at the overhead, his hand wrapped around the handle and his finger on the trigger. Arch Penney could see that finger, see that the assault rifle would go off with the slightest squeeze of that trigger.

Mustafa turned toward him and made a show of looking at the clock on the bulkhead, a clock that had somehow survived the RPG attack and all the shooting. He strolled back until he was in front of Penney, who was standing in front of the unmanned helm.

"Which one?" he asked.

Penney stared at him without expression. He hoped. Actually the revulsion he felt was plain to see, and Mustafa saw it.

The pirate snarled, "You think, he will not shoot. He is not serious person. He is *reasonable.* You think that, do you not?"

Mustafa's fetid breath washed over Penney, who thought the smell was caused by rotten teeth. Mustafa's body odor was undoubtedly due to the fact he never bathed. "No. I think you are a bloody raving murderous asshole," the captain said evenly.

"Call engine room," Mustafa said.

Arch picked up the direct line handset. He could hear it ringing. Finally someone answered. Harry Wooten. "Captain here. How much longer?"

Mustafa put the rifle barrel under Penney's chin and took the handset from him. "Two minutes," he said. "In two minutes I shoot someone on the bridge."

Arch could hear Harry Wooten's strident voice. "It will take at least another thirty minutes. I promise you—"

"Two minutes. I let you listen." He dropped the handset, which fell to the length of its cord, an inch or so above the deck.

"Which one?" he asked Arch Penney.

"Me."

"Ah, you think I would not. Your officers can drive the ship. I do not need you."

"Shoot and be damned."

Mustafa glanced at the clock, took a few steps toward the bridge wing, leisurely, just strolling, then turned back. He stood there with that rifle pointed up, glancing occasionally at the clock.

The second hand swept up toward twelve. The man seated against the wall was moaning gently now, almost mindlessly. Penney wondered if he even realized he was making the noise.

Mustafa pointed the gun at Penney.

The captain closed his eyes. Took a deep breath, forced himself to exhale, relax. As Marjorie said, everyone has to die once. But only once.

He was standing there, his hands at his side, his eyes closed, when he heard the shot. He opened his eyes.

The man who had been moaning and sobbing was lying on his side with his eyes frozen, a smear of blood on his chest. His heart must have stopped instantly.

Mustafa picked up the handset. "Did you hear?"

He paused, then said, "In thirty minutes I shoot another one. Work quick, or I start shooting one every five minutes."

Mustafa al-Said walked to the wing of the bridge and looked again at *Chosin Reservoir* and the Ospreys flying back and forth to a destroyer. Several more Ospreys were overhead, several thousand feet up. Two more destroyers . . . a helicopter.

He could feel the situation slipping out of his control. With the ship moving toward Eyl, which was only a couple of hours away, there was little the Americans could do to stop him. But here, dead in the water, drifting, the Americans had more options. Mustafa didn't know exactly what they were, but he felt the threat—and he was worried.

His men were pirates, not soldiers. They wanted money and were willing to risk their lives to get it. But they weren't willing to die for nothing. That was a hard fact. If pressed . . . well, if pressed hard, Mustafa didn't know what they would do. Surrender, he suspected. A man could always go pirating another day.

They had already seen what the Americans could do. The pirate killed by a sniper after he shot a swimming passenger had been an object lesson. Mustafa wondered if any of his men could be induced to kill another passenger.

He stuffed another wad of khat in his mouth. The khat would keep his fingers from shaking.

Admiral Toad Tarkington believed the pirates would surrender rather than drown or be shot. He was acting upon that belief.

Toad, his chief of staff, Captain Haducek, and his ops officer had a plan, and they were busy telling everyone their part in it. People who jumped would be pulled into rafts. Anyone armed would be shot.

The pirates couldn't fight it out. Shooting hostages would do no good. They would be in a real corner.

"Have the captains check out their loud-hailers," Toad reminded Flip Haducek. "I want Somali speakers on those things."

"Yessir."

"We may have casualties," Toad told his staff. "Passengers may jump into the water; we must be ready to rescue them. Innocent people may get shot. I know all that. Still, I think the benefit of rescuing these people and thwarting the pirates is worth the casualties, which we will do our very best to minimize. I want Recon marines to rappel onto that ship as soon as the pirates surrender. They are to check below deck for casualties and evacuate any wounded they find. Kill anyone who offers resistance."

"Sir, *Ward* has its marines aboard."

"Very good. Load up the Recon guys and let's get this show under way."

Colonel Zakhem had marines in helmets lining the flight deck walkways. Several platoons waited on deck behind the island for the flight deck to clear.

Watching the ships, Ospreys and helicopters through binoculars, Mustafa al-Said realized that the Americans were up to something, and whatever it was, it was going to happen soon.

He couldn't shoot it out with the Americans. He couldn't run. His only option was to threaten the hostages. He had serious misgivings, but no other options, so that is what he decided to do.

He gave terse orders. His men were to herd the passengers up on deck and line them up against the rails. They were to hide behind them, and shoot them if he gave the order.

Mustafa didn't think it would work. He knew his men. Oh, they were perfectly willing to kill people, but they weren't willing to die to win victory. After the hostages were dead, what then? The Americans would slaughter the pirates, and they all knew it. Still, maybe the Americans would chicken out. Maybe they didn't have the stomach for blood.

He used the ship's loudspeaker system to give the orders in Somali. In seconds he could hear shouts and screams and the sound of running feet.

This would work or it wouldn't.

Mustafa had a man on the bridge take the two women out on the wing of the bridge and stand behind them. He grabbed the captain and led him to the other wing of the bridge. Jammed his rifle in his back.

USS *Chosin Reservoir* was a mile away from *Sultan,* making two knots, when a yeoman ran up to Toad on the flag bridge and handed him a message. *Richard Ward* was approaching the cruise ship from the other direction, which was bow on to her. Marines with rifles were all over the weather decks.

Toad took a deep breath, exhaled and glanced at the message. From Washington.

"Reference your message"—there was a date-time group—"notifying us of your plan to confront the pirates. Permission denied. Risks to noncombatants judged to be too great. Do not allow any of your vessels to approach within two miles of *Sultan* without permission from this headquarters. All flights to remain clear by at least two thousand yards."

Toad Tarkington wadded up the message with one hand.

"Sir, lookouts report civilians are lining the rail of the cruise ship. Some pirates with weapons behind them."

He could just ignore the order and proceed as if he never got it.

Even as he weighed it, he knew he wasn't going to ignore a direct order from the National Command Authority. Wanted to . . . knew his plan would work . . .

God damn!

Haducek was standing beside him. "Tell the captain to veer off. Tell *Ward* to do the same. Tell them to take up station five miles on either flank of the cruise ship."

"Jesus, Admiral. What—?"

Toad handed him the wadded-up message. "Just do it, Flip. Have the marines stand down."

Mustafa heard the ringing of the engine room telephone as he watched the amphibious assault ship turn away and accelerate. Captain Penney heard it, too.

Penney wrenched himself from al-Said's grasp and walked over to the phone. He grabbed it. "Captain."

"Port aft pod has power. Use the bridge controls."

"Thank you."

Penney went to the power control station, advanced the power lever for the port aft engine, made sure the turn-rate controller was centered so he could see how much he would have to turn the engine to make the ship go straight. He felt the screw bite. Almost imperceptibly, but he felt it. Saw the RPM needle come off the peg.

. . .

"*Sultan* is under way, sir."

Toad bit his lip. Even with the ship under way, his show of force would have worked.

He took off his baseball cap and crushed it with his left hand. The flag lieutenant was standing a little distance away. Toad glanced at him. "I believe I'll have a cup of coffee, Mr. Snodgrass."

"Yes, sir."

Afterward Snodgrass told his fellow officers, "You should have seen the old man. Ice water in his veins."

CHAPTER EIGHT

ETHIOPIA, NOVEMBER 10

I settled myself into the earth and pulled the stock back into my shoulder, welding my cheek to the stock. The scope picture was right there, clear and crisp. I settled the crosshairs onto the target, a black circle inscribed on the side of a cardboard box with Magic Marker, and snicked off the safety.

The box was only two hundred yards out there. This rifle, a Sako TRG-42, was theoretically capable of putting a bullet into a one-inch circle at that range. No wind. If the shooter was capable of matching theory to practice.

The rifle was chambered in .338 Lapua Magnum, which fired a 250-grain very-low-drag bullet at a muzzle velocity of 3,000 feet per second. In the warm African air, the bullet remained supersonic for about 1,500 meters; in the hands of an expert, which I wasn't, this rifle/bullet combination could take down a man-sized target about 80 percent of the time at that distance, penetrating five layers of ballistic material to do it. It had more capability than the 7.62 mm NATO bullet, and less than a

.50 caliber Browning machine-gun round. Even though it weighed almost thirteen pounds with the scope, the gun kicked pretty good, so it was no rifle for anyone suffering from flinching.

To maintain expert proficiency with a sniper rifle, you should fire about two thousand rounds a year through your weapon, making every shot count. Needless to say, camping out with the CIA part of the year and doing the usual burglaries, safecracking and bug planting they expected of me the rest of it, when I wasn't doing paperwork, I didn't have that kind of time.

Nor had I ever had expert proficiency. At anything. In my whole life.

Still, I liked the rifle. If you were going to murder someone, this Sako was just the tool for the job. You could comfortably hunker down a goodly distance away, like a kilometer, set up with a tripod or bean bags, measure the range with a laser rangefinder, adjust your scope, and have a good chance to assassinate your man when and if he showed. Suck down water, shoot from a shady spot . . . all in all, this was the rifle for the gentleman sniper, which of course was the category I tried to fit into. No diapers, no camouflage, no lying motionless while insects chewed on your parts. Then, after you had done the dirty deed, you had an excellent chance of getting away clean since the unhappy people who had witnessed their friend's death were a kilometer or more away. Snipers always worried about the getaway. Being a burglar, I did, too.

The Sako carried a 24-power telescopic sight that had turrets for changing the vertical and horizontal settings. Back when we were younger, my team members and I had shot this rifle and developed a table for the various ranges and possible wind conditions. The crosshairs were adjusted with the turret settings so that the shooter could put the crosshairs precisely where he wanted the bullet. The rest was breath and trigger control. Sounds simple, and at five hundred yards it was no great feat to hit a man-sized target. That's military-ese for hitting a standing man holding stone stock-still just to make your task easier. Few of them do.

Beyond a thousand meters, which was about as far as a guy with my skill level should attempt a shot at our theoretical suicidal standing man, the rifle required a master's touch. Sniper rifles defined the phrase "precision instrument."

Today in Africa I concentrated on holding the crosshairs steady despite the heat mirage. I took a breath, exhaled, then ever so gently squeezed the trigger just the way those marine gunnery sergeants told me to in sniper school. The trigger on our rifle was adjusted for a feather-light two-pound let-off, so she went off while you were still thinking about it.

When I recovered from the recoil and steadied the scope on the target again, I could see the bullet hole. The round-spot target was roughly an inch in diameter, and the hole was about a half inch outside at the 10:30 position. Hmmm.

My second shot was just touching the circle at 3:00.

Good ol' Number Three. Squeeze ever so gently . . . and it was maybe an inch below the spot. Like a two-and-a-half-inch group. Sigh.

"Your turn," I told Travis Clay. He was the best shot we had, and he was no expert either. Still, he could routinely hit targets that I could only dream of whacking. Second best was a former Special Forces sergeant named Elvis Duchene. We called him Erectile Dysfunction, or E.D. He would answer to E.D., but not the other.

When we finished with the short-range stuff, just to verify the scope hadn't been knocked out of zero, we took boxes to five hundred and a thousand meters and left them there. Then we got serious.

We had two rifles, both of which had been packed in aluminum cases along with ammo, logbooks and data sheets. We played with the range finders, ensured they were working properly and we knew how to use them, then settled down to some serious shooting at a dollar a shot.

I heard a buzzing sound, faint, while I was concentrating on a shot. I tried to ignore it. A good shooter gets in the zone, concentrates on the mechanics, sight picture, trigger squeeze, wind, target movement, all of it. A burglar never gets in the zone. Ever. A burglar must be constantly aware of everything in his universe, sights, sounds, smells, heat, light, searching for the most minute warnings of things not the way they should be. Unfortunately I was a burglar first, shooter second.

I looked up. Couldn't find the buzzing. Then I saw it. Twelve feet above me. A maple seed, rotating . . . floating on the breeze . . . no. Not floating. Flying against the breeze. It dropped down, hovered just two feet in front of me. A drone, weighing less than an ounce. I knew the operators, Wilbur and Orville, were a hundred yards away, watching me on the drone's sensor. I stuck my tongue out at the thing, then settled in again with the rifle.

I heard the buzzing growing fainter, until it was lost in the African day.

Two shots later I saw another drone. The guys were working with our big night flyer, a Dragonflyer X6. It had six counter-rotating props arranged in three pods, each pod sporting a top and bottom rotor. It measured thirty-six inches from rotor tip to rotor tip and weighed about two pounds. Carried a good digital video camera with a zoom lens and an IR sensor, plus a transmitter.

Wilbur and Orville were making sure their toys were in working order. Sand and dust were the enemies of precision machinery and electronics; in this desert we had plenty of both. The other guys were cleaning weapons and doing routine maintenance on our com gear. When they finished that, there were the usual camp chores.

We gunnies finally knocked off for beer. I had a sore shoulder and tried not to show it. I owed E.D. twelve dollars and Clay eighteen. We didn't have any money here and would have to settle up later. I wasn't flustered because I intended to welsh.

"So, E.D., you did this for a living back in the day," I said. "How many kills did you get with a sniper rifle?"

E.D. was from New Jersey and still had the accent. "None. I wasn't a sniper."

"Any long-range shots at Taliban, bomb planters, suiciders . . . ?"

"Nope."

"Don't even ask," Travis Clay said. "I ain't ever fired a bolt gun at anybody, near, far or in between."

I contemplated my toes.

"Not even going to bother asking you, Carmellini. I can see it in your face."

"Three fucking amateurs," Erectile summed up succinctly.

"Hey," I said, remembering that I was supposed to be the leader and in charge of morale and all that, "we're the good guys. Truth, justice and the American way. That's our edge."

"Pot, chicks and porno flicks," E.D. sneered and drained the rest of his beer. He crushed the empty can in his fist and threw it as far downwind as he could. It was still flying through the air when he got his first shot off with his Kimber 1911. Missed. Then the can hit the dirt and he used both hands and kept it skittering along until the slide locked open.

Eyl, Somalia

Sultan of the Seas crept across the underwater sandbar that the river had formed two miles from the mouth. Once over, the cruise ship moved slowly toward the river mouth. There was a cape to the north that gave the harbor rudimentary shelter and a promontory several hundred feet high to the south, but that was about it. The city sprawled on both sides of the river, which wasn't much, a trickle of water coming down to the sea from a jagged tear in the caprock. A sandbar essentially choked the river, which had just a small cut to flow through. The fishing boats and pirate skiffs were pulled up on the beaches to the right and left and the sandbar willy-nilly, above the high tide mark.

From the sea the town looked like what it was, a typical third-world tropical shithole made of a few good old buildings and lots of rusted corrugated tin and steel arranged horizontally to provide shelter from the rain and sun and vertically to provide rudimentary privacy.

On the northern cape, Bas Ma, stood the crumbling remains of a colonial fortress built in the era before naval guns fired explosive shells. It was large, low and squat, with dark, gaping gun ports looking out to sea. In places the sand had drifted against the masonry right up to the gun ports.

Most of the fishing boats were on the beaches while their owners and crews went pirating. About a dozen oceangoing freighters and container ships were aground in shallow water north and south of the main channel, right where the pirates put them when they brought them in from the high seas. The crews were ransomed but the ships stayed, abandoned and rusting and looted by the locals, at the mercy of the occasional storm coming in from the sea.

Mustafa al-Said had Captain Arch Penney anchor *Sultan* off the sandbar at the river's mouth.

A small boat was pushed down the beach into the surf and came motoring out to the ship. Mustafa told Penney to open the pilot port in the starboard side, and he gave the orders over the handheld. Ten minutes later a large pirate with half his teeth and a scraggly beard walked onto the bridge accompanied by two bodyguards wearing pistol belts and machetes. All three were chewing khat.

Ragnar, for that is who the head dog was, slapped Mustafa on the shoulder and embraced him. They went out on the wing of the bridge and gabbled away excitedly while Arch Penney used binoculars to inspect the various beached ships and look over the town, trying to get a firm grip on himself. Behind him on the deck sat his wife, Marjorie and George from New York.

The pirates had thrown the body of the man Mustafa shot into the sea. The bullet that killed him, Arch had noted, had gouged a serious dent in the bulkhead after it had gone through him. There it was, in the middle of a grotesque little bloodstain. Another one. Arch thought he could smell the blood.

Over on the wing of the bridge Mustafa was issuing orders. Apparently Ragnar didn't speak English, or if he did, he was keeping quiet about it.

Five minutes passed. Then two pirates marched a passenger into the space and handed Mustafa his passport.

Penney recognized the man: Mike Rosen, from Denver. The talk-show host.

Rosen looked ashen.

"So Meester Ro-sen," Mustafa said jovially. "You have been sending computer messages to America all the time we try to get this ship to Eyl."

Rosen said nothing.

Mustafa looked amused. He glanced at the captain, then remarked, "He has given you much publicity, Captain. Your name, your ship, my men, we are famous. All over the world. People see and hear. Television, computers, newspapers, radio—all of it. All because of Ro-sen."

Rosen tried to control his face.

Mustafa continued. "Meester Ro-sen, you will do one more computer message to your radio station in Deenver. You will tell them you and everyone aboard *Sultan* are prisoners of Sheikh Ragnar." Here he gestured grandly at the large happy slob on the wing of the bridge.

"You tell them that Sheikh Ragnar release all of you—everyone—and your ship, if he is paid two hundred millions American dollars. Cash. Old money, not new. If no pay, you all rot in Eyl. You may buy food, but when money runs out, you starve. Two hundred millions American dollars, Meester Ro-sen. Now go, write and send your message."

Mustafa rattled off something in Somali to the two guards, who hustled Rosen off the bridge.

Mustafa and Ragnar conversed some more. Ragnar walked around, looking at everything, including the two women—especially the two women—and the bloodstains and the various displays and controls on the bridge.

A parade of small boats was coming out to the ship from the beaches. All those boats that Penney thought abandoned—well, here came most of them. Everything that would float. Some were rowed; some had engines; some were towed behind boats with outboards.

Ragnar and Mustafa walked over to where the captain stood. Ragnar spoke and Mustafa translated.

"Sheikh Ragnar says Americans on ships will try to rescue you."

"Sheikh Ragnar says we take all passengers and crew off this ship."

"Where are we going?" the captain asked.

Mustafa merely pointed at the fortress on the promontory as he listened to Ragnar's next pronouncement, given as if Ragnar were one of Mohammed's other sons.

"Sheikh Ragnar says you may take food from ship. When runs out, you must buy food. He is very generous."

"Sheikh Ragnar says you tell everyone on ship they must cooperate. Do as they are told. If they do not, they will be instantly shot."

"Sheikh Ragnar says surrender passports. To get off ship, everyone gives passport. If not, we shoot them."

"Sheikh Ragnar says, tell everyone."

Captain Penney reached for the ship's loudspeaker microphone. He caught his wife's eyes. She was staring at him. So was Marjorie.

Penney averted his eyes from the women, looked out the window at the brown river and shantytown and abandoned ships grounded in the mud, all under the merciless African sun, keyed the mike and began talking. "This is the captain . . ."

The captain's voice on the ship's loudspeaker system was heard in every compartment, stateroom, crew bunkroom, lounge and workspace. Everyone who heard it was horrified. Still, they had been waiting for the other shoe to drop, so in a way, it was a relief. They were leaving the ship, going to an old fortress. Crew would bring cooking utensils and all the food they could transport. Passengers were to bring all medications, at least one change of clothes, towels from the restrooms and all the toilet paper they could lay hands on. Passengers and crew would surrender their passports as they left the ship. Obey the pirates. Do as they directed.

The captain finished with the comment, "We are in a difficult position. We must do as these people direct because we have no other choice. Please help one another, give all the assistance you can to those who need it, and God will look after us. That is all."

Benny and Sarah Cohen heard the announcement and sat stunned. "Leave the ship."

"It will be all right," Sarah told Benny. "We have each other. All we need to do is trust in God and go forward."

Benny stared at her as if she had lost her mind.

Suzanne and Irene listened to the announcement as they watched the ragtag flotilla navigate across the harbor through their porthole.

"You heard that bit about the toilet paper," Suzanne said. "I didn't like the sound of that."

"What's in that old fortress, anyway?"

"It's where the pirates keep their victims until somebody pays the ransom. I suspect the No-Tell Motel would be ten rungs up the ladder."

Irene said a dirty word. She had been doing a lot of that lately. By God, Denver was going to look good when she got back there. Her husband was still there, presumably alive, but even he was preferable to the pirates. As she contemplated imprisonment in the old fortress just visible through the porthole, eating whatever, shitting in a hole in the floor, running out of toilet paper, dirty beyond description, Irene vowed to get a divorce when she got home. Pope or no pope, church or no church, she promised herself she would chuck that son of a bitch and live in her own house all by herself and stay home. *Home!* If she ever got back. She was going to call the lawyer from the first airport she arrived at in the U.S. of A. Tell him to draw up the papers and be damned quick about it. *So help me God!*

"This is our last cruise," she told Suzanne.

"I know," her sister said. "I'm ready for a five-star resort that doesn't move. Wish I was there now." A tear leaked down Suzanne's cheek.

Irene wiped it away with a finger. "We'll get through this, sis," she said.

They hugged each other fiercely.

Mohammed Atom heard the announcement and dismissed it. He had a Saudi passport. He would wave that thing in front of these pirates and demand they release him immediately. Ransom! Of all the insults . . . He was devout, a good Muslim. Ransom, as if he were a slave woman captured in war. He had heard of those days, but they were long past, long past. No one did that stuff anymore.

He certainly didn't intend to carry all his luggage when he left the ship, but he packed everything. The pirates could come get these suitcases, help him get them to the airport. They certainly weren't stupid enough to screw with the Saud family, their entourage, their friends.

He was in a foul mood as he carefully folded his clothes and packed them in the suitcases. Really.

Mike Rosen was typing his last e-mail to his radio station when the captain's announcement came over the loudspeaker. He jotted it down, quoted it in his e-mail. Passengers and crew were to be removed from the ship, held in the old fortress, two hundred million dollars ransom or else the pirates would let the captives starve. He typed it all as quickly as he could, read it while the pirate in the door watched with a bored expression. Corrected all the typos he saw. Changed a sentence around to improve the syntax.

Then he paused for thought. Decided to describe Sheikh Ragnar, big, fat and dirty, with a lot of missing teeth and a scraggly beard. He had no idea if the beard was a religious thing or if the guy was just too damn cheap and lazy to shave. Maybe he thought the scraggly chin hair gave him a unique look, gave him a leg up with the local trollops. Rosen wrote all this down, because he could and his psyche worked that way, and wondered what else he should say.

He had seen the blood and bits of flesh stuck to this and that on the bridge. He added a paragraph about that in the proper place. These pirates were homicidal—everyone ought to know it.

Added several paragraphs about the captain, who he was, how he looked. Rosen recognized the captain's wife seated on the bridge, and he wrote about her, about what she must feel watching these pirates force her husband to do their bidding. What she must have felt as she watched them murder passengers.

He was bitter and he wrote as fast as he could pound the keys.

He was still going at it when the pirate in the door said something in Somali and gestured with his rifle. The meaning was unmistakable. Wrap it up.

Rosen did, and clicked the SEND icon. The screen blinked, and the e-mail was launched into cyberspace.

Then he signed out. Found out he had spent another $27.89 on Internet charges. His credit card would be charged.

The captain's announcement gave Heinrich Beck a real problem. He had two kilos of cocaine stuffed in an air-circulation vent high in the wall of his stateroom, behind the metal intake screen. After the ransom was paid—Beck knew the pirates would demand one, although he didn't know how much—would the passengers be put back aboard the ship? Or not?

Two kilos of cocaine, nearly five pounds of the damn stuff, was a serious investment for Herman Stehle. It was not to be lightly abandoned. If Beck could deliver it in Doha, Stehle would pay him a hundred thousand euros. If he didn't get it there, well, Stehle would be a tough sell on the innocence defense. The risks were high, of course, which was why there was so much money to be made. Usually it was cops and customs inspectors who could ruin him. Or in Doha, an executioner's sword. Now he was dealing with pirates who might rob or kill him.

And if for any reason he didn't deliver the stuff, there was good ol' Herman Stehle, a friend of all mankind.

Optimism was not one of Beck's virtues. He knew in his bones that if he left the cocaine hidden in the vent, he would never see the ship again. If he took both packages with him, with all the risk that entailed, he would wind up right back in this stateroom in a week or so.

He decided to hedge his bet. Take one package with him and leave one in the vent. He removed a small piece of metal from the heel of his shoe and used it as a screwdriver on the two screws that held the vent screen in place. Pulled out one package, laid it on the bed and replaced the vent screen.

The backpack, he decided. Nearly two and a half pounds of coke was too much for his pocket, and he certainly didn't have the materials to break it down into smaller packages.

The pirates weren't in the business of enforcing drug laws. If they caught him with this stuff, he wasn't going to be prosecuted—they would merely take the coke and laugh in his face. Cocaine was valuable in Africa, too, although the folks in these climes rarely had the money to buy the stuff. They would happily snort it up their noses, though, if he wasn't very careful.

His decision made, Heinrich Beck packed his backpack. Several sets of underwear, one shirt, toilet articles, his blood pressure pills and his cash. Some socks and one sweater. His toothbrush. All the toilet paper in the bathroom.

That was it. The rest of his stuff he left right where it was. If fate allowed him to return to this room, the coke would still be in the vent. He didn't care a whit about the extra clothes or shoes or dinner jacket. He pocketed his wallet and passport, opened the door and went out, making sure it locked behind him. A few other people were already in the passageway.

One of them smiled bravely at Beck, who wasn't the smiling type. He bared his teeth anyway in what he hoped was a friendly manner and settled the backpack on his shoulders.

CHAPTER NINE

The helicopter from Langley flew under low clouds, through a cold, rainy, miserable day, across New Jersey and New York Harbor. It settled to the tarmac at a New York heliport, where Mario Tomazic, director of the CIA, and Jake Grafton got out after thanking the crew. The Justice Department had a black Lincoln Town Car waiting. After creeping for a while over glistening wet Manhattan streets, through the usual heavy traffic, the car deposited the two men at the secure entrance to One St. Andrews Plaza, a building adjacent to Foley Square in lower Manhattan, the building that housed the U.S. attorney's office for the Southern District of New York.

An escort was waiting, a handsome young lawyer in a tailored suit. He took them via elevator to a conference room high in the building, where they were met by an assistant U.S. attorney in his fifties. His suit wasn't tailored and his tie was crooked. He was at least three weeks past his haircut due date.

After the introductions and handshaking, he got right to it. "The attorney for Omar Ali has requested a plea bargain."

Grafton and Tomazic both remembered Ali, the computer geek for Sheikh Ragnar that Tommy Carmellini and his team had snatched from a building in Mogadishu, Somalia, three weeks ago.

"I thought he was going to plead not guilty and take his chances," Tomazic said grumpily. His low opinion of the American justice system's ability to successfully prosecute terrorists—and pirates—was well known in government circles.

Grafton, ever the pragmatist, asked, "What's he got to bargain with?"

"His attorney says that he has knowledge of a terrorist plan to assassinate the passengers and crew of *Sultan of the Seas,*" the government lawyer said.

"The pirates didn't capture the ship until yesterday. How could he know that?"

"He says Ragnar has been planning the attack on the *Sultan* for over a month."

"The question remains, What could he know?" Tomazic said curtly. "The son of a bitch has been locked up in the States for three weeks."

"He knows that the Shabab plans to murder everyone after Ragnar collects his ransom." The Shabab was the Islamic extremist organization that had been waging civil war with the Somali government for seventeen years.

"Does he have specifics?"

"His attorney says he does."

"Oh, poop," Tomazic said and raised an eyebrow at Grafton. He had learned through the years of their association that Grafton was a competent, levelheaded operator who never panicked. The retired admiral was at his best in high-pressure situations that called for Solomon's ability to weigh risks and possible outcomes. On the other hand, as Tomazic well knew, Grafton was at heart a gambler, a man willing to stake everything to win everything. In fact, he was the exact opposite of Mario Tomazic, a career army officer who had risen to the top of his profession by avoiding risk with the fervor of a devout Baptist avoiding sin.

Still, the measure of Tomazic's leadership ability was that he allowed a man like Grafton into his inner circle and listened carefully to his counsel. Mario Tomazic believed in winning. For himself, for his agency, and for America. And Jake Grafton was a winner. He made his own luck. Sometimes, Tomazic knew, the wisest course was to give Grafton his head and let him run while chugging Pepto-Bismol.

"We've passed this on to the White House," the assistant U.S. attorney said. "It was too hot for us."

Tomazic and Grafton traded glances. They knew precisely what the lawyer meant. If Justice discounted Ali's tale and the Shabab did indeed attempt to murder the *Sultan*'s people, they would be pilloried. Yet if Omar Ali sold them a bill of goods, they would be pilloried for being too easily manipulated. In other words, a lose-lose situation.

"We would need details," Grafton said, "all we can get, and we'll check out his story. Keep you advised. If he's telling the truth, we'll let you know. If he's peddling bullshit, we'll let you know that, too."

"Off the record, have you guys heard anything about a planned mass murder of the *Sultan*'s people?"

Tomazic's bureaucratic instincts took over. "That's something we would have to talk to the White House about. Not here."

The prosecutor examined their faces. "No, you haven't. I thought not."

"So how does this work?" Jake Grafton asked. "We want everything this guy can tell us, and if it turns out to be true, you can do any deal you like. A light sentence, kiss his ass and send him home, or give him asylum and a job sweeping around here at night. Your call. But we can't evaluate his story until we've heard it and asked questions."

Tomazic nodded his concurrence.

"The White House told us to give you everything we can get."

"Let's get at it, then," Tomazic said and rose from his chair. What he hadn't told the Justice Department lawyers was that he had already had extensive conversations that morning with the president's national security adviser and chief of staff. The credibility of Omar Ali's story would determine whether the United States was going to pay the ransom Ragnar demanded or mount a military mission to rescue the *Sultan*'s passengers and crew. Tomazic was not about to share those conversations with the lawyers at Foley Square, who didn't need to know.

. . .

Two hours later, when Tomazic and Grafton got into the limo for the ride back to the heliport, they didn't know a lot more than the prosecutors or the White House had told them. Ali said that he had told a high official in the Shabab about Ragnar's plans to hijack the cruise ship. The terrorist had wanted to know everything Ali knew, and had a bunch of questions that Ali didn't have the answers to. All these questions, about where the passengers and crew would be held, how many pirates would be guarding them, when the ransom exchange would take place, led Ali to believe that the Shabab was interested in a lot more than stealing the money from Ragnar. Or sharing a goodly portion of it. Ali thought the Shabab leadership would try for a terror event that would break the shaky truce between the terrorists and pirates, and reignite holy war in Somalia.

Tomazic was in a foul mood. "He doesn't actually know anything," he muttered.

Grafton held his tongue.

"There was not one single fact capable of being checked," Tomazic added. "We don't even know if he really met this Shabab dude, Feiz al-Darraji, or if he's making it all up."

It was still raining. Grafton sat looking out the window at people holding newspapers and umbrellas over their heads, trying to hail taxis.

"So what do you think?" Tomazic asked at last.

"I think Ali really believes what he is saying," Jake said slowly. "At least, he thinks it is highly probable. He knows we'll check it out. There is undoubtedly a guy named Feiz al-Darraji. We sure won't get any answers out of him, if we can find him. If events turn out the way Ali tells us they will, he'll get a plea deal. If they don't, he'll get a long stretch in a federal pen, which is precisely what he's looking at anyway."

"He's just buying a lottery ticket," Tomazic countered.

"Ali's not the most sophisticated man I've met lately."

Tomazic mulled it over for several blocks. "The White House meddled in Task Force 151's efforts," he said. "Arguably Admiral Tarkington could have forced the pirates to surrender and we'd have all the hostages back if the White House savants had kept their mouths shut and let Tarkington do his job. When the dust settles, Congress is going to have a field day investigating."

"There's that," Grafton said dryly. "So far, the White House staffers haven't covered themselves with glory."

Tomazic grunted.

"Ali's tale will force their hand," Grafton continued. "They can't pay the ransom and hope for the best. Shooting Ragnar isn't going to solve their problem. They are going to have to send in the marines."

"So what should I tell them?"

"Tell them they have run out of choices. No more hand-wringing and fretting about what the Europeans will think. No more sitting around worrying about all the things that could go wrong. It's time to suck it up and fight."

Captain Arch Penney watched from the bridge as a small armada of fishing boats and skiffs was overloaded with people and sent scurrying across the brown water toward the crumbling piers under the old fortress. Several times the boats were so overloaded that they shipped water over the gunwales, but he didn't see any sink or overturn. A minor miracle, he thought.

Julie went below, presumably to pack a few things. Mustafa stood beside Penney watching and issuing orders on a small handheld radio. Actually, he seemed to have this evolution organized fairly well, because it came off without a lot of aimless milling around.

The key part of the operation was getting enough food ashore to sustain nine hundred people. The food and cooking utensils were being off-loaded onto skiffs through the port pilot's landing. The chief steward was in charge of that operation and would undoubtedly do his best.

Penney knew damn well it took a lot of food to keep everyone eating for any length of time. Once food was removed from refrigeration, it wouldn't last. Mustafa's remark that Ragnar would sell them food had left him a little queasy. Nine hundred Western stomachs couldn't make it on roasted goat.

Well, he thought, a little belt-tightening wouldn't do anyone any harm. As long as they had adequate clean water.

There was little he could do about any of it except argue with Mustafa, and he suspected that would not get him far. Still, even Ragnar and Mustafa al-Said must be smart enough to realize that ransoming dead people was not a viable business.

Finally Mustafa herded Arch below to the captain's cabin. He and Julie didn't have any time alone. He was ordered to carry their stuff and prodded off for the pilot's port where everyone was embarking.

It was only after everyone was off the ship that Ragnar and Mustafa sat down with the passports and began trying to evaluate who they had and how much their lives might be worth. Normally Omar Ali would use his computer wired to the Internet to get this information.

Since Ali was now firmly grasped in the bosom of the Americans, they made do with what they had, which was Mike Rosen.

Ensconced in the e-communications lounge, which Rosen swept clean of broken glass and spent brass while the brain trust noodled over the passports, they looked a little befuddled. Mustafa spoke some English but read little of it. Ragnar, Rosen soon decided, was essentially illiterate. He liked looking at the photos in the passports and studying the stamps to see where the owner had been. He quickly tired of it, though, and let Mustafa do the heavy lifting.

Mustafa soon turned to Rosen.

"We use computer," he said and gestured to the desk unit in the little office.

Rosen logged on. Went to his e-mail account and found he had over a hundred new messages. He opened the first one, but Mustafa had other ideas.

"No, no, no. We search." He shoved a passport at Mike. "This man. Type in his name. Find out who he is."

Rosen didn't hit the Google search key quickly enough, and Mustafa rapped his knuckles with his pistol barrel.

"You do as I say, and when I say, or I don't need you anymore."

Mustafa put the barrel of the weapon flush against Rosen's left temple and pressed lightly.

"You think you only man use computer?"

Well, he had Rosen there. Probably 90 percent of the passengers and crew were computer literate. Mike made an instant decision to do precisely as Mustafa asked. He had no choice and he knew it.

As he typed names into the Google search engine and printed out search results for Mustafa to study, Mike realized that there was a book in his future. He was going to make a real bundle writing a book. Probably as much as Mustafa al-Said would earn in a lifetime of pirating. Maybe more.

Life isn't fair.

The old fortress was a ruin, Captain Penney found, but the walls and ceilings were remarkably intact. Crumbling in places, but still habitable. If the roof didn't fall in.

The old cannons that had once stood in the casements were long gone, if they had ever been installed. The people were herded into these rooms, each of which held thirty or so people.

Unfortunately the place was filthy with the trash of prior tenants—apparently the pirates had used the place as a jail for years—and human waste. There were no restrooms, merely rooms with holes in the floor. From the smell, the cisterns under the holes were not empty.

Penney's officers had taken charge and were getting the place cleaned, using every able-bodied person. A gunpowder storage room near the center of the structure had had a hole hacked in the overhead at some time in the historic past, so they built a fire under the hole and set up a makeshift kitchen.

The chief steward had even remembered to bring battery-operated emergency lanterns, so they would have a little light at night, as long as the batteries lasted. Just now he handed Julie Penney a cup of tea, then gave one to the captain.

A grateful Arch Penney greedily sipped the sweet hot liquid.

"Don't stint on the food," Penney told the steward. "Use it before it spoils. Where are you going to get water?"

"There's a well behind this place. You lower a bucket."

"How are you going to purify it?"

"Only way we can. Boil it."

"Okay."

"We'll do our best, sir," the man said. That simple statement and the trust it implied brought a wave of emotion over Penney. Fortunately the light was so bad no one could see his face. His wife, who was holding his hand, sensed how he felt and squeezed his hand.

Most of the passengers acknowledged his presence with a nod or word and let him move on. A few wanted a lot more.

One old lady, whose name Penney didn't know, gave him a blast. "I want to tell you right now, young man, that this outrage is *your* fault. Do you know that there are rats here? Right where we are going to sleep! Rats! It's *your* fault, and *your* company's fault. You people said this cruise was safe. When I get home, I intend to sue your company, and you, for every penny you people have or ever hope to get."

"Yes, ma'am. That is certainly your right."

"I know my rights, Captain, and I don't need you telling me what they are. A damned outrage, that's what this is. People are going to get sick and catch their death in this squalid building. And it's all your people's fault."

Penney's wife was tugging at his hand, trying to get him to move. "Don't forget the pirates, ma'am. You might want to include them in your suit. Except for the rats, lovely accommodations, don't you think?"

The gray-haired woman was so angry she spluttered. A younger woman said, "Now, Mom, Captain Penney is doing the best he can. So are his officers and crew."

Penney smiled his thanks at her and let his wife pull him away.

Two of the passengers who heard this exchange, Suzanne and Irene, tried to apologize for their female colleague. Penney waved them off with "Do your best. We'll all just have to make do the best we can."

The place was almost dark. Penney sent a man who was cleaning up garbage with a board to tell the steward to get the emergency lanterns distributed and lit.

It was going to be a long night. One man found the captain and told him the crew had made a place for him and his lady. He was tempted to tell him they would sleep with the passengers, but his wife was leading the way in the direction the man indicated, so Penney followed.

At least the place was ventilated. The sea breeze sweeping in the open gun ports smelled of the sea, and it was relatively cool.

Oh, he wished he were out on that sea tonight with a ship full of happy passengers anticipating the adventures of tomorrow.

The e-mail from Mike Rosen went from Denver to Washington in nanoseconds. Within minutes the White House staff had it, as did every media outlet in America and Europe. Switchboards lit up in capitals all over the world.

Again Jake Grafton was summoned, this time to the White House.

He drove himself through the crowded streets. Rain drizzled down. Grafton gave the guard at the White House gate his name and was admitted. A valet was waiting to park his car. He went in and soon found himself in a conference room.

Tomazic motioned him over to sit by him. The president and his right-hand man, Sal Molina, were there, as were the national security adviser, the chairman of the Joint Chiefs and the chief of naval operations, plus a dozen or so staffers and functionaries Jake didn't recognize. The uniformed professionals nodded at Jake, who stopped to say hello before he dropped into the empty chair beside Tomazic.

A copy of Rosen's e-mail to his Denver radio station was on the desk in front of Jake. He noticed that everyone had a copy. He was reading his when the lights went down and the briefer began. The capture of *Sultan of the Seas* was summarized and the current situation explained, quickly and succinctly. The briefer even had an old photo of Sheikh Ragnar that had appeared in a French newspaper several years ago. Some aerial photos of Eyl, and that was about it.

The president and several other people had questions, but most of the people in the room just kept their mouths firmly shut.

The attorney general got the floor when the president nodded at him. He informed them that Omar Ali, a Somali pirate in U.S. custody, had revealed that the Shabab, the Islamic fundamentalist rebel group in Somalia, was, he believed, going to attempt to murder the *Sultan*'s passengers and crew after the ransom was paid.

The president nodded at Tomazic, who expanded upon Ali's tale. "He says he talked to a Shabab lieutenant named Feiz al-Darraji. We believe there is such a man, but beyond that, we have at this time no verification for Ali's story."

So there it was. Jake and Tomazic sat silently as the big dogs worried the bone.

As Tomazic had predicted eighteen hours before, the politicians were unwilling to discount Ali's tale. It became the fulcrum on which the U.S. response would turn.

The president finally made a statement. "Lord knows I didn't want us dragged into the Somali pirate mess, and none of our allies want to get tarred with it either. We can't solve Somalia's problems. We can't go to war against the Shabab, we can't give troops to the government, we can't stimulate a moribund agrarian economy, and we can't feed the whole population. It may sound brutal, but the hard fact is that the Somalis are going to have to work this out for themselves, one way or another.

"That being said, we are going to have to do something to clean up these damned pirates, who are interfering with world trade and endangering the lives of everyone aboard a ship that transits those seas. Thomas Jefferson faced the same problem over two hundred years ago. He acted decisively and made the Mediterranean safe for U.S. merchants and, incidentally, everyone else.

"So, I have decided, we aren't paying ransom. Nor will we deliver it if someone else comes up with two hundred million dollars in cash. I don't even know how big a pile that would be. That said, what are our options and your recommendations?"

They argued a bit, but everyone could see that a fight was the only move on the board.

"So who is going to be in charge of this operation?" someone asked.

Glances went around the room. The silence didn't last long before the CNO said, "The best man is sitting beside Tomazic."

Every eye in the place swiveled to Jake Grafton.

"If he's so good, why wasn't he a four-star?" the national security adviser asked the CNO. His name was Jurgen Schulz, and he was a Harvard PhD on sabbatical, loaning his vast intellect and learning to the government for the greater good of mankind. Schulz had never been a Grafton fan; his antipathy was in his voice.

The CNO gave him a salvo in reply. "We thought other people would be better at kissing politicians' asses. Grafton was the warrior. Still is."

The silence that followed that remark was broken by the president. "Mr. Chairman, your thoughts?"

"Grafton."

The president didn't hesitate. "Admiral Grafton, your thoughts."

Jake Grafton opened his mouth, closed it, took a deep breath and spoke. "How much authority would I have?"

"There's no such thing as carte blanche," Jurgen Schulz said curtly.

Grafton squared his shoulders, looked the national security adviser right in the eyes. "The pirates would probably have surrendered if you and your staff had had the good sense to keep your mouths shut and let Admiral Tarkington do his job. Now we're going to need a lot more people and spill some serious blood to fix this mess."

Schulz turned livid. He was ready to fire a salvo when the president intervened smoothly. "Your point is well taken, Admiral. We expect you to work with the Joint Chiefs and fleet commanders. You'll need their cooperation. I expect you to listen carefully to whatever professional advice they think important to offer. We'll give you the responsibility and authority to do the job, and hold you accountable for the results."

"Yes, sir," Jake said, the relief evident in his voice. "I would be delighted to undertake this assignment under those conditions."

The rain had stopped and the sun was burning off the overcast when Jake Grafton got his car and headed out the White House gate for his office at the CIA facility at Langley.

A line of thunderstorms built up to the southwest of our camp in the Ethiopian bush late in the afternoon. They were dark and huge, their spreading anvil tops towering into the stratosphere. I had sentry duty that evening and was in our lookout post a bit away from the camp.

Just before the sun set, I saw movement toward the southwest and steadied the binoculars on it. Some kind of antelope, it looked like, maybe a half dozen. Three miles away, at least.

We hadn't seen much wildlife while we had been here. Three snakes and a couple of large mice or small rats was pretty much it. I sat watching the antelope graze as the sun slipped below the horizon and cast the earth in shadow. The sun shot the thunderstorm towers with golden fire, at first full blast. As the sky darkened, I could see flashes of lightning low in the storms.

When next I looked, the antelope had disappeared in the gloom that was obscuring the savanna. The last of the sunlight faded from the top of the storms . . . and their lightning hearts became brighter, flashing almost continuously. They were also, I realized, drifting our way. There wasn't much wind, just a zephyr out of the southwest, but it was enough.

I walked down the hill in the darkness, refusing to use the flashlight and trying not to trip over a rock or pebble or incongruity.

I said a few words to the guys, who were playing cards, told them the storms were coming and to batten us down, then got a beer and went to my personal tent. I was the only guy who slept alone, but being the exalted, esteemed leader, I figured I deserved the privilege. I hung every piece of gear I had up off the dirt floor. Tied my boots together and put them on a hook where I could get to them easily. Checked that the M-16 was loaded and handy. When I heard the first faint rumble of thunder, I turned off the propane lamp and crawled under my sheet. Arranged my Kimber 1911 .45 under the pillow and settled down for a good rain.

I like rainy nights. We didn't get a lot of them in Southern California where I grew up, so they were sort of a treat. A sloppy wet kiss from Mom Nature.

The wind blew hard at first, strong continuous blasts that stretched the tent fabric and made it flap furiously. Thunder crashed and rolled. After a few minutes of that, the first big drops splattered on the tent, then came in a torrent. I pulled my army blanket around me. Snug as a bug.

Went to sleep to the sound of the rain. Was sawing some zees when the buzzing of the satellite phone woke me. The thunder was gone and the rain was just a gentle pattering. I grabbed the flashlight. It was about

5:00 A.M. Water was running through the floor of the tent, even though I had personally ditched around it. Yep, I could hear the damn phone buzzing.

I got my boots down, put them on, stuffed my Kimber into my pocket and went out into the rain, which was down to just a drizzle, almost a mist. Slogged the forty feet through the mud to the com tent.

It was Grafton.

"Tommy, sorry to wake you, but there has been a change in plans."

CHAPTER TEN

Eyl, Somalia, November 12

It was a bad night in the fortress. The people imprisoned there were too keyed up to fall asleep easily, yet when they finally became tired enough they had to sleep on a stone floor with their own clothes as blankets and pillows. Due to the amount of garbage that had accumulated from past imprisonments of merchant mariners, the place was infested with rats and mice, which scurried about fearlessly in the dark hunting for food. People screamed, cursed and swatted at them, which merely sent the rodents to entertain a new audience. There were also snakes, hunting the mice, but they were shy and avoided people, if they could.

Already the toilet facilities reeked. There was no privacy, not with all these people trying to use just three holes in the floor. Many people found squatting difficult, especially on a wet, filthy, slick floor amid the miasma of human excrement.

Eight hundred fifty tired, dirty and emotionally exhausted people welcomed the dawn.

Captain Arch Penney, who had only managed two hours' sleep and spent the rest of the night reliving the murders of his officers and men, went to see his chief steward, who soon had water boiling for tea. The chief had a small army of crewmen carrying water, cooking and trying to scrape up old garbage for removal.

Penney took a cup of tea back to his cubbyhole for his wife, who accepted it gratefully. Marjorie had joined them and was still asleep beside her.

"What's going to happen to us, Archie?" she whispered.

"I don't know."

"We can't stay here very long. The older people are going to get sick. Soon we'll have people in real medical distress."

"All I can do is talk to the pirates. I think we are here because they have nowhere else to put us. Still, dead hostages won't get them any money. I'll see what I can do."

In the early light he could see her smile, a wan, tired smile. She squeezed his arm and went back to her tea.

The ship's doctor was a Nigerian in his early thirties, educated in London. He looked stressed to the max. "I brought the medical supplies I could carry with me, Captain. Left a lot aboard in the dispensary. I am afraid we are going to need everything and then some. I'd like to go back to the ship with some crewmen and bring everything."

"I'll talk to the pirates," Arch Penney promised.

People buttonholed him right and left, some with complaints and some with suggestions. Everyone wanted bedding and blankets and more eating utensils.

"I'll see what I can do," the captain said.

But he knew he could do little. Only what the pirates permitted, and the hostages' comfort was not their concern, he thought. The Somalis he saw through the cannon ports on guard duty outside the fortress were in foxholes watching the sky, waiting.

Waiting for an assault, he suspected.

He went to the entrance of the fortress, which had no door, and told the guards there he wanted to talk to Mustafa al-Said. "Mustafa al-Said," he repeated, slowly and loudly. "Talk."

They merely nodded and motioned him back inside.

Through a cannon port Arch glimpsed the sun rising on a shiny sea.

Indian Ocean, November 12

Admiral Toad Tarkington read the messages over his morning coffee. Jake Grafton was in charge of the *Sultan* hostage "situation," he read, and smiled grimly. Toad had been Jake's aide, then executive assistant, for years. If the powers that be had put Grafton in charge, Toad suspected the pirates were in for a rough time.

One of the messages was a personal from Grafton asking him for his recommendations on several questions. Could the hostages be rescued? How would he do it? How would he transport them if the *Sultan* were inoperable? What resources did he have that he could use, and what did he need? The message also asked for all the reconnaissance Task Force 151 could muster. Grafton wanted to know what was happening in Eyl every hour of every day.

Toad called his staff together. They discussed the problem over breakfast in the flag wardroom.

"Why a rescue?" Flip Haducek wanted to know. "Are the ship owners going to pay the ransom, or not?"

"Two hundred million dollars?" Ops asked. "Are you nuts?"

"The pirates will take less. That's just their opening position for negotiations. And that ship is worth more than that. Maybe twice that. The insurance company will fall all over themselves taking the cheapest option."

"So what are the people worth?"

"In this day and age, not much. World is full of people."

"We should offer the pirates ten bucks and their lives and see what they say."

Tarkington cut off the chatter. "I don't know what our government intends. I don't know what the ship's owners or insurance company want to do. I don't know what other governments think or their intentions or willingness to cooperate. Let's answer the questions we have been asked, and people paid more than we are can worry about all of that. Get your people together and start planning. In the meantime, shut down all unofficial Internet access from this task force. No satellite telephone calls. I want no leaks. None."

"I think there is a journalist aboard, sir. From France. It's a woman, I believe."

"She is now incommunicado. Nothing goes out but official encrypted message traffic. Jump on this recon request ASAP."

"Aye aye, sir."

Several hours later Toad took the time to read the routine messages, which had been sorted by date-time group and placed on a clipboard. It was then that he learned the Justice Department had decided to try the three Somalis the task force had pulled from the water. The admiral was told to put them on a carrier-on-board delivery plane when able and send them to the States, where they would be indicted and tried for piracy.

Well, we gotta do something with them, Toad thought, *but we're so far behind the eight-ball it's pathetic.*

He said a common, crude word, and turned to the next message.

Washington, D.C.

Jake Grafton soon found himself awash in information from *Sultan of the Seas.* The pirates had Mike Rosen pounding out e-mails to his radio station, and the folks there immediately put them on the wire services as news. Grafton got it about the same time as the cable news shows, which was within minutes after Rosen clicked on the SEND icon.

Rosen could have put everything in one giant e-mail, but he didn't bother. When he had filled up a page or so, he sent it and began another missive.

Mike was handicapped by the fact he was being held aboard ship and his shipmates were all ashore, except for a couple of guys in the engine room keeping the diesel running that turned the generator that provided a minimum power level to the ship—and to the e-com center and server. He was putting anything that Ragnar wanted the world to know in the e-mails, such as the amount of ransom it would take to buy the kidnapped passengers and crew out of hock, the names and nationalities of the people Ragnar held, how wonderfully they were being treated and vague threats of what might happen to them if the ransom demands weren't met. The hostages were, Ragnar said through Mustafa, under

Ragnar's protection, secure from the terrorists and unwashed savage hordes that roamed the northern Somali coast. Without the benevolent protection of Sheikh Ragnar . . . well, the reader was left to consult his fevered imagination for the answer to that contingency.

Yet after he had typed the messages from Ragnar to the world, Rosen typed what he, Mike Rosen, wanted the world to know about the passengers and crew of *Sultan of the Seas*. The pirates didn't care what he wrote. After all, they couldn't read English. Rosen wondered if they could read any of the earth's languages. The pirates merely talked back and forth between themselves and watched him type.

He e-mailed physical descriptions of Ragnar and Mustafa al-Said, described what he had been told by various witnesses about the events aboard ship, and editorialized shamelessly, which after all was his shtick at the radio station.

A half-dozen of these cyber essays landed on Jake Grafton's desk at Langley all in a heap. It was late in the evening in Washington and the admiral was exhausted, but he had another sip of coffee and settled down to read them in the order in which they were sent.

Thirty minutes later, just as he finished that pile, his secretary brought him two more. Man, that Rosen could type!

He was just about finished when his desk phone buzzed and his secretary informed him he had a visitor, Sal Molina. A lawyer from Texas in his former life, Molina was the president's right-hand man. Or executive assistant. Or chief hatchet man. No one knew Molina's real title at the White House; perhaps he didn't have one. Apparently he got paid regularly with taxpayer's money, and he certainly had the Big Dog's ear.

Molina looked right and left and parked his butt on the couch.

"Congratulations."

"For what?"

"For screwing Jurgen Schulz in front of an audience. If you'd told me ahead of time you were going to do it, I'd have paid money to film it. How did you know it was his staff that jerked Tarkington around?"

"I'm psychic."

"I doubt that. I call it shit-house luck. What if it had been the president's two favorite butt-boys who had their fingers in the pie?"

"You would have cut their fingers off."

Molina chuckled. "So how in hell are you gonna get those *Sultan* people outta there?"

"I don't know. Yet."

A young aide appeared in the doorway. She had a sheaf of file folders in her hand. "These are just the first ones, sir. They'll have more later today, they said."

"Fine. Thank you."

Jake opened the folders and spread out the contents, which were satellite photos of Eyl, Somalia. They were taken on different days, at different times, at different angles, as the satellites, for there were more than one, swung over the area. The information their sensors obtained was radioed to the National Geospatial-Intelligence Agency, which used computers to construct these images.

Jake sorted them by date and time as Molina watched.

"You couldn't have obtained all of this since the president appointed you."

"No. I ordered this stuff as soon as Tomazic and I got back from New York. Took a while, but the info is beginning to dribble out of the pipe." Grafton got a magnifying glass from his desk and began scrutinizing selected photos.

"You didn't know you were going to get this job."

"Of course not. Still, Omar Ali had something interesting to say, so I thought I had better get started checking it out."

"You mean about the Shabab murdering everyone?"

"Oh, no. The interesting thing was that he said he knew about the assault on the cruise ship weeks before we snatched him."

Molina the lawyer was dismissive. "He may have been lying just to get some leverage with the prosecutors. Hell, he had three weeks to offer us something, and he didn't."

Jake put down the magnifying glass. "Either the pirates were out there on the ocean randomly cruising around trolling for prospects, or they planned this assault. At least six pirate skiffs—one report says eight—simultaneous assaults on two cruise ships, shooting when threatened . . . No, this was carefully planned." He tapped his fingers on the photos. "Ragnar had plenty of time to prepare his defenses, make a plan with a high probability of success. Not just to capture a cruise ship full of people, but a plan to prevent their rescue unless someone paid his price."

"So they planned it. So?"

"These people aren't stupid, Sal. The plan to capture the cruise ship is worthless unless they can force someone to pay ransom. The pirates have to plan for the worst. What is the worst thing that could happen, from their point of view?"

Molina's eyes narrowed. "A military attack to rescue the hostages."

"Right. They knew that when they contemplated capturing a cruise ship. *That* was the problem that they had to address and solve." Grafton stirred the photos around. "We'll have these gone over by experts tomorrow. I'm just an amateur."

"So . . ."

"Sal, you and I and the pirates know we can apply overwhelming military force. Anyone who refuses to surrender immediately will die. Their only defense is the threat to harm the hostages. How? Shoot a few as we come thundering in? Or murder them all if we pull one trigger?"

"So what's your timetable?"

"We'll have answers in few days, I hope. A week. Maybe a little longer. What we need is time."

Molina frowned. "We're going to have to say something to the press about the ransom demand. The news is all over every network on earth. Got any suggestions?"

"The usual," Grafton said airily. "We're consulting with the owners of the ship, the insurance company, the British government . . . Add anyone you like. And get those aides pounding the phones. Do consult. Make it look good."

"The press will ask bluntly if we will pay if the Brits won't."

Grafton propped his feet on the lower drawer of his desk. "Don't give me that shit, Sal. Your press guy can dance around a direct question like that for weeks. We're negotiating. The president is pondering, consulting Congress and the UN, reading tea leaves . . . whatever. Just don't commit us to anything until I give the word."

Molina looked amused. "You'd lie to the press?"

"Everyone else does."

"That Rosen guy will probably tell us what the pirates' sword of Damocles is."

"He'll tell us what the pirates tell him to say. Be kinda nice to know the true facts before we put people in harm's way."

Molina sighed. Through the windows one could see the lights of the grounds, very tasteful and decorative, designed to make security airtight. He could hear the faint sounds of classical music emanating from the window-pane vibrators, sounds so faint he couldn't even follow the music. It was just noise. Molina hated this building. Hermetically sealed off from the outside world and the rest of humanity, the secure spaces reminded him of graves.

"The president says not a dime."

Grafton waved away that comment with a dismissive flip of his fingers. "If you're willing, I have a favor to ask," Grafton continued. "When the sun comes up, how about talking to the secretary of the treasury. I need two hundred million counterfeit dollars, just in case. Make it hundred-dollar bills."

Molina rolled his eyes.

Grafton pretended not to notice. "We need to keep all our options open until we figure out precisely what Ragnar has planned, what his capabilities are. We may have to buy him off, get the *Sultan* people out, then go back and liberate the money and whack him. Or we may decide to pay the ransom with counterfeit bills. We'll make the decision, real or fake, when we know what cards Ragnar is holding."

Molina's face now wore its usual expression, eyebrows up, brows knitted, jowls sagging, his lips slightly pursed.

"The Shabab guy, Feiz al-Darraji," Grafton added. "We'll have to string him along, too. If we buy off Ragnar, we want the people out, not murdered. We don't want the Shabab to get homicidal before we are ready."

"Counterfeiting, now."

"Ink and paper are cheap. The stuff's gotta be good enough that it'll pass for real, yet later we can tell the world the bills are bad and what to look for. Tell Treasury to get cracking. I need it in three days."

"Just a thought," Molina murmured. "If Treasury prints it and the government issues it, the courts may decide it's real money, even if we put Johnny Depp's picture on it."

Jake Grafton snorted. "If I had a fart in me, I'd turn it loose, Sal. We get the hostages home alive, everybody safe and sound, I don't give a damn what the courts decide five years down the road."

They talked for another few minutes; then Molina left.

Grafton had had enough. He closed and locked his door, left the photos stacked on his desk, stretched out on his couch and was almost instantly asleep. He had met some pirates back when he was young, and he dreamed about them.

At seven that morning he made a telephone call to the Israeli embassy. At eight o'clock he entered a breakfast joint for working men and women in a strip mall shopping center in Silver Spring, Maryland. There was an empty booth in the back of the row, and he asked the woman at the register for it. He ordered coffee, eggs, bacon and dry wheat toast. He was sipping his second cup of coffee and waiting on the eggs when a man walked in wearing jeans and a sweatshirt and sat down across from him.

The man's name was Sascha Meissl; he was the Mossad liaison officer to the CIA. His official title at the embassy was something else; Grafton didn't know what it was, nor did he care. Meissl was a short, heavyset man with a square jaw and a head of curly, wire-density hair. He and Grafton conferred about once a week, on average. Grafton suspected Meissl had other espionage duties at the embassy, but he never asked and didn't want to know what they were. The FBI could worry about Mr. Meissl's extracurricular activities, if any.

After the usual pleasantries, Grafton got right to it. He explained that he had been appointed to be the chief negotiator for the *Sultan* hostage crisis in Somalia, and wanted whatever help Meissl's agency could give.

Grafton explained his theory that the pirates must have a deterrent to military attack already in place. "They have planned this for at least a month. And they are not stupid."

"A bomb," Meissl said, then watched the waitress approach. He ordered coffee and orange juice and a short stack of pancakes.

When the waitress was gone, Grafton resumed. "I need all the information that you can give me, and I need it yesterday."

"I thought you might call," Meissl said with a grin.

"I'm too predictable."

"We don't really know anything about Somalia. However, we think one of Hamas's head bomb makers went to Africa for a working vacation about six weeks ago. He went to Cairo, then disappeared. We think he's probably in Somalia."

"Name?"

"God only knows what his parents named him. He goes by the *nom de guerre* of Al-Gaza. About thirty to thirty-five, technically astute, believes in jihad, has built and exploded bombs in Iraq and Afghanistan and Palestine. His specialty used to be bus bombs, but he's branched out into bigger and better things."

"Could he work with ammonium nitrate? Fertilizer?"

"Sure. Detonators, radio controls, all of it. Rather good at what he does. Not suicidal himself, but he likes to help martyrs start their journey to Paradise. Or wherever in hell they end up."

The coffee and OJ came. Meissl sipped the juice, then attacked the coffee. The waitress brought Jake's breakfast and filled his coffee cup. Jake dawdled over the eggs.

"You got any guys who know this dude?"

Meissl nodded.

"I'd like to borrow them, if I could. For a couple of weeks, no more. Give them a free trip to Somalia. If they can spot this guy or whoever their bomber is, lend us some expertise, I'd really appreciate it."

"Al-Gaza might not be there."

"Someone there knows explosives. As a rule, pirates don't have much experience building bombs. The Shabab in those parts doesn't blow stuff up, either. Just shoots people, rapes women, steals food and fuel and weapons and anything else they can physically move."

"I'll talk to Tel Aviv. If these guys find our man, we don't want him walking away."

"Something can probably be arranged," Jake said dryly. His eyes crinkled and the corners of his lips turned up slightly. That was his smile. Sascha Meissl smiled back, showing his teeth.

CHAPTER ELEVEN

Eyl, Somalia

The fortified lair of Sheikh Ragnar, the big banana of piracy, Somalia-style, was an old hotel right on the waterfront in Eyl. Six stories high, from the upper story it had a fine view of the harbor created by the two small promontories. Ragnar had knocked down superfluous walls on the top story to create a penthouse. His men were on the floors below, and he had four machine guns mounted on the roof, one on each corner, just in case.

From time to time Ragnar glanced at the captured cruise ship anchored in the river's channel and permitted himself a smile. Ragnar was not his real name. He wasn't a sheikh either; he was a vicious, amoral sewer rat who shot first and asked questions later. With his greed, sewer smarts, violent disposition and respect for nothing, Ragnar had what it takes to succeed as a pirate.

So far he had done very well at the trade. The ransoming of *Sultan of the Seas* and her passengers and crew would be the capstone on his career. He intended to retire and live like a pasha on his ill-gotten millions. He would have all the good food, liquor, women and drugs he could possibly want to eat, drink, screw or snuff up his nose—yet, in truth, Ragnar had that now. Still, like humans everywhere, he wanted more.

More.

He wondered if there were any attractive women in the fortress. Might not a new one be a delicacy in bed tonight? Young, white, with dark hair and shaved legs and big, luscious tits. Ragnar liked big tits and tight, wet pussies with a triangle of curly dark pubic hair. White skin made the dark pubic hair vivid, irresistible. He would ask Mustafa.

Forty miles south of Eyl, Somalia

I lay there in the dirt/sand mix of Africa trying to get comfortable. I was on my stomach, with my head resting in the crook of my arm, trying to ignore the hot sun slowly baking me and the itch that had developed on my right ankle. I didn't think the ants had gotten that far, not yet, anyway, but no doubt if I lay here long enough they would. Ants that would disassemble me piece by tiny piece and carry me away to Ant City to feed the little ones. I was in no mood to be recycled just yet.

It was quiet. Peaceful. Like everyone else on the planet was dead and I was the only one left alive, listening . . .

As I lay there I thought about many things. How Mrs. Carmellini's only boy, Tommy, wound up in the African dirt. She wanted me to be a professional something, work in a nice office, marry a nice girl, have 2.5 kids and invite her to visit for the Christmas holidays. I even got a law degree along the way. However, certain character flaws reared their ugly heads and the CIA latched on to me . . . so there went the nice wife, the kids, and Mom's Christmas vacation.

An ant crawled up onto my hand. I decided to risk it. I squashed the little bastard with my other hand, moving as little as possible.

I started out in the Company as a burglar and wish I could have stayed at it. Gadgets, bugs and safecracking were my Company specialties, although in the last two years Grafton has sent me to every military and Company school he could think of to teach me tradecraft and unarmed combat. Armed combat, too. I knew how to recruit and run agents, set up drops and lie convincingly. I also knew how to jump out of a plane, kill people with knives, garroting wire and high explosives, could tear down, repair, clean and shoot any weapon in any military arsenal, and could even swim fairly well, although the SEALs refused to certify my swimming skills. Said I wasn't proficient enough.

I didn't care: I didn't want to be a SEAL. What I got out of SEAL training was an abiding loathing of water—I limit myself to showers and an occasional glass of water between meals.

Another school he ran me through that I didn't do great at was Marine Corps sniping school. Oh, I could shoot fairly well, but I refused to get with the program and commune with blood-sucking insects and lizards, become one with the dirt and sweat, which is what marines are all about. Lying motionless under a bush for days at a time, pissing and shitting in an adult diaper, just to pot someone if he or she happened by was a skill set that I decided I could probably do without. Grafton knew the marines also sent me home without a graduation certificate, although he pretended he didn't.

The irony of all that training and my current predicament almost brought a smile to my face. Almost.

If worst came to worst, I planned on getting a job at Starbucks and to hell with all of it. At Christmas maybe I'd send Grafton a card, maybe I wouldn't. I could send Mom a fruitcake.

I was getting really relaxed, itches and all, when I heard the faintest sound of an engine. A gasoline engine. I listened and tried to stay totally relaxed.

After a bit I realized there were two of them, some ways off. I only heard the sounds when the engines revved or topped a little rise.

I knew what they were. Technicals, which were Jap pickups with a machine gun mounted on a swivel in the bed. They were the tanks, jeeps, supply vehicles, scout cars, VIP transport and mobile antiaircraft units of both the pirates and the Islamic fundamentalist rebels hereabouts, the Shabab, the holy warriors who had been trying to take over the country for the last seventeen years. The Shabab wasn't doing so hot right now, what with the famine in the southern half of the country and the universal opprobrium in which they were held, here and everywhere else. Three million people were in the various stages of starvation and the Shabab refused to allow international aid. Anything delivered anyway they stole.

The drivers of these two technicals were certainly taking their time. We spotted them with binoculars about twenty-five minutes ago and I had been lying here for fifteen, contemplating my itches and misspent life.

A voice in the earpiece. "About a quarter mile away now, Tommy. Act dead."

I took a deep breath and exhaled slowly. Tried to relax every muscle, become one with the earth.

"Two guys in each truck."

I could hear the engines clearly now. One had the remnants of a muffler; the other was reduced to a straight exhaust pipe, which blatted fiercely.

The two trucks were coming along this dirt road from the south, headed, presumably, toward Eyl or one of the villages farther up the coast. We were inland a few miles from the coast road, which was fairly well traveled. This rutted track through the desert was much less so. There hadn't been any other vehicles in over an hour.

Not that many people in Somalia were out on the roads. Without a government, with a civil war raging, with pirates along the coast, the country was swarming with armed, hungry men willing to rob, loot, pillage and rape about anybody. Anywhere you went, you needed to be in an armed group that the locals didn't want to mess with. Sorta like Europe in the Dark Ages, I imagine, or perhaps Wall Street today.

As the trucks approached I practiced being dead.

They were loud and right there when they stopped and the engines dropped to idle RPM. I tried to breathe ever so shallow.

Heard a door slam. Then another. Still, the kick in the ribs a few seconds later was kinda unexpected. I grunted.

A foot in my ribs rolled me over like so much dead meat. I blinked at the light, looked up. Saw a head wearing a rag blotting out the sun. The rays of the sun behind him left his face in shadow.

I realized he had a pistol in his hand.

The guy beside him said something. This guy was maybe twenty, wearing a rag and filthy trousers and shirt. There were two more of them, off to my right.

They jabbered.

The guy who had kicked me before kicked me again, and I curled up into a fetal position.

More jabbering. Laughter. Out of the corner of my eye I watched the closest man. He raised his pistol, cocked it with the thumb of his left hand and drew a careful bead on my little cranium.

I scrunched my eyes shut. Wondered if this was gonna be the big It. All my life, just to get to this.

Then I heard the thunks, the sickening impact sounds of big bullets striking living tissue. I felt a fine spray of liquid. I felt rather than saw two bodies falling.

About two seconds later I heard the shots, just one booming sound, rolling through the low hills and acacia bushes.

Two more heavy smacks, one potato, two . . . and, again, the report, just one bang.

"Tommy?"

I moved my hands and keyed my mike. "Yeah."

"They're down. All four."

"Yeah."

I pushed myself to my knees, then stood. All four of them were dead. Ratty clothes, sandals, Russian weapons, scraggly beards and head rags. One guy had guts hanging out. Blood sprayed everywhere. I felt the puke coming up my throat and managed to shut my eyes and keep it down.

The trucks were still idling.

My part in this little murder scene was designed to get them out of the trucks. We didn't want the hardware damaged.

I was checking out our new rides when the guys came down from the hills carrying the Sakos, E.D. and Travis Clay. They paused to inspect the corpses.

E.D. looked me over. "You got sprayed with blood," he said.

I used my sleeve to wipe my face.

"So what are we going to do with them?" He gestured at the corpses.

"You shot 'em, you bury 'em. Better be quick about it. Someone might come along before long, and we gotta be outta here. Keep their weapons."

"Yeah, Tommy."

I felt like shit. Yeah, they would have killed me in another few seconds—I know that. But still.

As Clay and E.D. dragged the corpses into the brush, I climbed into the trucks and inspected the machine guns. They were dusty but looked as if they had been cleaned and oiled in this decade. Lots of Russian brass, relatively shiny. Not too green.

OK.

Truck tires had a little tread left, not much, but maybe enough for thin mud.

I got behind the wheel of the first truck and checked out the fuel gauge. It read zero. I got out, unscrewed the cap and ran a stick down the pipe. Last four inches were wet. There were two five-gallon cans of fuel in the bed of the thing. The other one had three cans in its bed. Some blanket rolls that were probably full of lice, a metal pot containing some greasy meat. Probably dead goat. It stunk a little.

Two old milk jugs contained water. It looked kinda brown. Dysentery in jugs. Somali cocktails. I wondered what creek they got it from.

E.D. and Clay came in from the brush.

"So what were they?" I asked. "Holy warriors or pirates?"

"Like I can tell the difference," Clay said. "What they weren't was goat herders or farmers."

"You get them under?" I asked.

"Not very deep. Next good rain . . ."

"Let's load up and roll."

E.D. rode with me while Clay drove the other truck. He lit a cigarette, took a few quick hits off it. After a while he said, "I guess you're tired of living."

When I didn't reply to that, he said, "That guy was about a half second from doing you, Tommy. We fired as soon as we had a good shot, but shit, I was about peeing my pants."

"I have faith in you."

"Fuck you do, asshole. I think you're just tired of living. There were a half-dozen other ways to set this up without you lying down beside the road asking for it, fucking human tiger bait."

"So, if you lived out here, what would you be? Pirate or goat herder or holy warrior?"

He didn't say anything to that. We jounced along in silence, the shock absorbers being about as dead as the guys we buried. He glanced at me once or twice, finished his cig, then wadded his sweatshirt up and used it to brace his head. Closed his eyes.

I could still hear the whacks of the bullets hitting them, feel the blood spray, see guts hanging out of horrible wounds, smell the blood.

We had to kill them. Couldn't steal their rides and leave them to tell everyone they met that someone had ripped them off. I knew how it would be when we discussed this beforehand. I just hadn't yet seen their faces. And I didn't want to walk up behind them and shoot them in the head.

At least they didn't see it coming.

Jesus.

I felt my mouth watering. I slammed on the brakes, stopping the truck, opened the door and vomited in the dirt.

As I waited for my stomach to settle down, I wondered if I would see it coming. Or care.

"Tommy . . ."

"Just shut the fuck up, man."

Eyl, Somalia

Yousef el-Din was a devout fundamentalist Muslim. His god was fierce, strict, ruthless and unforgiving, and He liked the sight and smell of infidel blood. Those qualities also defined Yousef el-Din. He was the senior Shabab leader in the Eyl area. For years the Islamic revolution had been waged full tilt in the southern part of the country and Eyl had been a relative backwater. Recent military and political reverses in the south, which was suffering from a famine caused by the worst drought in centuries, had given new life to the movement in the north.

The north was actually doing worse in the rainfall department, but the people hereabouts didn't live on agriculture. Also, the north, Puntland, was infested with pirates, which meant money, weapons, imported food. Prosperity. Here were the resources to sustain a revolutionary movement.

The man responsible for most of the prosperity, Ragnar the Pirate, watched from his penthouse balcony as Yousef el-Din got out of his technical. His bodyguard coalesced around him. Yousef's truck had been the third in a five-truck convoy. Each truck had contained three or four men, all armed. This ragtag band of heroes swarmed like a hive of bees around their queen, Ragnar thought as he watched from his perch high above.

Ragnar saw Yousef look left and right, watched him spend a moment looking over *Sultan of the Seas* riding at anchor, then walk toward the entrance to Ragnar's building.

Ragnar toyed with the butt of the pistol sticking out of its holster on his belt. He had an uneasy relationship with Yousef el-Din, as he had with his predecessor, Feiz al-Darraji. Last week Ragnar had al-Darraji killed. Quietly. His corpse and those of his two bodyguards were now fish food, at least two hundred miles out. The three were captured by two of Ragnar's sons and Mustafa al-Said, his number two, as they left a whorehouse. They were put aboard a boat and given a long ride east. Then they were thrown into the sea. Not being fishermen, they couldn't swim, so didn't last long. Since they were devout Muslims, their souls were probably in Paradise now, Ragnar thought. Or maybe not. He had a healthy skepticism about all that holy bullshit.

The women could be relied upon to remain silent, Ragnar believed. They really knew nothing, and they had better remember that if asked. If they didn't . . .

His sons Nouri and Muqtada were in the anteroom, waiting at the top of the stairs. Both were armed. Yousef would be alone. His men would have to wait in the lobby downstairs.

He could hear Yousef's footsteps in the stairwell. The elevator hadn't worked in years; it was actually stuck between the fourth and fifth floors, its door permanently open.

Ragnar poured himself a cup of tea and sat down in his favorite chair on the balcony, with the harbor at his feet, and waited. He could feel the breeze coming in off the sea, gentle, cool, salty sea air.

Yousef came out onto the balcony, with Nouri and Muqtada behind him. Ragnar gestured toward a chair, and Nouri went to get the guest a cup of tea.

After the social preliminaries, doubly important because Ragnar wanted a hint about Yousef's state of mind, the men fell silent and sipped their tea.

Yousef el-Din's face was a mask, Ragnar saw. He had only seen the man on three or four occasions before al-Darraji's untimely departure, and had paid little attention. Ragnar would not miss al-Darraji, with his love of power, an aggressive personality and the manners of a goat, a man used to pulling the trigger and watching other people die. A man who expected everyone to kneel before him, including Ragnar. No, he would not be missed.

"Feiz al-Darraji has disappeared," Yousef said sadly, breaking the news. "His friends and soldiers cannot find him."

Ragnar shook his head sadly. "When was he last seen?"

"A week ago."

"Ahh, that is a long time. A week . . ."

"We have been looking, interrogating people who might know something."

"Of course. I have heard of your inquiries," Ragnar admitted, "but I hesitated to ask why."

"Two bodyguards are also missing."

"We live in dangerous times. Who, I ask you, is truly safe?"

"Since al-Darraji is gone," Yousef said without inflection, "I have been appointed to take his place."

Ragnar nodded, as if the appointment were inevitable. "May he rest in peace," Ragnar answered piously, "but it is the way of the world. We are but flesh and blood, temporary creatures, until we meet the Prophet in Paradise."

A trace of amusement crossed Yousef's face. He sipped tea. Glanced at the *Sultan* lying in the harbor.

"The news of your success has gone to the ends of the earth," Yousef el-Din remarked, a rather abrupt change of subject.

"We have made a start," Ragnar replied. "We will not succeed until the ransom is paid."

"They will pay. And you will pay us." The "us" he was referring to was the Shabab, as Ragnar well knew.

"Let us stop circling the fire," Ragnar said, his eyes pinning Yousef el-Din. "Al-Darraji intended to kill all the prisoners after the ransom was paid. He had his reasons, and no doubt you know them. Now I will tell you the reality of our situation. We can capture ships and demand ransom only because when it is paid we turn over the ships and crews. If we do not, they will never pay again. The money will stop coming. Without money, we will starve. That is, we will starve if the military forces of the West do not invade and kill us first."

Yousef said nothing.

Ragnar continued, "Feiz al-Darraji did not care about us. He only wished to lead a glorious jihad against the unbelievers. He cared not for us, whether we eat or starve, whether we live or die. As long as he and his men could march into Paradise with the blood of infidels on their hands he would sacrifice us all."

"So you killed him."

Ragnar rose from his seat and drew his pistol. He checked to see that it was loaded. He pointed it at Yousef. Walked toward him until the muzzle of the weapon was only a few inches from Yousef's head.

"As long as the Shabab stays out of my business we will get along. For only that long."

He holstered the weapon and made a dismissive gesture with his left hand.

"Go," he said. "This time, you live. The next time, you will not."

Yousef stood. "I am but one man. The Shabab is thousands. They will destroy you if you stand in their way."

"Perhaps," Ragnar said, "but you will not live to see it. And the mullahs will not see any money. Believe that. Al-Darraji did not care whether he was in this world or the next. He did not care about money. So he said. He is now in the next world, and he went penniless. Your revolution progressed not a millimeter. I doubt if Allah gives a damn."

Yousef shook with fury. "Do not blaspheme," he roared. "Our jihad is *holy.* On the Prophet's beard, do you understand *holy*?"

Ragnar turned his back. He heard steps, then silence.

When he turned around Yousef was gone. Down the stairs. Nouri nodded at him.

CHAPTER TWELVE

Mike Rosen stayed aboard *Sultan* in his own cabin. An armed pirate sat in the passageway outside his door day and night. Food was delivered occasionally, the toilet still worked, water trickled from the sink taps and showerhead, and the air-conditioning was out. Fortunately Rosen had a balcony and French door or he would have suffocated. As it was, he spent most of his time sitting on the balcony scribbling in a notebook.

He intended to sell a book about this adventure for serious money, just as soon as he got home. He was writing it now. Even added a paragraph to an e-mail yesterday telling the people at the radio station to call his agent and get him started calling New York publishers.

Strike while the wound is still bleeding.

Yesterday that prick al-Said had come for him in the afternoon and accompanied him to the e-com center, where his computer now resided on an apparently permanent basis. He had been given a list of names of passengers and crew and had to type every one of them into the computer and fire it into cyberspace.

Of course, he also had to print out all the e-mails that had accumulated in his account. A few were private messages from his ex-wives, an occasional one from his kid. The radio station was forwarding a lot of material to him, mostly news articles. And the station's executives had oodles of questions and advice. When the session was over, Mustafa al-Said took with him all the private e-mails and news stories, plus the dirty jokes Rosen's family and friends forwarded and the spam that had trickled past the filter, all of it, every single piece of paper. The guard brought Rosen back to his cabin. Perhaps al-Said wanted to show the stuff to his boss, Ragnar, who reportedly couldn't read any language on earth, nor speak English.

Obviously somebody in Eyl was reading the e-mails and translating for the pirates. Rosen wondered who.

He looked up from his notebook at the city and harbor and the coast of Africa stretching away to the south. The head of the promontory and the old fort blocked the view northward.

Rosen squinted at the fortress, shading his eyes to see better, but it didn't help. He couldn't see a soul at this distance. He sighed and went back to the notebook.

Someone pounded on his door.

He tossed the notebook aside—he didn't want Mustafa to steal it—and went to the door. Al-Said and the guard motioned him out. He went.

There was a man waiting for them in the e-com center, an overweight white man with short sandy hair and wearing a linen sport coat over a dirty white sport shirt. Sandals on his feet. He was sitting in one of the chairs and helping himself to a glass of clear liquid from a large bottle, which sat on the desk in front of him. A gin bottle. He reminded Rosen of Sydney Greenstreet in *Casablanca,* which was probably a slander on Greenstreet.

He glanced at Rosen, took a healthy sip of straight gin, then stuck out his hand and said, "Geoff Noon." British accent.

Rosen ignored the proffered hand. "Mike Rosen."

Noon withdrew his hand and addressed the gin. "Well, well."

Rosen dropped into the chair in front of his laptop.

Noon eased himself in his chair, finished the gin and wiped his mouth with his sleeve. "Young al-Said here wants me to do a bit of translating. Hope you don't mind."

"You from around here?"

"Airport manager. They need someone who speaks English, international language of aviation and all that rot, and who can help them order little luxuries from here and there . . . all for hard currency, of course."

"Of course."

"Ten years this past June I've been here. Seen it all. Revolution, murder, piracy, what have you. Still, a chap could do worse."

Rosen didn't see how, but he held his tongue.

"Don't know a thing about computers," Noon continued, "but I can read English. Rare skill around here. You type it and I'll read it, then you can send it on its merry way to a waiting world."

"I see."

Noon paused to pour himself another little tot of gin. Al-Said and the guard watched impassively.

"So, this fellow tells me Ragnar wants you to send a message to the world, especially the ship owner, telling them that he wants two hundred million American dollars. Cash."

"Already did that."

"Deadline is next week. This day next week, at twelve o'clock."

"High noon?"

"Well, had to pick something, didn't he? I suggested a week. High noon. You remember the movie? Poetic. That's what my friends and colleagues in aviation call me. High Noon."

"I'll call you asshole."

Noon flipped his fingers. "Start typing. Let's see how you do."

"Deadline is unusual for a pirate, isn't it? I thought they just kept their victims until the ransom was paid, no matter how long it took."

"That's the hoary, age-old custom, tried and true, yes. The men and old women were enslaved, the young women went to harems. But in our new modern age Ragnar dares to be different. He has no facilities to hold almost nine hundred people indefinitely. They'll start to get diseased, die on him from this and that; he has other uses for his men."

"Right."

"It's the return on capital equation. He has a lot of assets tied up in this."

"Capitalism is a wonderful thing."

"Makes the world go round."

Rosen got on line and called up his e-mail account. In the six hours since he was online he had received forty-seven e-mails. He ignored them all and addressed a new one to the manager of the station. Wrote out Noon's demands.

Noon read over his shoulder. When he had it down, Rosen asked, "So what happens if they don't pay by the deadline? What's Ragnar's threat?"

"Oh, death, of course. He'll kill them all."

"I'm one of them."

"Sorry about that, old man. But we must keep life in perspective. No one lives forever." Noon pointed at the keyboard. "Type it out."

"He can't be serious!"

Noon shrugged. "Humor is not one of his virtues. He has mined the fortress. If anyone attacks him or attempts to rescue the prisoners, he will kill them all with explosives. Blow it up, bury them under the rubble."

"How do you stand yourself, you fat slob?"

"I live here, Mr. Rosen. I act as a translator occasionally for any of the locals who need one because I have to go along to get along. I don't work for Sheikh Ragnar. His business is his business."

"I'll bet he greases your filthy palm with a little bit of blood money from time to time. Is that it?"

"Even rats have to eat, Mr. Rosen. Now write it out and I'll read it to see if you are an honest scribe. Then you can send it."

Rosen did as he was told. Noon poured himself another drink.

When that e-mail was on its way, Rosen settled back to read his incoming mail. He printed each one out after he read it. Nice notes from both exes. A long one from his station manager posing a dozen questions, copies of wire service stories on the *Sultan* capture, the headlines of which Rosen only skimmed, and a request from his producer to somehow record some of the conversations with the pirates. That brought a sneer to his lips. A joke from a fan who apparently didn't know or care that he was a pirate captive: It was raunchy but not funny. Offers to enlarge his penis, insulate his house, buy Viagra, get a break on membership from a local singles Web site and help a Nigerian banker move money from an abandoned trust account into the States. That was the crop. As the e-mails scrolled off the printer he passed them to Noon, who read each one with interest while he sipped gin.

"You should try this Viagra supplier," High Noon said finally. "They send me mine."

"I'll keep that endorsement in mind."

Noon handed the pile of papers to al-Said and hoisted himself from his chair. He stuffed the big gin bottle in his side pocket. He had another one sagging the pocket on the other side, to balance him out, so to speak.

"I see the ship's bar is still open," Rosen said acidly.

"I didn't think the cruise line would mind if I helped myself," Noon said, adjusting his coat on his rotund frame. "Be a shame to waste it. The misfortunes of others are sad, yet life does go on." He walked out, gin bottles and all, and al-Said followed.

The pirate guard motioned with his rifle for Rosen to get up. He followed the American back to his stateroom. Some locals were mining one of the ship's storerooms and staggering along the passageway with their loot. They ignored him. At his stateroom the pirate pulled the door firmly shut after he went in.

Eyl, Somalia

We were sitting on a small rise about a mile west of the Eyl airport. The hillock we were on only rose about fifteen feet above the plain, just enough to allow us to see over the brush to the two old hangars and a small building that looked as if it were sided with tin. That was probably the terminal.

We had the pickups parked behind the hill, out of sight of anyone there. Waist-high brush ran off in every direction. Behind us were the mountains, stark eroded desert mountains. Here on the coastal plain, the land was flat, but not rolling. The place reminded me of the Mojave, or perhaps Baja California.

From where I sat, using binoculars, I could see that there was some kind of draw between us and the flat place where they put the strip. Didn't look as if they did a lot of earthmoving before they paved it. If it was paved. I assume so. Amazingly enough, this was Eyl International. Or Eyl Intergalactic, if aliens ever decide to visit.

Using a tripod to hold the 12-power binoculars, I slowly scanned everything in sight. After working behind us and to both sides, I began really examining the airport. Saw some people in a small tower near the terminal. No glass, just a pole tower maybe twenty feet high with a tin roof to shed sun and rain. I could just make out three figures . . . and a machine gun on a mount.

A pickup parked nearby with a machine gun in the bed. A technical. No, actually two of them. And a car. Maybe a sedan. No other vehicles. No signs of life around the hangars.

As I watched I became aware of a piston engine drone. Very faint at first, then growing gently in volume, a deep sound. Pleasant. Radial engines, sounded like, coming from the south.

I took the binoculars off the tripod and scanned the sky. Spotted it. A speck with wings. Low. I used the glasses.

"DC-3, I think," I muttered to E.D., who was lying beside me smoking, scanning with his own binoculars.

In about a minute I was sure. I could see it clearly now, dancing in the binoculars. Yep. An old DC-3.

On final approach. It settled and landed on the runway, which was oriented north and south. Seemed like it would always have a crosswind, but I suppose that was the flattest layout, so that was where they put it. The plane eventually came to a stop and turned around on the north end of the runway, then taxied back to the terminal, where it parked and cut its engines.

The runway was a couple of miles from town, according to my satellite photos. The photos noted they had about five thousand feet of asphalt. Probably soft and crumbling, but sufficient for old prop jobs like the Douglas, which Grafton said came and went from Mombasa to Eyl, with a stop at Mogadishu, twice a week and return.

Air service.

I studied the photos, which had been annotated with contour maps. Looked like the airport was maybe four hundred feet above sea level.

The dirt road into town wound down a canyon to the plain by the sea. If we got over there on the rim, we should be able to see the town and harbor—and the old fortress.

"So what do you want to do?" E.D. asked.

"Wait until dark, then I need to go over there, check out the airport. See who they got guarding the thing."

"That tower."

"Yeah. Machine-gun nest. There have got to be a few more, I'm thinking."

"We're sorta hanging it out here if those guys do any kind of patrols," E.D. pointed out.

"See any tire tracks?"

"Not around here."

"This will do for a few days," I said, with more confidence than I felt. I glanced at my watch. Two hours till sunset, then another half hour to true darkness.

"What's for dinner?" I asked.

"Chef's Special, dude. MREs with Tabasco sauce. I get the applesauce."

"Better set up camp and get grub cooked. No lights after dark."

"Got it." E.D. arose and walked down the hill toward the pickups.

I noticed an old stick lying about five feet in front of me, at the foot of a bush. The reason I noticed it was because it was straight as an arrow. I got it, played with it a bit, then got out my knife and scraped off the bark on the bottom six inches. Then I put the thing down on a rock and cut off that shaved half foot. Whittled on it a bit, until it was smooth and straight. Then I put it in my pocket.

I couldn't see who got out of the old airliner or who got in. The door was hidden by the plane's fuselage. Forty-seven minutes after it landed, the engines started with clouds of blue smoke; then it taxied out and took off. Did a turn toward the town, away from us, and headed off to the south.

I lay in the dirt with my binoculars listening to the music of the engines fade away to nothing.

After a while Travis brought me a beer from the cooler. Although the ice in the cooler had melted during the afternoon, the beer was still cool and tasty.

WASHINGTON, D.C.

Rosen's e-mail containing Ragnar's ultimatum arrived on Jake Grafton's desk about an hour after he sent it. It had gone from the radio station to the FBI, then to the White House and Pentagon, and finally from the Pentagon to the CIA and Grafton. It hadn't cooled off on the way.

Grafton read it once, then put it facedown on the desk and went back to studying the satellite images spread on the credenza behind him. Three photo interpreters were seated around the credenza, which was just a large table, with a high-magnification, dual-lens device, a computer and a monitor sitting on it. Every now and then one of the experts slid another photo into the low-tech gadget and studied it. The computer was their primary tool, however. Software programs allowed them to take satellite images apart and analyze them. These were young people, a man and two women, CIA staffers. They studied satellite images for a living and were damned good at it.

A half hour after the e-mail arrived, Grafton received a telephone call from Sal Molina.

"We need a briefing," Molina said.

"Who is we?"

"Me and the Schulz."

"Got all my stuff over here. You want me to bring it over, or you want to come visit over here?"

"See you in an hour."

Actually, it was closer to two before Sal and Schulz and another man came through the door. Sal was in shirtsleeves, wearing a jacket due to the weather. The national security adviser was togged out in academic tweeds and sported a bow tie, which emphasized the swell of his paunch.

Sal introduced the third man to Jake. The British ambassador, Sir Ronald Dahl. He was lean and had a little mustache that stopped halfway to his nose, with gray spots in his brown hair at the temples. Jake thought he was the kind of diplomat who would look snappy in striped trousers, but he wasn't wearing them. Instead he was in a perfectly fitted dark brown suit with tiny blue pinstripes that must have set him back a couple of thousand pounds. White shirt with cufflinks. His tie was yellow, but not gaudy. Silk, undoubtedly.

"I never met a knight before," Jake said as he waved them into chairs.

"You'll be underwhelmed, I'm sure," Dahl said. He flashed a tiny grin. Very upper-class.

Jake motioned for the imagery experts to leave. "You guys go get coffee or pop or something. See you in a while."

"You've seen the latest, I guess," Sal said.

"The ultimatum? Pay or we kill them all?"

"Yeah. That one," Schulz said.

Jake picked it up from the desk and fluttered it.

"How will they blow up that old fort?"

"Fertilizer—ammonium nitrate. They captured a ship full of it two months ago. The crew was ransomed, but the ship is sitting on a sandbar just under the fort. Old tramp, rusted. The owner decided to let the insurance company buy it, and they left it right there in the mud. The pirates could have off-loaded some AN, stuffed it in the bottom of the fort, made a bomb out of it." He tossed a couple of satellite images at the two guests.

"Will that work?" Schulz asked as he examined the first one.

"It'll go boom," Jake answered. "If they did it right. It's not TNT or plastique, but a couple hundred tons or so of the stuff laced with diesel fuel, set off with a proper detonator, will make a hell of a bang. They'll hear it in Cairo and Mecca."

"What about his deadline?"

"What about it?"

"Can we get those people outta there by then?" Schulz demanded.

Grafton eyed the three of them. "We'll do the best we can. How we doing for money?"

Sir Ronald spoke. "The cruise line is insured by Lloyd's. They have decided to pay the ransom. They are scrambling to assemble the cash. They can fly it to the Middle East as early as tomorrow."

"Has there been any announcement about Lloyd's being willing to pay?" Jake asked.

"That's what we're here to talk to you about. The families are raising hell and pledging money to ransom their loved ones. It's all over the press."

Jake twiddled the pencil between his fingers, then tossed it on the desk. "I suggest you announce that Lloyd's has decided to post the money, but delivery methods are still under discussion. Have someone figure out how much all that cash weighs, how bulky it is. Make a big deal about it. Anyone who wants to contribute money to buy out his family members should write a check to Lloyd's. We'll make sure Ragnar gets the money."

"Really?" Dahl inspected Grafton's face. "You Americans are going to do a military assault to get those people out, aren't you?"

"That's a secret," Jake replied.

The British ambassador said a dirty word.

Sal Molina threw up his hands. "Okay, okay. Treasury is printing bills. This is a couple of tons of paper, by the way. The lawyers still don't know if it will be real money or not. The money is just a stage prop for Jake. The president said no ransom, although if the British wish to provide tons of real currency, we can probably deliver it."

Now Schulz said a dirty word. Two, actually.

Jake waved away the subject of filthy lucre. "MI-6 says Feiz al-Darraji, the Shabab general, is dead," he said. "Murdered by Ragnar. They can't confirm that, but they think it's solid."

"So?"

Jake shrugged. "I don't know if that is a good or bad thing."

"One less terrorist in the world is always a good thing," Jurgen Schulz intoned.

"Righto," said the ambassador. "Is there anything I can pass on to my government?"

Grafton stood. "Sir, we'll do our very best to get every man, woman and child who was aboard *Sultan* out alive. Whatever it takes."

Schulz popped up and walked out. Sir Ronald shook Jake's hand, muttered, "Good luck," and followed him.

When the door was closed and Sal and Jake were alone, he said,

"Okay, you pissed Schulz off. Now, what the hell are your plans? What do I tell the president?"

"Sit down and I'll brief you." Grafton reached for a map of Eyl.

Thirty minutes later Schulz scratched his head and eyed the admiral. "Think it'll work?"

"It should. The only question is how many *Sultan* people or marines get killed."

"I know you'll do your best."

"Every man in uniform will. Tell the president that."

"Okay," Molina said.

"Tell me about the money."

Molina took a bill from his pocket and passed it to Grafton. A century.

Grafton rubbed it between his fingers, held it up to the light, then put it on his desk and used a magnifying glass to study it. He looked at the serial number, the little curlicues, all of it.

Finally he said, "Looks real to me as if I'd know."

"Oh, it's real as a heart attack. Right paper, ink, plates, secret marks, consecutive serial numbers, everything. Except I am named as treasurer of the United States, and I signed my name on it."

Grafton used the glass to look again. There it was. Sal Molina. He passed it back to the president's man. "Congratulations on the promotion. I hope the pirates don't have an expert inspect the bills. Why did the flaw have to be so obvious?"

"The treasury secretary had a conniption fit. This was the best I could do."

"Okay."

Eyl, Somalia

High Noon drove an ancient Chevrolet station wagon. The seats were tattered, two windows were missing, and a cloud of blue smoke followed it everywhere. He parked it beside the airport terminal in the last of the daylight and managed to extricate himself from the vehicle.

He adjusted the gin bottles in his coat pockets, then walked unsteadily into the terminal. To his amazement, he found nine men and a woman sitting there on silver aluminum cases. Lots of them.

One of the men approached him. "Mr. Noon?"

"That's right. Who are you?"

"We're newsmen. Some of these men are photographers, and this is our equipment."

Noon took off his coat and arranged it on the back of the chair behind the only desk. Then he sat in the chair and looked at them. It was obvious who the photographers were. They wore jeans and had unkempt hair, several had tattoos, and one wore a muscle T-shirt. The well-dressed ones looked like they got their clothes from some sort of safari outfitter and were on their way to assassinate elephants.

The man in front of him wore a button-up shirt and had a colorful handkerchief wrapped around his neck and arranged just so. A full head of curly hair and a huge mustache. He said his name as if Noon should recognize it. Ricardo Something.

Noon just nodded. Settled himself comfortably in his chair and scrutinized the woman. She was slim, wore her hair in some kind of flip and was striking. Not beautiful, but striking. She held his eyes. "I am Sophia Donatelli," she said in English, "with Mediaset." Mediaset was, Noon knew, an Italian television network.

"We need transport to the hotel in town," the man standing in front of him said. "For us and all our gear. And we need the services of translators. Three, at least. And if someone could arrange an introduction to this pirate, Ragnar? You know him?"

"You have been misinformed, sir. Eyl doesn't have a hotel."

"Well, where do people stay when they visit?"

"Don't get many visitors around here since we are infested with pirates and Shabab holy warriors. They don't like visitors. Rob and kill them. Most unpleasant."

Ricardo Something rubbed his hair. "We're the press," he explained.

"I got that."

"Television networks. Fox, the BBC, and Mediaset."

"No television around here. We get a few radio stations, but they're down in Mogadishu. One from Mombasa."

"Ragnar. You know him?"

"Oh yes. Difficult man. Doesn't speak English. Shy, retiring. Doesn't give interviews, I don't believe."

"Can we get in to see the *Sultan* passengers? The ship's officers?"

Noon tore his eyes off Sophia Donatelli and looked Ricardo up and down. "Are you crazy?"

The reporter pulled a wad of bills from his pocket. "I saw you drive up. We can pay for a ride to town."

"Perhaps I could take Ms. Donatelli."

"No doubt."

Noon sighed. He uncorked a gin bottle and took a little tipple.

"A hundred dollars a trip."

"You pirate!"

"You will have to make your own arrangements for lodging and meals when you get to town. If you can pay . . ."

Sophia Donatelli sat beside him in the car. She even smelled good. She smiled at Noon and he smiled back. Dust came in the broken windows and settled on her and she made a face. God, she was cute. The other two passengers tried to keep the dust from their hair and eyes.

The breeze was off the land now, hot and pungent. Smelled of Africa. And road dirt.

He dropped them in the old square as half a hundred men and women looked on in the lantern light. Many of the men were armed. One of the male passengers paid him as the others unloaded their aluminum equipment cases. Then he drove back up the arroyo toward the airport for another load. The Chevy's one working headlight bravely stabbed the darkness.

CHAPTER THIRTEEN

Eyl Airport

There is a school of thought that postulates the best time for a breaking and entering is in the wee hours of the morning, "when life is at its lowest ebb," which is a fancy way of saying most folks are asleep or wish they were. Another school of thought, equally valid in my opinion, is that the best time to do a breaking and entering is when they least expect it, regardless of the position of the sun or the hands of the clock.

I figured these airport guards—I'm being charitable here—would be most relaxed right after sunset, at dinnertime. So that's when I planned to do my scout and see what's what. I didn't know how many there were, where they were, or how diligently they performed their guard duties. I needed to find out so I could tell Grafton.

If we didn't use the cruise ship, airplanes were going to be necessary to get a large number of troops in and passengers out—and this was the only airport.

As the last of the light faded from the sky, I used pliers to pull the bullets from six of the machine-gun cartridges arranged in links in cans in the back of the pickup I was driving. I poured the powder on the ground, tossed the empty cartridge cases in the back of the truck with the others and pocketed the bullets. I was dressed in black trousers and pullover, so to complete my ensemble I smeared black grease paint on my face, neck, ears and hands. Finally, I checked and stowed my gear in a backpack.

The guys and I sat around finishing the coffee until the darkness was total, enlivened only by stars. It was night as dark as you could find in Africa, and it was only seven o'clock, according to the hands of my luminous watch. Wind was out of the west, off the desert, as usual, at about ten knots, gusting to fifteen.

"Don't wait up for me," I said, adjusting my night-vision goggles and radio com headset. Wearing all that stuff, I felt like a Martian. Probably looked like one, too, but I hoped no one would get the chance to see me.

"Look me up the next time you're in town, baby," E.D. said. He was wearing a headset, too, so his voice sounded in my ear.

I hoisted my backpack and began hiking.

Night-vision goggles are tricky. The more you wear them, the better the experience. If, like me, you don't use them often, the transition from looking at something far away to something just in front of you, like a path through and around the scrub brush, can be jarring. The neophyte stumbles and bumps into things a lot. Then there is the lack of peripheral vision. That is the corner-of-the-eye stuff you don't think you use much until you strap something to your face that restricts it.

So I hiked along, staying in the waist-high brush. This place reminded me of Arizona after a wet summer. Normally the Somali state of Puntland was extremely dry; sometimes years would pass without rain due to the prevailing wind off North Africa. I realized I had been lucky the other night to witness a rare thunderstorm.

As I walked I looked. Yep, fires on both ends of the airstrip.

Approaching the airfield, which was unlit, I had a decision to make. Should I go left around the north end, or right around the south end? Eeny meeny miney moe . . .

I went left. The fire was up ahead, offset just a little from the bitter end of the crumbling asphalt. There would be people there guarding the airstrip, against what I didn't know. Nor did I know why they needed a machine-gun nest in the tower structure by the terminal.

I took my time approaching the fire. Stopped under a swaying bush fifty feet away and surveyed the scene. Wind whipping at the fire. Three guys visible, one old pickup. The machine gun was mounted on a tripod that sat on the ground behind a bush of some type to make it a bit more difficult to visually acquire quickly. It allowed the gun to be fired by a man standing erect behind it, and he could swivel it in any direction and elevate it as required, all by merely circling the tripod. An ammo box was attached to one side of the thing, and I could see the belt going into the gun.

No one was around the gun. They were over by a fire, cooking something. God knows what. I could hear their voices, and an occasional laugh. The joys of the military life. They were doing the male-bonding thing, farting and telling lies and not working or fighting. While getting paid for it. Welfare in the fourth world.

I sat in the dirt watching. Finally, when I was sure there were only three men, I moved on, between their camp and the vast darkness that was the runway.

Walked and looked and paused to listen. The whispers the wind made in the brush masked sounds, a mixed blessing. I couldn't hear the bad guys and they couldn't hear me.

The terminal and hangars were about a half mile south on the east side of the runway. I took my time. When I got there I could see that there was no one in the tower. All the guys were gathered around an open fire between the pickups, which apparently contained food, fuel, ammo and whatnot.

I raised the goggles to my forehead and waited for my eyes to adjust.

Taking my time, I moved over to the tower. There was a ladder, so I went up it carefully, watching everything. Got to the platform and found the machine gun I knew was there. It was mounted on a tripod identical to the one at the north end of the field. Since there was a roof above it to keep off the tropical sun, it couldn't shoot at airplanes overhead. A couple of boxes to sit on. Discarded food cans underfoot. These guys weren't neatniks.

I got a bullet from my pocket and inserted it into the barrel of the weapon. Tried to push it in with my thumb and got the nose started in. I used the butt of my pistol to tap the base of the bullet flush with the muzzle. Tiny little sounds, which sounded to me like someone using a sledgehammer on a garbage can. The locals didn't hear it, though. I got out the stick I had whittled that afternoon and put it against the bullet. Used the butt on my pistol to tap the bullet about five inches up the barrel.

I could hear the voices around the fire, hear the clanking of a metal spoon on a pan.

After one last look around, I climbed down the ladder and faded around the corner of the hangar. Got my goggles down, checked around in starlight and infrared. I was alone.

There was an open door in the side of the hangar, inviting. No light inside. I slipped inside and waited for the goggles to adjust. The only light came through the open door and a few cracks in the siding. Just enough.

The only thing in the hangar was another pickup with a machine gun mounted in the bed. What the heck. I climbed up and forced a bullet down the barrel. Anyone who fired that weapon was also in for a surprise.

The other hangar was empty. Just a few tools scattered around and a couple of cases of oil. For the DC-3, I guessed. Just in case.

Another long walk to the south end of the field. No surprise, I found another camp. The fire was only coals. Time was marching on, and the people here were settling in for the night. No one on guard. Using the goggles on infrared, I located four men.

Moved on toward the west side of the field and started back to our camp. I knew my guys would be alert and ready, so I used the mike to call them.

"Have a nice walk?" Travis asked.

"You bet. Outposts on the north and south end, guys in the watchtower, at least five pickups with guns. I managed to spike the gun in the tower and one in a pickup in the hangar. No airplanes."

"What about the others?"

"We'll take them out if and when."

"Did you leave tracks?"

"Yep. Nothing I can do about that. Dirt is pretty hard, though. I'm betting they don't notice them. Just in case, we'll keep one guy on guard duty around the clock. Four hours on, eight off."

"Want a beer?"

"Sure."

I had about finished it when Jake Grafton called on the satellite phone. I made sure the others weren't listening. When I had reported, he gave me a tentative "this is what we're planning" heads-up. I listened, didn't say anything. He told me about Mike Rosen's e-mail, relaying a threat from Ragnar to kill everyone if the ransom wasn't paid within a week.

"How the hell is he gonna do that?" I asked. "Machine-gun them?"

"If anyone runs, yes, he'll probably do that. Now, tomorrow, next week. But we think he's off-loaded tons of fertilizer from a ship he hijacked in September. The insurance company wrote off the ship, which is lying in the mud below the fort. It's possible he stuck some of that stuff under the fort, or in the old magazines and sealed them off. We've got some aerial recon from the navy, and we could use anything you guys can get with the drones."

"Been windy here today, too windy for the drones. Still blowing pretty hard."

"Then go eyeball it up. Tonight."

"Roger, eyeball."

"Even if we pay the ransom," Grafton said, "the Shabab may try to kill the hostages. Probably by setting off that crude bomb."

"You know that for a fact?"

"I don't know anything for a fact. I have rumors and possibilities. Threats. I want you to check out what is physically there, to the extent you can."

I took a deep breath. "Okay."

He told me what he knew about the fort. I had already studied the satellite images, but he told me things the images didn't reveal. I didn't ask where he got his information, although of course I was curious. I didn't have a need to know. That's sorta the way it goes in the CIA, the mushroom agency.

When he ran down, I told him, "When this is over, I want out."

"Out of what?"

"The CIA."

"Any particular reason?"

"A dozen or two. First and foremost, I am tired of killing people."

"Yeah."

"That's at the top of the list."

"I understand."

"Do you?"

"Tommy, there are eight hundred fifty civilian prisoners in that fortress, give or take."

I didn't say anything.

"These pirates are not nice people," Grafton remarked. "The Shabab dudes are even worse."

He had a bad habit of stating the obvious when I wanted some insight, profound or stupid. I thought I was used to it, but it irritated me occasionally, like now.

"The only nice person I know is my mom," I shot back, "and I'm not really sure about her." That was a lie, but I was in no mood for a pep talk from Grafton . . . or anyone else.

Grafton apparently got the message. "Let me know how it goes," he said, quite superfluously. "Good night." He hung up.

I sat there a while with the phone in my hand, then put it back in its cradle.

Yeah, the world is full of assholes. We can't kill them all. Even if we could, what would that make us?

The Fortress

The people in captivity settled down to another long evening. Somehow the ship's cooks managed to prepare enough food to feed all eight hundred fifty people, which was quite a feat over open fires. They even made enough tea to give everyone two cups. Coffee was more precious, and was all gone by the time Suzanne and Irene got to the pots. They took tea and loaded it with sugar, a treat women their age didn't often put in their mouths.

The sisters found a spot to sit while they nursed the cups of hot, thick, sweet tea. "What is that smell?" Irene asked. "This place reeks of it."

"What I wouldn't give for a bath," Suzanne mused. "Hot water, shampoo . . ."

All around them tired, hungry, dirty people were gobbling the food as fast as they could shovel it in. Not everyone was eating, though. Some of the elderly people didn't bother. Merely drank tea or coffee and sat staring at nothing at all, or holding hands, or whispering with someone beside them.

The ship's crew, men and women, didn't mix with the passengers. They hung out in little groups, apparently self-selected because of nationality. The Brits in one group, the Indians in another, the Indonesians in a third and so on.

"Have you seen Rosen?" Suzanne asked Irene.

"No."

"I hope he's okay."

"Yeah."

Suzanne got up to get a refill on her tea. Her route took her past a knot of ship's officers, who apparently didn't realize she was in earshot.

". . . took her this evening," one of them said.

"Did they say why? When they'd bring her back?"

"I only know they took her. Didn't say a word. Just grabbed her by both arms and hauled her off. Her daughter had hysterics. That al-Said rotter was leading them."

Suzanne butted right in. "Who did they take?'"

"Nora Neidlinger. From Denver."

"You're kidding!"

"Unfortunately, I'm not."

"What are you people doing to get her back?"

The captain came over. Arch Penney. "Suzanne . . . sorry, Ms. . . . ?"

"Ranta."

"Ms. Ranta, we're doing everything we can."

"Which is nothing."

"Ms. Ranta—"

"They're going to rape her."

The statement hung in the fetid air like a wet fart. "I don't know, Ms. Ranta. They told us nothing. Merely took her."

"Jesus, you can't—"

"Ms. Ranta," the captain said in his best no-nonsense tone. He could have stopped a riot with that steely voice. "Get a grip. We are doing what we can, whenever we can. The object of this exercise is to feed and house everyone . . . keep you alive, get you home safely."

"Remember Nine Eleven?" Suzanne demanded.

"Nine Eleven?"

"They wanted to murder everybody. This Shabab thing is part of al Qaeda."

Arch Penney seized her shoulders and looked into her eyes. "We are doing everything we can," he said softly, almost a whisper. "It won't help for you to panic these people. Look around you. Don't you see? They're right on the edge now."

Eyl Airport

I talked to my drone guys, Wilbur and Orville, just to make sure. Those weren't their real names, of course, but they answered to them. Orv whipped out a pocket device he held up in the wind. It had an analog wind speed gauge attached.

"Gusting over twenty," he said. "Might crash it or lose it, and we can't get more of them out here."

Travis, E.D. and I put on our night-vision goggles, picked up our gear and set out. The best way to get to the fort was to walk since it and the airport were on the same side of the river. I just needed help spotting the people so I could avoid them.

When we got to a little rise where we could see the fort, we used the infrared scopes on the silenced sniper rifles—not the big Sakos—and night-vision binoculars, to check it out. We could see the black presence of the old fort, the roads, the paths, the guards—I assumed they were guards—around that big pile of masonry, and we could see a hot spot that had to be the remnants of the evening cooking fire.

I tried to memorize where everyone was. It was going to be iffy.

"You gotta watch me," I told Travis and E.D., "and let me know if anyone is close or begins to approach me."

"Sure."

We decided E.D. would move around to the north, find a spot where he could observe the north and eastern sides of the building. Before he set off, we went over every contingency we could think of. I put new batteries in my headset and night-vision goggles, we checked everything one more time, then E.D. headed out. It took him twenty minutes to get into position, then I moved. Took my time, checked in with the guys every few minutes.

Walking along in the darkness and wind, under the African stars, I was nervous. Grafton wanted me to check out the fort and leave undetected. Which meant he didn't want me leaving any bodies lying around. That was the rub.

Of course, Grafton was half a world away, and I was the guy who would do the bleeding if they caught me. I had my Marine Corps Ka-Bar knife, my silenced Ruger .22, and my Kimber .45. If they caught me, some of them would already be dead. If the thing went down that way, Grafton could fret about it and apologize to the politicians.

If it got rough, Travis and E.D. would help out with the silenced rifles.

"You guys see me?"

"Oh yeah. You're the tall cool dude waving your middle finger."

"If you lose me, for even a second, sing out."

"Yeah."

The town to my right was very dark. The only electric lights seemed to come from Ragnar's lair. Everyone else was using lamps or candles.

Using the goggles, I could see the harbor between the buildings, and every now and then get a look at the *Sultan*. She had a few lights on, but only a few. The other boats in the harbor were all dark.

The old fort loomed above me on the ridge, black and massive. I worked my way through the brush. As I did, I realized a sliver of moon was peeping through the clouds over the sea. Still stars above me, so the clouds were only over the water.

"Two sentries ahead," E.D. said softly in my ear, which startled me somewhat because his voice was unexpected. "If you go to your right about twenty feet, then go straight for the fort, you should avoid them."

I clicked the mike twice in reply and dropped into a crawl. Kept looking for the two dudes E.D. said were there. I finally saw one on the ground, lying down . . . maybe asleep. I crawled a few feet, stopped and listened, then crawled some more. Saw the other guy lying down too. Both asleep, apparently.

Of course, if E.D. or Travis missed a sentry, the evening was going to get exciting very quickly. I crawled slowly, like cold molasses, then paused every five or six feet to look and listen.

I came up to the fortress on the western side, the only entrance to the place right in front of me. The road came up from my right. Several pickups with unattended machine guns were parked haphazardly in front of the place. There was no door to the fort.

I counted carefully. Seven men in sight. The trucks were empty. I lay in the dirt between low bushes and watched, relying on Travis and E.D. to let me know if anyone approached me from the back or sides. No one did.

Fairly quiet, except for the constant whisper of that desert wind, blowing out to sea. Then I became aware that I could hear someone crying hysterically from inside the fort. The pirates outside shifted their weapons from hand to hand and looked bored.

I moved around to the north so I wouldn't have to cross the road. Took my time, spotted the sentries, which were in pickups or lounging near foxholes. Here and there a machine gun pointed skyward.

Slowly circling the building, I could see nothing out of the ordinary. The gun ports were windows allowing entry or exit, without bars or chains, but once the prisoners were outside, there were the guards.

On the southwest corner of the building I hit paydirt. Literally. Found soft disturbed earth. I knew what it was the instant I stepped on it and sank in a half inch or so. I squatted for a closer look. Got a handful and smelled it. Some kind of petroleum smell. Then I recognized it. Diesel fuel. Just a hint.

Crawled to the wall. Found that the earth had been trenched along the wall, and now filled in. There certainly could be explosives buried there. But were there?

I watched for my chance, then stood up beside a gun port and listened carefully. Looked in and saw the heat from living bodies. Asleep, I figured.

Well, if I went in there, sooner or later, I was going to run into someone who wasn't sleeping . . . or wake someone up. A scream or two and I would have more trouble than I could handle.

I turned and surveyed the darkness. Three long strides took me into the brush, and I sank down to watch and listen. Finally I returned to the wall, still looking for sentries.

More disturbed earth. Someone had done a lot of digging here. I could hear voices. Sentries.

Then I found it. A wire coming out of the earth and going up the side of the building. I flipped the goggles to ambient light and tried to examine it. Felt it. Insulation for about four feet, then bare wire. It was taped to the stone. It ran up, up, out of sight.

An antenna. To pick up a radio signal. Oh boy. I wondered what freq it was listening for. Thought of all the VHF and UHF frequencies the military used, the freqs the headsets were on . . .

I got the itch just squatting there. This trench bomb could explode at any moment. I could feel the hairs on my arms coming erect.

It took an act of will to keep going. In the next half hour I found four more antennas coming out of the dirt. By then I had crawled completely around the fortress and could see the entrance. On the left side of the entranceway was a roll of wire. It seemed that one end went into the earth. The other end went off the ridge into the brush.

Eight people here now, all men. All armed. Another pickup. Lights. Television lights. A portable satellite dish. A gasoline-driven generator. And some idiot standing in front of a camera with a microphone in his hands.

I knew the signs. The press was here. I didn't recognize the media dude, but the mustache looked familiar. He was dressed in the latest safari fashions from Cabela's. The man he was interviewing apparently spoke some English, because there was no translator.

As I watched, another pickup rolled up and more press people piled out. One of them was a woman. Lights were set up quickly, and her cameraman took his position. Then she joined Mr. Mustache.

The pirate was obviously uncomfortable. Talking to a foreign reporter while the lights shone in his eyes and the camera rolled was one thing, but to a Western woman? In a designer dress, it looked like, with hair just so, a scarf around her neck, dark hair and high heels. The pirate tried to ignore her, but that proved impossible.

I crawled down the hill, hoping to intersect that wire and find out where it went.

In Washington Jake Grafton and Sal Molina sat watching the live interview of Mustafa al-Said. "Two hundred million American dollars, or we blow up the fort and everyone in it." Al-Said showed the television crew the rolled-up wire, with one end leading into the dirt near the fort. "We have mined the fort with explosives. If the Americans try to rescue the hostages, we kill them all. Boom. Or if we are not paid."

"Well," Molina said, "that's certainly clear enough."

Grafton grunted.

The camera jiggled and they got a glimpse of the woman reporter, about a second's worth. It was enough. She was a knockout. Al-Said studiously ignored her, even when she tried to ask a question.

"We are going to have to say something to the press," Molina said to Jake. "Schulz wanted to make a grand announcement, but the president vetoed it. Still, the reporters at the White House Briefing Room will be in a feeding frenzy in a few hours."

Grafton sighed. "Get the head of the shipping line to make an announcement in London. They said they would pay. Now they can tell the press."

"What about the U.S. government?"

"Make no commitment. I'm going to Somali to see Ragnar, and I'll need some wiggle room."

They watched the segment until the end, then turned off the television. Grafton was on the phone making preparations for his journey when Molina left for the White House.

. . .

Rear Admiral Toad Tarkington got the feed live via satellite on his flagship, *Chosin Reservoir.* His staff was there, Marine Colonel Zakhem, Lieutenant Angel Cordova, the captain of the ship. All watched without comment.

The technician pushed some buttons, and in a few seconds they were watching the satellite feed of the Italian cameraman. He got the interview, all right, but he left his camera running when he lowered it from his shoulder. It was about waist height, apparently, when it panned the pirates, one by one, then the entrance to the fort, then made a complete circle. It took a few seconds for the camera to adjust to the low light level, but adjust it did. The picture was still there. The camera lingered on the wire coming out of the dirt, then seemed to follow it off down the hill.

Now someone jostled the camera, and it came back to the Italian lady, Sophia Donatelli, who summed up her report in Italian.

"They should have let us take them down," someone commented.

Tarkington didn't have much to say. He had a stack of classified messages in his hand, and he waited until the broadcast was over to start reading them. Everyone else wandered out. Lieutenant Cordova was using a cane. The admiral concentrated on his reading.

I saw a man come out of the fort, slip behind the cameramen and talk to one of the guards. The guy was wearing a backpack, it looked like. The sentry led him to a man standing by a truck near where I lay. I crawled three feet closer and listened carefully.

Yes. English.

". . . to trade for my freedom." The guy was like a magnet. In seconds he had three pirates around him. One on either side and the guy in front.

"You have money?"

"Something more valuable. Smaller. Easier to carry." The guy had an accent, but I was too far away to place it. He was medium-sized, perhaps a hundred and fifty pounds. I tried to guess his age by the way he carried himself. He was no youngster. Nor was he a geriatric.

Two more men drifted over to join the group.

I crawled on.w

Found the wire. Felt it, then saw it with the goggles on the ambient light setting.

Decided I had crawled far enough. Got up, stayed crouched, followed the wire. I am not sure what was going through my mind. I was fed up, and maybe I was looking for someone to take it out on. I was in the mood to break someone's neck.

Fortunately the moment passed, just as I saw a little building up ahead. I automatically went down on my stomach. A shack. Made of scrap wood and a few tin sheets. I had my fighting Ka-Bar knife in my hand, the one with the seven-inch blade with a razor edge. A surgeon could take out an appendix with that thing.

It took me at least twenty minutes to crawl up to the shack and satisfy myself that it was empty.

I stuck my head it. The goggles let me see just enough. There was a box with a handle sticking out of it. Wired up. I backed out and quickly crawled about fifty feet up the hill. Got out my knife and sawed through the wire. Then heaped some dirt on the ends.

I decided this might be an excellent time to make tracks. Got up and began walking. When I was up on the ridge, walking away from the fort, I keyed the mike on my headset.

Nothing. Not even a click. I played with the controls.

Damn thing was dead as bin Laden. I wondered how long it had been that way.

Found I still had the knife in my hand. Put it back into its sheath, felt the gun butts, drew as much air in as possible and let it out slowly.

About a hundred yards later I started to shake. The shaking subsided after several seconds. Thought I might vomit, but I didn't. Spit in the dirt a time or two and walked slowly on into the night.

CHAPTER FOURTEEN

Two pirates escorted Nora Neidlinger up the stairs in Ragnar's lair. All six flights. Led her into the living room and pointed to a chair. She sat, with her knees together and her purse on her lap.

Ragnar was conversing with a Somali, using Arabic. She had no idea who the man was or what was being said.

The man was Yousef el-Din, and he was unhappy. Ragnar had refused to let his men in to see the captives, or to help guard them, or to talk with the journalists who were doing interviews in the town and with al-Said in front of the fortress.

Ragnar quickly deduced that Yousef wanted to be on television himself, and he was merely talking around that fact. He wanted to tell the world about the prowess of the Shabab, of the power of Islam. He wanted the world to see *him*. Presumably if his fame as a holy warrior were to spread far and wide, his standing in the Shabab would be enhanced.

Ragnar considered the matter carefully while he eyed Nora Neidlinger and her magnificent chest. He had never before seen a surgically enhanced bosom, and the sight fascinated him. The possibility that those two flesh melons might not be homegrown never entered his head.

He forced himself to come back to Yousef el-Din and his television ambitions.

"The object is to force the British and Americans to pay the ransom we have demanded. Seeing a man high in the Shabab here might complicate things."

Yousef was working himself up to a tantrum, but Ragnar forestalled it. "After we have the money, then will be the time for you to talk to the television men. Explain to the world the demands of fundamental Islam, the inevitability of its triumph. Explain about martyrs and Paradise and houris and all of that."

El-Din didn't like Ragnar's edict, not a whit, so he argued for another fifteen minutes, then stomped off down the stairs.

Meanwhile another man was escorted into Ragnar's lair. A European. He clutched a backpack in his arms. He was perhaps sixty, with close-cropped salt-and-pepper hair, a medium-built man, close-shaven, in contrast to the pirates, who didn't shave, nor did they have full beards. They were like adolescent boys, with mere tufts of facial hair or none at all.

Ragnar listened to his men explain in Arabic; then one of them spoke in broken English. "Ragnar says give him bag."

"Explain to Herr Ragnar that I wish to trade the bag for freedom."

The pirate translated, and Ragnar ripped the bag from the man's hands. One of the pirates grabbed the man from behind and held him. "My name is Beck," the man explained. "Heinrich Beck. I am a businessman, like Herr Ragnar. I do business with important people in the Arab world. I have many friends . . ."

Heinrich Beck ran down as Ragnar unzipped the bag, revealing a carefully wrapped package. Heavy. Several pounds, in fact. Ragnar hefted it and glanced at Beck. He said something, and the pirate translated. "What is?"

"Cocaine. Pure. Refined. Worth at least two hundred thousand American dollars. I wish to give it to Herr Ragnar in return for my freedom."

Ragnar and his son Nouri took the package to a table and carefully unwrapped it, revealing a zip-lock bag full of white powder. Nouri unzipped it, took a pinch and sniffed it up his nose. He smiled at his father and zipped the bag shut.

Ragnar said something, and one of the pirates slapped Beck. "Where is rest?"

"Rest?"

"More. Where is more? This not all. Where is more?"

"Listen. I am a businessman, like Herr Ragnar. I wish to trade—"

Another command, and two pirates, one on each arm, physically dragged Beck through the French doors to the balcony and across it to the low wall that formed the safety rail. They hoisted him up on it and held him there.

"Where is more?"

Beck looked down, terror written on his features.

"If there is more cocaine," Nora Neidlinger said loudly, "it is probably on the ship, in his stateroom. Why don't you look there? And let the poor man go."

This was translated.

Ragnar looked at Nora and laughed. His men laughed. After a moment Ragnar made a gesture and someone gave Beck a gentle push. His arms flailed the air, he teetered on the rail for just an instant, then he fell. Screaming. All the way down.

For the very first time in his life, Arch Penney felt completely helpless, unable to cope. Even when the pirates were capturing his ship, he had some control. Now, a prisoner in this old fortress at the entrance to the little harbor of Eyl, he knew he was unable to help himself and everyone else in his charge, including his wife.

She sensed his mood. As his strength ebbed, hers increased. She went among the women, talking, touching, listening, doing her best to maintain morale. Penney watched. Guilt washed over him like a tsunami. If only he had ran the ship at full speed, or chosen another route, or . . .

He still had bloodstains on his uniform, which was now filthy and rumpled. He hadn't thought to bring more clothes from the ship . . .

Unprepared. He had been unprepared. Hadn't really thought the problem through before the crisis presented itself. So he had been improvising. And he had failed.

"Archie," his wife whispered. "Don't get so down on yourself. Nothing you could have done would have made any difference."

He grunted. He didn't believe that, and doubted that she did.

He sent her to see the chief steward, to check the menus. Keep her busy. Make her responsible for something. That would keep her mind off this total, absolute . . . debacle. Disaster. Failure. Death for some of these people. Maybe all of them. Certainly more than had already died.

He went to the gun port and looked out into the night. The guards were out there, of course, although he couldn't see them. Beyond this strip of loosely packed earth, out there somewhere in the brush.

He could crawl out this portal, start running. Run until they shot him. Then it would be all over. Mercifully over.

"Captain."

It was the ship's doctor.

"We have some people coming down with dysentery. The toilet facilities . . . there isn't enough water, no soap . . ."

"Yes," he said as he stared into the darkness. Stared at the surface of the ocean, illuminated by starlight.

"Do what you can."

"Yes, sir." The doctor went away, leaving him at the portal looking at the ocean, as far beyond his reach as the lunar seas.

She was living a nightmare, Nora Neidlinger thought. A cluttered bedroom that smelled of unwashed bodies and semen. Filthy, stained sheets, the mattress on the floor, a spider's web in one corner. Insects flying around naked lightbulbs. An African whorehouse. Her revulsion made her skin crawl. She hugged herself.

Ragnar pushed her onto the mattress. Made a gesture, plainly, *Take off your clothes.*

She didn't think physical resistance would get her anything but a beating. She complied. Started with her blouse. Then the bra. Ragnar stood watching with his mouth open. She kicked off her shoes, wriggled as she pulled the slacks down over her hips. She was wearing granny panties, but apparently Ragnar didn't notice. Or care.

Before she could get them off he launched himself at her and buried his face between her breasts.

Mike Rosen was frustrated. Alone on an anchored ship with only emergency power, he felt as if he were the last man left alive on Spaceship Earth. Obviously there were some crewmen aboard in the engine room spaces, making sure the emergency generator stayed online, but he didn't see or hear them. They were imprisoned there, and he was imprisoned in his stateroom or the e-com center. Every now and then he heard noises, which he assumed were guards or Eyl citizens scavenging.

He wondered about Geoff Noon. The Brit was filthy—and so, Rosen suspected, were most of the things and people in northern Somalia—and an alcoholic. The possible fate of Rosen and the other people from *Sultan* didn't seem to cause him a moment's angst. Doesn't give a damn about anyone or anything except his bottle, Rosen decided.

Gin. What a pissy drink.

Rosen opened the door to his stateroom. The pirate was right there, sitting on a chair, chewing khat.

"I'm hungry."

The man stared at him uncomprehendingly. "Food." Rosen pantomimed eating.

The pirate gestured, *Back inside.* Jabbed at him with his rifle barrel, trying to force him back in the room.

"Prick," Rosen said. "You are a scummy little prick and your mother was a mangy hound dog."

He was just getting wound up when the man jabbed him in the chest with the rifle so hard he involuntarily stepped backward into the room. The pirate pulled the door shut.

"Asshole," Rosen roared at the closed door. "Fucking asshole."

He was furious at himself. He should have grabbed the rifle, jerked it out of the pirate's grasp and shot the son of a bitch with it. Blown his fucking khat-addled brains all over the corridor.

Well, why hadn't he done that?

. . .

The black inflatable boat was powered by an electric motor that made no noise. The U.S. Navy SEAL lieutenant in the bow, Bullet Bob Quinn, could hear the tiny slap-slap of waves as the boat worked through the seas, but that was the only sound.

Quinn surveyed the Eyl harbor and anchorage with night-vision binoculars. He had the magnification set as low as possible due to the motion of the boat, which made it difficult to keep the binoculars focused on any one item.

When he was satisfied that there were no boats under way in the harbor, he turned his attention to a ship that was grounded against a sandbar on the south side of the harbor. Her anchor was out and she was listing slightly, but not a light showed. From all appearances, she was a derelict.

Her name, he believed—he couldn't pronounce it—was Greek. Someone said the ship was named after a goddess. Bullet Bob didn't know if that was true, nor did he care. The message traffic said she had been captured several months ago. The crew had been ransomed, but the insurer refused to pay ransom for the ship, which was almost forty years old, so, Greek goddess or not, she had been abandoned to the pirates.

Her bow was pointed toward the town, her stern the open ocean. From her bow to the pier in front of the largest building in Eyl, Ragnar's six-story skyscraper, was a distance of 842 yards, according to the air intelligence techs who studied the drone photographs and compared them to satellite imagery. From her bridge to the fortress on the northern peninsula was 3,100 yards, over a mile and a half. The *Sultan* lay between, anchored in the main channel, 712 yards from the derelict's bridge.

Satisfied that no one was aboard the Greek freighter and the harbor was still, Bullet Bob tapped the man beside him on the shoulder, pointed to the freighter and gave a thumbs-up. The man checked his luminous wrist compass, then rolled backward off the gunwale of the inflatable, holding his mask and mouthpiece in place. He was wearing scuba tanks, but Quinn hoped the man could make the swim on the surface. The tanks were for an emergency, if he had to get below the surface and stay there.

Ten seconds later, the second man followed the first into the water.

Quinn checked his watch.

The coxswain throttled back, put the engine in reverse and kept the little black boat almost stationary against the tide, which was coming into the harbor.

There were four men left in the boat: the coxswain, Quinn and two more SEALs. All wore black wet suits and carried black gear. Submachine guns were snugged up tight to their bodies, short-barreled things. The boat rocked gently in the swells.

Bullet Bob found himself checking his watch. As usual, there were time constraints. He wanted all his men and their gear aboard the derelict and the boat out of the harbor into the open sea by moonrise, which was only an hour and a half away.

He looked back at the open sea, using the light-gathering binoculars, trying to spot the two skiffs that were running back and forth, patrolling the entrance to the harbor. Yes. They were still going back and forth, slowly, from north to south and back again. These were the lookouts, tasked with warning the pirates if enemy ships or boats appeared. Quinn's inflatable had slipped by them by hugging the shore, almost in the surf. A black boat, black-clad men, a dark night . . . the gamble had paid off. They were inside with the pirates none the wiser.

He hoped. Well, if there had been radio transmissions, the tactical watch officers aboard ship would have been warned him on his handheld.

Twenty-two minutes after he dropped the swimmers, his handheld radio did come to life. "We're aboard."

"Roger."

Now the men had to check out the ship, to ensure that they were the sole occupants. This would take another fifteen or twenty minutes. They would use black light, invisible to the naked eye, to find their way around inside the ship, where the darkness would be total.

The waiting was the toughest part of the job, Bullet Bob thought, much more difficult than being in motion, doing something. Anything. When you waited you thought too much.

He looked again for the skiffs. He spotted them with the night-vision binoculars, still moving slowly on their patrol routes. When he lowered the glasses the darkness hid them. As it hides us, he thought.

The minutes dragged. Quinn heard a boat motor fire up inside the harbor. He looked. Yes, a boat near the beach, men in the surf, climbing aboard.

Harbor patrol? A fishing boat? Or a skiff getting under way for a pirate cruise? He tried to count people. About a dozen, he thought. Which would make it a pirate boat. Two or three men would be enough for a harbor patrol.

Quinn watched the crew get the boat got under way. In just a moment it was motoring past the *Sultan* for the open sea. Speeding up, making a nice bow wave. The pirates were past the harbor mouth when their wake rocked the inflatable as the SEALs clung tightly to the lines.

Then the sound faded and the harbor again grew silent.

"Night Owl, come on in."

Bullet Bob clicked his mike twice and motioned to the coxswain, who had heard the transmission.

In two minutes they were on the side of the Greek freighter that faced the shore. Several lines dangled over the side. The coxswain hooked the inflatable to the lines and held it there with the engine while the men in the boat snapped lift lines to the largest black bag in the bottom of the boat. Up it went, slowly. The lines came back down and two more bags went up. Then Quinn and the two men went up.

On deck the lieutenant took a look around with his regular night-vision goggles.

"Two men were aboard. We took them out."

"Let's get the boat up."

The coxswain hooked the inflatable to the lift lines, and it was the last thing brought aboard.

The SEALs quickly went about their business. The largest bag contained a .50 caliber machine gun. This was carried to the bridge. The second bag contained two .50 caliber Barrett sniper rifles, and the third, the heaviest, food and ammo.

On the bridge Bullet Bob again used the night-vision binoculars. Yes. This would be a good place. The town of Eyl, the *Sultan,* and the boats on the beaches were all in range of the .50s, which were effective to a mile and a half. The machine gun and sniper rifles were, in effect, light artillery. When the time came to sanitize the *Sultan,* they could simply motor over in the boat, taking their weapons along.

As the men set up the guns a sliver of moon rose over the ocean. It didn't throw much light, but it made the harbor and town and abandoned ships easier to see with the naked eye.

Quinn supervised the placement of the weapons, reported via radio to the flagship, then settled down with his men for a snack and drink of water.

"I'll need a million bucks in fifties and hundreds, used, packed in a duffel bag," Jake Grafton said as matter-of-factly as he could manage. "Put a lock on it and give me the key."

Sal Molina looked up from the messages he was reading and eyed Grafton warily. "I'd like a million in cash myself, just for pocket change, you understand."

"This will be a down payment on the ransom. Proof of my bona fides, so to speak."

"What about the other hundred and ninety-nine million? The funny money you wanted Treasury to make."

"Pack it on pallets. Damn stuff will weigh about four and a half tons, I figure."

"Pallets."

"Then send it to Admiral Tarkington aboard *Chosin Reservoir* as soon as possible."

"FedEx or UPS?"

"What's your beef, Sal?"

"Why are you going to Somalia?"

"The name of this game is rescuing as many of the *Sultan* people as possible, with the minimum amount of friendly casualties. I want to see the situation, smell it and touch it, then we'll figure out how to unscrew this mess."

"You really think you can pull this off?"

"Pretty sure. The only question is how much blood it will cost. We have Jurgen Schulz and his staff to thank for maneuvering us into this corner."

"You're not going to make that crack to a reporter, are you? Or to Congress?"

"Hadn't planned on it. However, if Schulz tries to sit in Washington and tell me what to do, then I might."

"You obviously think you can wow this pirate, Ragnar, convince him not to kill you."

Grafton smiled.

"What if you're wrong?"

"Well, Sal, I expect you to wear a decent suit and tie to my memorial service. None of those rag-bag Texas lawyer threads. And send some flowers. Callie likes flowers."

Molina stood. "When are you leaving?"

Grafton glanced at his watch. "I'll be leaving for Andrews in about an hour, after I talk to the director. We'll take off whenever you get that bag full of money onto the plane. In the meantime, have the Fed put out a call for hundred-dollar and fifty-dollar bills to all the national banks. Get some stories in the press. We're lucky they asked for used bills. That gives us some time."

"Okay." Sal Molina stuck out his hand. "Luck," he said.

"Yeah."

After Molina left, Jake opened his desk drawer and took out a pistol and ankle holster. He strapped the holster to his left ankle and checked the pistol, a Walther in .380 caliber. The magazine was full. He chambered a round, popped out the magazine and added one more cartridge to it, then put it back in the pistol. He holstered the weapon and pressed the Velcro safety strap firmly in place.

He debated taking another magazine. He didn't think they would search him, but if they patted him down, he didn't want them to find a magazine in his pocket.

No. One magazine-load would have to be enough.

Grafton shook his trousers down and checked his image in the glass of the window. He saw a lean man in his mid-sixties with short, thinning salt-and-pepper hair combed straight back and a prominent nose. Clean-shaven, square jaw, a reasonable tan. He was wearing a fairly expensive gray suit and off-white shirt, no tie. Leather shoes.

He looked, he hoped, like a pirate's idea of a successful senior bureaucrat or political appointee. Not the Sal Molina type, but the Jurgen Schulz type. On a sabbatical from Wall Street or the Ivy League. A guy who could talk about a couple hundred million as if it were small change.

Jake Grafton ensured all the drawers and cabinets in his office were locked, then picked up his small suitcase and walked out, turning the lights off before he pulled the door shut.

Ten miles north of the promontory that formed the northern side of the Eyl harbor, six SEALs in wet suits crawled through the surf onto the beach. They put out sentries, checked the consistency of the sand, which was hard above the high water line, then hoisted their boat, which contained their bags of gear, and trotted into the dunes.

Thirty minutes after they arrived, they established radio contact with *Chosin Reservoir* and reported beach conditions, distance to the dunes, the fact that the beach was deserted in every direction as far as they could see. Inland, the dunes turned to desert scrub and ran on for a mile or so before the foothills started. The hills were low and irregular, covered with scrub.

The senior man, a first-class petty officer named Ben Bryant, thought this beach would make an excellent landing area for marines, and he passed that observation on to the ship.

The only problem, as he saw it, was the tracks of pickup trucks in the sand above the high water mark. Up and down the beach, again and again. They had made a rutted road. Apparently they liked to drive the beach and look for things or people who shouldn't be there, like shipwrecked millionaires or stranded submarines . . . or U.S. Navy SEALs.

Ben Bryant told the folks on *Chosin Reservoir* about the tracks, and began looking for an ambush site. He figured the time might come in the not-too-distant future when the bad guys' beach rides might become an annoyance. If and when, that was an itch he could scratch.

Another SEAL team landed on the beach six miles south of Eyl. Again, the beach was straight, the sand was packed hard above the high water mark, and the dunes behind were empty. A half mile south of their landing place stood a fisherman's shack on the edge of the dunes. A boat rested on the beach, tied to a rock so a large wave couldn't carry it away.

Without a word, two SEALs trotted that way to check it out.

There were two men and a woman asleep in the shack. No kids. No weapons. No food in the place except for a couple of half-rotted fish. The SEALs used plastic ties on the Somalis' wrists, binding them in front, and fed them MREs. They wolfed the food down.

There were tire tracks on the beach here, too. The Somalis couldn't speak English and the Americans not a word of Somali, but through signs the Americans came to believe the pickups came by every two or three days.

The SEALs looked at each other. A pickup truck with a machine gun in the bed would be a nice souvenir of their African adventure. Perhaps they could even find a proper use for the gun.

Ten miles farther south along the beach, a helo settled onto the dirt road that led to Eyl and a team of six Force Reconnaissance marines piled out. They carried two machine guns and several cases of ammo in addition to their packs and personal weapons. The chopper was on the ground less than a minute, then rose and skimmed the earth eastward, toward the sea.

Two other roads led into Eyl. One from the north and one that wound its way through the mountains from the interior. Both were dirt, mere rocky tracks through the desert. Teams of Recon marines were landed in both places.

The teams quickly took positions, positioned their machine guns to control the roads, sent out scouts and reported back to the ship.

Eyl was cut off. No one was going in or out without a fight.

It was nearly eight o'clock in the morning in Eyl, Somalia, when the door to Mike Rosen's stateroom opened and Geoff Noon walked in. "Good morning."

"Knock next time, shithead." Noon was wearing the same clothes he wore yesterday. Maybe he slept in them.

"And a pleasant morning to you, too, sir. If it's not too much trouble, the gentlemen of Eyl request that you accompany me to the computer center, where you can check the news from Merry Old England and the former colonies. If you please."

Noon smelled of gin. Already. Bastard had already had his morning tots. More than one, Rosen was sure. As they walked, with the pirate guard trailing, whiffs of Noon's body odor nauseated Rosen.

"When was the last time you had a bath?"

"What a coincidence you should ask! My chambermaid is drawing my bath as we speak. When we are finished with our errand, I shall leave you to enjoy the squalor of this abandoned ship and go home to my mansion on the hill, to a luxurious hot bubble bath, clean clothes and a noon feast prepared by my personal chef and served by professionals in white livery. Then gin fizzes on the verandah and a wonderful Cuban cigar. One can live quite well in these climes on a modest income, as I do."

"I haven't had anything to eat since noon yesterday."

"I'll talk to the pirates."

"Great."

"They're roasting a goat on deck by the pool. Perhaps—"

"No goat. I can root around in the galley and find a can of something, if they'll let me."

In the e-com center Noon settled into a chair like a bird returning to its nest and took a nip from his gin bottle. Rosen fired up his laptop, which was sitting just as he left it. As long as the pirates left it alone, Rosen mused, it was probably less likely to be stolen here than at Rosen's condo in Denver.

Almost sixty e-mails awaited his attention. He scanned the list. A U.S. military sending address caught his eye, so he opened it.

This is what he read:

Mr. Rosen,

The company that owns MV *Sultan of the Seas,* the company that insured it, and the governments involved have appointed me chief negotiator for the release of the passengers, crew and ship. I will arrive in Eyl tomorrow evening. Please pass this message along to the pirates and ask them to meet me at the Eyl airport.

Sincerely,

Jacob L. Grafton

Rosen printed out the message and handed the copy to High Noon, who put on his glasses and perused it. "Any previous messages from Mr. Grafton?"

"No. That's the first one."

"What does 'MV' mean?"

"Motor vessel."

"Tomorrow evening. Didn't give a time. Probably arrive after tea, on the flight from Mombasa. The wogs have plenty of time to arrange a reception."

Noon read the e-mail again. "Chatty chap, isn't he? Why don't you google Mr. Grafton and see what comes up."

Rosen did so. Noon pried himself out of the chair and came over to squint over his shoulder at the screen. The gin and body odor made Rosen breathe shallow.

"You can sit here if you like," he offered.

"This is fine. Hmm . . . American naval officer. Two star. Retired. Well, that should be enough for Ragnar, I think."

Noon went back to his chair and settled his bulk.

Rosen continued to scan the list of documents that mentioned Grafton. "This guy has testified at various congressional hearings, on at least three occasions."

"Ragnar won't be interested in that," Noon said dismissively. "He's a pirate. Pretty good one, as a matter of fact, but quite ignorant. Doesn't know a thing about Congress or condoms. Educating the wog bastard would be a complete waste of time and brain cells. Let's do the rest of the e-mails. Print out each one, and if something deservers an answer I'll give you any hints that pop to mind."

"Oh, thank you, thank you. I would have been quite at a loss."

"Bloody cheeky blighter. Try to behave yourself. Let's see if you and I can get through this little adventure alive, with all our body parts still firmly attached, shall we?"

CHAPTER FIFTEEN

When Geoff Noon arrived via boat at the beach in front of Ragnar's lair, the press was waiting. Both the Italian and Fox News reporter/photographer teams were there filming him arriving in a punt powered by an outboard motor that gave off great clouds of white smoke.

Geoff waded ashore with his battered leather attaché case right into the middle of the mess.

"Mr. Noon, are you going upstairs to see Sheikh Ragnar?"

"Yes."

"We wish to interview him."

Noon ignored the Fox man with the massive mustache and concentrated on the Italian woman, Sophia Donatelli. He couldn't help himself. He smiled at her.

"Where are your colleagues from the BBC?"

"They are filming 'human interest' stories," Ms. Donatelli replied cheerfully, demonstrating her excellent command of the English language. She had a small, delightful accent. "How the people of Eyl live in their tropical paradise, fishing for fun and profit, the jolly life of a pirate at home . . ." Her cameraman was filming the conversation.

"What do you wish to ask Sheikh Ragnar?"

Mr. Mustache jumped right in. "It would be great if he could repeat his ransom demands on camera, and his threats to murder everyone if not paid."

"I see."

"That would be terrific television."

"Doubtlessly. Anything else?"

"We want access to the fort to interview the prisoners. People all over the world are watching in huge numbers."

"A perfect market," Noon murmured. Ms. Donatelli grinned at him.

"We sell beauty soap, automobiles, wine and soft drinks," she said cheerfully.

"If you will wait here," Noon said, "I will go upstairs and ask Sheikh Ragnar if he will cooperate in your efforts to keep the wheels of commerce turning vigorously."

With that, he walked toward the hotel, trailed by two pirate bodyguards.

Ms. Donatelli's cameraman was named Carlo Luria, although everyone called him Joe. Just now a feminine voice spoke in English in his right ear. "Pan the building and zoom in on each floor."

Unlike the other cameramen, who wore an earpiece in one ear so they could hear their producer's comments and directions via the satellite link, Luria wore two, one in each ear. His producer in Rome had his left ear and used Italian. His CIA producer in Langley, Virginia, had his right ear and always spoke English, even though she understood Italian perfectly and listened to everything Joe and Ms. Donatelli said to each other and to their Italian producer, who didn't know about the CIA connection.

Luria did as the lady in America requested. His camera habitually rode on his right shoulder so he had easy access to the controls with his right hand. With his feet planted, it was easy enough to scan the building, then zoom in and pan across each floor. A few seconds would be enough.

The digital feed from the camera was sent to a satellite transmitter that the third man on the team had set up in the town square, beside the satellite gear of both the other networks. All three transmitters were powered by diesel generators that were snoring loudly, making the necessary electricity. The satellite transmitters sent the signal up, and from there it went hither and yon.

Luria knew that in addition to the network control room in Rome, his digital signal was being recorded by the CIA in America. They could freeze the audio and video or slow it down and study it at their leisure.

The Americans rarely said much to him—only when they wanted a specific shot—and he only gave it to them when he thought his producer in Rome wouldn't get suspicious.

When finished with the building, Luria panned the pier, the boats and the harbor. He carefully focused the camera on the anchored cruise ship, *Sultan of the Seas,* and zoomed in. The only sign of life was a wisp of smoke from the stack, almost invisible.

He swung the camera on to every ship he could see, almost a dozen of them, anchored, run onto mud flats or sandbanks, rusty with peeling paint, glass gone from the bridge windows, lifeboats gone or hanging haphazardly from davits, lines trailing over the side . . . It was a depressing sight.

Soon a pirate came from Ragnar's building and motioned to the media people. They followed him inside and up the stairs. Luria kept his camera running, even though he carried it in his right hand as if it were an attaché case. The building reminded him of the crumbling tenement in Naples where he grew up, with the aroma of rotten food scraps mixing in with the smell of urine and feces.

Sophia Donatelli climbed ahead of him. He kept his eyes on her hips, which were the only things in Somalia worth looking at.

She was a smart, breezy woman, full of self-assurance, with a face and figure that blessed any camera that gazed at her. She was a reporter now, but in a few years, Luria believed, Sophia Donatelli would be one of the largest personalities on European television or a film star. She had it in her.

She marched right up to Ragnar and stuck out her hand. "Sophia Donatelli."

The pirate was visibly taken aback. Carlo Luria caught the moment. Mustache came charging into the picture, babbling something. The fact that Ragnar spoke no English hadn't sunk in. One of the pirates grabbed

Mustache and jerked him away from the chief. Another stuck a rifle barrel in his face.

With the translation help of Noon, who had watched that little scene, an interview of sorts was accomplished. Ragnar leered at Donatelli, ignored Mustache, and generally proved he was a wart on the world's ass.

"We are poor men," Ragnar said. "They have stolen our fish and dumped poison in our oceans. Our people are starving. We will do as we must to live. We have no choice."

"Do you condone murder?" Sophia asked. "The slaughter of innocent people?"

"We are pirates. Buccaneers. Gentlemen of adventure." Ragnar had gotten this last phrase from *Pirates of the Caribbean,* the favorite movie of everyone in Eyl, but Donatelli didn't know that. "We do not apologize. We have chosen this way of life in order to eat, to feed our families. Our cause is just. We do what we are forced to do. The ransom must be paid. Without it, the prisoners will die quickly and we will die slowly."

Donatelli waited to ensure Ragnar had run down and Noon had finished translating. She said, "Various international aid agencies have tried to relieve the suffering of starving Somali people, yet armed bands of men prevent the delivery of aid. They steal any food and medicine that is delivered, sell it on the black market. They abandon the helpless, condemn them to starvation and death. Do you condone this behavior?"

Ragnar was frowning as he listened to this soliloquy by Ms. Donatelli, and was answering before Noon could finish the translation. "We have fought the Shabab and won here, in Eyl. They are strong other places. They fight for Islam. We fight for survival.

"But I did not make the world. The strong will live, the weak will die. It is that way. Since forever it is that way. You in Europe and America are strong. We have been weak. Europeans pollute our oceans and kill our fish. We will take what we must have. We will be strong."

The pirate chief refused to answer more questions.

Ricardo tried anyway. He requested an interview with the captain of the *Sultan*. To his surprise, Ragnar nodded yes. Pirates escorted Mustache and his cameraman to the stairs and prodded them downward. The little procession was not seen again.

"You stay," Ragnar told Donatelli. Soon tea was brewing, then being served. Ragnar laughed and joked with his men. Noon translated a word here, a word there, but contented himself with slurping tea. Donatelli looked calm and cool, as if she were drinking tea at a restaurant in Davos while the world's economic leaders vied to be interviewed by her. She had that ability.

Carlo Luria captured it all on his camera, and his transmitter outside in the square fired it up to the satellite.

Ricardo and his cameraman rode in a technical to the fort and were reintroduced to Mustafa al-Said. "It is I who captured *Sultan,*" the pirate bragged, so Ricardo gave him a few more minutes of fame. After he got a quickie version of the action, Ricardo asked to see Captain Arch Penney. Last night he had not been permitted to see Penney, nor to enter the fortress. Al-Said led the way into the fortress.

They found Penney in the cooking area. The cameraman arranged and turned on his portable spotlight.

Penney's clothes were rumpled and filthy. He was unshaven. Words were unnecessary. His haunted visage told the story. Still, he spoke slowly and softly into the microphone Mustache held near his lips. "Two passengers died last night of dysentery. Dehydration. We have almost no way to keep clean, the toilet facilities are holes in the floor, the people have nothing. All of us will eventually sicken and die unless we are released."

Al-Said stood watching. He was happy. The suffering of the infidels would soon bring money. Much money. The more suffering the camera revealed, the sooner the money would arrive. In truth, he was used to suffering. He had watched children die of starvation all his life, had watched people waste away from terrible, untreated diseases, had lived with the rats, lived like a rat. He was a survivor who cared about no one but himself.

Ricardo interviewed some other people, who to their credit didn't complain. One man, from the Midlands, praised Captain Penney and his crew. "They have done all they can do."

"Should the owner of the ship pay the ransom?" Mustache asked callously, and the Brit turned his back and walked away.

He buttonholed a man standing nearby and asked him if his family would pay ransom to win his freedom. Two women shed tears in front of the camera, which Mustache encouraged with leading questions that would have wrung tears from a stone. "Do you miss your children? What will they tell your grandchildren if you are murdered by pirates, or die of some preventable disease? Do you have any last message for your loved ones?" Subtlety was not his shtick.

He would have probably interviewed everyone in the fort if his cameraman hadn't told him the batteries in the camera needed recharging. The spotlight was also draining juice quickly.

Mustache decided to move his operation outside, and spoke to al-Said about it. To his amazement, he was told no.

"No. You no leave. Ragnar's orders."

"Wait! You don't understand. We are members of the press. We are not passengers or crew of this ship you captured. We report your story to the world. We tell the world what is happening."

"Tell it here," al-Said said firmly. "You stay."

And he walked out. Ricardo trailed behind him, protesting vigorously, but the guards at the entrance stopped him and the cameraman. They stood watching as al-Said climbed into the pickup that had brought them here and drove away.

When he had composed himself, Mustache assumed the position with his microphone in front of his mouth. The cameraman used the last of his battery juice to broadcast the sad truth: He and Ricardo were now prisoners of the pirates and wouldn't be broadcasting anymore unless and until they found a way to charge the batteries in their equipment.

Then Mustache had one of those moments that earned him the big bucks from Fox News. He said, "So we too join the prisoners from the *Sultan.* We too will die here in this filthy, rat-infested fortress unless the ransom Ragnar demands is paid. Like all these people trapped by an evil they can not control or even comprehend, we hope that statement is not our epitaph." He managed to say it matter-of-factly, with the emotion just under the surface, summoning his courage and steeling himself for the ordeal. He was commenting in the shadow of the gallows.

As he predicted, it was terrific television.

. . .

Rear Admiral Toad Tarkington watched the Fox News and Italian transmissions to the satellite in the Flag Ops spaces aboard *Chosin Reservoir.* Unfortunately he was not a connoisseur of cable news, so he almost gagged at Ricardo's histrionics.

He had the technicians play Sophia Donatelli's interview with Ragnar twice while he studied the man's face, his expressions. He learned nothing that he didn't already know. The pirates were vicious men playing hardball. So be it. The U.S military played hardball, too.

Soon the admiral was watching technicians in an intelligence space put together a model of Eyl on a large table that was usually used for map study. The model was being constructed with sand, plaster of Paris and wood bits that were used for buildings and shacks. The info to construct the model came from satellite and drone imagery, and was checked and verified against the images from Carlo Luria's television camera. Distances had to be correctly measured, the topography of the terrain accurately reproduced, buildings correctly placed, at the right height and aspect.

The admiral was most interested in the area below the fort, near the road that led to the entrance. The wire from the fertilizer bombs ran down this road, and Carmellini said it terminated in a small shack with an old-fashioned DC generator. No one knew where the detonators were located in the explosive mixture. Carmellini had also reported antennas. If there were some kind of radio controls, there must be batteries and a capacitor. How many radio controls there were, their location and who had access were all unknown. With a push of a button or flip of a switch, the bomb could be detonated at any time.

Finally, the admiral and his experts didn't know where the Shabab soldiers were located. There seemed to be a large number of armed men and pickups in a district, actually a separate small town, about a mile upriver of Eyl. Were these men Shabab, or pirates under Ragnar's control? They had to be one or the other. In Eyl there were very few neutral persons.

Tarkington's staff fired off a Top Secret message to Washington asking for any information the CIA had about the Shabab in Eyl. Hours later, the For Your Eyes Only, Top Secret reply was placed in Tarkington's hands.

The lead paragraph stated that Tarkington was to reveal the message's contents only to those officers who needed the information for operational purposes.

Tarkington quickly realized why. He was reading a carefully written, detailed intelligence summary. The message named every Shabab soldier in the Eyl area, where he lived, who he lived with, the weapons and other military equipment the Shabab possessed and their communications setup. It included descriptions and summaries of the abilities and prejudices and weaknesses of Shabab commanders, from the top down.

It was brutally obvious that the information could have only come from a spy on the ground in Eyl, someone who knew every man in town. No doubt that was why the information was not to be shared.

The admiral went into the space where the mock-up of Eyl was taking shape and compared buildings to the locations set forth in the message. Yes, the Shabab warriors were concentrated in the village neighborhood in the old wash west of the downtown area. Aerial reconnaissance imagery clearly showed the armed pickups parked willy-nilly, and fuel tanks here and there. When Colonel Zakhem came into the space a few minutes later, Tarkington handed him the message.

"It's gold or bullshit," Zakhem said after he had carefully read the message twice and handed it back.

"We're going to find out, Colonel," Toad Tarkington said with a smile. "Want to make a small wager on which substance it is? Like a steak dinner next time we hit port?"

Zakhem laughed. "You want me to bet on bullshit, right?"

"I like filet mignon."

I took E.D. and Travis with me when I went sneaking that night. We all had knives and .45s, and they carried silenced submachine guns, MP-5s. Me, I was loaded down with night-vision goggles and binoculars.

We hiked through the brush to the sentry outpost on the northern end of the Eyl airport and settled in for a good look around.

Yep, the pirates or Shabab holy warriors, whichever had the duty tonight, were doing their relaxed campout. No sentry. Nice fire, way too big, on which they were frying something in a big pan. Some kind of fish, I figured. Or a dog. Or a couple of rats. Perhaps I didn't properly appreciate the local cuisine.

Two pickups parked nearby. One of them had a machine gun mounted in the bed, and of course there was that tripod-mounted machine gun that commanded the runway. It was perfectly adequate to perforate any airplane landing or taxiing or taking off. If these guys didn't like you, you weren't going flying.

The three of them were sitting around the fire laughing and jabbering, probably telling lies about their sexual exploits.

I lay there in the brush on my belly watching. They had a plastic can strapped to the side of one of the trucks, and occasionally one of them would wander over for a drink from it. Water, I suspected.

A couple hours passed. A bug somehow got inside my lower trouser leg and decided to feast on the lean white flesh he found there. Moving as slowly as possible, I squashed the little bastard and itched the bite. Wished to Christ I were in Paris with a gal I know and happen to like, eating French grub at some white-tablecloth place with a bottle of good vino in easy reach, and contemplating the prospect of getting laid later.

Finally, as the fire began to die and the three warriors for truth, justice and the Muslim way got busy spreading blankets and rags, I started crawling. Crawled completely around the fire and got the pickup with the water between them and me. Worked my way right up against that thing, where I could see them by looking under it.

Finally they lay down in their blankets. Arranged weapons within reach and settled in for a pleasant night.

I waited another hour, until the moon sliver was up, then got to my feet and walked carefully around the pickup. Took the cap off the water can and dropped in three pills. I was about to screw the cap back on when I thought, what the hell, and added two more. That should be enough dope to knock out an elephant.

We left them there, sound asleep, and E.D., Travis and I hiked the length of the runway.

The guys on the other end were already asleep. One was in the cab of his pickup, and the other two were near the fire, which was burning nicely. They had piled such woody roots as they could find on the thing to keep the snakes and critters away.

I waited for half an hour, just to be sure, then doped their water can. Then I saw another can, so I doped it, too.

When we were hiking to our hidey-hole, E.D. asked, "How long do you want them asleep?"

"Until Grafton's plane gets here tomorrow afternoon."

"If they drink some of that spiked water in the morning, they may be awake by the afternoon. Or somebody may find them all sprawled out."

"It's a risk, sure. If you got any other ideas, let's hear them."

"We'd better get there around noon and check on them."

"If they are asleep, spike the machine guns."

"Okay."

"If they are awake when the plane lands and it stops at their end of the field, kill them and haul away the bodies in one of their pickups," I said. "That's Plan B. It's our only possible choice."

Neither man said a word in protest. Those guys had to be asleep or dead when that DC-3 landed. We didn't want witnesses. So maybe they were going to die tomorrow. On the other hand, maybe we three fools would.

I assured myself that the *Sultan* passengers and crew had an excellent chance. We all had an excellent chance. Yeah.

Hell, we had Jake Grafton.

CHAPTER SIXTEEN

I heard the radial engines murmuring gently.

"It's coming," I said into the handheld.

"Asleep North."

"Asleep South."

So there would be no witnesses awake to tell the sheikh that this Carmellini guy didn't arrive with Jake Grafton.

I used the binoculars. Yep, the DC-3 was low to the south, coming straight in. I was across the runway from the terminal. I duck-walked back to the little draw that paralleled the west side of the runway and started trotting toward the northern end of the runway. Running, actually. I had a half mile to do, and in this heat it was a chore.

The wind was out of the west, hot and dry, right off the Sahara. It was pushed up and over the coastal mountains, so cooled a bit on being elevated; if there was any moisture to be squeezed out of that air the mountains got it. Still, here in their wind shadow it was a little bit cooler than it would have been without the mountains' help.

I had been sweating anyway. I had bathed as best I could and shaved. Was now wearing a set of rumpled khakis and a button-up short-sleeve shirt from Sears. I was still in my desert boots. My backpack was packed with extra underwear and my toothbrush, plus the Kimber .45, the Ruger .22 with silencer and my knife. The pack bounced up and down as I ran because I didn't have the straps tight enough.

Since I was about to join the diplomatic corps, I didn't figure that the bad guys would search me. After all, there were fifty or a hundred of them and only one of me. If I got out of control they could always pop me. Even if they confiscated my weapons, I could always take a shooter from one of their warriors when I needed one.

Little puffs of dust rose from my footfalls as I booked it. The engines were plainly audible, even though throttled back. I kicked it into overdrive.

The plane was on the ground. I heard the engines pulled back to idle.

It went by me spewing choking dust, and I sprinted the last two hundred yards. I got there just as the tail kicked around and the guy goosed the outboard engine. The passenger door was already open, which was a good thing because the plane didn't stop. Just completed its one-eighty and taxied toward the terminal.

As I hit the floor inside, Jake Grafton pulled the door shut and turned the handle.

He looked at me with a smile and said, "Nice run?"

His trouser leg was right there by my face, so I used it for a towel. His grin widened.

There were two other men in the passenger cabin. They were dark Middle Eastern types in ratty trousers, pullover shirts, and worn tennis shoes. They had AKs near at hand. Smallish men, less than a hundred and fifty pounds. They looked at me with dead eyes, expressionless faces. Except for us, the passenger cabin was empty. A single row of threadbare seats went up each side, so you got a window/aisle seat regardless of what you asked for.

Grafton introduced me as we taxied. Ben and Zahra. "They are on our side," Grafton said, and the men extended hands. I shook them. Firm, muscular, calloused hands.

"They are on our side, but you don't know them. Ignore them."

"Sure."

Grafton and I plopped into two seats near the rear door, with the aisle between us.

"Got a pistol on you?" the admiral asked over the rumble of the idling engines. With the engines at power this thing must reverberate like a kettledrum. I could see why. All the interior insulation was gone. Welcome to Africa.

"Yeah," I admitted.

"Put it in your waistband where they can see it. That bag there"—he pointed at a duffel bag two seats forward of mine—"is yours to guard. Full of money. Don't let them take it away from you unless I give the word. Put this in your backpack." He handed me a small handheld radio transceiver.

Amazingly, the air in the interior of that aluminum airplane was even hotter than the air outside. My heart rate was getting back to normal, but sweat poured off me, soaking my shirt. I noticed Grafton looked a little travel-worn, too.

"Enough money for me to retire on?"

"Only if you want a shack in Somalia." He must have thought that was droll, because he knew I was a Paris kind of guy.

I fished the Kimber out of the backpack and stuck it in my belt. Put the radio in the bag and zipped it up.

"How was your trip?" I asked.

"Long."

Another minute, and our pilot cut the left engine. The plane rolled to a stop in front of the terminal. Grafton opened the door while I got the duffel bag and luggage—my backpack and his soft travel bag. I passed them out to him. The pilots never left the cockpit. Ben and Zahra followed us off the plane, their AKs in one hand and a little bag of personal possessions in the other, and wandered off.

As I stood on the dirt in front of the terminal, with the tower and machine-gun nest to our left, Grafton closed the door and made a vague wave at the pilot. We humped the stuff toward the terminal as the left engine made noises and spewed smoke while the prop began to turn.

Then dirt was flying and the plane was moving.

I tossed the duffel bag on my shoulder. I guessed it weighed at least eighty pounds. Grafton got our two bags and we strolled toward the half-dozen armed Somalis waiting for us.

"I'm Grafton. Anybody here speak English?"

"Aye, yes, sir," came a voice from inside the tin terminal shack, and a white man appeared. Fat, balding, wearing a dirty button-up shirt, filthy slacks and sandals. "Welcome to Eyl. My name is Noon. I'm the airport manager."

Grafton took a good look around, his first. "Who paved the runway?"

"The Chinese, in a fit of capital expenditure designed to capture our hearts and open Eyl to international development . . . by the Chinese. About twenty years ago, before the unpleasantness started."

Grafton nodded and glanced over the armed men. "Who are these guys?'

"Your bodyguard. Ragnar wanted to extend every hospitality."

"The customs of the country, I suppose."

"Precisely. Every man of substance has an entourage."

Grafton sighed. "You have a restroom?"

Noon smiled and gestured grandly. "All of Africa is your urinal, sir. If you have other ideas, you might try the brush behind the building. Other people have been there before you, so watch where you step."

"Welcome to Somalia," I muttered as I readjusted the duffel bag on my shoulder. I saw Noon glance at the pistol behind my belt.

Grafton said, "Mr. Carmellini, my aide."

"Well, gentlemen, after you refresh yourself, we will depart for town and your interview with Sheikh Ragnar."

Carrying that eighty-pound duffel bag full of folding green up six flights of nonventilated stairs in the desert heat was the mustard on the shit sandwich. Fortunately I was a studly young man in the pink. Even so, by the time we reached the top I would have traded the entire contents of the damned bag for a cold beer.

The room at the top was full of pirates—and one woman, a white woman, who sat in the corner. Her clothes were not the cleanest, and she wore no makeup. She eyed me coldly. I ignored her and concentrated on the men, standing around their leader, Ragnar. There was no doubt who he was. He was the tallest and fattest, and in absolute command. He radiated power.

I looked the entourage over while Noon mopped his brow with a mechanic's rag and fought to catch his breath while giving Ragnar the lowdown on us, I suppose. Most of the guys to the right and left wore sidearms, and a few had AKs cradled in their arms.

When Noon ran down, Grafton introduced himself and me. Noon translated.

I lowered the bag to the floor and held it upright with my left hand. I could see some of the pirates eyeing that Kimber in my belt. I ignored them and watched Ragnar.

He introduced his sons and a couple of his lieutenants. Skinny, medium-sized guys, the Somali body type I had come to expect. None of these people got enough food when they were growing up, regardless of who their daddies were.

"I have come on behalf of the ship owners and insurers, and the governments involved, to negotiate a release of the ship *Sultan of the Seas,* and its passengers and crew."

Ragnar set his jaw and jabbered awhile. Noon said, "Ragnar says the ransom amounts and time deadlines are nonnegotiable. If you have come to arrange payment, you are welcome. If you have come to try to save yourself some money, you waste everyone's time."

Grafton didn't blink. "I have authorization to arrange to pay one hundred million. Nothing else. For the ship and crew and passengers. Before I pay that, I will have to talk to the captain, ensure everyone is well and in good health, treated with dignity and respect, given adequate food and water."

Ragnar waved a sheet of paper and made a statement. Noon said, "He says he wants another million each for these eighty-five people. Unless you pay, they will stay behind when the others leave."

Their positions staked out, they thrust and parried back and forth. After about five minutes, when Ragnar was obviously beginning to lose his temper, Jake Grafton suggested a change of course. "If you will let me visit the captain and his crew, and the passengers, I will communicate with my government and tell them of your demands. Perhaps they will change their minds."

Ragnar was petulant. Negotiating was not one of his skill sets. He was accustomed to giving orders and watching people jump.

Jake Grafton was old Mr. Smooth. "As proof of my government's serious purpose, and as a sign of respect for Sheikh Ragnar, I have brought with me a gift for him. Tommy?"

I picked up the bag with my left hand and took a step up beside him. One of Ragnar's boys stepped forward eagerly as Noon talked, so I tossed the bag at him with my left hand. He put both hands up to catch it, and was unprepared for the weight. He lost his balance and fell. He gave me a murderous look while his pards beamed and Ragnar laughed. Grafton pulled a key from a pocket and passed it over.

The kid unlocked the padlock and spread the top of the bag. He reached in and pulled out bundles of money.

"I have brought the sheikh a gift from my government of one million American dollars as a sign of our good faith."

Ragnar looked at the bills, dug out a handful for himself, smiled and gave orders. We were going to see the prisoners.

Noon led us out. I got a glimpse of the woman sitting in the corner. Her eyes followed me, but her face was expressionless.

Aboard the grounded Greek freighter, Lieutenant Bullet Bob Quinn and his men made an interesting discovery. The ship contained several demolition charges set to blow holes in her bottom, and to set her on fire. She still contained a reasonable quantity of fuel oil, perhaps eight hundred or so tons, and the charges were laid to breach the tanks and ignite the oil.

Quinn and his men quickly determined that the charges were radio controlled, and soon had disassembled the devices by removing the wires from the batteries to the fuses. The bombs were now inert. Quinn turned on his encrypted radio and reported his discoveries to *Chosin Reservoir.*

"Tonight," the controller said in a few minutes, "could you and one or two of your men swim over to *Sultan* and board her? If that ship you are on is wired to go, *Sultan* might be, too."

"At dark," Quinn agreed.

He and his men sat on the bridge with binoculars and studied the *Sultan.* The pilot port was open, and the anchor chain looked inviting.

"When is the ball going to open?" Bullet Bob asked.

"Ahh . . . don't know. We'll pass that date and time along when we receive it."

Quinn turned off the radio and looked at his team members. "Heavies are still cogitating," he reported.

"They do that."

"They are slow cogitators."

"Old and decrepit."

"Not young and virile and handsome, like us."

"Amen."

The news of our arrival spread quickly. Sophia Donatelli from Mediaset, her photographer and a reporter/photographer team from the BBC were waiting in the square. Grafton graciously granted an interview. Noon and I stood to one side watching.

The questions came thick and fast. Grafton was here on behalf of the ship owners, he said, and at the request of the British and American governments. He had begun negotiations with Sheikh Ragnar for the release of the ship *Sultan,* the crew and the passengers. When an agreement had been reached, he would hold a press conference and inform them of the terms.

Needless to say, Sophia Donatelli had my attention. She wasn't a raving beauty, but she had presence. She glanced at me and I gave her a grin, and got a flash of one in return.

That warmed me right up, and I was beginning to feel better about this Somali gig when I happened to glance up. Ragnar was leaning over his balcony watching.

That did it for my bonhomie. I looked around, taking in the half-starved women and kids, the men with guns, the grungy boats on the beach, the brilliant sun, the empty sea, the hot wind off the desert, the derelict ships . . .

Maybe we are all coming to this, when there are too many people, not enough resources, people don't care about decency or their fellow humans or . . . Or maybe I'm an idiot.

One thing for sure: The CIA doesn't pay me to philosophize.

I made sure my pistol was riding properly, within easy reach, and concentrated on the interview. There were the usual questions trying to drag specifics from him, but Grafton deflected them all, smiling at everyone. As he made his escape, he nodded his head so I would know to follow. Noon was waiting to escort us up the hill.

We walked to the fortress. Noon was willing to drive, but Grafton refused. He said he had been sitting too much the last few days. Through the square, through a neighborhood of shacks and outdoor restaurants—maybe they served liquor—and past a couple of shacks with partially clad women sitting out front. Looked like whorehouses to me, but I have led a sheltered life.

Up the hill. Grafton and Noon were in an earnest, quiet conversation. I wondered what that was all about but was too conventional to ask. When Grafton wants me to know something, he tells me. Got that habit in the navy, I guess, and his wife never broke him of it. As we approached, I could see a lot of people on the roof, trying to get a bit of fresh air and sun. Got glimpses of them through the gun cuts in the wall, which as I knew was about six feet thick.

So we walked into the fortress, which stank despite the desert wind coming through the door and flowing out the gun ports. People packed in there like it was a Japanese railway car. I thought I could smell diesel fuel, but maybe not. Sure got a good whiff of human excrement and unwashed bodies.

Noon introduced Grafton to the captain, I think. He was wearing what had once been a white uniform and had four stripes on his shoulder boards. He and Grafton had another quiet conversation. The captain did a lot of talking and Grafton listened. When the admiral spoke, the captain listened carefully.

Those two were still at it when some television guy who said his name was Ricardo came blasting in, talking loudly. “You’re with the American government,” he said to Grafton. “We’re the press, and that pirate has imprisoned us. You must get us out immediately.”

“All these people have the same problem,” Grafton said mildly. “Why don’t you go sit down and let me finish my conversation with Captain Penney?”

“But we’re the press,” he howled. “Television reporters.”

“And these people are consumers of your wonderful product. Sit down, please.”

The fellow looked as if he needed a more forceful argument to persuade him, so I latched onto the back of his neck with one hand and squeezed a little. Marched him into the next room and found a vacant spot to drop him. He spluttered all the way.

Two women buttonholed me before I could get back to Grafton. “You’re with the American government?”

I admitted it.

“They took a woman from here. Nora Neidlinger. She’s—”

“She sorta slim, brunette, short hair, tan, with a nice figure?”

“Why, yes.”

“I’ve seen her.”

“Is she okay?”

“She’s alive.”

“Her daughter is beside herself.”

“I see.”

Truly, I didn’t know what else to say. I went on, saw an Arab in there, Atom something, some Italians, Brits, Americans from all over. All of them were in bad shape. Most of them seemed to be suffering from dehydration. All of them were dirty . . . they told me of dysentery, of the people that had died the previous night.

By the time I got back to Grafton I was ready to strangle some pirates. Grafton must have seen it in my face. He led me outside to where Noon was waiting.

“Mr. Noon, we’ll be down the hill shortly. Would you meet us in the square?”

Noon set forth down the hill. Grafton looked around, then faced me.

"I see the wires going up the building. You were right—those are antennas. We can't dig the batteries and capacitors and detonators up, so we must find the radio controllers."

"You know there are more than one."

"Your job tonight is to find them. Start with Ragnar's hotel. I'll tell you when."

"How are we going to know if we got all of them?"

"We'll have to ask Ragnar, of course."

He started walking. I caught up with him, matched him stride for stride. He walked with his head down, looking at the road, lost in thought.

CHAPTER SEVENTEEN

Those people are sick," Jake Grafton said to Ragnar. "Seven dead of dysentery already, and more will die today and tonight. They need medicine and clean water, and the sickest ones need to be evacuated."

Grafton sounded like a man ordering a pizza. Didn't raise his voice, didn't look nervous or flustered, looked like a man in perfect control of himself and the situation. He looked like a man used to command.

High Noon translated that bit while I glanced around. The woman was still there, sitting in the corner. Obviously American or European, well-endowed, tan, nice set of legs and arms, a face that showed nothing. I suspected she wasn't having a pleasant time of it. Ragnar had her sitting there to show her off, his trophy, to his men and Grafton and me.

Before Ragnar could reply to Noon's translation, Grafton started talking again. "Nora Neidlinger"—he gestured at the woman—"was a passenger on that ship. She is an American. I want her released right now."

Ragnar's face darkened as he listened. I glanced at Neidlinger, who was wearing the best poker face I had ever seen. I wondered if she was sedated.

The pirate chieftain erupted. Words poured forth, plus much

gesturing. He was nervous, couldn't hold still. He looked at his men as much as he did Grafton, and I realized he was playing to them. He had to hold on to their loyalty no matter what. If he lost it, the gig was over. Nothing was more important than that.

Noon started talking, even though Ragnar didn't even pause. "Two hundred million American dollars in old bills. Three days from now. Friday. At noon. Or we kill them all. Everyone. Old, young, men, women, sick, healthy, all of them. No medicine. No tricks. No one leaves. Pay the money!"

When he wound down Grafton spoke in the same flat tone he had used before. "I told him I would speak to my government. Perhaps they will authorize more money. Perhaps not. In the meantime, he must show good faith. He must release Ms. Neidlinger and allow medicine, water and food to be brought in by helicopters. They can land on top of the fortress. The sickest people will be evacuated. Two helicopters. Only two."

"No."

Grafton found a chair and pulled it around and sat in it. He slouched and crossed his legs. Comfortable. "How do I know that Ragnar will release everyone and the ship after the money is paid?"

"You have my word."

"How do I know that you have not made a deal with the Shabab to kill them after you get the money?"

"Do you take me for a fool? I know that once the hostages are gone, the Americans and Europeans can attack this town and kill everyone in it. What is to prevent them? Only my doing as promised. My good faith and honor keeps me alive. And all my men. The hostages have not been harmed. When the money is paid they will be released."

"I have been told the Shabab wishes to betray you."

"A lie."

"You cannot spend corpses."

"Your people will be returned alive."

"We will not pay for dead people."

Ragnar's eyes became cold, hard. "I know about Osama bin Laden. I know your government can kill anywhere. Anyone. I need no threats."

"The Shabab would like to see you dead."

This comment went through the group like chain lightning. They snapped at each other, fingered their weapons; Ragnar shouted at one of his sons.

"Two hundred million American dollars," Grafton said, "but only for all the hostages. Nothing extra for anyone."

As Noon translated, Grafton walked over to the duffel bag that contained the money. It was still half full. He picked it up, turned it upside down and let the bills cascade onto the floor. He picked up a handful, looked at it, then tossed it down.

"Two hundred times this much," he said, glancing at Noon, who translated.

Grafton took his seat again and slouched comfortably.

Three more minutes of thrust and parry, but Ragnar kept looking at the bills heaped up on the floor. I knew then he was going to surrender, and so did Grafton.

When the pirates quieted down Grafton returned to the subject of helicopters. More harsh words. Ragnar kept glancing at the money from time to time.

Finally Ragnar nodded. Grafton held out his hand to me for the radio. I pulled it from the backpack without letting my underwear or the Ruger fall on the floor.

He turned the thing on, fiddled with frequencies and volume, then made a call. It was immediately answered.

"This is Grafton." He explained what he wanted. Two hours, he was told. He apparently knew the person on the other end, and they made a few personal remarks. Grafton closed with, "And I want you to send a message to the powers that be. Tell them Ragnar wants two hundred million and won't take a penny less."

"Wilco."

"Thanks, Toad."

Grafton put the radio in his shirt pocket, leaned back in the chair and laced his fingers behind his head. "Tell him two hours," he said to Noon, then turned and glanced at Neidlinger. Motioned to her. She rose and came over, stood near him while Ragnar's face flushed. He was one mean bastard; I could read it in his face.

"I may be able to get you out of here," he said. "These people want money so badly that—"

"No," she said softly, looking at him, not Ragnar.

A look of surprise crossed the admiral's face, then disappeared. "Why?"

"I'm going to kill the son of a bitch."

Grafton thought about that, studied her face for a few seconds, then said, "A better option would be to ride a chopper out of here and leave Ragnar to me. Take your daughter with you."

"No." The word came quickly.

Grafton seemed to be searching for words. "Revenge is a wonderful thing," he said finally, "yet it comes in many varieties. There is something going on here I don't understand."

She shrugged. Walked back to the corner and resumed her seat.

Grafton glanced thoughtfully at me, and his mouth made a little O. Then he scrutinized Ragnar and his sons and lieutenants, taking a moment to examine each one, as if committing their faces to memory. He took his time, as if he had all the time in the world. It was Ragnar who got the fidgets.

Grafton wiggled one finger at High Noon. "Tell him I want the American television reporter and photographer released from that prison. As a sign of his good faith, his honor."

Noon did so. Ragnar nodded once. One of the lieutenants left the room and started down the stairs. When his footsteps had faded, Grafton stood and shook out his trousers. "Mr. Noon, perhaps it would be best if we left before we wear out our welcome with the sheikh. Thank him for his hospitality. When I hear from my government, I will return for another negotiating session."

Noon made this statement, drawing himself up as he did so. To my relief, Ragnar didn't object. I got the impression that Grafton didn't care one way or the other.

When we reached the bottom of the stairs and exited the building, Grafton had my arm. The reporters were out in the square and ready with cameras and lights. "We'll get to them in a minute," he said. He wrapped a hand around my arm and gently pulled me for a block or so, then into the doorway of a building so dirty and old that I looked for the sign DR. LIVINGSTON SLEPT HERE. With his mouth only six inches or so from my ear, he told me his plan, and my part in it. The exposition took fifteen minutes. I could feel the panic start way down inside me, well up like hot lava. The hairs on the backs of my arms and hands stood to attention.

I had objections, of course. What if I failed to achieve the results he wanted? What if the pirates killed me?

"They won't," he said dismissively.

There are some things about Jake Grafton that I am not skeptical about anymore. He is the coolest, most calculating gambler alive, he will stake everything on his ability to force events to unfold as he wills them, he has ice water in his veins and no nerves at all, and when he strikes, he does so suddenly, violently and ruthlessly, with devastating accuracy and effect. In truth, he is the embodiment of the perfect warrior.

There are days when I think he should forgo clothes and wear a steel suit, complete with helmet, chain-mail gloves, sword and lance. This was one of them.

"Sir Jake," I muttered as he went into greater detail about my role in his drama.

"What?"

"Nothing. A brain fart. Forget it."

Ten minutes later we went out into the square. Ricardo was getting set up. His photographer told me the generator would take a few minutes to get enough charge on his batteries to get him back in business.

Grafton wasn't waiting. He was chatting with Sophia Donatelli and the BBC dude, Rab Bishop. The Brit was pretty buttoned-down, I thought. He wanted to know Grafton's background, a subject the admiral wasn't interested in throwing much light on.

In a few minutes, Ricardo was ready to go. As the three cameras focused on him, Grafton spoke easily, as cool as a congressman just reelected by a landslide.

"I have been having discussions with Sheikh Ragnar. The sheikh has agreed to allow two helicopters from Task Force 151 to provide humanitarian aid to the passengers and crew of the *Sultan*. They should land on the fortress in a little more than an hour. Meanwhile, I shall relay his ransom demands to my superiors, who of course have given them careful consideration, and will do so again. The British and American governments are philosophically opposed to paying ransom to pirates, yet there are humanitarian considerations here that must be weighed carefully. Sometimes public policy must bow to the sanctity of human life. We will know more in a few hours, I hope. If you have any questions, I will try to answer them within the scope of my authority, which, as you may suspect, is very limited."

I knew Grafton was slick, but he had a talent as a liar that would have done credit to Bernard Madoff. He should have been a politician.

They had questions, and he deflected most of them. They would have to wait.

Then he was done and walked away. I went with him. The press got busy packing up and moving up the hill to photograph the choppers arriving and departing.

The evening was upon us. The ocean to the east was shrouded in darkness.

I was tired, and I realized I wasn't going to get any sleep. Grafton sat on a piece of a box that had washed up on the beach and talked awhile on his handheld radio. It didn't have much range, but he was chatting with Toad Tarkington aboard *Chosin Reservoir*; I doubted if the ship was over ten miles away. Just in case, I suspected the E-2 Hawkeye from the aircraft carrier farther north was overhead to relay the signal, and of course Tarkington probably had an Osprey or two aloft. Plus drones. I wondered if Ragnar realized how tight the net already was.

Ragnar, his two sons, and Mustafa al-Said huddled around a radio set up in a room on the third floor of his building. The radio had come out of a captured ship and could run through the UHF and VHF frequencies that the allied task forces used to communicate. The technician spoke some English, enough to get the drift of remarks, but tonight he was having his problems.

All the tactical transmissions among the ships and SEALs and planes were encrypted. About the only plain-language transmissions he could intercept were aircraft control freqs in use around the ship, and were quite useless to him, most of the time. Other than the fact that certain aircraft were airborne, and how many, a nonexpert listening to this stuff heard most of it as useless tidbits, and numbers could easily be over- or understated to confuse eavesdropping baddies.

However, tonight the technician had found and was listening to Jake Grafton's plain-language discussion with Toad Tarkington. Grafton told the admiral afloat that he wanted two helos, all the clean water they could carry, soap, medicine for intestinal problems and a doctor. He wanted the choppers to land on the roof of the fortress, off-load their supplies and evacuate sick people. The technician translated as much of that as he could for Ragnar and his men.

Then Grafton got into the amount of money Ragnar wanted. Toad read Grafton snippets of messages that, he said, were pouring out of Washington. After fifteen minutes, Ragnar learned that Grafton had the authority to agree to pay two hundred million in cash to Ragnar, but the money wouldn't arrive aboard ship until the following day. Toad recommended a delivery Friday morning, after Grafton had agreed on the amount and the method of transport of the prisoners after they were released.

What Ragnar didn't know, of course, was that all this was merely good theater. Still, he and his men discussed the conversation they had overheard, and were pleased. They had won. The allies were going to cave. They were going to be filthy rich.

Two miles inland, at the headquarters of the Shabab in the village beside the river, Yousef el-Din was also listening.

He and his lieutenants made their plans. If Ragnar and his pirates were dead when the two hundred million arrived, they could collect it in their place and use it to fund jihad. The irony of using infidel money to buy weapons from infidels to kill infidels was delicious to contemplate.

Of course, the Shabab would kill all the prisoners. "God's curse be upon the infidels," says the holy Koran. "Believers, make war on the infidels who dwell around you. Deal firmly with them. Know that God is with the righteous."

This triumph would be the ultimate terror strike against the Great Satan. The power of the Shabab would be on display for all the world to see. America and her allies would react violently, of course, and that bloodletting would unite the faithful worldwide in the ultimate jihad, the final cataclysmic battle between good and evil.

Since they fought God's battles, the warriors of the true faith would win, once and for all. Their reward in Paradise would be great indeed. The Koran promised endless virgins to deflower and boys to bugger, prospects that appealed mightily to Yousef el-Din, who did his best to anticipate his reward right here on earth.

Yousef el-Din and his lieutenants could scarcely contain themselves.

Allah akbar!

After a while Jake Grafton and High Noon strolled into Ragnar's building to see the man. No doubt they were going to negotiate some more on how much ransom the good guys were going to pay. I was sure Grafton would be a super-hard sell yet eventually capitulate, filling Ragnar's hard little heart with greedy hope . . . but, of course, I now knew that Grafton intended to pay nothing, nada, zip point zilch more than the million he had already laid on Ragnar.

Knowing Grafton, I suspected he would also figure out a way to get most of that million back. No doubt he planned a tiny role for me in that repossession.

I sat on a handy rock and surveyed Ragnar's building. The Italians built it, I knew, back when this was Italian Somalia. Balconies faced the sea, but the other three sides had only windows. The walls had the usual decorations, little ledges and cornices. I estimated the distance between them. Yes, the building could be free-climbed.

The windows were bright with electric lights. Obviously the building had a generator. As far as I could see, it was the only one in town. Everyone else had candles and lanterns to keep the night away, so the town was much darker than one would see in Europe or the Americas.

I sat watching the crowd as the evening deepened. One of the television reporters was busy chattering into the cameras as the portable lights illuminated the scene. The other two reporters were already up at the fortress. Hordes of local kids stood behind the reporter, mugging for the cameras. The technician running the diesel generators was passing out candy bars to the kids. He tried to make the goodies last, but soon he was out and the kids abandoned him to his noisy machine.

A few entrepreneurs had set up grills and were selling food. I wasn't tempted. The locals ate the stuff with their fingers. I didn't see a single Somali woman in the crowd. Lots of kids, men with AKs and unarmed men just wandering around, but no women. Every now and then one of the kids or men would relieve themselves in the sand. Or on the plaza.

A bonfire burned in the plaza. The flickering light made the scene look like something out of Dante.

The hot wind blew gently off the desert, and waves flopped on the beach. By all appearances, it was just another night in Somalia.

Up on the point I could see some light leaking out the gun ports of the old fortress. Eight hundred fifty people hunkered in there . . .

I stood up, dusted off my fanny and hoisted my backpack, and walked across the plaza toward the road that would take me up the hill. I wanted to be there when the helos arrived.

CHAPTER EIGHTEEN

Susan B. Grant was the name of the freighter lying in the mud below the fort on the north side of the harbor. The slope of the hill came down to the beach at perhaps a thirty-degree angle, and the beach was perhaps fifty yards wide. The six-thousand-ton bulk carrier lay two hundred yards from the beach. She had been anchored there in June. Her bulk had caused the discharge from the small river to slow there, and silt to accumulate. In addition, the natural movement of sand southward along the beach was disrupted, so sand mixed with the silt. *Susan B. Grant* now rested solidly on the silt-sand mixture, which was building up around her hull. At most, only ten feet of water circulated around her rusty sides.

Ten feet of water was plenty for the SEALs. Five of them swam in after darkness had fallen and used grappling hooks to scale the seaward side of *Susan B. Grant*. Once aboard, they began inspecting the ship, searching for pirates and weapons and anything else that looked interesting.

Petty Officer First Class Doggy Reed was the senior man, and he kept *Chosin Reservoir* Ops appraised of his progress. Thirty minutes after he and his mates had boarded, he was convinced that the SEALs were the only people aboard. They went into the hold and began testing the cargo. It was fertilizer, all right, with a lot of ammonium nitrate mixed in. A few simple chemical tests proved that.

The bad news was that hundreds of tons appeared to be missing. The stuff had apparently been shoveled out by hand; mounds of it were strewn about the weather deck. Not to worry, however; at least five thousand tons remained aboard in the holds.

Someone had squirted a large quantity of diesel fuel from the ship's bunkers into the fertilizer, perhaps a hundred tons of it, and the fuel had been absorbed by the fertilizer, discoloring it and giving it a distinctive petroleum odor.

The people who had rigged this crude bomb then placed five explosive charges to ignite it, charges that would be triggered by a radio signal. The radio receiver was there, the trigger mechanism, batteries, a capacitor and the explosive charges, the detonators, to ignite the whole mess.

Simple, crude and effective, Doggy Reed concluded, and relayed that opinion over the radio to the ship.

The SEALs then set about taking the pirates' radio receiver and controller out of the system. They merely unhooked the wires and carried the radio unit topside.

While his men finished the work, Doggy Reed went out on deck for a careful squint at the fort. Just for kicks, he used a laser range finder to establish the exact distance that separated the ship and fort. Three hundred twelve yards.

Oh boy. If the AN in the ship's hold exploded, the blast would probably collapse the nearest walls of the fort, which would bring the ceiling down and bury anyone inside.

Reed turned his night-vision goggles toward the town of Eyl, which lay about a mile away. The explosion might well flatten Eyl, too.

It would take a callous man to set off this bomb, Reed decided. He wondered who had rigged it, the pirates or the Shabab?

Five thousand tons of ammonium nitrate. God almighty!

His next thought followed that one. Had his team found all the original radio triggers? If they missed even one . . .

. . .

Aboard *Sultan of the Seas,* Mike Rosen was getting frustrated. His ship had swung enough on the tide that he had a quartering view of the Eyl plaza from his stateroom. He saw the television reporting teams' lights, and the bonfire, and knew in his bones that something important was happening. Unfortunately, High Noon hadn't been aboard all afternoon to escort him to the e-com center, so he had missed his evening Internet fix. He also hadn't had anything to eat since he gobbled some stale bread this morning, and he was hungry.

It was Tuesday night. The pirates' deadline wasn't until Friday noon, but there must be news on the Internet, maybe even e-mails from the newsroom of his radio station, about whether someone was going to pay the ransom. Or talk Ragnar into joining civilization.

He went to the door of his stateroom, unlocked it and jerked it open. His guard was squatting in the passageway, two doors down, taking a shit. Making progress, too.

Revulsion swept over him. Rosen slammed the door shut and locked it. Stalked back through the stateroom, around the bed, to the French door. Opened it and went out onto the little balcony.

No one in sight on the other balconies, no heads visible on deck above him . . .

Rosen made an instant decision. He leaned out to the next balcony rail, grasped it and scrambled over. The stateroom was empty. So was the next one, and the next.

Getting more comfortable now, he stood on the rail, grasped the stanchions of the balcony above and managed to haul himself up. He did it one more time, so he was on the same deck as the e-com center. He tried the French door on this stateroom. Unlocked. It slid right open. No lights except the emergency EXIT sign over the door and the faint glow of Eyl coming through the glass. He unlocked the door to the passageway and eased it open just enough to allow him to take a look aft. The passageway was lit by low-level emergency fixtures mounted near the floor. Empty. Another look forward. Also empty.

Listening carefully, hearing nothing, for at least a minute, Rosen looked around for a way to block open the door, since it would lock when it was closed. He stepped into the dark bathroom, got a towel and used a corner of it as a doorstop.

Listened another few seconds, screwed up his courage and stepped into the passageway. The door closed to within an inch. He checked the room number, then set off.

Made it to the e-com center without running into anyone.

His computer took its own sweet time booting up, giving Mike a bad moment. What a time for the thing to catch a virus! Boot up it did, though, and in seconds he was on the Internet.

He tried to get some news video from the reporters in Eyl, giving up after the computer stalled on each of several attempts. Not enough bandwidth.

Checked the KOA Radio Web site. Yep, plenty of news there, along with his picture and some of his e-mails reporting from the *Sultan*. Management was playing their access to Ragnar, through Rosen, for all it was worth.

Wire service reports were more current. The government was coordinating negotiating efforts. The ship's insurance company had agreed to pay what it could. The government had sent a negotiator, not named, to treat with Ragnar. The governments involved had pledged to do everything possible to ensure the safe return of the hostages. There were lengthy quotes from bigwigs: secretary of state, defense secretary, foreign secretary of the U.K. government, the foreign minister of France, some Saudi prince . . .

Rosen read it all.

Well, he thought, at least the politicians were reacting to the spotlight of public opinion.

Finally he tackled his e-mails. His producer was begging for all the info he could send. His ex-wives were worried, his kids were worried, his mom was worried, his brother was worried. His stand-in host for his morning talk show while he was abroad was also worried, but happy. "You're going to be famous," he said. "Someone will hire you away and I'll inherit your time slot."

Sure enough, there was an e-mail from his agent, who said he had fielded inquiries about Mike's contract from two networks, who were talking about an hour cable television show five days a week.

Mike Rosen turned off the computer and sat in the dark thinking about the situation. About the crewmen and passengers the pirates killed. About the semideserted ship. About how hungry he was. About the guard taking a dump in the hallway. About High Noon and his gin bottles. About scavengers rooting though cabins and storerooms. About starving Somalis. About pirates!

Aauugh!

His ruminations were interrupted by his stomach growling. He stood, looked out the window at the old fortress. The light seeping out the gun ports made tiny squares in the evening gloom.

He thought about taking his computer with him, then recalled the scramble along the balconies and left it on the table.

Listening, carefully looking around corners, Rosen made his way to the forward stairwell and went down it one deck to the dining room. It appeared empty, but in the semidarkness of the emergency lighting, he wasn't sure. Moving as quietly and stealthily as possible, he sneaked into the room and headed for the kitchen.

He had almost made it when he tripped on something.

Caught himself. Looked hard . . . and realized he was looking at a body. A pirate, by the look of his dark pullover shirt and trousers and sandals. A pool of blood by his throat. His head was tilted back at an unnatural angle, his arms and legs akimbo. No weapons visible.

Rosen stood frozen, with only his eyes moving. Sweat poured down his face, soaking his collar. His armpits were wet, his legs trembling. He tried to swallow but couldn't.

For the first time he was aware of noises. Little noises, random, of mechanical things. Little clicks and creaks and groans. And movement. Almost imperceptible, but definitely there, a gentle, rhythmic back-and-forth as the ship rode the Indian Ocean swells.

Steeling himself, Rosen stepped over the body and eased into the kitchen. His eyes were adjusted to the low illumination, and he had no trouble seeing that the space was empty of people. Full of stoves and sinks and cold lockers and worktables and pots and pans strewn about . . . and cans of food . . . Trying to be quiet, he found bread. Cheese. A knife.

Not much of a knife, but a sharp kitchen paring knife, which he pocketed. Some kind of canned spread. It was too dark to read the label, and he had no can opener.

Moving on, he found frozen bags of cooked food, to which he helped himself. It would thaw.

With his arms loaded, he looked for a bag, some way to carry his loot. Found a tray. Well, why not? He'd never get it over those balconies, but he could store the food in the stateroom he had exited from and nibble on it from time to time.

When he turned to go he got another shock. A man was standing in the kitchen doorway looking at him. A man all in black. Wearing some kind of goggles and headset. Carrying a weapon on a strap over a shoulder.

Rosen tried to speak, but it came out a croak.

"You crew or passenger?" the guy asked conversationally. American accent.

"Passenger."

"What are you doing here?"

"Getting something to eat."

A chuckle. "Got a name?"

"Mike Rosen."

"Ah, yes. They said you might be aboard. I've read some of your e-mails. Informative. Tell you what. Spread out your staff and have a picnic right there while I keep watch. I think we've got all the bad guys, but I wouldn't bet the ranch on it."

Rosen eased his burdens to a worktable. He was acutely aware of the knife in his pocket. The American was talking, apparently on a radio headset. "Okay, I found Rosen. He's here grazing in the eighth-deck galley . . . Roger."

Now Mike could see the man was wearing a black wet suit and had things strapped to him, pockets and such. "You kill that guy behind you?" Mike asked.

"One of my colleagues did, I'm sure. I don't know which one."

"Got a name?"

"Duff Finnorn. U.S. Navy. Petty officer."

"Pleased to meet you."

"Eat."

Finnorn was moving, checking the other entrances to the space.

Mike Rosen sat down and tore off a piece of bread. He stuffed it into his mouth and chewed. Finnorn came back in a few minutes, and they talked as Rosen ate.

Finnorn was a SEAL. Had boarded the ship about an hour ago, just after dark, along with six mates. They were eliminating the pirates.

"Killing them?"

"Or capturing them. Obviously, we can't take them anywhere, but we put ties on their wrists and hands and put them in a compartment, which we lock. Maybe they'll get rescued by their mates one of these days. Or they won't."

Finnorn spoke again into his headset. Rosen was drinking room-temperature tea from a quart container when two more SEALs came in. They ignored him and spoke to Finnorn.

"We've got them all, we think. Five dead, four locked up. Joe and Walt are checking the machinery spaces. Two Brits down there. The guy guarding them didn't make it. The Brits are coming here for food."

"I'll keep Mr. Rosen company for a while." The other SEALs flipped hands at Mike and strode away, their weapons at the ready.

From somewhere Finnorn produced a flashlight and began rooting in the cupboards and coolers, which were off. The food in there was spoiling. He found a can opener, however, and said, "Eureka. Now we feast. Better look at these cans. Heck, they got marmalade and caviar . . . How about caviar on crackers?"

Rosen was feeling human again. Americans. SEALs.

"Where you from?"

"Oh, hell, everywhere, I suppose. My dad was in the service and dragged us all over. You?"

"Denver." Mike swallowed hard. Trying to keep his voice normal, he asked, "You guys gonna get us outta here?"

"Absolutely. No question. Isn't that what the sports announcers say? Me and a lot of other folks. Let's not get into that. Sorta a secret. Oh, look! Peanut butter."

. . .

I was standing on the roof of the old fortress when the two helicopters approached from over the water. Their lights were on, they made lots of noise, and their landing lights were almost too brilliant to look at.

Captain Arch Penney was there beside me, along with the doctor and crewmen helping, half-carrying sick people. Almost two dozen of them sick with diarrhea and vomiting and a few other ills.

Three or four pirates were standing to one side, AKs on their hips, pointed up. They were young and I guess trying to look tough, but they only looked nervous. This was big doings for Eyl, I suppose.

The choppers settled down on the roof, raising a cloud of dirt and grit, and men sprang out with boxes of supplies and drums of liquid. Water. Wouldn't be enough for all these people, but it would help for a day or so. The water and supplies they stacked out of the way. One of the guys saw me, came over and handed me a radio headset. I put it on and was instantly on the net.

Crew chiefs were giving orders. An officer in blue navy camos, carrying a duffel bag on his shoulder, walked over to where I was standing. He talked to Penney, then began looking at the patients. The doctor, I figured.

The evolution went with little lost motion. When all the supplies were off, the crewmen began carrying the sick people out to the choppers and passing them to people on board.

Captain Penney escorted a woman to a chopper, got her aboard, then came over to where I was standing. "That's a woman named Dol Bass. Her husband jumped into the ocean and a pirate shot him. She doesn't need any more of this."

He made a few more remarks, and I gave him a smile. He looked as if he needed it.

These helicopters weren't large machines. I am no expert on choppers, but these were armed and had machine guns on them. Sensors sprouted like warts from their chins and sides.

I didn't think there would be enough room for the two dozen passengers, but the navy guys put them aboard anyway, then scampered aboard themselves. The lead chopper lifted off. More dirt flew around.

The second bird was right behind. They swung out over Eyl, turned and headed out to sea. The noise and lights faded.

I turned my attention to the doctor, who went down the stone stairs into the building with Captain Penney. In just a moment the top of that old place was empty except for me and the pirates.

I went down into the fort to see how things were. The *Sultan* crewmen were unloading the boxes, which contained MREs. To keep the pirates from getting ideas, I put my radio and headset in my backpack.

Penney pointed out one of the pirates to me. I had seen him with Ragnar and knew he was a big cheese. "Mustafa al-Said," Penney whispered. "He was the leader of the crew that captured my ship."

I made sure I would recognize him when I saw him again, then ignored him. He didn't know it, but he wasn't going to get much older.

Mike Rosen and Petty Officer Finnorn watched the choppers from the *Sultan*'s galley. Finnorn explained to Rosen what was going on. Supplies coming in, sick people going out.

"Ragnar agreed to this?"

"Yep. We got a guy negotiating. Fellow named Grafton. I hear he's one tough nut."

As the helicopters flew seaward, Finnorn produced a waterproof pouch from inside his wet suit. He opened it, extracted a piece of paper. "Is your computer still working? Can you still send e-mails?"

"Yeah."

"Finish up your chow and let's go up to the computer center. Here's an e-mail that the task force commander would like you to send."

"Hold that flashlight so I can read this." Finnorn did so.

Rosen couldn't believe his eyes. This is part of what he read: "The militant Islamic group Shabab is planning to wipe out Sheikh Ragnar and his pirates within the next twenty-four hours. Ragnar is aware of their plans, which have leaked, and plans a preemptive strike in the next few hours."

There was more, including the names of five Shabab officers, and some quoted communications with Shabab forces in southern Somalia. One of the quotes was from some Muslim cleric who gave the Shabab a fatwa concerning the righteousness of killing the pirates and infidel prisoners.

"Is this true?" Rosen asked, aghast.

"Man, I'm just a sailor who takes orders. Let's go get this on the Internet as written. No editorializing, no extraneous stuff, just the words on this paper."

"Wait a minute. What guarantee do I have that—"

"No guarantees, no explanations," Finnorn said bluntly. "The admiral wants this on the Internet. He wants you to do your e-mail trick to get it there. Now. Or sooner. You did a hitch in the army way back when and worked for several years as a civilian in the Pentagon. Maybe you remember how to salute and obey orders. Grab your sandwich and let's get at it."

"How do you know about my past?"

"You gotta be kiddin'! Of course the brass checked on you when you started e-mailing the hot steaming poop. If they didn't like the cut of your jib, you couldn't get your stuff on the satellite."

I wandered out of the fortress into the night. Passed the sentries, who gave me the eye but didn't stop me, and walked down the road that led to town. I checked, and no one followed me.

I was about halfway down when I passed Ricardo and his cameraman walking up. They ignored me. Just behind them came Jake Grafton and High Noon in Noon's old station wagon. Noon was behind the wheel. I leaned on the driver's door and got a snootful of gin smell. Apparently drunk driving wasn't a traffic offense in Somalia.

"Too lazy to walk?" I asked Grafton.

"Mr. Noon and I are in conference."

"I see that. You got any bright ideas on where the radio controls for the detonators are?"

"Mr. Noon assures me they are in Ragnar's palace, third floor. And guarded."

"What about hardwired triggers?"

"Geoff?"

"There's one in the shack on the side of the hill. That black wire that runs from the entrance of the fort off down the hill."

"Any others?"

"Not that I know of."

"You want to bet nine hundred lives on that?"

"Geoff is pretty sure," Grafton said.

"You seem to know a lot," I said, trying to see his face.

"MI-6, old chap. That's hush-hush, of course."

"Righto."

"Wear your headset. SEALs are going to assault the building. When they do, go in with them."

"When, do you think?"

"Before dawn, I suppose. Your colleagues will be standing by with their Sakos to give you cover, and the marines have some stuff on the *Sultan.*" He sighed. "Let the SEALs do the fighting, if there is any."

I was having my problems keeping my temper. "Jesus, where do you keep your crystal ball?" Amazingly, it didn't occur to me just then that Grafton knew because he had scripted it. "Before dawn?" I asked.

"I suspect the Shabab crowd will assault Ragnar's hideout, or he'll sally forth to wipe them out. Ragnar and the boys are going to realize they've been had when they see the SEALs, so we are going to do our best to help Shabab come out on top. With serious casualties, of course."

"Oh yeah."

"If the pirates and Shabab dudes party as scheduled, we'll invade tomorrow night."

The light began to dawn. I'm kinda slow on the uptake, but I get stuff sooner or later. "And if they don't?"

"We'll improvise. Maybe go to Plan B. We'll see."

"Why don't we just defend the fortress and hit the pirates and Shabab with air strikes from the carrier?"

Grafton shot me a sharp glance. "I considered that. I thought too many Somali civilians would probably get zapped, which would be politically incorrect. In this day and age you must win militarily *and* politically. I learned that in Vietnam 101."

"Uh-huh."

"Go up to the fortress and stay inside or on the roof until the fireworks start."

I addressed Noon. "You got any pearls of wisdom or suggestions?" I figured an MI-6 agent who had spent the last ten years in this shithole might have more insight than Grafton or I did.

"The pirates and holy warriors have let you and Mr. Grafton walk around unmolested because they think you will make them rich. If disabused of that notion, they will kill you without a qualm. It will simply be business as usual with Ragnar. The Shabab fanatics will kill you for the fun of it."

I slapped the car door, and Noon drove off. Another little cloud of dust. I held my breath until it settled, then walked back up the hill.

I was worried. If I had known more about Grafton's plan, I would have been petrified. Maybe it's a good thing I didn't.

CHAPTER NINETEEN

Sheikh Ragnar found out about the Rosen e-mail less than three hours after Rosen hit the SEND icon on his computer. The pirates and the Shabab had shortwave radio setups: the Shabab used theirs to communicate with fellow Islamic terrorists, and the pirates monitored international merchant ship traffic and the activities of the international antipiracy naval task force in Pirate Alley and the Indian Ocean.

The pirates' allies got on the radio first with the news, which was headline stuff in America, Europe and Asia. Ragnar, his sons and his most trusted captains, including Mustafa al-Said, conferred in the penthouse of his lair. Al-Said pointed out that Rosen was a captive aboard *Sultan,* incommunicado. "What could he know?" he asked rhetorically.

Ragnar instinctively knew that the truth of the e-mail was not the issue. The only question that mattered was how it would be received by the local Shabab leaders, whom he assumed already had it or would get it within minutes. Would Yousef el-Din discount the e-mail as a Western provocation initiated by the infidel Americans, or would he suspect the statements might accurately predict the reaction of the pirates to Shabab treachery?

Ragnar was acutely aware that el-Din, a homicidal paranoid sociopath, would shoot first and think later. He began issuing orders to call his men to arms.

As Ragnar suspected, el-Din and his lieutenants didn't even consider the possibility that the e-mail was a fraud. They heard about it from al Qaeda operatives in Pakistan, where the news of Rosen's e-mail was on television and the Internet. The Shabab indeed intended to betray the pirates, take the ransom money and kill all the hostages, so if the pirates learned of their plans, of course they would react violently. The only question in el-Din's mind was whether he could strike before the pirates were ready to defend themselves. The holy warriors awoke their troops, who grabbed weapons and ammo and ran to their armed pickup trucks.

"The Shabab is on the move in Eyl West," the drone controller reported to the Flag Ops Center aboard *Chosin Reservoir.* Everyone on the net heard the report in their headsets.

"They're excited in Eyl East," the drone operator reported less than a minute later. "Manning pickups, warming them up, armed men running to get aboard." I was wearing a headset and recognized Wilbur's voice.

I was standing with Jake Grafton, High Noon and the two Mossad agents Grafton had brought with him, Zahra and Ben, just inside the entrance to the fortress. Two emergency lanterns provided a little light, though not much. The Israelis were eyeing an Arab in decent, though rumpled, clothes who had had the ill luck to walk up on the group of strangers. The expression on his face was wondrous to behold as the fact sank in these two might be Mossad agents, or at least Israelis. Or perhaps it was just his conscience. He walked quickly away back into the gloom of the interior. The Israelis glanced at one another. I heard one say, "Mohammed Atom."

A pickup with a machine gun in the bed, a technical, came racing up the hill just as Wilbur announced on the net, "Lots of action in Eyl West. Armed men running everywhere." As I watched, a man got out of the passenger side of the pickup and conferred with the guards, who sent runners to pass the word to all the men in foxholes around the fortress.

Then the guy got back into the pickup and it roared off down the hill, its unmuffled exhaust rattling through the building as it faded.

When it was gone, I turned around, but the two Mossad agents had disappeared. "Who is Mohammed Atom?" I asked Grafton.

"An agent for Iranian interests throughout the Arab world. I think the guys would like to have a chat with him."

The television news teams were flaked out in a shack a hundred yards or so south of Ragnar's building, a shack with an old shirt for a door, candles for lights and a privy out back. The owner, a woman, was all smiles when they arrived, directed there by High Noon, who apparently knew everyone in town.

Sophia Donatelli got the best bed in the house, an old mattress suspended on ropes through a wooden frame. She inspected it while the BBC reporter, Rab Bishop, and Ricardo from Fox chattered away on their satellite telephones to their producers in England and America. Donatelli had seen worse accommodations, when she was just getting started in the business, and had thought that bug-infested beds and dirt floors were well behind her. She decided to sleep with her clothes on, as did everyone else. The ringing of a satellite telephone brought them awake about 3:00 A.M., which meant it was midnight in London and 7:00 P.M. in New York. While Rab Bishop was listening to someone tell him of the Rosen e-mail, they heard truck engines start, men running and shouting, and saw pickup headlights spear the night.

Ricardo grabbed his satellite phone and was the first to charge out of the shack. The rest of the crews were right behind him. They paused in front of the shack to watch. The sound of a distant machine-gun burst was quite audible and made the men boarding the pickups pause to listen.

"Whatever is happening, we'll have a devil of a time broadcasting it," Rab Bishop remarked. "Still, I suppose we can try. Let's get the generators going so we can datalink to the satellite."

Ricardo ran toward Ragnar's building. He was within feet of the door when he met a pirate coming out. The man had an AK at high port and was on a dead run. When he saw Ricardo with his satellite phone glued to his head, talking a blue streak, he halted.

He gestured once, back toward the south, and when Ricardo didn't instantly obey, triggered a burst right by the reporter's ear.

No fool, Ricardo turned and ran. Talking all the way, breathlessly. Literally a running commentary. His producer in the States put the conversation on the network. Within minutes, millions of people were listening to Ricardo's voice. The audience grew exponentially. All over America, people stopped what they were doing to watch Fox and listen to Ricardo.

The SEALs came out of the ocean silently, almost invisibly. They were in black wet suits, had black balaclavas on their heads and wore night-vision goggles. They crawled up onto the beach and scanned the empty Eyl town square and Ragnar's building with the night sights on their rifles.

Four pickups with machine guns surrounded Ragnar's lair. Other pickups roared up the river road toward Eyl West. Sounds of gunfire and muzzle flashes came from that direction.

The SEAL team leader, Chief Petty Officer Al Dunn, scanned the dark city with his night-vision binoculars. He saw men moving from house to house, carrying weapons. No women. No kids. Just armed men. He counted . . . and quit when he reached a dozen.

Dunn keyed the mike on his headset. "Blue Leader from Red Leader. Let's be ready with suppressing fire on those people in town when I give the word."

"Roger, Red Leader."

Aboard the *Sultan,* Bullet Bob Quinn settled in behind his .50-caliber sniper rifle. He could see people through his night-vision scope. His spotter, just beside him, would call his targets. Under the Rules of Engagement, he could only shoot people who had weapons. He relied upon his spotter to confirm the weapons.

Settling in a good shooting position with the rifle on a solid rest, loaded, Bullet Bob stared through his scope and watched the crosshairs move as the ship he was on rose on the ocean swells. The crosshairs moved regularly in a predictable, slow, sinuous dance.

The last of the pickups headed west on the river road, each crammed with armed men, some with RPG-7 launchers and bags of warheads, some with AKs, leaving only the four around Ragnar's building.

Through his night sniper scope, Quinn studied the four machine-gun emplacements on Ragnar's roof. He could see people moving around, standing up, looking here and there, carrying ammo belts.

Each gun was surrounded by a little wall of sandbags, making a nice little fortification for protection from small-arms fire. Nothing else. Still, since they were six stories above ground level, the machine-gun crews had positions that commanded the square and town.

Quinn took stock of his breathing and heart rate. Normal, he decided. He took several deep breaths, then willed himself into a shooter's calm.

Aboard *Chosin Reservoir* Rear Admiral Toad Tarkington checked to see where his drones were, then the fighters from the carrier. They were airborne and in about five minutes would be at the Initial Point, where they would hold until needed. If they were needed. Their ability to hold was finite. Fuel was always a consideration. Tankers were in the air, but they could merely top off tanks, not keep a strike force airborne indefinitely.

The MEU was not ready to storm Eyl. Tomorrow it would be, but not tonight. Tomorrow marines would come ashore in armored personnel carriers to the north and south of town. They would land on the beaches and get ready to roll into Eyl. They could kill every pirate and holy warrior in the place, rescue the hostages and be out of there in a couple of hours. Tomorrow.

Grafton's objective tonight was the radio controls for the bomb in the trenches around the fortress. The SEALs would neutralize the explosive potential of the cargo of the freighter grounded near it. If the trench bomb or shipload of fertilizer exploded, there would be no *Sultan* passengers or crew alive to rescue.

Jake Grafton wanted, if possible, to let the pirates and Shabab kill each other while he disabled the trench bomb. Every pirate and holy warrior who got launched for Paradise tonight was one less the marines and SEALs would have to face.

In the flag spaces aboard *Chosin Reservoir,* Rear Admiral Toad Tarkington tried not to think about the possibility of the bombs detonating. He already had SEALs on the beach and ships in the harbor. If those bombs exploded, he was going to lose American fighting men . . . and everyone in that fortress, including Jake Grafton, Toad's friend and mentor for many years. Toad tried to take his mind off Jake Grafton. Stop worrying about the marines. About the SEALs. About the eight hundred and fifty civilians imprisoned in that fortress. Stop worrying about how their families would feel losing these people. Think about how to win.

Toad knew what Grafton would say, because he knew Jake Grafton. *Put all those people out of your mind, Toad. Concentrate on the job in front of you. And with a free and easy mind, go forth and give battle.*

The battle west of town, up the river, was heating up. A cacophony of automatic weapons could be heard, almost a continuous background noise. The pirates and Shabab were shooting it out.

Jake Grafton took Captain Arch Penney's arm and pulled him to one side. I sidled closer so I could overhear what he said. Eavesdropping is one of my failings.

"The pirates have buried explosives in a trench around this building, Captain. Tons of them. They say they will blow the fort up and kill everyone if the ransom isn't paid. We need to find the radio receivers and batteries that power the detonators. To do that, we're going to have to eliminate the guards."

"Eliminate?"

"We are going to kill them," Grafton said flatly. "After we do, I want you to get some of your men and carry the bodies down to the beach. There is a sand overhang at the high tide level. Put them alongside it and cave it in, covering them up."

I could see Penney mulling it.

"What if some of them are only wounded?"

"Finish them off. Think you can do it?"

"They threw some of my wounded men into the ocean to drown. Yes."

Jake nodded, then turned to me. "Tommy, give me that Ruger." I had the silenced assassin's pistol in my hand.

That was Jake Grafton. Make no mistake, he could pull a trigger. One time in Hong Kong I saw him—

Now he glanced at the guards, who were intent on the drama in the plaza in Eyl, about a mile away but plainly visible. Muzzle flashes strobing the darkness, the burning pickup . . .

I pulled the Kimber from my waistband.

"No," Grafton said. "No noise yet. Give me the Ruger."

"No," I said. My voice came out a croak. "You're the brains. I'm just a shooter."

I knew this was coming, so I didn't freak out on the spot. I didn't think Mrs. Carmellini's boy Tommy was going to get much older, but what the heck! I had the silenced Ruger .22 in my hand. The magazine held nine rounds, and I had a spare loaded magazine in my pocket.

I looked at the faces around me, Arch Penney, his wife, the chief steward, and behind them passengers, their faces barely visible in the dim light.

Grafton slapped me on the back, then used his headset to tell E.D. and Travis I was coming out. Heard them Roger the heads-up. In a way, that was comforting. With night scopes on their rifles, those two snipers were almost as deadly after dark as they were during the day.

I stepped outside, walked toward the two gate guards, who were nervously watching the battle in the town. They glanced at me, didn't pay me much attention.

I put the pistol right behind one man's ear, pulled the trigger, then shot the other one before the first one hit the ground.

A forty-grain .22 bullet isn't much of a weapon unless it's fired into the skull at point-blank range and penetrates the bone into the brain mass. A solid point is best for this kind of work; a hollow point may explode against the skull and not penetrate the brain case. Still, only one bullet may not kill, may merely put the victim in the hospital with a horrible brain injury, making him a vegetable. Eyl didn't have a hospital, but still. I shot each man again in the head while he lay on the ground.

Then I picked up their assault rifles and the bags that held their extra magazines and hustled back to Grafton, who was standing in the portal to the fortress.

I gave him one rifle and an ammo bag, and he set off up the stairs toward the roof. I followed.

"We have to take out the men in the foxholes," he said over his shoulder. "The bomb dudes gotta disconnect the radio receivers from the batteries." On the roof he waved me toward the north side of the big roof, and he ran toward the south side.

The crenellations in the wall around the roof, designed so that cannons could blast away at ships in the roadstead or troops advancing along the beach, gave us excellent fields of fire. We were looking down into the foxholes, which weren't really foxholes at all, but merely mounds of earth. The guards had been on the outside, so they could look toward the fort and keep people from crawling out the gun portals, but now they were on the inside of the mounds, looking out. Survival instinct, I guess. Down there in the darkness were the muzzle flashes. Nothing was happening in the fort.

They were hard to see at first, but as my eyes became adjusted to the low light leaking from the gun portals I could just make out the guys hunkered down in the first guard position, with their backs to me.

Since I didn't have an ounce of sporting blood in me, I shot them both in the back as fast as I could pull the trigger. Ducked down and ran to my left, toward the next portal.

These guys were looking around in all directions, trying to figure out what was happening. I popped the first one, but the second guy hosed a bullet my way. Must have gone over my head toward Arabia, because I didn't hear it smack into the stone. I shot him before he got off a second shot.

Somewhere behind me I heard the boom of the Sako. E.D. or Travis was helping Grafton nail the guards over there. Grafton's rifle cracked repeatedly.

By the time I got to the third guard position, it was empty. The guys were probably boogying down the hill toward the beach. I got a glimpse of one and sent a bullet after him to speed him on his way.

The easternmost guard position was empty.

Grafton left me on the roof while he went below to get the bomb disposal guys into action. In a minute I saw the three of them working with a shovel below my position, along the wall of the fort, digging around an antenna that disappeared into the earth.

Things were quieting down in Eyl. Every now and then a heavy machine gun aboard *Sultan*—I saw the muzzle flashes—put a burst into Ragnar's lair, probably just to keep their heads down.

A couple of sharp cracks reached my ears, different from the reports of AKs or machine guns. Or the Sako. I couldn't place them.

"E.D., where are you?"

"In the brush up on the hill above the fort."

"Keep an eye peeled."

More gunfire. Several RPG explosions. I saw two launchings, the signature flames unmistakable, and heard the warheads detonate. Eight or ten minutes passed, and the battle up the river road quieted down. An ominous silence settled over this corner of Africa.

On my headset I heard the SEALs giving orders. Any pickups coming into town from any direction were to be disabled.

After perhaps ten minutes, Grafton called me on the headset. "Come on down, Tommy."

He was waiting at the portal with the Mossad bombers.

"It wasn't AN in that trench," he told me, his voice tired. "It's PVV-5A. Tons of it. Looks like they laced it with a little diesel fuel as a booster for the fuses. We found six radio-controlled detonators, each powered by three pickup-truck batteries. That's all of them, I hope, but who the hell knows? The only way to be sure is to find one of their garage door openers or radio triggers and push the button."

I just nodded. Grafton was a gambler with absolutely no nerves. He could clean out Las Vegas.

"We have to check out Ragnar's hive," he muttered.

I nodded.

Grafton keyed the transmit button on his belt and spoke into the headset mike. "Red Leader," Jake Grafton said. "This is Team Leader. Light them up."

"Aye aye, sir. Blue Leader, anytime you are ready."

I heard the words in my headset. Then I saw more muzzle flashes from the *Sultan*. A heavy machine gun sprayed the side of the hotel. I could see the sparkles of glass cascading down, hear the smacks as .50 caliber bullets tore into the side of the building, hear the ripping bursts carrying over the water.

For a second I thought of Nora Neidlinger, who was in that building, but then I pushed her out of my mind. She elected to stay . . . that was her choice.

By some miracle, Ricardo's cameraman had his camera running and the feed going to the satellite. He was standing in the door of the shack, Ricardo right beside him still on the satellite telephone, talking excitedly about what he could see.

The cameraman aimed his camera at Ragnar's building, scanned the pickups. Maybe it was instinct. Maybe it was luck. Whichever, he caught everything that happened in the next thirty seconds.

As the .50 caliber machine gun opened up, Bullet Bob Quinn settled on a machine gunner in the back of one of the pickups. The lights of the hotel were behind him, limning him. He was a nice target. The ship's movement brought the crosshairs onto him, and Quinn pulled the trigger. The recoil made him disappear.

"Got him," the spotter said. "Try the gunner on the truck to the left." Quinn shifted his aim.

Then an RPG round shot toward *Sultan* trailing a streak of fire, the rocket exhaust. Simultaneously the machine guns in one of the pickups opened up on the *Sultan*. It got off two bursts before the fifty chewed into it. Pieces flew, and the fuel tank exploded. Two other technicals got under way, only to be hit by automatic weapons fire that seemed to be coming from the beach. The last one started moving . . . and was hit by a rocket-propelled grenade. It too exploded and began burning brightly. A man with his clothes on fire managed to bail out and run about ten feet before he collapsed. The barrel of the machine gun in the bed pointed at Mars, up there somewhere in the night. Flames and flashes lit up the plaza as machine-gun ammo and RPG warheads in the beds of the trucks cooked off. It looked as if a string of large firecrackers was popping.

All four pickups had been destroyed in about fifteen seconds.

"Hellfire inbound." That was the voice of the controller aboard the flagship. The drones were shooting.

The first Hellfire missile exploded on the right front corner of the roof, a bull's-eye on the machine-gun nest. Two seconds apart, three other missiles impacted.

Through his scope, Quinn could see that the guns were gone, the sandbags lying about haphazardly. No one moved. No doubt they were all dead.

His spotter called a target, a man in the door of a house to the right, aiming an RPG-7 launcher. Bullet Bob fired first, and the RPG went soaring into the night sky. The rocket exhaust must have ignited the house, because it burst into flame.

"Go," Grafton said and slapped me on the back.

"Okay." I started walking into the darkness toward Eyl. The Israelis were right behind me. I keyed my mike. "Red Leader, this is Carmellini. Coming down."

"Roger that."

We broke into a trot, which soon became a run. Down the hill in the darkness, running, breathing hard, the sounds of gunfire in our ears . . . I confess, I was getting into the combat zone where it didn't matter if I lived or died. I had been there before, and it is addictive. Maybe it's the adrenaline. Or the knowledge you are cheating the devil.

The pickup that had been on fire was now just a glowing mass of twisted metal. Some bodies lay scattered about as I ran across the open space, followed by my two Israelis, but I was following a crowd. Four SEALs in black were ahead of me. I slowed my pace as they charged into the building.

There was the stutter of a submachine gun, just a short burst. Taking my time, I walked into the entrance and paused. The electric lightbulbs were still illuminated, so the generator was still going. Somewhere. I didn't hear it. A pirate's corpse was arrayed on the floor against the far wall, still bleeding from multiple chest wounds. Maybe his heart was still pumping. I didn't know or care. The SEALs were gone, up the stairwell.

The two Mossad agents had pistols in their hands. They looked around, then nodded at me. I could lead them or follow them. I was tempted to sit down in one of the old stuffed chairs and let them do their thing. However, if I did that and the trench bomb around the fort went off, destroying it and murdering everyone in the place . . .

That damn generator. Radio controls would probably be battery operated, but if there were a landline to the detonators, the generator was probably rigged to power it. It wouldn't be high in the building since it used diesel fuel. The pirates wouldn't want to carry cans up the stairs. The basement, then.

A burst of submachine-gun fire rattled down the staircase. Then a couple more. The SEALs were cleaning the place out.

I went around the stairs, found a door and opened it. There was an electric lightbulb on the ceiling, illuminating stairs going down. Now I could hear the low, steady throb of a diesel engine.

I found the Kimber .45 in my hand. When I drew it I don't know. Suddenly I realized it was there. I cocked the hammer and put the safety on. Some people carry those things cocked and locked, but without a holster to put the thing in, I never had that kind of sangfroid. Sooner or later I would have managed to shoot myself. I laid the assault rifle on a chair and, with both hands on the pistol, started down.

Mike Rosen was in the e-com center aboard *Sultan* when he heard the .50 caliber machine gun the SEALs had brought aboard open up. There was no mistaking the trip-hammer rips of a heavy machine gun firing bursts for anything else.

One of the windows popped. Rosen could see a hole in the glass, small, with cracks radiating out from it. Although he didn't know it, a bullet from the machine gun in one of the pickups in the Eyl square had found its way here. Just one. The only casualty was the glass.

He looked out the window and saw the burning pickups in the square in front of Ragnar's lair, saw muzzle flashes from automatic weapons and the distant flashing on the hills, up toward Eyl West.

He got back on his computer and began typing. The words poured out as fast as he thought them. He was a good typist and he was good with words, which were his stock-in-trade. Every minute or so he hit the SEND button; the Internet could crash anytime, and even if it didn't, he wanted to report as close to real time as he could.

At Rosen's radio home, KOA Denver, the e-mails were put on the Net at the same time the announcer read them over the air. All up and down the front range of the Rockies, people pulled their vehicles to the berm of the highway or the edge of the street and turned the volume of their radios up. Rosen wrote for them. He could see them in his mind's eye, and he wrote word pictures just for them.

"Captain, we have all three pirate skiffs on radar."

"Range?"

"Eight miles."

USS *Richard Ward,* an Arleigh Burke–class destroyer, approached Eyl from a course slightly north of west. The commanding officer, Commander Millicent C. Fjestad, had her ship inbound at ten knots. Her crew referred to her as The Old Woman, just as male commanding officers were traditionally called The Old Man. Less reverently, she was called Big Mama behind her back. Still, every man and woman aboard *Richard Ward* respected the captain. She was a highly competent naval officer who cared about her crew.

Her mission tonight was to sink all pirate skiffs at sea off the port of Eyl so that SEALs could egress without opposition. "Sanitize the area and keep it sanitized," flag ops said.

Like all American destroyers now in commission, *Richard Ward* had but one gun. It was a dilly, a Mark 45 Mod 4, in caliber 5"/62. This weapon fired a shell five inches in diameter weighing 70 pounds at a muzzle velocity of 2,650 feet per second. Its effective range was over 20 miles. Aimed by radar and computer, it was accurate and deadly.

The pirate skiffs, however, were not conventional enemy warships, with decent freeboards and a superstructure. They were boats, and their gunwales extended about a foot above the water. They were small, difficult targets. Big Mama Fjestad didn't intend to miss. She wanted them closer, not hull down on the horizon.

She worried about the depth of the water as she approached the Somali coast. There was a submerged sandbar about three miles offshore, and the channel across it was farther north. Of course the skiffs were inside the bar, cruising up and down, looking for God knows what. The sonar was giving the bridge crew a constant real-time reading on the depth of water.

Not a light shown from *Richard Ward* as she glided toward the coast. On the deck forward the gun barrel was alive, tracking the northernmost target as the destroyer closed the range.

At three miles from the skiffs, five miles offshore, the water shallowed to less than a hundred feet. Commander Fjestad turned her ship northward to parallel the coast.

Meanwhile, aboard the skiffs, the fireworks and muzzle flashes from Eyl were plainly visible. The crews were not searching the dark sea for enemy ships, but staring toward Eyl as their captains tried to raise someone on their hand-held radios.

Ten seconds after *Ward* was steady on her new course, the tactical action officer (TAO) called on the squawk box. "We are stabilized on all three targets, Captain. Request permission to shoot."

"Send them to hell," Big Mama said, then stuffed her fingers in her ears.

Two seconds later the Mark 45 rapped out three shots, about a second apart. The propellant gases still burning as the shells left the gun muzzle strobed the darkness. Now the gun barrel traversed at 30 degrees a second to the second target and stabilized. Boom, boom, boom, three more ear-splitting reports assaulted the bridge team, most of whom had fingers in their ears or were wearing ear protectors. Traverse to the next target, three more muzzle flashes and trip-hammer reports.

It was all over in twelve seconds.

Five seconds later the bridge squawk box came to life. "Captain, the targets have disappeared."

"Good shooting, people! Well done."

The Hellfire missiles that took out the machine guns on the roof of the lair cratered it. Chunks of brick, mortar, concrete and wooden beams were blasted down into the penthouse. Sheikh Ragnar was hit by a large piece, which knocked him unconscious. His two sons were there, and they too went down under the onslaught.

Nora Neidlinger was in the bedroom, under the bed, when the roof caved in. She wasn't hurt. For a long moment the air was opaque with dirt and dust and explosive residue, but gradually the sea breeze carried it out. From the outside it looked like smoke.

She crawled out and looked around. The lights were still on. She made her way through the rubble and found the three pirates on the floor of the main room. U.S. currency notes were scattered everywhere, like confetti. One of the sons was obviously dead, with a large splinter of wood through his neck. He had bled some, but not much. She couldn't see his face, which was covered with dirt and small debris.

The other son was still alive. The butt of his rifle was under him. She grabbed it and tugged. It came slowly, then quickly when out from under his dead weight.

She examined it, then pointed it at the man's head and pulled the trigger. Nothing happened.

She fiddled with a lever on the side. Tried it again. This time it hammered. The recoil was unexpected and the rifle leaped from her hands. Fell into the blood-and-grime mess that had been his head.

Nora went over to Ragnar and scrutinized him. He was lying faceup, with a bloody spot on his skull, in a bed of currency. His eyes were open and blinking. He was trying to swallow.

Not too much stuff on him. She found his pistol on his belt and jerked it out. Threw it across the room.

Turned and wandered away. There was a rope in the corner, coiled up. Not too thick. Clothesline thickness. But long.

She went into the kitchen area, also a shambles, and rooted through the debris until she found a knife. Went back to the rope and began cutting six-foot lengths. It was difficult. The knife was not very sharp, so she had to work at it.

CHAPTER TWENTY

Jake Grafton, Arch Penney and four of the *Sultan*'s officers and supervisors were standing by the portal to the fort when a technical roared out of the brush and screeched to a halt in a shower of gravel. It had come cross-country, avoiding the road. A man swung the machine gun in the bed back and forth, looking for targets, as another man jumped out of the driver's seat and ran for the entrance. Penney and his officers ran for cover.

Jake propped the AK against the stone that formed the side of the entrance, took careful aim and fired a single shot. The man on the machine gun toppled. The other man slowed. Grafton put a bullet into the dirt at his feet. He stopped dead, his weapon in his hand.

"Drop it!"

He knew enough English to understand that command. The assault rifle fell to the ground.

Penney came over to Grafton's side. "That's Mustafa al-Said," he said. "He led the pirates that captured my ship. He killed my officers. Murdered my passengers."

Grafton handed Penney the AK. "You do the honors. Get him in here. Don't kill him. We may need him later."

Penney walked out with the rifle at his shoulder, aimed. He took a pistol from al-Said, then marched him toward the portal.

Once they were there, Penney handed the pistol to Jake Grafton. Al-Said stood with his hands up. Grafton said to Penney, "Get something to tie him up with."

"We don't have anything. Someone will have to watch him every minute."

Jake Grafton bent over, checked the pistol in the dim light. Then he pointed it at al-Said's leg and pulled the trigger. The bullet tore into the pirate's knee; he toppled, screaming.

Grafton walked over to him. At point-blank range he shot him in the other knee.

"He'll stay put now," Grafton told Penney. "Get the keys to that truck. We may need it later." The *Sultan*'s officers were gawking at him, with their mouths open.

The admiral handed Penney the pistol, then climbed the stairs leading to the roof. He wanted to see the rest of the battle, what there was of it, and radio reception was better up there.

The problem with going down stairs is that your feet arrive before you do. The sound of the shot in that basement was like a cannon going off, but I didn't notice. The bullet burned my left leg and it folded, which was just as well. By then I was in the process of diving toward the bottom headfirst.

Saw the guy to my left with a pistol trying to get a clean shot at me. I didn't wait. I got one into him by the time I hit the floor like a sack of potatoes. I rolled right, pistol out, and got him framed in the sights. He was sagging against the wall, staring down at the red spot on his dirty shirt. I wasn't in the mood for a long-drawn-out dying scene, so I shot him again, then scanned the rest of the room. No people in sight.

The room was big and half-filled with crates stacked floor to ceiling. I scrambled up, cussing at the pain in my leg, and went exploring. There was another room behind this one, just as big, but completely filled with crates and weapons piled here and there. I gave it a cursory glance, then went back to the generator, which was throbbing along. For the first time

I realized the room was filthy, with trash that had been piled in there since the Italians left. Rat shit all over the floor. I had been rolling in it. No doubt dozens, maybe hundreds, of generations of rodents had lived out their life cycles here.

My leg wasn't bleeding too badly, and I could flex it, but it burned like hell. I rubbed the rat shit off my face and hair and spit on the floor, just in case.

Ben and Zahra came down the stairs. They glanced at the dead pirate, then ignored him. They went into the other room with their pistols out and ready. I kicked some of the trash around, looked for odd wires. Some rats scurried out of one pile and ran into another.

The generator had a fuel line gravity-feeding from a huge tank sitting beside it, against an exterior wall, mounted up on some kind of wooden supports. There was a valve on the line. I was looking it over when Zahra came back for me. "Carmellini!"

I went. In addition to the crates in the second room, in one corner were stacks of AKs, hundreds of them. I examined some of the crates while the Mossad agents scanned the others. The writing on the crates was in Cyrillic. A few of the wooden crates were open, so I looked in. The first box I looked at contained belts of machine-gun ammo. So did the second. The third one contained boxes of AK stuff, 7.62 x 39 mm. Hundreds of RPG-7 launchers were stacked like cordwood along one wall, with piles of warheads, and there was box after box of MON-50 mines, Russian claymores. They weighed maybe five pounds each, were packed with hundreds of steel bearings that the explosive propelled out like a shotgun blast. They were deadly as hell within fifty yards, and hit-and-miss out to maybe three hundred. I estimated that at least a hundred of them were piled here.

"Look at this."

Ben pried the lid off one of the large boxes.

"PVV-5A," he said. "Several tons of it, I think."

"Detonators?"

"In this lot somewhere." He stood looking around. "Over here are a couple of machine guns."

I went back to the generator. Started cranking the fuel valve. The engine sputtered. The lights in the basement flickered, and died when the generator did.

The two Israelis already had their flashlights out and on. I hadn't been smart enough to bring mine. I followed them back up the stairs.

They were pros. They held the flashlights out in their left hands while they scanned them around the lobby of that dump. It was still empty. I talked a bit on my headset with the SEAL team leader, Red One, or as he called himself, Red Leader.

"Check out the north room on the second floor," he said. I clicked my mike and motioned to Ben. We headed up the staircase, Ben leading with his flashlight.

The second-floor north room was the com center. A modern shortwave set sat on a table. Ben didn't waste much time—he used his pistol to put three rounds through the main radio. There were radio controls for model airplane rigs and garage door openers, all right, and batteries. Also two dead men. The Israelis looked them over, but they didn't recognize either of them. They settled in to examine the radio controls, one holding the flashlight while the other scrutinized them.

I checked in with Grafton on the net.

"Grafton, Tommy. Found the radio room. A shortwave set and batteries and RC control units."

"In the com center?"

"Yes."

"Ragnar will have the hot one in his pocket. Get it and bring it to me."

"I'm trying to figure out why they didn't push the button to blow the fortress when the shooting started."

"Thought we were Shabab, maybe," Grafton said. That Grafton! He didn't sound too interested. Fucking guy had ice cubes for balls. Everyone was still alive, so . . .

"Red Leader, I'm coming on up," I said.

Heard some more gunfire above me. "Come on," he said.

It was a nice early November evening in Washington, not too cold, with almost no wind. The president and his leadership team huddled around a television in the Ops Center in the basement. They sat silently listening to Ricardo—he was using his microphone now, he said—and watching war on television. Real war. In a shitty little place. Mostly the show consisted of random flashes and a cacophony of small-arms fire, overlaid by Ricardo's fevered descriptions.

In London it was past midnight, and the prime minister and his lieutenants were similarly engaged at 10 Downing Street watching the local Fox network. On another television tuned to the BBC, they had only audio from the satellite telephone of the BBC's man in Eyl, Rab Bishop. A scrolling legend on the bottom of the screen pleaded technical problems and promised video momentarily.

"All that money for the BBC," someone remarked, "and this is what we get."

Both the prime minister and the president had satellite telephone connections with Admiral Tarkington aboard *Chosin Reservoir*. The admiral had apprised them several hours ago that the action would soon begin, but they had expected that when they read Mike Rosen's first e-mail.

"Wouldn't it have been better to wait until the marines were ashore tomorrow before launching this party?" the foreign minister asked the PM.

The prime minister knew little of military affairs, a fact he was willing to admit publicly, and he had learned not to trust generals and admirals, who were, in his opinion, far too quick with victory predictions and clueless about political realities. Today his misgivings over the handling of this crisis grew with every machine-gun blast and Hellfire impact on the screen in front of him. Still, he wasn't going to call the admiral for reassurance. If he had any to give. Or those ninnies at the White House. The bald fact was the horse had left the gate and was running the race.

He contented himself with the comment, "If anything happens to those *Sultan* people, there will be bloody hell to pay."

On the far side of the Atlantic, the president was also examining his hole card. Giving Grafton command of this operation looked smart last week, but if this thing turned into a civilian bloodbath . . . A congressional investigation was the least that would happen. His handling of the military would be questioned. Foreign affairs . . . His enemies, of whom he had many, would wave the bloody shirts as proof of his and his administration's incompetence, which would have incalculable political effects.

He felt like a man on a runaway horse, with no control whatever, just trying to keep from being thrown.

The president glared at Sal Molina, who had lobbied hard for Grafton.

As machine guns chattered and muzzle flashes strobed on the television screen and that nincompoop Ricardo had oral sex with his microphone, the president dug a packet of cigarettes from a drawer and lit one. Blew smoke at the NO SMOKING sign. Mouthed a dirty word but didn't say it.

The SEALs were certainly thorough clearing Ragnar's lair. I counted five bodies as I climbed the stairs. Passed a troop of women and kids going down the stairs. I knew from the net that the SEALs had found them upstairs in the living quarters below the penthouse and were sending them down. Eight women, eleven kids, three being carried. I saw no blood. Just scared helpless people.

The penthouse was a helluva mess. The four SEALs were standing around looking for someone to shoot while Nora Neidlinger sat on the floor, working in near darkness cutting rope. Fifty dollar bills and C-notes were scattered everywhere.

"One alive, these other two are dead," the SEAL team leader reported.

"Got a flashlight?" I asked.

He gave me his.

"Have you searched them?"

He handed me a small RC control unit with three little arms and a red button. "Ragnar had it on him. No battery. The battery was in the other pocket." He gave me the battery and I pocketed it. Stuck the controller in my other pocket. It just fit.

I took a look at the pirate still alive. Ragnar! He was trying to talk. Had stuff covering his feet and hands, and one eye didn't focus. Concussion. No weapons in sight. The SEALs had confiscated them.

"Thanks," I told the SEAL guy. "I'll take it from here."

They turned and trooped off.

I squatted by Nora. She hadn't said a word. Just sawed that dull knife on the rope.

"Wanna go get a beer?" I asked.

"No."

"What are you going to do with the rope?"

"Tie him up."

"I see."

"Do you?"

I took out my Marine Corps fighting knife with the seven-inch blade and handed it to her butt first. "This is sharper."

She quickly finished cutting the rope into the lengths she wanted. She pulled all the trash and debris off him, then tied a rope around each of Ragnar's wrists and ankles. Then she tied the other end to any heavy thing in reach. Worked on those knots. Got them good and tight.

I went into the bathroom. The water wasn't working, naturally, since the electricity was no longer powering the water pump, but there was water in the toilet. I used a gourd I found in the kitchen to scoop out some.

Went back and poured it on Ragnar's face. He started coming around.

"Why don't you just kill him?" I asked. "I won't tattle."

"You can leave now," she said. She was watching Ragnar. She didn't even glance at me. She was holding that Ka-Bar with both hands.

"If you want, I'll do it for you."

No response. I put the flashlight on the floor and went.

Nora Neidlinger made sure Ragnar was trussed up good. The ropes holding his arms were tight, the knots snugged down. In fact, his hands were beginning to turn white from lack of blood.

She had tied one ankle to a fallen ceiling beam and one to a heavy chair. She used hundred dollar bills to gag him. Wadded them up and stuffed them in his mouth, and tied them in place with a piece of his shirt. Made sure he could still breathe. He was good to go.

Unfortunately he was still groggy from the concussion. She went into the bathroom and got more water from the toilet. She dribbled it on his face until his eyes flipped open.

"Hey there, asshole."

He seemed to become fully conscious. Looked around, tried to talk, struggled against the ropes.

"Try harder," she said and showed him the knife. Then she cut off his trousers. Rubbed his cock with her hand, waited for a response. Oh yes. She got a death grip and pulled it straight.

Ragnar bucked like a man possessed. "Have you ever been raped?" she asked conversationally, as if getting raped were equivalent to getting a parking ticket.

"Have you any idea what it's like? You ignorant raghead devil worshippers rape women, kinda like breeding a dog. You pour acid on their faces, beat them, sometimes to death, and it's just a ho-hum thing. Can't wait to get to Paradise so you can butt-fuck little boys. Isn't that what that pedophile Mohammed promised?"

She sighed. The bastard didn't understand a word. Even if she could have spoken Somali, he wouldn't understand. It was like talking to some slimy thing that lived in a sewer and came out when it was hungry to rape women and eat kids.

"Going to cut this off," Nora told him. She made the first incision. Blood spurted.

"You won't need this anymore," she said. "You are all done screwing. Finished."

Every muscle in Ragnar was taut, and his stomach was arched toward the ceiling. He was moaning through the gag.

"You should have known us back in the day," she said, just talking. "Back in Cherry Hills. My husband wanted me to be the perfect little piece of arm candy." Nora showed him his member, then tossed it through the door onto the balcony.

"He told me my boobs were too small so I had to get fake tits. Stay trim, look good for him. He was a car guy, seven dealerships, all kinds of brands, and gave money to every civic organization in town, all the charities. We went to every dinner, every function, got photographed for the society pages a hundred times. There I was, the perfect little wife, all dolled up in designer duds to show off my fake tits, smiling at everyone. And every evening the son of a bitch was fucking the babysitter when he took her home."

She worked as she talked. "Her parents finally caught on, of course. She was sixteen and in love, love, love, going to marry him and be on his arm instead of me. She wrote all this in her diary, and her mother snooped and found it. Mothers do that, you know. Snoop."

Jesus, the bastard could bleed, even though the ropes were tight.

"Statutory rape, of course, due to the age difference, and the fact it started when she was fourteen. It was pay big money or go to prison, so the bastard bought his way out of it. The parents wanted money. They really didn't give a damn about the daughter, as long as he paid them four million dollars. They sold her. You see that, don't you? Isn't that what you ragheads do—buy children to fuck?

"My husband could have probably made a better deal if he had gone to them up front," Nora mused aloud, "and said, 'I'll give you a million dollars if you'll let me fuck your daughter on the sly for the next three years.' A bang a month. Sometimes two. Call it fifty fucks in three years. A million bucks for fifty fucks." She giggled. "They would have gone for that."

Sweat was pouring off Ragnar's face. Blood was seeping out his mouth around the gag. The shit had bitten his tongue. Idly, she wondered if he had bitten it off.

"One day the bank called the house to verify a check while he was making the rounds of the dealerships. I went to the bank and took a look. Can you believe it? The idiot wrote it on a joint account. Four million bucks. That was a damn big pop for us. I had the locks changed on the house that afternoon and filed for a divorce two days later.

"He tried to keep it all hushed up, but I fought to get the money back, so it became a huge stink."

She stared down into Ragnar's eyes, which still tracked.

"You haven't understood a word I've said, have you? It's too bad, really. But even if you spoke English, you wouldn't have understood. Men seldom do. And you don't strike me as the empathetic type.

"I'll bet you were a pretty good pirate. My husband was, Honest John, but the divorce and publicity cost him the dealerships. They even threw him out of the country club. He became an alcoholic. Pickled himself, and his liver gave out last year. That's the way it goes, I guess. You wear out your turn, then it's someone else's."

Nora wandered around the room, touching this and that, paused to wipe the blood off her hands and arms on a blanket in the bedroom, then went into the living room and sat in a chair with her back to Ragnar. Amazingly, she spotted her purse in the rubble of the main room, right where Ragnar had tossed it several days ago.

She got it, rooted in it, found some cigarettes and lit one. It tasted delicious. She sat looking into the night as she smoked it. Above her, through the holes in the ceiling, she could see stars. Heard the desert wind whisper through the holes.

I stood in the doorway of Ragnar's lair listening to what remained of the battle between the Shabab and the pirates. An occasional distant automatic weapons burst, then long moments of silence. An occasional explosion, no doubt from an RPG. Someone was cleaning up, executing the last of their enemies. Burbles of conversation on the tactical net in my ear. The SEALs were still on the beach, drones were overhead, the controllers were reporting on the battle. It was a bit like listening to a baseball game without the crowd-noise background or commercials.

My watch said it was a little after 4:00 A.M. I was almost tired enough to sleep standing up, even with the nicked leg. The bleeding had stopped. Slowed, anyway. Smarted a good bit. I needed to get a bandage on it.

The shards of war were scattered all over. Burned-out pickups, bodies, pieces of bodies, crap from the face of the building, glass all over, spent cartridges . . . Even with the breeze, I could smell cooked meat. A couple of women were examining the bodies. Maybe looking for their men. Or sons. Nora Neidlinger was upstairs carving on Sheikh Ragnar, the terror of the Somali coast.

Here came the television people with flashlights, picking their way through the trash, absolutely certain no one would ever want to shoot them. Poor deluded fools. Cameramen, reporters, engineers toting gear . . .

Donatelli looked tired and a little the worse for wear. One-star accommodations can wear you down. Still cute, though.

The group came toward me and obviously intended to enter the building. I stopped them. "Don't go in there. Off-limits to the press."

"That's the best vantage point for filming," Ricardo explained, pointing upward toward the penthouse. "Great background. Anyway, we want to interview Ragnar. He's still in there, isn't he?"

"I am not his press secretary. He has other people for that. But I doubt if he wants to talk to you. Beat it."

That got them.

"Who are you, anyway?" the BBC man demanded.

"Nancy Pelosi. How do you like my disguise? No one is supposed to know I'm here."

"Don't you understand? We're the press! The whole world wants to know what is happening."

"I don't give a damn if you're the pope's eldest son. Take your act and git. Go interview a corpse." I waved the Kimber around.

They went, carrying their gear, threading their way through the remnants of the pickups and bodies and pieces of everything, some of it bloody. They hiked off toward the fortress. If they knew about the trench bomb, they were the pride of their networks. I doubted if they did. Ricardo hadn't impressed me as that kind of guy.

I was sitting in the doorway with my back to the pillar watching the sky brighten to the east when the drone controller announced that apparently the Shabab had won and were boarding pickups. They would be here in short order, he said. I looked at my watch. Almost 5:30 A.M.

I hiked back up the stairs to collect Nora Neidlinger. Met the two Mossad guys coming down. Each of them was carrying a couple of those Communist claymores. Souvenirs.

I found Nora sitting in a chair in the main room calmly smoking a cigarette. She had bloodstains to her elbows and on the front of her blouse. Lots of blood. The remains of Sheikh Ragnar were there on the floor, still trussed up. I tried not to look.

"Come on. Some bad guys are coming and we gotta get you outta here."

She was in no hurry.

"I mean now. Unless you want to let the holy warriors rape you to death."

She picked up her purse, stood and headed for the stairway. She didn't even glance at Ragnar.

"I'll need my knife."

She jerked her head back toward the chair and kept going. I found the knife on the floor. Used a wad of currency to wipe as much of the blood and gore off the knife as possible—taking care not to look at Ragnar—put it in its sheath, threw the bloody money on the floor and followed her down the stairs.

Jake Grafton was waiting when I came out of the building. He had one of the pickups. Ben and his buddy were sitting in the bed, one on either side of Mohammed Atom, whose wrists were held together with a plastic tie. Grafton took a look at Nora and then at me. Didn't ask any questions.

"Get her in the surf," he said. "Wash her off."

I took her elbow and walked her toward the ocean. We passed a couple of SEALs lying on the beach. They were wearing those black wet suits and were difficult to see until I almost stepped on them. If Nora saw the SEALs, she paid no attention. We passed them by, walked into the water to our knees. It was warm, wet and black, with rollers flopping on the beach and running back into the sea.

She handed me her purse, then took off her blouse and began handwashing it in saltwater. Dark as it was, I couldn't see any blood. She scrubbed her hands and arms and shoulders slowly, as if she were washing up after a tennis workout. She was calm. Dead calm. I was worried about her. Wondered if she'd crack.

I suppose I should have been horrified about what she did to Ragnar, but I wasn't. If she hadn't been in that penthouse, I would have shot him. Good-bye, and bang. Can't say he didn't deserve it. Hell, all these pirates deserved it. Arch Penney would swear to that. One of the great philosophical issues of our time is why so few people get what they deserve. Good or bad.

Grafton was waiting for me when we walked off the beach. He was standing beside the pickup. The Israelis were not in sight. Grafton's headset was draped around his neck. He must have had a dozen questions for me and Neidlinger, but he didn't bother. One of the lessons he had undoubtedly picked up somewhere along the trail was that you can't testify about things you don't know about. It was a thing to remember.

"The Shabab will be here in five minutes," he said. "I'll stay to meet them. Tommy, you get Ms. Neidlinger up to the fort. Get her some food and a place to lie down."

"Too bad we can't gun them and waltz our people out of here."

"Too many of them, and the planes won't be here until tomorrow evening. Getting the radio controls to that trench bomb was the best we could do tonight. And eliminate some of the opposition."

"What about that ship full of fertilizer, the *Susan B. Grant*? If she explodes—"

"She won't. The SEALs blew a dozen holes in the side of the ship while the battle was going on. The seawater will ruin the fertilizer. Ship's still there, of course—can't sink, since she's already resting on the bottom."

"What about—"

"No time. Hustle out of here and get that leg looked at."

I went. Got Nora to march. We got into solid darkness and walked as fast as my leg would allow. The wound was bleeding again. We were climbing the hill when a dozen or so pickups rolled into the plaza, one after another, and braked to a stop. I glanced over my shoulder and saw Grafton wandering over to the first one. I quit watching and climbed on up the hill, steering Nora along.

Yousef el-Din watched as armed men from the pickups behind him piled out and ran for Ragnar's lair. Others set up a perimeter. Men at the machine guns mounted in the bed of every truck kept their weapons moving as they searched for targets. The vehicle headlights lit up the plaza as if it were a baseball field.

More pickups rolled through the plaza and took the road to the fortress.

The bed of each contained eight to ten men, all armed, all hanging on tightly as they bumped and rattled up the dirt road.

Jake Grafton stood watching with professional interest. Any ambushing force could have decimated the column as it drove up. Yousef had a lot to learn, if he lived long enough. On the other hand, he obviously knew more about ground combat than the pirates—he was still alive.

El-Din climbed from the passenger seat of the lead pickup and was instantly surrounded by a small retinue of armed bodyguards. They kept their AKs at the ready.

Grafton stood with his arms folded. El-Din strolled over, in no hurry.

"Your men made short work of these pirates," Grafton remarked, looking around. One of el-Din's aides translated.

The bearded terrorist sneered. "Where are your men?"

"Not here. We used drones for this."

The word "drone" threw the translator.

"Little unmanned airplanes. They carry weapons." Grafton pointed toward the sky.

"Are they up there now?"

"Of course."

From his pocket Yousef el-Din produced an object. He displayed it to Grafton, who recognized it. It was a modified garage door opener. Yousef talked, and the translator jumped in without waiting for a pause.

"With this I can set off Ragnar's bomb around the fortress, and collapse it. The explosion and falling stone will kill everyone inside. My men will kill everyone outside. If the British or Americans attempt to betray us, or fail to pay the money, I will kill all these people, including you. *Allah akbar.*"

Grafton donned his headset, which had been arranged around his neck. He keyed the mike with his belt switch. "Toad, this is Jake."

"Roger."

Grafton repeated el-Din's threat. As they discussed it Grafton heard a shout. He looked up in time to see a body falling from the penthouse balcony. It hit with a dull splat. Then another, and another.

Several of el-Din's entourage ran over for a look. They came back with the news. Jake didn't need a translation. Ragnar and his sons were dead.

Yousef el-Din's eyes crinkled, and inside his beard his lips twisted. This was his smile.

He spouted more words, either Arabic or Somali, Jake didn't know. The translator said, "You come with us. You will talk for us. Any tricks, and you die."

Jake repeated that to Toad Tarkington, then added, "I'm turning this headset off to save the battery. I'll call you tomorrow to find out when you are ready to deliver the money."

"Fine."

As the pickups came up the hill toward the fortress, I put my weapons in my backpack and set it inside where it was hard to see. Thank heavens someone had dragged off the bodies of the sentries I'd killed. No doubt there were small bloodstains, but who would know? Or care?

Here they came, a couple dozen of Allah's finest. Ahmad the Awful spouted gibberish at Captain Penney as I listened on my headset to Grafton talking to Admiral Tarkington.

I heard Grafton say el-Din was making him a prisoner. So they were kidnapping the negotiator!

One of the pickups was backing toward the entryway. It stopped twenty feet or so away, and the man at the machine gun pointed it at us, scowled fiercely and wiggled the barrel. If the trench bomb went off while he was sitting there he was going to join the ranks of the recently departed. Maybe he didn't know that.

The three network reporters were trying to get an interview, but the head dog wasn't having any of it. Maybe he didn't speak English. He smacked a light with his rifle barrel, breaking it, and pointed toward the fort. The message was unmistakable. Get inside!

The media people obeyed with a lot of wasted motion. Generators died and lights were extinguished.

I keyed my headset. "Red Control, this is Tommy. Can you track Grafton with the drones?"

"We should be able to do that."

"Wilbur, Orville?"

"We'll try, Tommy."

"Everybody, I'm going to turn off the headset to save the batteries. I'll call before dawn for a report."

"Roger."

I switched the thing off, passed behind Captain Penney as I retrieved my backpack and headed for the stairs to the roof. I needed a few hours' sleep. I wondered if I would get any.

Julie Penney escorted Nora Neidlinger to where Suzanne and Irene were trying to sleep, after the battle sounds died away. Marjorie was there, too. The women made a fuss over Nora, whose clothes were still damp.

"We must find her something dry to wear."

As they did that, Suzanne got right to it. "How are you, Nora? Are you okay?"

In the gloom, it was impossible to read her face. "Fine," she said. "Fine."

When her daughter was led in a few minutes later, Nora grabbed her and held on tightly.

Someone asked, "Have you had anything to eat?"

"I'm not hungry. Honestly."

"Pirate adventures are a good way to lose weight," Irene remarked.

"Two more days," Julie told the women. "Arch talked to the negotiator, a Mr. Grafton. The money is coming. Just two more days and we'll be free."

When Nora finally lay down and closed her eyes, she tried to get some perspective on her life and her recent adventures. She often did that in the moments before sleep overcame her, but tonight the emotions threatened to overwhelm her. She needed to surpress them, try to wall them off. She certainly didn't want to think about the details of the torture of Ragnar, which had been a catharsis, a break.

I've broken with my past life, she thought. *From here until the end it's a new adventure.*

That thought allowed her to relax, and she slept as the dawn turned into day and the first rays of the sun sneaked through the gun ports into the fortress.

Jake Grafton was also lying down, trying to relax enough to sleep. He was in some ramshackle dirt-floored building a couple of miles up the river from the beach town, Eyl proper. East Eyl. Eyl Beach. Eyl by the Sea, the jewel of Somalia.

Around him he could hear men farting and snoring and coughing, and the groaning strain of the cots on which they lay.

He was acutely aware of the Walther in the ankle holster. They didn't search him, merely took his com unit and headset. Told him where to lie down. He had obeyed.

Of course, the act of pulling that pistol from its holster would get him shot immediately. He had no intention of doing so. Not anytime soon, anyway.

He lay there listening to the night sounds and wondered if Yousef el-Din's pocket radio controller would indeed trigger the trench bomb. He and the Israelis thought they had disabled all the detonators and antennas . . . But! Maybe they missed one. Or two. Maybe it wouldn't be a really big bang, but a little one. Maybe there would be no bang at all. If Yousef pressed the button and nothing happened, he was going to be very surprised. Also very unhappy. Disappointed, too.

Maybe . . .

Jake Grafton was still going over the maybes when he drifted off.

CHAPTER TWENTY-ONE

WASHINGTON, D.C.

Encrypted Top Secret Flash messages were launched into the ether at the speed of light from desks in Washington, Langley and the Indian Ocean, and at most of the military commands in between, and other encrypted Flash messages came zipping back, again at the speed of light.

Toad Tarkington received an avalanche of demands to be told in exquisite detail all that had happened in Eyl to date and what was going to happen in the future. Was or was not the trench bomb safe? Tarkington was given orders to report on the state of health of the *Sultan* prisoners, the status of the television news teams and the status and circumstances of any civilian casualties caused by the U.S. military or anyone else.

For his part, Toad informed the bureaucrats that Jake Grafton, the American envoy, was the prisoner of Yousef el-Din, the local Shabab banana, and that Ragnar was dead.

Toad and Grafton had a plan, of course, that they had made and massaged since the president appointed Grafton, and Toad undertook to state to the powers that be that the plan didn't require any participation from Grafton.

Then he turned the whole message mess over to his chief of staff, who could draft answers and kiss ass at the speed of light whenever required.

In Washington the president took another smoke break with Sal Molina. "Whaddaya think?" the elected one asked after that first blessed drag of cigarette smoke.

"You know Grafton," Molina said. He stretched out his feet as far as they would go and jammed his hands in his trouser pockets. "Ragnar got his lesson, and now it's the Shabab's turn. The thing about Grafton: Anything can go wrong, and if it does, he has probably prepared for that eventuality."

The president spun his chair so he could look out the window at the floodlit Washington Monument rising like a giant phallic symbol against the black night sky.

"This military adventure won't go over very well in Europe. They call us unprincipled cowboys now; if there are any significant casualties, they'll call us worse."

"The Shabab did the pirates. God only knows how many of those bastards they slaughtered, but *we didn't do it.*"

"Grafton's a genius."

"Maybe the queen will knight him."

"I just have this suspicion," the president mused, "an inkling perhaps, just an itch between my shoulder blades, that this whole thing is out of control. It's like a televised debate, with the cameras on and the swine reporter grinning like a moron on crack, and you just know the son of a bitch is going to ask you an unexpected question that will make you look like a friggin' idiot in front of everyone on the planet. That's the feeling. I got it big-time. This whole pirate gig is going to turn out badly."

"Grafton is the best—"

The president smacked the table with one hand. "Homicidal Muslims, grinding poverty in Africa, people starving by the millions, polluted oceans, vicious pirates—this isn't Johnny Depp swaggering in front of a camera wearing more eye shadow than a whorehouse full of sluts. This is real as a heart attack. That Grafton . . . he can certainly smash things. That's the easy part. *I* have to pick up the pieces."

Sal Molina sighed. After twenty-five years in politics, he thought most politicians had the courage of mice, present company included. They were constantly congratulating themselves on having the fortitude to take political risks, when the worst that could happen was losing some votes. Molina tried to recall just what the president had done about poverty and starvation in Africa, vicious pirates and polluted oceans. Maybe he made a speech or two. Tut tut.

All the guts inside the Beltway wouldn't be enough for a Vienna sausage, Molina thought savagely.

I woke up with the sun in my eyes. I got up, went to the eastern edge of the roof and pissed through a gun port as the warm desert wind pushed on my back and the sun warmed my face. One of the guards eyed me, thought about shooting me and apparently changed his mind. Everyone has to piss, even infidels. He settled for a rude gesture.

Ahh, morning in fabulous Eyl. With any luck, this would be my last one. Tomorrow morning I'd either be dead or someplace else.

I turned on my headset. Not a lot of battery left, but maybe enough.

"Red Control, Tommy. Where is Grafton?"

"Good morning, Tommy. All indications are he's in a hut in West Eyl. We've counted over two hundred armed men in that vicinity."

"Thanks. I'll get back to you."

I went downstairs and found Arch Penney, who was conferring with his crew, trying to figure out how to feed eight hundred fifty people and not poison them. It was a tough problem. My personal contribution was to refuse to eat anything. Fasting wouldn't give me the trots, although the water might. I had to drink it anyway.

"Did you bring binoculars from your ship?" I asked the captain.

He nodded.

"May I borrow them?"

His wife had them. He told me where she was and I went.

Nora Neidlinger was still asleep, and the women were talking in hushed tones. Nora's daughter was asleep beside her. No one asked me what had happened to Nora, and I wasn't letting on that I knew.

Lying on my belly on the roof, looking through a gun port, I surveyed the beach. A few kids were fishing in the surf, but there were no SEALs lying around. I wondered where they were. Looked the *Sultan* over. Probably aboard her, but I saw no one. She appeared to be a derelict.

Lots of guys with assault rifles wandering around Eyl. Up on top of the lair amid the rubble, in pickups in the plaza, stealing food from the locals. I could see men literally carrying pots out of the houses scattered about while women screamed at them and children cried. Those holy warriors . . . The distance was too great to see much detail. I needed to get closer.

I needed to get out of here. I got up, put the binocs in my backpack and wandered along the wall, looking at the guards and brush and considering possibilities.

In midmorning two guards came for Jake. He hadn't eaten, nor had he been given any water. He was hungry and thirsty, but tried to ignore it.

His captors put him in a pickup, and away they went driving fast toward the beach. Roared into the plaza and screeched to a stop in front of Ragnar's lair. Grafton saw that the plaza had been cleaned up, somewhat. The remnants of two pickups were still there, but the less-damaged ones had been removed, no doubt to be mined for parts, and the bodies carried off.

A group of hard cases with AKs watched Grafton get out of the bed of the pickup, and watched his two escorts take him inside.

Although he didn't know it, Yousef el-Din had had a group working for hours cleaning up most of the mess in the penthouse. They disposed of broken glass and rubble and trash by the simple expedient of tossing it off the balcony and out the windows on the south side of the building, none of which had any glass left.

Jake was prodded up the stairs, all of them, to the penthouse. The roof looked as if it would cave in if even a mild breeze arose, but most of the rubble was gone. The bodies of the Ragnars, father and sons, were somewhere below under all that debris.

Yousef was waiting in the penthouse, seated on a carpet with his legs folded, looking every inch like an Arab slave trader waiting to haggle. Standing beside him was Geoff Noon, High Noon himself, still wearing that filthy old white linen sport coat with a bottle of gin in the side pocket. The pocket on the other side was empty, so he looked unbalanced. He glanced at Grafton but showed no sign of recognition. Also standing there was a white man of medium height, trim, wearing slacks and a short-sleeve pullover shirt with a polo pony on the left breast. He was obviously the cleanest man in the room.

"I'm Mike Rosen," he said to Grafton, extending a hand.

Grafton shook and pronounced his name.

"Yousef wants to talk about money," Noon said.

"Okay."

"When and how it will be delivered."

"Tell him that two helicopters will arrive at noon tomorrow. Each will have money suspended on a pallet below it. The choppers will put the pallets in the plaza, then fly over to the fort and land on the roof."

Noon chattered a while, then listened as Yousef talked; then they went back and forth. Grafton put his hands in his pockets and inspected the holes in the roof. Those Hellfires had done a job.

Finally Noon asked, "Why pallets under the helicopters?"

"Two hundred million dollars in currency weighs over two tons. That is a ton for each chopper. In this heat, that is a safe load."

More jabber.

Grafton interrupted. "Of course, after the money is paid we will want to transport all the people in the fortress out of here. We will use helicopters, take about a dozen people at a time. It will obviously take the rest of the day to fly eight hundred and fifty folks out to the ship. As each helicopter is loaded and takes off, another one will land on the roof."

Yousef listened impassively to this statement.

Grafton continued, "I suspect that Yousef and his followers will wish to take the money and leave immediately. If they try any treachery, we will of course kill every single one of them and take the money back or destroy it."

Yousef's face darkened as he listened to Noon, and he rose swiftly to his feet. He had a pistol in a holster on his belt, and his hand went to the butt.

"We are Muslims of the Shabab," he said, according to Noon. "Not liars and thieves and blasphemers and sinners, like the pirates were. They are dead, gone. The Shabab will not be insulted." The men standing around listening made appreciative noises upon hearing this. They were Allah's chosen. "You will do as you have said. If you try to betray our agreement in any way, all the hostages will die. Every last one. They will be shot and bombed until every single one of them is but crushed bone and bloodstains on the stone."

He pulled a radio control device from his pocket and tossed it on the carpet on which he had been sitting.

Jake Grafton didn't seem impressed. "We'll want the *Sultan,* too," he said. "A team of sailors will arrive tomorrow by boat after the money is paid. They will go aboard, start the engines, raise the anchor and sail her away."

Yousef wanted more money. Grafton stood his ground. He had made a deal with Ragnar. There was no more money.

"Two hundred million for the people, another hundred million for the ship," Noon reported.

After thinking it over, taking his time, Grafton said, "We will sell him the ship for a hundred million. We will give him a hundred million for the people and he can keep the ship. Maybe start up a cruise ship line. Eyl to Rome, via Suez and Athens."

It was an argument for show. Yousef played to his followers, with much back-and-forth with them that wasn't translated.

After a while Yousef caved. "Two hundred million, and you can have the people and the ship."

Grafton merely nodded. He looked a question at Noon. "You taking Rosen back to the ship?"

Noon nodded.

Grafton turned toward Rosen and said, "Put it on the Internet." He turned on his headset, arranged it on his head and had a short conversation with Admiral Tarkington. Then he turned it off to save the battery.

Yousef issued orders, and Grafton's escorts led him to the stairs and down. They ended up in a room on the third floor. Still some trash about. Grafton looked out the shattered window and the one that still had glass, then sat down. He paid no attention to the guards.

High Noon accompanied Mike Rosen back to the ship. They waded out from the beach and managed to heave themselves into the boat without tipping it over, and the boatman started the little one-cylinder engine. Away they putted.

When they were back aboard the *Sultan of the Seas* and climbing stairs to the e-com center, Rosen asked, "What happened to Ragnar?"

"He is no longer with us."

"And the rest of the pirates?"

"The same, I am afraid. Yousef el-Din and his men did their level best to kill them all. Oh, no doubt a few of them are hiding in the brush, but only a few."

"That e-mail I sent?"

"Oh, yes. It stimulated them vigorously."

"And whose idea was it to send that?"

Noon grinned and didn't answer.

When Rosen's computer was online, over a hundred e-mails vomited forth.

"We will send the Shabab's communiqué first," Noon said, "then the substance of the conversation between Yousef el-Din and Mr. Grafton." He extracted a grimy sheet of paper from a pocket. "Send them to your radio station. Your colleagues will, I assume, put them on the Net where the world can read them."

He handed the paper to Rosen, who spread it out on the desk and read it carefully. It merely stated unequivocally that unless the two hundred million dollars was paid by noon tomorrow Eyl time, the Shabab would kill all the prisoners. A couple of sentences of boilerplate followed, exhorting the faithful to jihad.

"Apparently Allah's soldiers have inherited the pirates' business," Rosen muttered.

"Their assets and their debts," Noon said, uncorking his gin bottle. "Start typing."

It was close to noon when I heard trucks coming up the hill toward the fort. A man would have had to be deaf not to hear them, since none of them had a working muffler. Sounded like a NASCAR race.

I figured the guards were going to change, so trotted over to the other side of the fort. Sure enough, the holy warriors were walking around the fort. For just a moment, there was no one on the eastern side. I didn't waste a second; just vaulted over the side into the loose dirt twelve or so feet below. Then I shot off down the hill toward the beach. Went about fifty yards and then flopped onto my belly.

Waited a minute or so for shouts, or shots, or someone running after me. Nothing. I started crawling. My leg hurt every time I moved it.

After I had done about a mile on my stomach around the north side of that rock pile and was thoroughly fagged out, with cactus stickers in my hands and knees, I decided to get on the net. Got my headset on and turned on the transmitter/receiver and keyed the mike. "Control, this is Tommy. Where is the admiral?"

"He's in Ragnar's lair."

"E.D.? Travis?"

"Yo."

"Where are you? We need to talk."

Julie Penney was standing at a gun port looking at the sea when Tommy Carmellini landed in the dirt in front of her, picked himself up and galloped into the brush.

She recognized him, even though she didn't see his face. Big, rangy, athletic, lean . . . Grafton's assistant, the man who brought Nora back from Ragnar's hellhole.

Marjorie was there and came over to the porthole. She had gotten a glimpse of the falling body, but hadn't seen who it was.

"Tomorrow's the deadline," Marjorie reminded the captain's wife. "One more night."

Suzanne Ranta heard that remark and joined the conversation. "Out of here tomorrow. Or we'll be dead."

"Arch says the ransom will be paid," Julie Penney reminded them. "Let's keep our chins up."

"Stiff upper lip," Irene mocked, as British as she could.

Julie Penney wandered off to check on other passengers. She had had a little talk with her husband in the wee hours of the morning, after the shooting died down, and he had said, "It'll be tonight." She asked why, and was told, "The locals can't see in the dark. The Americans prefer it. If there is going to be trouble, it will be tonight."

Tonight. Conceivably, this could be the last day of life for a great many people.

So . . . if you knew this might be your last day, how would you spend it? Almost by instinct Julie Penney chose to spend it trying to buck up her husband's passengers.

It was nearly four o'clock when I reached the rendezvous, what with crawling and sneaking along. The Shabab had patrols out, and they kept showing up at inopportune times. Sometimes I am lucky that way.

Our rendezvous was a big pile of rock overlooking Eyl West. It was just below the rim, a pile of hard rock that had resisted the rain and wind through the ages. I wouldn't have been surprised if hundreds of thousands of years ago *Homo erectus* hadn't huddled on random nights on the very spot where Travis had built a tiny, smokeless fire to brew coffee and warm up MREs. In Africa, you think about things like that.

It wasn't just Travis and E.D., either. It was my whole snatch team. Harry, Doc, Willis, Buck, Wilbur . . . all of them.

"This is like a high school reunion," I said. "Who brought the beer?"

"Jesus, Tommy, you look bad! What did you do, crawl the whole way?"

"Damn near. Where's Orville?"

"Up on top of the rock. We have a drone up keeping watch."

"I'll recommend a Christmas bonus for all you guys."

"Want a beer?" Buck asked.

"You are a prince among men. Wanna meet my sister? I'll fix you up."

E.D. handed me the satellite phone. "The navy wanted to talk to you as soon as you showed up."

"I kinda thought so."

"They weren't expecting Admiral Grafton to get himself into a hostage situation. I think they want you to take care of that."

"Did you guys get all those radio detonators?" Willis asked me.

"If you hear a really big bang, the answer is no." I opened a can of beer and looked at E.D. "Anything else they want to ask me?"

"Now, Tommy, no one knew if you were going to get out of that fort before dark. We were Plan B."

"I see."

"What with you here, we'll go back to Plan A."

"The airport?"

"Yep. The Shabab boys are sitting up there looking mean. Kinda too bad about the pirates. When the Shabab came in shooting, the pirates' machine guns split their barrels when the first round was fired. The battle was a little lopsided. Very tragic."

I set about making the satellite phone do its magic. By the time the task force ops officer was on, I was halfway through my second can of beer. Even warm, it tasted delicious.

While I talked the guys worked on my leg. Got an antibiotic on it and a coagulating pad, then a tight bandage. At least now it wouldn't bleed. Damn thing was sore, and the best I could do was a hobble.

When the ops officer was finished and had answered my three questions, I turned off the phone. I looked at my little band and told them, "We eat, then get at it. Timetable is unchanged. The airplanes are in the air." They knew all that, of course. "E.D., you and Travis are going to cover me with the Sakos."

They just nodded and handed me some MREs. I began wolfing them down. Damn, I was hungry.

E.D. sat down beside me. "I heard some shooting last night. Did you guys get any kills?"

He shrugged. Looked around to see who was listening to us. Apparently no one. "We missed," he allowed in a low voice.

"Oh, come on!"

"Shit, Tommy. Shooting at people running around like crazy in the dark isn't like shooting at a damn target. You know that! The damn guys wouldn't hold still."

"I thought you guys—"

"For the love of Christ!" he hissed, trying to keep his voice from carrying. "Of course I've been in combat before. A dozen times. Sprayed lead and threw grenades and called in air strikes and patched up wounds and all that soldier shit. We got those guys about to do you on the road, didn't we? Sure, we were trying last night, but the crosshairs kept dancing and those guys wouldn't hold still. You know what I'm saying?"

"It'll be my neck on the chopping block tonight," I pointed out.

"We scared 'em last night. Kept their heads down. When they got their heads down they're outta the fight. We'll take care of you."

"Yeah. Sure. Anything happens to me, you'd better get off this planet. Shoot straight, damn your eyes."

"Oh, of course, Tommy. Sure as shootin'."

"Fuck you, Erectile Dysfunction."

"*Hey!* Watch your mouth."

"Fuck you, Limp Dick. Is that better?"

"Cocksucker."

"Don't drink any more of this horse-piss beer before we go, either."

Properly motivating people is a fine art. It comes natural to me. It's a gift.

We sorted our gear, made sure everyone had what he needed. Willis Coffey was leading the rest of the guys to the airport. Since they had farther to go, they left early. E.D. and I helped ourselves to more water. The sun had slipped below the hills to the west, but still made the ocean sparkle. When the sun was gone and the ocean turned gray, we started sneaking.

For some reason, the sky turned bloodred as the night came on. Perhaps the upper atmosphere was full of dirt from the desert to the west. Some kind of lensing effect, I suppose.

We finally reached our position just after dark. E.D. settled in beside me and set up the legs of the Sako's bipod. Got his spotting scope beside him, focused it on Ragnar's lair, used the laser range finder . . .

"Two hundred ninety yards," he whispered.

That was well within the capability of the night scope on the rifle. Unfortunately it was too close for comfort. One of the advantages a sniper enjoys is that he can kill from beyond the range of enemy weapons, and it is this edge that often is the only thing keeping the sniper alive.

Using the night scope, we checked for other positions. After a couple of shots, E.D. was going to have to move. Probably retreat, if the opposition tried to encircle him with more people than he could take down. We picked out places.

"Just don't shoot unless you have to," I told him. "But if you do shoot, kill the son of a bitch. One shot, one kill."

He didn't say anything. The dumb bastard. Shooting and missing last night! Jesus! Sniper my ass.

I lay there stewing as I looked over Ragnar's lair with binoculars. I could see people in some of the windows, and people in the penthouse. A couple on the balcony. None of them was Grafton, not that I expected to see him. They probably had him in one of the back rooms under guard.

In the plaza were six pickups with machine guns, technicals, tastefully arranged around the burned-out hulks of the two trucks that caught fire last night.

The gunners in the trucks were nervous, and kept looking out to sea, scanning. They weren't stupid. The truck carcasses and side of the building had plenty of .50 caliber bullet holes. Anyone with eyes could see that a heavy weapon had been used. From a patrol boat? A launch? Or from the *Sultan*?

Even as I watched, two squads of armed men, about eight in each bunch, walked out to the beach and carried two boats into the surf, where they climbed aboard. Other men brought them machine guns, one for each boat, which the people in the boat mounted on a tripod.

They didn't waste any time, but set sail immediately for the *Sultan*. Once there, the first boat went alongside while the other laid off about a hundred yards and covered it. Six or so of the Shabab warriors went aboard. Truth is, these guys should have done this twelve hours ago. Maybe el-Din just thought of it, or maybe he was too busy praying or writing reports to his superiors to attend to business.

I hoped the SEALs were ready. It was a couple hours too early for the party to begin. A shootout aboard ship would alert this bunch here, complicating the problem of extracting Grafton. And the *Sultan* passengers. And crew. Plus my snatch team. And me.

Bullet Bob Quinn saw the boats set off from the beach and assumed the worst. Like Carmellini, he knew that shooting at dusk would jeopardize the entire operation. He and the men could just go over the side and swim away . . . but there was the big fifty on the bridge. One look at that gun and its ammo and the Somalis would catch right on. At least now they were only suspicious.

He sent a runner to the e-com center to warn Rosen and High Noon. The Somalis expected them to be there, so that was fine. Indeed, that was where some of them would go first, just to check. He stationed two men there.

He and the other SEALs took up positions here and there throughout the ship. He hoped to take out the holy warriors one at a time, if they would just cooperate.

Bullet Bob stood just around a corner from the pilot landing, which of course was still open. He heard the boat bump against the grate and heard them clamor aboard. These guys weren't silent. Didn't know how. People were supposed to flee from the righteous violence of their guns, from the wrath of Allah.

The pirates hadn't, and their corpses were lying in a pile between Eyl East and West. Of course, most of them had been ambushed, but . . .

Quinn waited until the last man had taken a ladder upward, then followed him. At the top of the staircase he saw the guy looking around, slightly awed at the size and opulence of the ship, and apparently undecided about which way he should go. The man paused to listen, held his rifle tightly.

He made a selection and walked along, looking at this and that, obviously ready to shoot someone if only he could find someone. Anyone.

Bullet Bob kept low, stayed behind, as quiet as a shadow. His chance came when the pirate thought he heard something behind a closed door and approached it, intent upon it.

Quinn's garroting wire went over his head and the SEAL pulled with all his strength. The rifle fell, the man grabbed at his throat. They all did that. It was instinct.

As violence goes, garroting ranks right up there with slashing with a cutlass. To be good with a garroting wire you have to like the weapon. You must like pulling with all your strength on the handles and feeling the victim buck and writhe helplessly as the wire cuts into his throat, then slices into his jugular veins, severing them. The lack of air would eventually kill the victim, a strangulation, but the loss of blood to the brain brings an almost instantaneous unconsciousness. The victim never wakes up.

The trick is to keep tightening the wire after the victim passes out. Tighten until it cuts the veins. It helps if the man pulling on the handles is strong, with well-developed shoulders and back muscles. Bullet Bob was. He was only a few inches taller and twenty pounds heavier than the Somali male, but he was twice as strong. It wasn't a fair contest. It was a quick, silent assassination.

When the blood erupted from the holy warrior's neck, Quinn lowered him to the floor. Pulled his wire off and wiped it on the back of the man's filthy shirt in a place the blood had yet to reach. Then he moved on.

The SEAL lieutenant was on the bridge, hidden in the doorway of the navigator's office, when he heard a man come along the starboard passageway and pass through the open door. Sure enough, he saw the big machine gun lying there on the floor immediately and stepped toward it to take a look. As he passed the open door, Quinn stepped out behind him, grabbed his mouth with his left hand and cut his throat with his right. The fighting knife slashed through tissue as if it were soft cheese.

Quinn stepped back into the office and waited. Sure enough, within less than a minute another Somali came exploring. He saw the first guy lying on the deck in a pool of his own blood and stopped. This put him about six feet from the doorway. Quinn launched himself toward the man, with his knife swinging. The swipe caught muscle, tissue, tendons and cartilage; blood erupted from the man's neck. His eyes glazed and he tumbled to the deck, unconscious and bleeding out.

Five minutes after they came aboard, it was all over. All six were dead. One of the SEALs skinned out of his clothes, donned a dead man's, grabbed his AK and went on deck to wave off the two circling boats.

Quinn watched. It was a necessary gamble.

It paid off. The boats moved off to the other ships.

Bullet Bob went up a deck to the e-com center. Noon was fairly well pickled, his usual late-afternoon condition, and Rosen was working on his e-mails. Neither knew the Shabab warriors had come aboard, and Quinn didn't tell them.

"We're going to have to get ashore before the darkness becomes too thick," Noon said. "I must signal for our boat."

"Plan on staying aboard tonight," Quinn said. "If the boat comes, we'll wave them off."

"I wonder if the cruise line would mind if we helped ourselves to some of their fine cuisine?"

Rosen turned off the computer. "I know where the peanut butter is, and if the bread hasn't spoiled . . ."

The SEALs were in the kitchen and had a simple dinner prepared when Quinn came in with Rosen and Noon. The two ship's engineers were already there, drinking their pints, celebrating their return from belowdecks. They looked happy and serene; no doubt they would get happier and more serene if they kept swilling the beer.

The last of the light was fading from the sky.

Quinn checked his watch, then said to Finnorn and the others, "You guys get that gun mounted on the bridge. Show starts in two hours and five minutes. While you are going that way, throw those corpses over the side."

Rosen stopped forking food. "Corpses?"

"We had uninvited guests. They are on their way to Paradise. Or Hell. Allah will figure it out."

. . .

As the light faded completely, I switched to night-vision goggles. I had everyone located, I hoped. There were the six pickups, all in the plaza, all illuminated by the evening fire. No women or children around, just men, and all armed. They were roasting something in the fire . . . If there was a pickup on the far side of the building, I couldn't see it from my vantage point.

The generator was running again, powering lights in every room. I got glimpses of people in the penthouse, two visible on the second floor . . . a couple guys on the balcony with rifles, walking around looking things over.

I could see two machine guns mounted on the roof. They were the belt-fed 7.62 mm Russian models that were in all the pickups. These two must have been carried up from the weapons horde in the basement.

When the night was as dark as the inside of a black cat, I pointed out my route to E.D., who wasn't talkative. "Don't shoot unless it's absolutely necessary. If you do shoot, don't miss."

He grunted.

My leg had stiffened up. Oh, man, that thing was sore.

I crawled forward.

Aboard *Chosin Reservoir,* Rear Admiral Toad Tarkington was watching the action unfold on computer screens. Real-time video and infrared presentations from three drones over Eyl played on monitors. SEALs were in the water and approaching the Eyl beaches. Marines were landing on the beaches above and below the town in armored personnel carriers. They had some light artillery and plenty of machine guns with them. Three Ospreys carrying SEALs were orbiting high over the Eyl airport. They would parachute into the airport and help Tommy Carmellini's snatch team secure the place after the CIA operatives had taken out as many of the defenders as possible. Carmellini's team would attack at the airport at the same time SEALs crawling onto the beach assaulted Ragnar's old lair, the move that would open the ball. Thirty minutes prior to the assault, F/A-18s and F-35s would launch from the aircraft carrier seventy-five miles offshore; they would be overhead with plenty of ordnance, should it become necessary.

The whole plan was overkill: the naval intelligence professionals thought the Shabab around Eyl had at the most 150 men, and probably less after last night's battle. Tarkington was hitting the place with enough firepower to destroy a division. Simply, he could not be certain that Grafton and his Mossad colleagues had managed to disarm the detonators for the trench bomb. He needed to hit the Shabab with overwhelming force, take them down within seconds, and make any resistance impossible. Tarkington was trying to save lives—the hostages in the fort and the marines and SEALs.

He had had several satellite conversations during the day with his boss, the fleet commander, the Pentagon and the White House. All offered advice, no one issued orders. It was a military miracle, Toad thought. Yet there are two sides to the total responsibility coin: Screw this up and you alone take the fall.

"Swarm them," he told Sal Molina at the White House this evening, "and we'll have minimum casualties. Piddle around and it's going to be a mess."

"Why don't you just blow up Ragnar's building with missiles?" the president had asked. "Obliterate it."

"That was the original plan, sir, but Admiral Grafton is being held hostage in there. So I've changed the plan."

"I see," the president said thoughtfully. What he meant was, his hands were clean. *If Grafton or any of our guys get killed, I'll give them a medal. Spend an hour in the East Room in front of cameras holding hands with the widows.*

Politics. It was enough to gag a maggot.

Toad wasn't betting everything on the initial assault. He had every destroyer in Task Force 151 in a trail formation, one behind the other, ready to steam just off the beach and shell any target. He had every marine in the MEU on alert to go ashore as fast as helicopters and Ospreys could get them there. He had airborne ordnance from the aircraft carrier USS *United States* that could be delivered in a continuous stream as fast as the carrier's crew could work the flight deck and rearm the planes.

Finally, all the destroyers and both cruisers had targets selected for their Harpoon missiles.

Tarkington had enough military power at his command to wipe this corner of Africa off the map. If anything happened to the hostages, he intended to use it. He had told all his superiors that, and none of them said no.

Yet, if anything happened to the hostages, he and Grafton had lost.

Tarkington didn't intend to lose.

Just now he watched a small green spot moving on an infrared image captured by a drone over Eyl. There were plenty of other green spots, some of them moving, but the computer techs said this one was Tommy Carmellini crawling for Ragnar's lair. Jake Grafton was in there.

Toad tried to see the telltale traces of SEALs crawling up onto the beach. Nothing. Since they were wearing wet suits, which were indeed wet, their forms should be colder than the sand still warm from the sun. As the water dried, the cold signature would disappear. As the heat of the men's bodies slowly exceeded the temperature of the cooling sand, they would again become visible in infrared. But not yet.

Tarkington hoped the Shabab didn't have night-vision or infrared technology. He and Grafton had made this plan assuming that they didn't. Watching Carmellini creep along, Toad crossed his fingers.

"Thirty minutes, Admiral. Battlestar"—the *United States*—"is launching aircraft."

"Thank you." Toad arose from his chair and went to the head. There wouldn't be time later.

Yousef el-Din had spent most of the afternoon and evening in conversation via shortwave with his colleagues in southern Somalia, who of course knew his plans quite well. They informed him about media coverage of the *Sultan* hostage incident, and the fact that the two hundred million in cash was on its way to the task force via air. That fact had been splashed across every newscast in the world.

Ragnar's shortwave radio was in shambles, so the Shabab had transported theirs from West Eyl to the lair and lugged it to the penthouse, where the reception would be better due to the height, and the fact that, unlike East Eyl, the beach town didn't sit in a river valley surrounded by rimrock hills.

When he wasn't chattering to his colleagues, Yousef el-Din prayed on his regular schedule. He normally prayed five times a day, unless he was in combat.

Yousef was deeply devout. He knew that he and his men would need Allah's help after they had the money and killed the hostages. Still, the Shabab's friends all over the Muslim world would grow in prestige and power, and Allah be praised, the final battle between good and evil would be one giant step closer.

Yousef did not think he would survive the wrath of the allied task force. To go to Paradise as a martyr, with the blood of infidels on his hands, after having fought Allah's war against the nonbelievers . . . well, it was heady stuff for Yousef el-Din. He could feel the Prophet's spiritual presence, giving him strength for the days ahead.

When he finished praying, he thought again about the money. Two truckloads of currency. He would have his men hide it in the desert, at a place known to his Shabab colleagues in the south. If he didn't live, they would find it and use it to fund jihad.

Allah akbar.

But the Americans! After he blew up the fortress, or machine-gunned the hostages, they would be outraged, naturally, and would lash out, like snakes. One of the places they would storm was this building—and the basement was full of explosives! He had inspected the weapons treasure trove earlier this afternoon.

The weapons were tempting, enough to outfit hundreds of men, but with two hundred million dollars the Shabab could buy a shipload. Perhaps even several nuclear warheads. The North Koreans were a reliable source, and of course there were the Bulgarians. And these days the Iranians were anxious to tangibly assist anyone who was the enemy of their enemies, of whom they had many.

After his evening prayer, Yousef gathered his lieutenants and issued orders. They must be ready for tomorrow.

CHAPTER TWENTY-TWO

I managed to reach the back corner of the building without being seen. I had crawled the whole way, taking advantage of every shadow, every turned head, and eventually I reached the corner of the building on the dark side, away from the fire in the plaza.

I had my headset on, so I could hear reports from everybody involved in this operation, if they were on my freq. I thought the SEALs were, but they hadn't said much. A few minutes earlier I had heard Willis Coffey say that he was in position. I triggered the mike. "Tommy going in." I got a Roger.

I took one more quick look around, then began free-climbing the building.

I had studied that building since I arrived in Eyl, and knew precisely how it could be done. During my college years I was a rock climber, which was the perfect sport for a guy who aspired to burglary. I had an interesting youth, one that I tried to avoid discussing in polite company. Of course Jake Grafton knew—he knew everything. The thought occurred to me a few years ago that he had spent so much of his life around straight arrows that he was amused by bent ones.

I gained the second floor in just a few seconds, hauling myself up by my fingertips. Try it sometime. If you think chin-ups are difficult, this will be an interesting challenge for you.

I reached a window, devoid of glass. Maybe it had been shot out in the excitement last night . . . or some kid threw a rock through it just to piss off Ragnar.

I looked in, saw no one and crawled through in less time than it takes to tell.

The lightbulb hanging from the ceiling was lit. I reached up and unscrewed it. It's something in my character—I feel safer in the dark. I pulled the Ruger from my backpack and checked the safety.

The hallway was empty. I checked each room, then listened in the stairwell. Heard people coming down. Ducked into an empty room and waited. I felt naked with all these lightbulbs burning. Should have completely disabled the generator, not just turned it off. Maybe I should ask for a do-over.

Three of them, by the sound. They went on down.

I went back to the stairwell, listening carefully. Went on up to the next floor and eased my head around the corner for a look. There sat a guy on the floor outside one of the rooms. No one in the other direction.

The man was about twelve feet from me, more or less. Chewing khat and looking bored. His rifle rested on his lap. If I didn't drop him with the Ruger and he shouted, this gig could go south fast.

For a few seconds I hoped he would get up, walk away, or toward me. Anything but just sit there. Yet even as I thought about it I heard someone come into the lobby down below. Two of them, and their voices came up the stairwell, which was a sounding pipe. I heard footsteps on the stairs.

Out of time. I stepped out, squared around and, as the startled guard turned toward me, shot him in the face. He swayed, his mouth opened to scream. I ran the three steps to him, put the muzzle of the silencer against his forehead and pulled the trigger.

Tried the door. Unlocked. Pushed it open, grabbed the AK and dragged the guard inside.

Jake Grafton was sitting against the far wall, watching me. He started to say something, and I put my fingers to my lips, silencing him.

The guard was still alive. At least his eyes were fluttering, though unfocused. I don't know much about brain injuries, don't want one myself, and if I ever get one, hope someone will quickly send me along to the next adventure. That's what I did for the guard. Took his head in one hand, twisted sharply and broke his neck. His body went limp.

Voices in the hallway were coming this way. I left the guard where he lay, tossed Grafton the AK and stepped back out of sight.

Voices. Gabbling. Probably remarking that the guard was supposed to be here. They came through the door together, saw the guard and froze for just a second. I shot them both above the ear. Down they went.

"I've got Grafton," I whispered into my headset mike.

"Roger that."

I helped myself to an AK, motioned to Grafton, and we slipped out the door.

Paused to listen.

Down the stairs to the second floor. Grafton wasn't quiet. He was trying, but to me we sounded like a symphony warming up.

I froze to listen some more. People talking in the lobby.

We had to chance it.

Down to the ground floor. A squint into the lobby. Two guys standing there talking, one with an AK, the other with an RPG-7 launcher and a bag of warheads over his shoulder, looking out into the plaza. Fortunately the window glass was long gone, so there would be no reflections.

I could just hear the hum of the generator in the basement.

I motioned to Grafton. I wanted him to step through the door, then turn left and go down the stairs to the basement armory. When I saw that he understood, I checked the guys, then gave him a nudge. He went. When he had made it, I followed. The diesel generator was louder here.

Going down was going to be iffy. Someone in the basement was going to get another free shot at our legs.

Well, we couldn't stay here, and the noise helped mask our footsteps. *Suck it up and do it, Tommy.*

I led off, the Ruger in my right hand and the AK in my left.

Thank God the room was empty. We cleared the stairs and I walked over for a look into the other room. Just piles and piles of weapons.

Grafton didn't say anything. Just stood and looked.

He wandered into the other room.

After he had had his looks, he whispered, "Thanks, Tommy."

"Do you still have your pistol?"

"Still do. A little hideout popper."

"When the shit hits the fan in a few minutes, one of these guys may rush down here to shoot an RPG into this mess. Blow us all to kingdom come."

Grafton didn't say anything to that. He started walking, looking at everything.

In less than a minute he stopped and pointed. I looked. He was pointing at a battery. From a car or truck. Wires on the top. We walked toward it. Saw that there were actually three batteries, wired in series. The positive and negative wires ran to a radio-controlled switching unit, then into a box of PVV-5A.

"It's set to blow when someone triggers it," Grafton said. He walked over to it and crouched down. I was right behind him.

"This wasn't here last night," I told him.

"Ragnar wasn't in a hurry to get to Paradise," he replied.

The simplest way to safety the thing appeared to be to merely pull the wires off the batteries' terminals. Grafton must have thought so, too, for that is what he did.

"Look around," he hissed. "See if there's another rig like this."

There wasn't.

Grafton, Mr. Sunshine, said, "Well, if there is another trigger unit we'll find out soon enough."

With the generator droning monotonously, we hunkered down in the doorway arch between the rooms where we could watch the stairs. Grafton must have been glad to see me, because he punched me once in the arm and gave me a quick grin.

I looked at my watch. Three minutes to go.

Two companies of marines were spread out on the dunes above the beaches, one company to the north and one to the south. They had spent the last two hours getting into position, aided by armored personnel carriers that delivered them to within a few hundred yards of their combat positions.

From where they lay, they could see the plaza and the numerous armed pickups that sat there, and those that buzzed around aimlessly, apparently piloted by nervous drivers.

The guards at the fortress never heard or saw the British Royal Marine commandos. They came out of the darkness like ghosts, cut throats and pulled the bodies into the brush. The whole job took two minutes.

Then they sifted into the fortress through the gun ports. The lieutenant found Captain Penney standing by the kitchen area with his officers and saluted.

"Lieutenant Mick Laycock, sir, Royal Marines."

Arch Penney's jaw fell. As the marine held the salute, he realized he should return it, and did.

"The admiral asked me to inform you, sir, that transport has been arranged. Your passengers and crew will be driven to the airport as soon as possible."

"The airport?"

"Yes, sir. Transports, sir. I don't wish to be forward, sir, but I suggest you inform your people and organize them as you wish."

"Yes, Lieutenant . . . What did you say your name was?"

"Laycock, sir. Royal Marines."

"Indeed."

"If I may make a suggestion, sir? You might wish to get your people away from these openings in the wall. As a precaution, sir."

Arch Penney grabbed the young man and gave him a bear hug.

Bullet Bob Quinn was watching from the *Sultan*'s bridge. Mike Rosen and High Noon were there, too, sharing the binoculars and night-vision scope. Two other SEALs manned the Big Fifty machine gun, one to shoot and the other to ensure the ammo belt fed properly. Quinn had the Barrett .50 caliber sniper rifle lying nearby on the deck, but he thought the guys on the beach and the marines on both sides probably had enough firepower. Really, there is such a thing as enough.

Rosen was excited. He could feel the tension, tangible as smoke.

For the last ten minutes Quinn had been watching a boat being launched from the beach. Apparently the holy warriors were coming out again to check the ships and harbor area. The boat was under way now, heading straight for the anchored cruise ship.

Bullet Bob keyed his headset mike. "Vince, do you see the approaching boat?"

"Roger."

"Take him out when I give the word."

"Roger."

Vince was standing on the topmost deck of the liner with an M-3 recoilless rifle on his shoulder. This reloadable weapon fired an 84 mm warhead and could take down anything up to a tank. This one was equipped with an ambient-light-gathering sight, so the boat showed quite clearly on the dark sea. Vince could even see the crewmen. He counted heads. Eight. Fairly small boat propelled by an outboard engine. The exhaust of the engine whispered in the night air.

Another SEAL was on the pilot sponson, actually just inside the ship, waiting, in case the fighters boarded before the bell rang.

Out at the airport, Willis Coffey looked at his watch, misread it and told the guys on his net to start shooting. The sniper rifle boomed, submachine guns opened fire, and within seconds all the Shabab warriors in the five positions they occupied around the airstrip were dead, wounded or standing with their hands up. The CIA team ceased fire and moved in.

As they did, one of the standing men leaped to a machine gun in a truck bed and cut loose. He managed to spray the area and wound a man before he was killed.

When the controller aboard ship said, "Go," the SEALs on the beach cut loose with submachine guns and M-3s. Aboard *Sultan,* Quinn's men opened up on the trucks with the Big Fifty.

On the upper deck, Vince fired his M-3 at the approaching boat. The charge literally went through the boat and detonated in the water, lifting the boat and breaking it in half. It quickly sank, taking most of the men with it. Two managed to stay afloat until the SEAL in the pilot sponson shot them; then they slipped under.

A Shabab lieutenant standing on the balcony of the lair saw the muzzle flashes coming from the beach, aimed his RPG-7 and triggered off a rocket. Fortunately he had launched an antiarmor warhead, which vented its main charge into the sand. One man was injured. Before the holy warrior could reload, he was cut down by a .338 Lapua Magnum slug fired by E.D.

The recoil of the Sako jerked the rifle off target, so E.D. brought it back to the balcony as he chambered another round. He looked for his man, and saw only a hand hanging over the lower railing.

I got him! Holy damn!

E.D. scanned with the rifle scope and found a man who had apparently bailed from a pickup running toward the entrance to the building. It was actually a fairly difficult shot at a moving target, but E.D. didn't miss this time. The 250-grain bullet striking with about three tons of energy swept the man off his feet, killed him instantly and dropped him on the plaza like a sack of rocks, and continued on its way. It struck a stone a half mile out, ricocheted and plunged into the ground five miles southwest of Eyl.

Meanwhile the trucks in the plaza were being riddled. One was already on fire, with RPG rounds cooking off in the bed.

E.D. chambered another round.

Yousef el-Din heard the racket. It sounded as if World War III had started right outside, all at once. A fervid believer in the efficacy of treachery, he instinctively knew that the Americans had lied. They weren't coming tomorrow with two tons of currency: They were here now with enough firepower to overwhelm the Shabab's men, and quickly.

He extracted the radio controllers from his pocket—he had two—and turned them both on. Waited for the little green lights. First the *Sultan* prisoners.

He looked at the fortress, a massive dark shape up there against a dark sky. He pushed the button.

Nothing happened.

He pointed the device at the fortress and pushed the button repeatedly.

Those damned pirates! Doubtlessly they improperly installed the radio controls and detonator. Incompetent fools!

Well, he still had the unit to blow this building. The batteries and radio control and fuse were installed by al-Gaza, the Hamas expert. It would explode. But the time was not yet. He would explode it when the building was full of Americans. A true believer to the core, Yousef was ready to die. He would take the American infidels with him to Paradise to prove his faith to Allah.

Meanwhile he shouted down the staircase to the men on the floor below. They were armed with RPG-7s. "The fortress," he shouted. "Shoot at the fortress!"

The fact of the matter was that the fort was a bit too far for the RPG-7 rockets, which had a maximum range of a thousand yards, a few feet more than half a mile. Unfortunately, the fort was almost six thousand feet away from the lair. Yousef didn't know the range of the rockets; technical matters were a bit beyond him. On the floor below three men fired rockets—lots of back blast that nearly asphyxiated them and their loaders on the spot—that went zipping off trailing fire from their rocket exhaust. The trajectory of one of the rockets was insufficiently elevated; it went into the ground and exploded at eight hundred yards. The other two were elevated enough, but the warheads self-destructed at a thousand yards, making a flash and spraying shrapnel in a cone-shaped pattern ahead of them.

From the lair, the fact that the rockets hadn't reached the target was not readily discernible in the darkness. Looking up the fiery trail, it appeared the flashes had actually occurred on or around the fortress.

"More," el-Din roared down the staircase. "Shoot, shoot, shoot at the infidel dogs!"

Three more grenades roared out on their rockets, trailing fire.

The second salvo was the last. The Big Fifty aboard *Sultan* chewed into the room in a long rolling burst. When it ended, the three RPG men and their three loaders were dead or bleeding to death.

Meanwhile, on the plaza below, all six of the pickups were either on fire or being riddled with automatic gunfire. A few of the men were still alive, huddling under a truck chassis or behind the stones around the fire pit. A thoughtful observer would note that the scene looked much like the one last night, only the actors were Shabab warriors, not pirates.

Amazingly, the evening fire in the cooking pit was still burning. Its glare competed with the light from the burning trucks. Several of the tires had caught fire, and they burned with little intensity but gave off copious quantities of noxious black smoke. There was little wind, so the tire smoke lay over the area like fog.

The generator in the basement of the lair was still running fine. The lights were still on in the old pile, which was beginning to resemble a burned-out tenement building in Philadelphia or the Bronx.

The marines were advancing toward the town. They had to be careful when they used their weapons so they wouldn't shoot each other. They came under fire from fighters in the brush and those in buildings or in pickups. Machine guns chattered, RPGs lit up the night, and assault rifles belched bursts.

At the airport, the parachutists were rounding up surviving Shabab fighters. They collected eight who were uninjured and three with bullet wounds. All eleven had their hands bound behind them with plastic ties, and their ankles tied together. The wounded were not treated.

Some of the Shabab warriors had hit the brush, running for their lives. The lieutenant in charge had expected that, and he didn't have the people or time to chase them. He merely kept some men on guard and hoped the Somalis kept right on running.

Ricardo, Sophia Donatelli and Rab Bishop from the BBC were beside themselves. They could hear the battle going on in the town, but they were stuck in this damned old pile of rocks. They made a corporate decision to move operations to the roof, film what they could, and send it to the satellites whenever they could get the generators running. If ever.

As they raced for the stairs carrying armloads of equipment, they passed by two Royal Marines in battle dress standing near the entrance with their weapons. Ricardo and Rab Bishop did a double take.

"I say, I think the cavalry is here," Bishop said.

"Damn, we're gonna get rescued," Ricardo echoed.

"Let's adjourn to the roof and get these cameras grinding," Sophia Donatelli told them. "We can interview the shooters later."

So they went. The cameras were on, recording muzzle flashes and RPG launchings, when a helicopter went over with its machine guns blazing at the lair.

Ricardo was beside himself.

"We're going to get rescued," he screamed into his mike, and the digital camera recorded it on the sound track.

This was the scene when the SEALs on the beach charged the lair. The Big Fifty aboard *Sultan* laid down covering fire; helicopters materialized out of the darkness and added their machine guns to the fusillade. The cameras on the fortress roof caught it all, for later rebroadcast.

The fusillade stopped as the SEALs gained the lobby. They went up the stairs in pairs, alert for grenades or booby traps. The surviving Shabab warriors were shell-shocked. They offered no resistance, so were quickly immobilized with plastic ties on wrists and ankles, searched for weapons and radio controllers, and left where they lay.

In the penthouse Yousef heard the infidels' footsteps thundering on the stairs, the shouts, the occasional shots, and knew the moment had come to leave this earth for Paradise.

He pushed the button on the controller that was to trigger the explosives in the basement, the trigger that the Hamas expert had assured him would work. The explosion al-Gaza swore would take him, el-Din and a hundred infidels to Paradise.

He pushed the button . . . and nothing happened.

El-Din's bodyguard had seen what the Shabab leader was doing, tossed down his weapon and curled up in a fetal position on the floor. Sixteen years old, he had been herding goats until six months ago, and had never imagined what it would feel like to be on the receiving end of a barrage from automatic weapons wielded by a modern military force. His nerves were shot. He was incapable of even standing.

As the SEALS topped the stairs, they saw Yousef el-Din viciously kicking the boy lying in the rubble, and cursing him and his ancestors. The SEALs swarmed them both, immobilized them in seconds with plastic ties and confiscated the radio controllers.

Outside the shooting was dying down. A burst or two now and then, and silence for long seconds. Then nothing.

In the fortress, people began cheering as the shooting trickled off. When the night was silent they filled the old stone fortress with shouts of joy and cheering.

One of the SEALS found Grafton and me in the basement, ready for anything. The generator was still snoring, the light was on, and the wet-suit-clad man with a submachine gun looked like an apparition from the black lagoon. Still, he was the best sight I had seen in years. I almost kissed him while he tried to salute Jake Grafton.

"Admiral Grafton, Admiral Tarkington's compliments, sir. He said we would find you and Mr. Carmellini in the basement."

Even though he wasn't in uniform, Grafton saluted him back. "The fortress? The hostages?"

"They're okay, sir. The building is still standing. The Royal Marines secured it."

Grafton got a sappy grin on his face, grabbed the SEAL, who was built like a middleweight prizefighter, and gave him a hug that nearly crushed him.

We went up the stairs, through the lobby, and walked out onto the plaza. The stench of burning trucks and tires almost gagged me. We were just in time to hear the swelling of jet engines passing overhead.

"Globemasters," he said by way of explanation. "C-17s. We're flying the hostages out of here."

Even as he spoke, two choppers with landing lights ablaze were landing on the roof of the fortress to pick up people and transport them to the airport. They settled in like birds on their nests. Over the water were other choppers, all with their external lights shining brightly and landing lights stabbing the darkness.

Grafton was soon surrounded by officers, SEALs and marines. The senior marine was Colonel Zakhem. He saluted, and Jake Grafton grabbed his hand and wouldn't let go. Kept pumping it.

I wandered off and found a place to sit. My leg was throbbing and I felt drained. Exhausted.

I looked at my watch. Only nine thirty. The whole damn thing hadn't taken an hour.

The arrival of the choppers, the news that they were leaving tonight, now, flying home, reduced many of the hostages to tears. Suzanne and Irene cried and laughed at the same time and hugged each other fiercely, then started hugging everyone in sight.

The *Sultan*'s crew began herding passengers up the stairs to the roof in groups of twelve or so. There they were led to the idling choppers and helped aboard. When the chopper crew made a sign, the passengers backed away to wait for the next one, which was hovering nearby. The loaded chopper lifted off and the next one landed.

Two marine armored personnel carriers pulled up to the door, and the Royal Marines led people out. Someone suggested the women leave first, but Arch Penney nixed that. Families, he said. Keep the families together. So they went in couples, usually holding hands, carrying what little they had. Some were sobbing, all were joyously happy.

Arch Penney stood with the Royal Marine lieutenant keeping an eye on the operation, and he wore a broad smile.

Julie and Marjorie materialized beside him. "Go," he said. "You two get on the next vehicle. I'll be along after a while."

"We'll wait for you."

"I'll see you wherever the planes take us. I have to ensure we get all the crew out of here."

Julie locked him in a hug, and Marjorie did likewise. And they went.

Penney murmured the names of his passengers, all those he knew, as they walked past. "Mr. Jones, Harriet, Reverend Franklin, Mr. and Mrs. Cohen . . . Benny. I'm sorry about all this. I'll get your address from the company and write you when I have time. Thank you for your courage and example."

Others got the same treatment. Von Platen with his three friends, a farm implement dealer from Iowa, a bookseller from Birmingham, a retired schoolteacher and her companion from Stoke-on-Trent . . .

Over their heads the helicopters were coming and going. More APCs rolled up, more smiling marines helped people into them . . .

Arch Penney wiped the tears from his eyes and kept shaking hands.

Sitting in the plaza made me restless. Everyone was busy except me. I tried my headset. "E.D.?"

No answer. I tried three or four more times, but he didn't reply. Willis Coffey called from the airport and wanted to tell me all about what had happened out there, but the controller aboard ship shut him up with a curt admonition to keep the net clear.

The shooting seemed to have stopped, but who knew? Anyone could take a potshot at an infidel at any time. I kept my Kimber in my hand and started walking toward the location where I had left E.D.

Found him there. Dead. Chopped up pretty badly by shrapnel. Looked like an RPG warhead to me. The Sako was there, damaged. I scanned about with my penlight. Found six empty .338 Lapua cartridges lying near him in the dirt.

He hadn't moved from this position after he started shooting. I told him to, but he didn't.

I picked him up, got the corpse over my shoulder, managed to bend enough to snag the rifle and walked toward the plaza. I wasn't leaving E.D. in Somalia. We could bury him back in the States.

I laid the body in the plaza. Had blood all over me, and I didn't give a good goddamn. Blood everywhere on everything. My leg screamed.

I sat a while. Some marines came along with a body bag and took E.D.

They were bringing the prisoners in trucks. Marched them into the building. Other marines were carrying in armloads of weapons. Machine guns, AKs, RPG-7 launchers and bags of warheads.

I don't know how many prisoners they put in there—at least fifty, maybe seventy-five. More or less. I wasn't counting, and I don't guess anyone else was.

The two Mossad agents showed up with one, a guy who had been shot through the lower body sideways, it looked like. He was obviously bleeding from a torso wound. The two Israeli agents were supporting his weight, but his feet were dragging along. So they had found the Palestinian bomber, al-Gaza.

They dragged the guy into the building.

One of the marines, a sergeant with lots of stripes, checked the prisoners as they were led out of the truck, or carried out. Some of them were bleeding from horrific wounds. I saw him pick out a few, and they were loaded into another truck.

Curious, I walked over. "You're letting these guys go?"

"Kids. Got one who weighed sixty pounds and was just five feet tall."

As I was standing there I saw a woman with an AK approach one of the vehicles. She came out from behind a pickup. How long she had been there I don't know. A group of prisoners was being herded toward the building.

The marines tensed.

"Stand easy, men," the sergeant said in his parade-ground voice, not shouting, but with a voice that cut through the noise.

The woman was perhaps middle-aged. She didn't hesitate or break stride. She was staring at one Somali. She stopped about fifteen feet from him, lifted the AK and gave him a burst in the gut. Two Marines swung their weapons, ready to kill her, but the sergeant roared, "No."

He walked slowly over to the woman, held out his hand, and she handed him the rifle. Then she turned and walked away, back toward the huts that comprised the town.

"What was that all about, Gunny?" one of the marines asked.

"God only knows," the gunnery sergeant said. "Maybe he killed her man. Or raped her. Or raped her daughter. She figured he earned it. You people pick him up and carry him inside."

The marines didn't even check to see if the guy was dead. They carried him into the building and threw him on the floor.

"How'd you know she wouldn't shoot our men?" I asked the sergeant.

"After three tours in Iraq and two in Afghanistan, you get a feel. The aggression, the bad vibes. I just knew."

The thought crossed my mind that you only have to be wrong once to end up dead, but I kept my mouth shut.

The gunnery sergeant had some more to say in that gravelly, parade-ground voice. "These women have been taking shit from these ragheads all their lives. The times, they are a-changin'."

I looked around for Grafton. Didn't see him. Wandered into the lobby past the rows of prisoners lying on the floor trussed up with plastic ties and looked down the stairs. Heard a noise and saw Grafton coming up with the two Israelis.

He didn't say anything. Just slapped me on the shoulder. Then he saw a young marine in battle dress standing there amid the prisoners lying on the floor, trussed up with plastic ties, tearing pages from a book. Maybe it was the Koran.

Grafton went over to him and took the book from his hands. Tossed it on the floor. "This isn't good for your soul," he said. He put a hand on the young man's shoulder and guided him out. I followed him into the plaza.

He stood looking, watching the prisoners being marched in, the weapons being policed up. Marines were carrying them into the building by the armload, then hustling back for more.

An APC came down the hill from the fort and stopped in front of the lair. Four Royal Marines carried three wounded men from the APC into the building. Grafton nodded at one man who had apparently been shot through both knees. He was screaming as they toted him in, one holding his shoulders and one his ankles. "That's the pirate that led the team that captured the *Sultan*. Killed some crewmen, threw the wounded overboard to drown, murdered several passengers."

"Maybe we should take him back to the States. The defense lawyers would love you for it."

Jake Grafton made a rude noise. "His pirating days are over," he muttered. Then he turned to me. "Tommy, you did well. I thank you."

"Yes, sir."

"Hitch a ride up to the airport. Get all your guys. Keep them alert, guarding the planes. Then put them on the last plane out. You, too."

"What about you?"

"I'll be along after a while. Gotta make sure we get all the hostages out of that fortress. We're not leaving anyone behind."

"Yes, sir."

He walked off to talk to a knot of marines. I called Willis on the net, told him E.D. wasn't coming, and relayed Grafton's order that the CIA team was to be on the last plane.

Then I started walking up the hill toward the fortress. My leg needed some exercise to work the soreness out.

It was almost dawn when the last of the *Sultan*'s crew were evacuated. I was sitting with my back against the parapet of the roof when Captain Penney and a few of his officers boarded the last chopper to the airport. The Italian and BBC news crews were already aboard. At the last minute Ben and Zahra, the two Mossad agents, came over with Mohammed Atom, who had his hands cuffed with a plastic tie behind his back. They put him on, then climbed aboard after him.

Ricardo refused to go. I saw that he was shaking his head violently, and strolled near enough to hear the argument over the noise from the helo's idling engines. "There is another story here. What about the people of Eyl, after the battle is over? I am staying to do this story."

"We aren't keeping a plane at the airport to wait for you."

"I understand. I absolve you of all responsibility. My cameraman and I will find our own way home."

"Jesus, you are a stubborn son of a bitch. There's dozens, maybe hundreds of those murderous Shabab assholes out there in the brush. They'd love nothing more than to do you, just for the fun of it."

"This is my job," Ricardo said heroically.

The loadmaster threw up his hands and waved to the chopper. It lifted off, and we were swamped with silence.

I headed down the stairs. Walked through the fortress one last time—

a few of the emergency lanterns from the ship were still lit, but mainly the place was dark. A rat shot through the beam of my penlight. I suspected the locals would mine the trash when the sun came up.

I left the fort, waved to a Royal Marine standing at the entrance with his weapon cradled in his arms and started hiking for town. The U.S. Marines were still there, though most of the fires had burned themselves out. A couple of APCs had their headlights and spotlights on, lighting up the plaza.

Willis Coffey called me on the net. He was a happy fellow. "We're ready to get aboard this last plane, Tommy. Where are you, dude?"

"Go on. I'll catch a ride with the marines. See you in Langley."

He didn't argue. "Adios, amigo," he said.

I turned off the com unit and stuffed it and the headset in my backpack.

When the sun came up, the marines started to pull out. Machine guns were broken down, packed up. Ammo stowed in boxes. Water cans picked up and stowed in the APCs. Then the SEALs and marines piled in, and they headed off up or down the beach to the landing craft that were waiting to take them back to the ships.

A U.S. Navy destroyer was anchored near the *Sultan,* and small boats were coming and going. They were going to tow her away, I thought.

Jake Grafton was still in the plaza, standing beside an APC, a commandeered pickup and some marines. One of the marines was a captain.

Grafton asked him, "Did you get all those people evacuated from those huts?" He nodded toward the village.

"Yes, sir. Made them walk at least a mile. Some of the old women and kids we gave rides to."

"How many rations did you leave?"

"Two pallets, sir. One of rice, beans, canned meat, juice, lots of stuff from the ship. The other was MREs."

Grafton eyed me. "I thought I told you to take a plane."

"I disobeyed orders. Thought I'd ride along with you. Wheedle some leave out of you, maybe a pay raise while you're so full of cheer and love for your fellow man."

He merely nodded and climbed into the truck's passenger seat. One of the marines got behind the wheel, and two jumped in the back. I didn't jump, not with my leg. I eased myself aboard and swung my sore leg in.

The APC preceded us. We hadn't gone a hundred yards when we saw Ricardo and his cameraman hiking our way, waving their arms.

The truck stopped, and he rushed over. Maybe he didn't recognize Grafton, because he asked the buck sergeant driver, "Where are all the civilians?"

"I think they cleared out, sir."

"But where?"

"I don't know. Now you'd better get in the truck."

"We're not leaving," Ricardo said flatly. "We're the press, and we don't take orders from anyone."

The sergeant made a gesture with his hand at the two marines who were riding in the bed. They jumped off, picked up Ricardo bodily and threw him in the truck bed. The cameraman decided discretion was the better part of valor, hoisted his camera in, and climbed up under his own steam.

The truck rolled. We were up near the fortress when the truck stopped and Grafton got out. He was standing beside the truck, right beside me, and I think I was the only one who saw him pull something from his pocket. He fiddled with it for a moment, then pointed it at Ragnar's lair.

The building exploded. The explosion started in the basement and just kept getting bigger and bigger, I guess as more and more of the PVV-5A and ammo and RPG warheads got involved. The noise and concussion felt like a punch, even at this distance. The fireball rose and turned into a mushroom cloud.

Grafton dropped the controller and climbed back into the truck. The sergeant started it moving. Everyone in the bed was looking at the still-growing cloud. The blast knocked down most of the shacks in Eyl. Little bits and pieces began raining from the sky. I covered my head with my hands.

As the truck topped the crest I got my last look. The breeze had moved some of the cloud to seaward. Ragnar's lair was no longer there.

. . .

Mike Rosen was in *Sultan*'s e-com center typing, as usual, trying to get the events of the evening into e-mails. He had stopped and was sitting looking at the town of Eyl in the early-morning sun when Ragnar's building went up in a cloud of smoke and fire. He watched it for a moment, typed out what he had just seen and hit SEND. Then he turned off his computer.

He went up on deck and watched the giant mushroom cloud drift toward the *Sultan*. Looked at the destroyer and the boats and saw that one of them was towing a hawser toward *Sultan*.

An hour later the ship was free of her anchor and moving. Sailors were aboard on the bridge, using handheld radios to talk back and forth to each other and the destroyer, *Richard Ward*.

Sultan was turned toward the east and the destroyer towed her toward the open sea. Mike Rosen stood on the upper deck watching Africa slowly recede. An hour and a half later, all he could see in every direction was water, and some navy ships. High Noon joined him. Amazingly, his coat pockets were empty and he was drinking coffee from a ceramic cup.

"There's coffee in the galley," he said and leaned on the rail.

"Where's your gin?"

"Oh, that. I poured gin on myself from time to time, but the bottles held mostly water."

"Who do you work for? MI-6?"

Noon grinned. "Been in Africa over twenty years," he mused. "Time to go home. Fact is, I think I've worn out my welcome."

"What am I supposed to say when people ask me about that e-mail I sent Wednesday evening? How the Shabab was going to kill the pirates, steal the ransom and kill everyone in the fort."

"Oh. Amazingly accurate prediction, that. True, even."

"Yeah."

"Why don't you just say you overheard some people talking, and let it go at that?"

"The e-mails from the States had a lot to say about this Grafton fellow. That he was in charge of the rescue. You know him?"

Noon laughed.

"I was going to write a book about the *Sultan*'s capture, but I am re-thinking that."

Noon emptied the last of his coffee into the sea. The wind whipped the liquid away.

"The truth is, I don't know very much."

"Life's like that. I could use some more coffee. Want some?"

They headed toward the galley.

"Fact is," Rosen said, "I've been offered an hour show on a cable television news channel, five days a week. Big pay increase. I'm going to take it."

"Congratulations. Something good came out of this mess, after all." Noon took a deep breath of the sea air. "I always wanted to take a cruise."

"Enjoy."

"I intend to."

CHAPTER TWENTY-THREE

I went back to the States via Rome. Got a room in a modest hotel and looked up Sophia Donatelli. She had a few days off, so we spent them seeing Rome. She knew it backwards and forwards. I liked her a lot. She liked me a lot, too. Say what you will about Italian politics, but the women there are the most beautiful in the world, and the food!

From there I went to Paris and visited a friend I happened to know. She was gorgeous too, and the food!

My leg was well by the time I got to Washington in the last week of November, Thanksgiving week. The weather was mild. I didn't bother taking my coat to work—my sport coat was enough.

Ricardo had broken the story about the Shabab warriors being murdered in an explosion after the Eyl battle. It had been all over the news in Europe, America and I suppose everywhere else. Al Qaeda had sworn revenge.

Ricardo had waited until the media hubbub over the returning hostages had died down somewhat. Everyone had had their fifteen minutes, or less, and life was returning to normal when Ricardo hosted a one-hour news show. He had lots of video, but none of the explosion. The camera had stayed on him as he related the tale of murder of defenseless men.

The press loved it and kept it alive. Congressional investigations had been threatened and scheduled. Subpoenas had been delivered.

An FBI agent and two congressional investigators were waiting for me at Langley that November morning when I unlocked the door to my tiny office. They escorted me to the conference room outside Grafton's office, got the tape recorder and camera rolling and started questioning me. Having a legal education and some less-than-upright incidents in my shady past that I didn't wish to discuss, I immediately refused to talk.

That upset them. They made unhappy noises while I worked on the coffee I had bought at the Starbucks stand in the lobby of the building. I smiled.

"Refusing to talk to us could cost you your job," said the lead dog, a heavyset female with a rather large jaw.

"Really?" I replied and made a slurping noise with the coffee. "Fact is, I haven't yet written my operations report. When I get it done, of course it goes to my boss. It'll be classified. If you want to know anything about what my orders were, what I did, saw, said, witnessed, whatever, ask my boss for a copy of the report."

"There is a report that one passenger from the *Sultan* was removed by Israeli intelligence agents, a Mohammed Atom. Do you know anything about that?"

"You have got to be kidding."

"Did you know that there were two Mossad agents on the ground in Eyl?"

"For all I know, there could have been a hundred. Lots of shady characters running around there. Pirates, holy warriors, spies, SEALs, marines, British matrons and innocent babes like me. Take that Ricardo guy from Fox News—I thought he might be Russian intelligence, but damn if I know. I certainly didn't ask him. Ask the boss for a copy of my report when I get it written."

Some hot tongue work for a couple of minutes got them no place, so they turned off the gear, packed up and left.

I went in to see Jake Grafton. He was in his office with Sal Molina.

"Tommy Carmellini, Sal Molina."

He asked how I did and we shook hands.

"Sal wants to ask you some questions," Grafton said. He leaned back in his chair and ran a pencil back and forth through his fingers.

I mentioned the FBI and congressional investigators and my refusal to talk. "Fact of the matter is," I told the president's man, "my report will be everything I have to say about Somalia. If anyone asks about anything not in the report, I intend to take the Fifth Amendment. Everyone should do it at least once, so I thought, why not now?"

Molina stared at me stonily. "Have you been reading the papers?"

"I just flew in from Paris yesterday," I said. "Read newspapers on the way. Some of the op-ed pieces read like the author belonged to al Qaeda. I've heard they can join that in college now, like they can the Communist Party."

"The administration is under severe political pressure to explain the events that happened in Eyl."

"Alleged events," I said brightly, using my legal training.

"Tommy," Grafton said, "I think we owe Mr. Molina an off-the-record oral statement. He can do with it what he will. Tell him what you personally witnessed in Eyl."

I thought about it, took a moment to arrange my head and started with my team's arrival near the airport after the *Sultan* was captured by pirates. My exposition took twenty minutes. I confess, I sanitized it somewhat. I never mentioned Nora Neidlinger, and I didn't mention the RC control units. I did tell him about the woman who gunned the Shabab guy while he was in custody. I didn't think the marines were at fault—who knew what she might do?—and said so.

Molina zeroed in on the wired-up batteries, the radio-controlled receiver and the explosives in the basement. "So you saw the three batteries?"

"Yes."

"And you saw Admiral Grafton safety them by removing the wires from the terminals of the batteries?"

"Yes."

"You didn't reattach the wires?"

"No."

"Do you know who did?"

"No."

"Two Mossad agents were in Eyl. Could they have rewired the batteries and triggered the blast from a distance?"

I shrugged. "Anyone could have. I didn't, and didn't see anyone do it, but it was a long night. The building was used to hold Shabab prisoners. The explosion of the weapons cache could have been an accident. There were over two tons of Russian PVV-5A in there, hundreds of RPGs, tens of thousands of rounds of AK and machine-gun ammo, MON-50 Russian claymores . . . the whole basement was an explosion waiting to happen. And it did."

I shrugged again. "I repeat: I had nothing to do with that explosion. But if I had thought of it, I would have been perfectly willing to go down to the basement, wire up the detonators and push the button on a radio controller from a safe distance. If someone did that, they did the world a favor. That part of the world, anyway."

"The prisoners had surrendered."

"I am sure Allah considered that when he totted up their accounts. Do surrendered martyrs get fewer houris, fewer little boys?"

Molina grimaced. "The president is out on a limb, and you are doing nothing to help him get off it."

"I didn't hold a ladder for him to get up there," I stated, "and I won't hold a ladder for him to get down."

Molina looked at me awhile, then transferred his gaze to Grafton, then back to me.

"We only lost five killed, eight wounded in the rescue operation," Grafton said. "The president should be crowing about that. And giving out medals to the families in a White House ceremony."

"Does that include me as a wounded casualty?" I asked.

"No."

I pulled up my trouser leg and showed Molina my scar. It was still pink. "Nine wounded."

"You clown," Molina said to me. He told Grafton, "We're doing a ceremony."

Grafton opened his drawer and took out a piece of paper. He passed it to Molina. Looked like a hundred-dollar bill to me. "The counterfeit money went into the ocean with bin Laden. He can spend it in hell. The paper will eventually decompose. Here's a souvenir."

"No one knows that money was counterfeit," Molina said, fingering the C-note.

"My suggestion is we leak the story. The administration can deny it at first, then sheepishly admit it. Everyone will have a good laugh on the pirates, and the president will look tough. That will get him part of the way off the limb, anyhow."

Molina smiled. The smile turned to a chuckle; then he laughed out loud. "Jake, you are one amazing son of a bitch. Okay. Okay."

"I know a guy over at the *Post*. Jack Yocke. I'll call him and send him this bill. He'll be delighted to break the story."

Molina laughed his approval. He tossed the C-note on Grafton's desk, got out of his chair and retrieved his sport coat from the couch. Put it on.

"What happened to that million dollars in real money that you took with you?"

"I gave it to Ragnar. Maybe it's still in Eyl. Consider it an investment."

Molina walked over to a print on Grafton's wall of a naval battle in the age of sail and stood scrutinizing it. "We'll probably never know exactly what happened after the battles in Eyl," he said soberly, all trace of mirth gone from his voice, "and perhaps that is best. Just so it stays that way."

He turned around. "Merry Thanksgiving to you both," he said and trooped out.

When the door closed, Grafton asked, "How was your French lady?"

I sighed. "*Très bien*. Very *très bien*."

"Welcome back to the world." He leaned forward in his chair and picked up a file, passed it to me. "I've got another assignment for you."

I looked at the cover for the file. Didn't open it. "I hope you intend to send me somewhere that has ceramic conveniences and toilet paper. I'm really tired of squatting over a hole and using leaves. Or pages from the Federal Employees Handbook."

"Tommy, Tommy, Tommy." His eyebrows danced, and a grin crossed that leathery face. "I've put you in for the Company camping award. If you win, you get a CIA coffee cup and an embossed compass at the Christmas party. Tough competition, though."

"I feel so lucky! I'll buy a lottery ticket on my way home tonight."

He nodded at the file in front of me. "The IRS says an international ring of thieves is defrauding the government by submitting false income tax returns claiming refunds for people with Puerto Rican Social Security numbers. The real people don't even know about the returns. Puerto Ricans don't pay federal taxes. The FBI and IRS want our help. *You* are the help."

"Not the revolution in Mali? I thought I was in line for a government-paid trip to Timbuktu. 'Them being three and us being two . . .' I have thought up an excellent list of reasons why I shouldn't go. Want to hear them?"

"Some other time."

We talked for a half hour about my new assignment. As I was leaving he came around the desk to shake my hand. "Thanksgiving dinner at my place, Tommy," he said. "Anytime after noon."

I grinned, then headed off to study up on IRS refunds—and write an ops report. A little fiction never hurt anyone. Hell, maybe fiction was my calling, the start of a new career.

ACKNOWLEDGMENTS

For their kindness in reading portions of the manuscript and offering suggestions, the author wishes to thank Gilbert Pascal, Jerry A. Graham, Dr. Donna S. Johnson, and RADM Stanley W. Bryant, USN (Ret.). A special thank-you to Mike Rosen, 850 KOA Denver's ace talk-show host, who graciously agreed to act in the author's drama. Any errors are, of course, the author's sole responsibility.

The author owes a special debt of gratitude to his editor, Charles Spicer of St. Martin's Press, whose patience, wisdom, and enthusiasm are unsurpassed.